A HUNDRED LIES

JEAN M. GRANT

A Hundred Lies

Copyright © 2020 by Jean M. Grant

All rights reserved. Printed in the United States of America.

No part of this publication may be reproduced, distributed, or transmitted in any form or by any means, including photocopying, recording, or other electronic or mechanical methods, without the prior written permission of the publisher, except in the case of brief quotations embodied in critical reviews and certain other noncommercial uses permitted by U.S. copyright law. For permission requests, write to the author using the contact form on jeanmgrant.com.

This is a work of fiction. Names, characters, places, and incidents are either the product of the author's imagination or are used fictitiously, and any resemblance to actual persons living or dead, business establishments, events, or locales is entirely coincidental.

Book cover and scene break art by AK Westerman, AK Organic Abstracts | OA Graphic Design.

Map by David Lindroth Inc.

First edition, 2020

Print ISBN 978-1-5092-3197-3

Digital ISBN 978-1-5092-3198-0

Second edition, 2024

Print ISBN   979-8-989-8854-7-3

Digital ISBN 979-8-989-8854-6-6

www.jeanmgrant.com

To my readers,
whether this is the first book of mine you've read,
or you've been journeying with me through this entire
trilogy, thank you for your continued support.

ENGLAND AND SCOTLAND

1322

The Scottish Cause has failed after years of conflict and uncertainty. For now, England and Scotland live in a delicate peace as they await confirmation from the Pope that Scotland will be its own sovereign nation.

Rich, noble-born wardens control the tumultuous border regions. An unsuccessful English baronial revolt against King Edward II of England led by several of these wardens has resulted in harsher rule and tension among the English people. Many resort to questionable tactics for power and security, falling upon murder, exploitation, and superstition...believing any lie they are told if it means a chance at a new life.

CHAPTER ONE

Summer, Northern English Border

R osalie Threston reached across the table and took Marin's palm.

She pretended to study the lines with a focused brow, but the answers to her "reading" lay ready to be spoken. Analyzing the palm just helped the lies go over with plausibility. She had overheard Marin's husband, Jon, boasting to a friend in the tavern last night about the baby and his new position with the village armorer. "I see another baby." She traced the lifeline, then the mounds.

Marin gasped.

Rosalie internally breathed a sigh. "What's this? Jon has come upon fortune. Please congratulate him upon the new position with the armorer."

Marin's early pregnancy complexion glowed. A gullible smile tipped the edges of youthful lips. It must be the season. Pregnancy signs were easy to tell if one just spent some time actually looking at the woman, and even easier to glean among town talk. Marin cooed, "Your gift, Rose! Nobody knows but me and Jon."

That's what you think. "A teller knows, Marin. The baby will bring you joy and a sibling for wee William."

"Boy or girl?"

Rosalie kept her face unrevealing. Marin's cheeks were rounded this time, early in the pregnancy. She had a fifty percent chance of accuracy. "Girl."

Rosalie would be on to the next town before the babe was born anyway, so she allowed herself some guesses.

"Is it, the, er, what's that mound called? The one that shows life?" Marin withdrew her hand and nibbled on her fingernails, a nervous habit. They were shorter than usual.

Hmm. "Here." Rosalie took Marin's hand again, swiping a finger softly across her palm to both demonstrate and distract. "The heart and fate lines tell me." She paused, pretending to scrutinize, before saying, "You're having problems again with—"

Marin grimaced, then sucked her teeth. "Oh...Jon's mother. She's such a hen, nosing into our business."

She listened as Marin divulged about her troublesome mother-in-law. Finally, taking a breath, Marin said, "Can you see your own future, Rose? Perhaps a man?" Bright eyes stared back at her, hopeful, innocent.

Rosalie's cheeks warmed with the sensitive subject. "It doesn't work like that. I can't see much in my own palms." A twinge of envy filled her chest. Marin was her age and already married with one child and another on the way. She had an adoring husband. A steady income. A family.

Only wishes for Rosalie.

Jon appeared in the doorway and cleared his throat. Marin dropped a penny into her hand and drew closer to whisper, "Thank you. This covers payment for the last time, too. You've always been kind. When my sweet girl is old enough, and with Jon's new work, I can buy one of your necklaces for her. I'll pay with a coin instead of eggs, I promise." Marin drew a finger along the display set on the table. "You've a talent. The Sight *and* your crafting. All the bright colors." She danced fingertips upon the painted stones strung together.

A tingling sensation swept up the back of Rosalie's neck. "Thank you."

Marin added, tying her shawl as she made for the door, "A soothsayer should be working for lords. Your fortunes are precious to us. Mr. Barlow told me how you'd warned him of the misdoing with his brother, and well, he caught 'im with his trews down indeed." She tsked with a bob of her head.

Rosalie nodded, and ushered Marin closer to the door as she took in Jon's less credulous gaze and shifting of feet. "I prefer to help people like you and Mr. Barlow over pretentious lords."

As she saw Marin and Jon out and mentally counted the earnings from today's successful readings and sales, Rosalie pondered what to make for sup. A dozen eggs, two pennies—both from past-due patrons for multiple readings—a jar of fresh milk, thread and fabric from the weaver, a new set of brushes for her paints... Her uncle would be pleased about the coin, not the bartered items. But, people paid with what they had. She'd not refuse the payments. She always found a use for them. Her stomach growled. They could butcher the hen that had stopped laying. She salivated thinking of the rich stew she could cook, and bone broth to jar.

"Rosie!" a voice screeched from behind.

She turned to find a winded Oswell, who must have come in through the rear door. "What's wrong, Uncle Os?"

He rushed to her side, his eyes wild and wide. "You must hide! No, leave, for the night. Hurry to Marin's croft."

"Whatever for?" As she said it, she ducked behind the counter, checked on her cats—safe in their crate—and then felt her apron for the coins. All there. She always kept her money on her person. She glanced around the meager shop, expecting somebody to burst through the door.

"Lady Brantingham. She was asking about you at the tavern."

"Does she seek another reading? She knows where to find me." Why had Oswell been at the tavern at midday? Gathering information for her fortune-telling business she hoped, and not spending their coin on cheap ale. He knew better. She trusted him. Her stomach hardened. "She's one of my best patrons. What's wrong?"

"I-I—" He coughed, tapped his chest. Once the phlegm cleared, he continued, "I heard her—my, what a tongue for a noblewoman—proclaiming you lied to her. Told her false fortunes. That you're a ruse."

Rosalie looked over her shoulder in the empty shop. "Well, I am." After all these years, why did those words bring shame to her mind? It was just work. It kept their stomachs full.

"She made threats. Go. I'll handle it."

"But—" Aunt Nelda hadn't returned from her day's work at the castle.

"Please. I'll be alright. I've not done anything to upset the lady. You know if she is out and about, it's important. She hardly ventures from that tower of hers."

Her stomach twisting in knots, Rosalie left reluctantly. Commotion sounded behind her as she darted out the rear door. Lady Brantingham, if she was there—and Rosalie guessed she was, for she knew her well—silently watched, allowing her men to deliver her message.

Wood cracked, pots broke, and trinkets scattered. Each item breaking ran numbers through Rosalie's mind. Oswell pleaded between gasps as if he'd been punched. Instead of running far, Rosalie ducked behind the neighboring shop, well hidden, but within earshot, in case.

She had just started to like this village.

A few days later, on the move again, the cart jostled and creaked along the heavily trodden road. They ventured into new territory this time: Scotland.

Competition had grown fierce in the wake of the baronial revolt, forcing them to resort to the land where folk hid in the heather and danced with faeries at night, and where men fought brazenly, wielding broadsword and axe...according to Nelda. Rosalie shivered. Then again, Nelda's mind had grown dimmer with each passing day. Rosalie was no young girl anymore, believing all Nelda's stories.

Tall tales aside, the revolt was only part of their reason for a hasty departure. She shot a gaze behind them. The true reason lay south, in England. Lady Brantingham.

Rosalie tightened her threadbare shawl, the summer's sun obscured behind large, looming clouds as dusk called. She dipped a quill into her ink jar, precariously balancing it between her knees. "What is that place there, Uncle Os?" One crofter had paid for her services with an accurate map of northern England and southern Scotland, which Rosalie now augmented with notable landmarks.

"What?" Oswell didn't look at her.

She pointed ahead of them at the sandy gray stone arches of a cathedral. Much of it remained hidden behind a verdant hill and thick canopy of mature trees. Rooftops in a nearby town poked through. "There. The cathedral?"

He shrugged. "Look at the other map I got you. I believe it's an abbey. Jedburgh Abbey, where the St. Augustine monks reside."

"Can we stop there?" Though she couldn't read the books, the monks were known for their calculations and mechanical drawings. Artwork, too. Portraits mostly, but she loved learning about new paints and processes for creating them.

Oswell slapped the reins and cursed at the slow-moving oxen, their last two large working animals, other than the two sheep and one pig squealing in the cart's bed beside Rosalie. She missed their cow, Tilda. The old beast had ceased producing milk, and Oswell sold her to an unsuspecting crofter. The cow would likely end up butchered.

"No time. Sorry, Rosie. We'll make camp for the night farther 'long the road."

"Pippy, calm yourself," she said to the chubby pig. Nelda was fast asleep in an herbal-induced fog, the two sheep dozing beside her. Their three cats her uncle used for his rat catching in castles meowed as they hit a bump, then settled in closer to Nelda. They'd grown accustomed to their journeys, too. Rosalie seldom put them in their crate anymore. She scratched Duo under his chin, and gave Trēs a maternal pat.

She drew the symbol of a cross on her map and a simple square with an arch. "Jedburgh? A *g*?"

"No, a *j*. Take the quill, draw a line down, and then a hook up, on the left. Left is your non-writing hand's side."

She did her best to make a letter *j* and then put her quill and jar away. Oswell always appreciated her precision with maps. Something to add to the trinkets she sold. She had nearly all of England mapped out. On to Scotland...

Her stomach growled. She wondered if Nelda would be capable of maintaining work in a castle kitchen, for they counted on her aunt's monthly earnings. Lately, Nelda performed mending and cleaning, shoddy quality at best, and Rosalie was left covering her aunt's mistakes. The efforts brought in more coins per month at least.

Nelda's working days were diminishing. "Hush, Pippy," Rosalie said to the anxious pig.

"How many times have I told you not to name the animals? That pig will be ready for slaughter come fall. He'll make a hearty sup and provide enough salted meat to last us through winter," her uncle chided her like she was a young girl, not an adult of twenty.

"Every creature deserves a name." Even those without a family name...or parents, she wanted to say.

He mumbled under his breath.

She stuck her chin out. "He's a *she*, Os."

He ignored the comment with a "hrmmph."

"You're certain about traveling north? There must be work at the keeps in Northumberland or Cumberland. Or we try south again?"

"Yes, we must. The revolt has cost the lords heavily. There's no work for us in England, Rosie. And Lady Brantingham..."

She grimaced. "North it is. How has it come to this? Our business thrived during the months leading to the revolt."

"Exactly. There was coin to be made from it. But no more." He lowered his voice, though there was no waking Nelda from her nap, as he said, "Your auntie can't get in with the kitchen cooks or servants to garner information for you to use anymore. Rats, aye, rats are less of a priority when war is stealing sons and lords from their homes and returning them in boxes."

She shivered, despite the warmth in the air. They'd made it safely across the turbulent border, through the far western region of the marches to avoid Warden Brantingham's territory. They drew upon— "Where in Scotland will we stop? Have you decided?"

No answer.

The pig settled in a corner of hay beside her aunt, so Rosalie edged closer to the front. She held the wooden divide firmly, lifted her leg, then the other, and plopped into the seat beside Oswell. "We've made it across the border. Where have you decided to set up shop?" she asked, louder. She shook her head. Her aunt's cloudy mind, and her uncle's hearing. It was no wonder she talked to the animals.

He avoided her question. "You're to assume your auntie's role in the kitchens or with the ladies. We could dress you in a finer gown and bring you to court, but you're not Scottish, so I'm not certain the nobles will take a liking to you. You've got a fetching beauty though," he continued, his gaze on the road.

Her cheeks burned as he spoke like she wasn't there. He meant well, but there was no way she'd play coy with the heathens and be used as...as what? He'd marry her off? No. He had always allowed her to make her own choices with love. She'd find another way to acquire information for their fortune-telling business. Make friends? What Scottish woman would befriend her, a poor Englishwoman who lied for a living? A kitchen job might be it for her. There, she could make coin, listen, and hide.

He scratched his head and coughed. She almost felt the rumbling wheezes in his chest. They'd depleted the special syrup of mint, sugar, and barley water the last healer had prepared. She'd buy more for him in— "Where, Os?"

"Edinburgh."

She swallowed, making mental notes of the road they traveled upon, always keen on directional observations. The abbey served as a good landmark.

Edinburgh. A larger town. With a court. A bold move. They could lose themselves there. Unless Lady Brantingham followed them across the border. Then what? If the lady didn't relent, they'd be clear to the northern isles by winter. She'd muddled it all, and hell was on their heels in the form of a silk-clad noblewoman.

Oswell's cough settled. He tapped her knee. "Don't worry yourself. We may be English to these heathens, but they've strong-rooted beliefs in the mystical. We'll profit well."

"Don't they have their own Seers?"

He waved a dismissive hand.

She nodded. "It's fortunate Nelda has taught me their superstitions, then."

"Yes, indeed. You are well-learned." He spoke to her like she'd been studying French or undertaking a noble's education. No, she was learning the art of lying. She couldn't even read. Reading palms was it. Except for arithmetic. She loved numbers. In all her efforts to learn to read, only numbers stuck in her mind.

The sun lazily settled behind the horizon. By her calculation on the map, they'd reach Edinburgh in a few days.

Nelda snored blissfully unaware behind them, her sleep spiked with poppy and heavy cider.

Rosalie slid her hand into her thinning, homespun gown's pocket and rubbed the gold bracelet without removing it, lest Oswell see. She traced the memorized ridges and the lone gemstone, a garnet, she thought, by its brilliant red hue. All her years of bartering educated her in a variety of stones and gems.

Her fingers never lied. Nor could people. Their faces usually revealed answers, and Nelda had taught her all the tricks. Along with Nelda's experience, the tavern and castle *gossib* revealed the information needed for successful readings. They had grown an adequate business. Enough to survive at least.

She had spent many years studying celestial and lunar movements and tales of the ancient gods of the Romans, Greeks, Norse, and isles people from other tellers. Understanding the sky helped in foreseeing weather, famine, droughts. It really was simple. All it took was patience and practice. Political discussion and superstition mixed well to create likely premonitions.

Except when their predictions had fared incorrect, but she refused to focus on that calamity.

Touch told more than faces did. The weathered knolls of fingers, the ridges and valleys carved into palms by their lines, and the calloused flesh of a working hand or supple skin of a fairer hand. The truth found residence there.

She released the bracelet, and it settled deeper into her pocket. Oswell never let her wear the bracelet in public, for he feared it would be stolen or their patrons would think they were too well off for the coin they earned. Sometimes, at night, she slid it on. It was all she had from her parents. Every now and then, when their bellies grew hungry and their coins sparse, she'd contemplated selling it.

Blinking, she leaned her head upon her uncle's shoulder, allowing daydreams to play in her mind.

She was a lady, in a fine hall, with men eager to woo her. She danced and laughed and smiled. One young man approached, caressed her knuckles, and swept her to the dance floor. The fiddles and harp played merrily. Her dance partner planted a tender kiss on her lips.

She heaved a weighted breath. Her daydreams couldn't appease her soul.

For what man would marry, let alone want to dance with or court, a liar like her?

A FEW WEEKS LATER

Domhnall Montgomerie turned onto the busy street in Edinburgh. He rubbed a knot in his neck and moaned. Kendrick liked to work the men so hard that they dragged their achy bodies into bed each night. Sometimes he thought his uncle—his great-uncle in fact, the oldest man in all of Dornie—possessed an unnatural, immortal ability. He had an unfathomable level of endurance and a mystical connection to horses, it seemed. Whilst Domhnall enjoyed his time in the stables, and appreciated his uncle's training, he gladly wandered the streets in the darkness of night. Away from it all.

He moved with purpose, gliding between throngs of people, with Hayden as always by his side. The occasional brush of arm or leg sent his heartbeat soaring, then recovering. *Nothing*, his inner voice reminded. He forced the beast down. A demon, more like it. It had been nearly ten years after all since the last clutch of death besieged him. If he avoided people, then he was well.

He twisted another wooden dial on the puzzle box in his hands. The Edinburgh woodwright used different types of wood on this one resulting in an eye-pleasing design. He favored the ones that were one working piece, although many had parts that came out and had to be put back together and he appreciated the challenge.

"You overpaid," Hayden said.

"It keeps my hands busy."

"And your mind distracted."

Exactly. "I can manage more than one task at a time, you know. Besides, I've not encountered a woodwright who makes these puzzle boxes as complicated as Athol does." He added, "Sometimes, puzzles hold multiple solutions."

"What is their purpose other than a waste of coin?"

"I support a local crafter. Besides, they pass the time." More like keep the whispers and visions at bay. They diverted his mind from hyper-focusing on everyone's proximity, wondering if today Death would reappear from a long dormancy. So aye, worth every coin.

They continued their route. "This is foolish, Domhnall. Foolish. If Constable MacCoinneach finds us nosing in these shops, he'll have our head. We need to be working." Hayden crinkled his nose and scowled with a gesture toward the questionable alleyway, the one off the main path. He hopped over a muddy puddle.

"You'd be surprised at how open-minded my uncle is. And quit your moaning. Also, he insists you call him Kendrick, too." Domhnall shifted direction, lured by the signs on the corner: *Apothecary, Herbalist, Brewer, Ratcatcher,* and... *Fortune-teller.* That was new.

His quickened steps matched his pulse.

"He's your family, not mine, and I prefer to call him by his proper title. He is owed respect, as are you." Hayden kept pace with him.

"I'm not laird yet."

"You will be. Might as well grow accustomed to it."

He'd rather hide under a rock. Thankfully, his parents were lenient with clan traditions, but his younger sister Aileana wasn't married yet and didn't want the obligation of lairdship for her future husband either. The people of Dornie expected the Montgomerie name to carry on.

Rather than rule, if he proved himself capable, he wished to be promoted to constable instead when Kendrick relinquished his position. If Aileana found a husband willing to rein her in—good luck to the man—her husband could be laird. She could follow in their parents' footsteps, for it had been his maternal grandfather, Simon MacCoinneach, who'd been the laird. Alasdair Montgomerie hailed from a noble bloodline in the south, but he was not a MacCoinneach. Alasdair had become the new laird, not Domhnall's uncle Edmund. Why couldn't his parents allow their children to do the same?

The Watch and streets held Domhnall's heart. The men of the Watch kept peace by night, and day when needed. He loved slipping into the cold, dark shadows of solace. Aside from the occasional disorder, drunkenness, or minor theft, watchmen led uneventful lives. Simple puzzles to solve. Order. Seclusion.

Time alone.

Except lately there had been thefts and wrongdoings with nobody accountable—yet. A puzzle to solve.

"Where the devil are we heading? I thought Const—Kendrick," Hayden corrected, "wanted us to get the goods on our list?" He waved the parchment.

"We will. Look," Domhnall said with a pointed finger to a sign down the way, "an herbalist, too. My mother would love a few more herbs. Her gardens weren't as bountiful after our hard winter. You know how she is."

They passed the apothecary and brewer.

"Wait, this one?" Hayden pointed to the apothecary.

"Nay, she wants raw herbs. No odd tonics. She can make her own."

Ah, there it was, farther, beside the herbalist shop.

He drew a slip of parchment from his tunic's pocket.

"Domhnall…"

"God's bones, you're crabbit today. Make haste. Let's try these shops. Work can wait."

Domhnall drifted down the stone-lined alleyway, mindful of puddles of water and other filth in the gutters. Walk and watch and observe. Take it all in. That is what he did. He'd spent many years as a watchman learning to be aware. Kendrick had trained him with the appropriate skills that had arisen innately—and strongly—years ago.

Skills?

Or as Kendrick called them—abilities.

More like inabilities. Afflictions.

Domhnall swallowed the bitterness in his throat. His pulse flittered. *Center yourself.* He returned to the puzzle in his hand. He banished his thoughts and kept the demons at bay, for every day was a reminder.

Being constable and overseer of all watchmen was his calling. It rumbled in his blood. Aileana would marry the future laird. She often preened over Hayden, but his best friend wasn't nobility. Or maybe his sister Gracie could find a lovely match. Alas, she was only twelve. Given his father's robust health, Domhnall had time at least. Time to discern his future.

If only he could convince his father.

"This way, Hayden. There's the herbalist."

A man stumbled into their path and grabbed Domhnall's arm, nearly pulling him down. Fumes of overindulging scented the man's clothes. "Och, sorry, sir. I..." He didn't unclasp his tightened hold on Domhnall. A squat glass bottle fell from the stranger's other hand and crashed into the road, its contents spilling in an astringent waft. "My last coin's worth, too! Mercy!" He wept.

He must have purchased something from the apothecary.

Domhnall's heart raced as he tried to pry himself from the man's grip. "Do be well." He froze, not wanting to shake the man from him, but also desperately wanting to be free. One finger at a time, he peeled the man's hand away from his forearm, each touch a shock wave. A hint of black, a slow, sly sludge, moved in from his peripheral vision. No, he commanded Death's malevolent hold, with gritted teeth that caused pain to shoot through his jaw. Four fingers, three, two... Booming thunder rang in his ears despite the clear sky. His breakfast threatened to come up as his mind spun. Not now!

Hayden stepped in. "Did you drink your senses away? Get off him. He's a laird's son, and you reek." He ripped the man from Domhnall's arm and walloped him across the side of his face. The man fell. Hayden kicked him.

"Stop, Hayden. He's sick."

"He's been in his cups." He poked the man in the stomach with his boot. "Drunk as a thrush."

Domhnall raised his voice. "Stop."

"You could have...did you..." Hayden snarled, then whispered, "...*see* something?" He caught himself and straightened his shoulders. "You're well?"

Domhnall brandished his hand and recovered his breath, the only sounds in his ears the muffles and shuffles of the crowded roads. He swallowed acid that had risen up his throat. "I'm well. He's no bother." He handed the man two pennies to replace his remedy and as an apology for Hayden's behavior. He inclined his chin to his friend. "Come, Hayden."

God, Hayden was prickly today. Likely riled about Aileana's upcoming birthday and her hopeful announcement of a suitor. The drunk man was another sore spot for his friend. He cleared his throat and stepped through the herbalist's shop door first, still shaking from the near vision triggered by the man's touch, now branded on him like a scar. His skin crawled with invisible touches, and he rubbed his arm.

Pungent mixed with sweet assailed him as he entered, encouraging a thought of Isolde of all people.

God, could his mind just rest for one day?

Isolde had always smelled like rosemary and tasted of berries. She had worked in the kitchen with their cooks until she found herself a noble match a few years ago. Fortunate lass, and fortunate him. She would not have been a good wife. The memory of their one time together still haunted him, compressing his chest like hooves were upon it and waking him with sweaty bedclothes occasionally.

It felt like a century since he'd touched someone, fully touched. He both yearned for it and dreaded it. He'd make a perfect priest. But, he missed a woman's touch, a kiss or two. Isolde had been a divine kisser when they'd absconded to the old rowan tree in the pass years ago.

Memories of earthly passion flooded his mind. However...she had lied to him. Used him. Thank God their union hadn't worked out.

Perhaps the other side of his bed would always remain empty.

"Christ's bones, it stinks." Hayden slid in silently behind Domhnall, his friend's ire already doused and back into watchman persona. Domhnall's own frustration, and frankly anger, at being reminded of his inability to touch people, slowly dissipated. As did his painful memory of Isolde.

"My mother has a list of herbals." He waved the parchment. Work beckoned.

CHAPTER TWO

The summer heat stifled Rosalie's energy. She moved through the stale air of the Edinburgh shop and propped the door open with a heavy clay pot filled with petite, periwinkle flowers. Passersby were likely to stop for an open door. *Be inviting. Entice them.* Oswell and Nelda's words. However, she refused to wear her dress with the low-cut bodice. Instead, she swept her hair up and wore her favorite colorful stone necklace she'd crafted herself. She owned no face powders or paints, but Nelda said she held a natural, alluring beauty...except for her plain green-brown eyes.

Ahh. Fresh air and the sounds of the town. She inhaled, then gagged on a whiff of something wretched and swiped her nose to erase the sullied odors. She could pretend.

"Rosie, why must you do that?" Nelda fluttered aimlessly about the shop.

Her aunt had yet to take her daily poppy, so she was as sharp as a nail, and her tongue sharper.

"The place could use life." She waved a hand, scrunching her nose at the burning incense. Their cramped shop reeked with whatever the previous owner used to sell.

She wondered sometimes if it had been a butcher or leatherworker's shop. The scents varied between cow hide, rancid meat, and a mysterious biting scent.

She approached the counter with a dozen eggs, payment from a patron this morning. She imagined Oswell's consternation. "Coins, Rosie, coins. Get me a chicken, but no more godforsaken eggs." She lined up knickknacks: thimbles, two brooches she'd received from ladies, and a delicate cat figurine she'd acquired in London. None were for sale today until she could determine a profitable asking price, so she tucked them on the lower level of the counter, hidden from sight. In their place, she laid her handmade beaded and stone necklaces.

So far, her patrons had been limited to crofters with questions about the fall harvests. It was only early summer, and the folks were already wary of crops failing or thriving. Even here in Edinburgh, common folk paid in trinkets and goods or commodities, sometimes with a penny if she was lucky. Coins usually came from the noble patrons and so few had yet to visit her shop. She varied her charge depending on the person or need. Some could hardly afford the eggs.

If her uncle wanted a chicken or coins, then he could march himself down here and entice someone with his rat-catching business. He was still asleep. Despite purchasing his syrup from the apothecary next door, Oswell had been up half the night with coughing fits. His lungs needed fresh air. With the upstairs more stifling than the shop, Rosalie insisted on sleeping downstairs most nights, her cot tucked neatly behind the counter. Perhaps she'd have enough money today for Oswell to visit the healer. The coins rattled in her apron. She had three pence from yesterday. She needed two more for a thorough workup with curatives. The cough could be helped, but his diminished hearing would only get worse. Soon, it might be her alone making the money. Three people and multiple animals to feed, plus rent, taxes, tithes... Her mind spun with the numbers.

Two of their cats, Duo and Trēs, skittered past her. "No, no! Furry beasts must remain inside, lest you be taken or eaten. You've work to do later with Uncle Os." She grabbed each under an arm and carried them upstairs. "Heavens, I shan't be the only one who works." She plopped them on the bed beside her snoring uncle. Quattuor, their third cat, slept soundly beside him. "Smart kitty," she cooed with a swipe along the cat's thick orange coat. Oswell had laughed when she named his cats after Latin numbers. She smiled. Numbers pleased her. The stars and calendar held many fascinating patterns, too. Not to mention folks clung to superstitions.

Numbers ruled her life. Numbers helped her determine if she was getting swindled by a person who didn't want to pay her price or thought her to be dimwitted. Trēs jumped off the bed and tried to follow her. "No, no. I'll bring you milk later, my rascal." A quick one, he scurried past her down the steps. "You devil." She chased him. He was probably hungry. With their cow gone, she'd been forced to purchase their milk from the herbalist next door who had a goat. She'd not yet convinced Oswell to sell a sheep and get a goat instead. She preferred milk and cheese over wool—which required further processing, so she just purchased their fabrics for clothes.

Sweat trickled between her breasts. She loosened the strings at the top of her bodice and fanned herself. Trēs paused near his empty dish behind the counter. "I miss it, too, sweet boy."

Nelda carried the flowerpot inside, knocking over a display in her efforts.

"No. Please, Auntie," Rosalie said with an agitated rise of her voice while picking up scattered trinkets. "People like a pleasant welcome. And it pleases me." Flowers cost nothing when she could find some in a nearby meadow.

Her aunt sucked her teeth. "They don't need flowers. They come with their own ideas already. People like the mysterious...and their own truths. Superstitious, themsfolk are. They pray to their heathen god here. They only like to hear what they want to hear. Best you remember, Rosie." Nelda's hands flitted through the drawer, seeking.

Rosalie shoved the flint and steel sitting in plain sight on the top of the counter into her aunt's hands. "Here, Auntie. There are Christians in Scotland. They share our God."

Gratitude lit her aunt's dark brown eyes as she took the flint and steel. "What about your lavender dress? The one with the sweet neckline? I got that fine fabric in..." She rubbed her head and moaned.

Rosalie politely waited, but her aunt's brow twisted, her eyes teary.

"Norwich was a lovely town."

Confidence returned to Nelda's face. "Yes. In Norwich. The best fabrics. Linen with a texture reminding me of silk." She smiled, her gaze glassy and distant. "It brings out the fairness of your golden hair. We can't do anything about your eyes though." She staggered, lighting candles to illuminate the shadows of the shop. She struggled with one, her hands shaking. She scowled until she got a spark.

It was too stifling inside to keep a fire going and use the hot embers to light the candles in summer.

Nelda should take a dose of the poppy, but not before work today. After. Rosalie loved Nelda, but she was a boar in the mornings. "There's nothing wrong with my eyes," Rosalie whispered. Self-conscious, she lifted the hand mirror on the counter. Staring at her were humble eyes. They weren't a Seer's enchanting eyes, for certain. Nor a lady's, with sweeping dark lashes or deep blue irises. They were a crofter's, a simple folk's eyes. Eyes told many truths. But eyes also lied. Oh, the truths she deciphered in eyes!

"Careful. That's for sale. Real silver. I expect no less than—" Nelda bounced her knuckles off her lips.

Rosalie waited. A frustrated moan came from her aunt.

Finally, she said, "Five shilling, Auntie."

"Yes, yes, five shilling. I must be gone, off to clean homes."

She was nearly to the door when Rosalie stopped her and shoved a folded page into her hand.

"What's this?"

"Uncle Os wrote the names and numbers for you. In order, see," Rosalie said, pointing, though she couldn't read the words. The numerals and map she added. She might be good at numbers, money, and bartering, but when it came to writing and reading, Oswell never thought she required the education. Her training had come solely from Nelda: gathered information from castles, houses, taverns, and streets. Of course, Rosalie was adept at all household duties, of which she found herself doing more daily with a sick uncle and senile aunt. Oswell insisted she had no use of writing or reading as long as she had her pretty face and "gift" of premonition.

"No need, no need," he always said. "People believe what they want to believe. One day you'll woo a man and have a household of your own. No more need for lies, Rosie dear."

She hugged her aunt and returned to the doorway. "Keep it close. In case?"

"I don't need no reminder." Nelda perused the list anyway. "Mrs. Abernathy. I haven't seen her in a while."

Try last week. Rosalie fought the frown and smiled instead. Her cheeks hurt from the act.

Nelda turned left.

"No, Auntie, that way." She gestured right. Oswell needed to start escorting Nelda.

Her meals had become a peculiar mix of foods, so Rosalie had usurped the role once her aunt had added chestnuts. Thankfully, Rosalie had seen them prior to a bite. She was horribly sensitive. Consumption of them constricted her lungs. Once the healer had been called. The incident had depleted their coin for the month.

Sloppy sewing, passable cleaning, and poor cooking: Nelda could no longer cope with the demands of working.

"Follow the oil lanterns, Auntie. To return. See." She pointed. "There are fifteen on the way to Mrs. Abernathy's house. Two on the corner, then turn. Look for our sign." She tapped a hand on the wooden sign.

Nelda tilted her head in an obedient nod. Loose gray curls, tucked haphazardly under a cap, broke free with the movement. Rosalie touched her own soft wavy hair. She always wondered if her mother had curls like Nelda.

She watched for a long moment, then as her aunt's short, round form was swallowed by the swarm of people, Rosalie knelt and picked dead blooms off the flowers in the pot at the door. She didn't know their name, but a good plucking encouraged growth. She topped the soil with water from her pitcher.

"Forget-me-not," a deep voice said from behind, causing her to spill some of her water.

Startled, she turned while wiping a wet hand on her apron. "Pardon me?"

"Forget-me-nots. Lovely if you ignore the belief behind their name," the stranger explained. He held Trēs in his arms.

What the—? How?

"Your cat, I take it? Little thing snuck out behind you while you were tending the flowers." He handed the cat to her.

She scooped Trēs into her arms after placing the heavy pitcher on the ground. "This one is trouble. Pardon me, sir. Sorry he bothered you." She stroked the furry scoundrel's chin, and he purred.

Every person was a potential coin, so she evaluated the man immediately. The first moments were the most crucial when a new patron approached. He stood a few steps back from her. He liked space?

How did he carry himself? Robust posture.

What did he have with him? Her cat. Kind to animals.

When a person entered, what did they first inspect? Hmm, he wasn't inside. Yet.

Clothes, voice, eyes. All admirable. Her breath caught. He was devastatingly handsome.

Finally, she analyzed hands once she got a person to sit with her.

She repositioned her wiggly cat in her arms.

"Forget-me-nots," he repeated, with an eyebrow raise. "Your flowers."

"Oh? What an interesting name for them." Knows flowers—check. Odd trait for a man.

"Aye, my mother loves gardening."

Ah. She loved when people unknowingly gave her the answers.

He wore a finely crafted pouch on his belt. A subtle whiff of him gave off the remnant odor of betony and sage. He had visited Edith, the herbalist.

Well-groomed. Refined speech. Flower knowledge, herbs. Mother.

The man was a nobleman, likely. Unsoiled tunic, leather belt, clean boots, shaven face.

"Why are they given such a name?" She allowed his nearness, but when she stepped a fraction of a step closer, she felt his hesitation, so she backed up...one foot in her door. *Draw him in. Smile.* Heavens, she'd be an old lady with horrible smile lines. Nelda held none though and she had done her share of fortune-telling in her younger years. Her aunt's ways were not as gentle, though. Less honey, more spice had been Nelda's method. She'd practically scared them inside. Not Rosalie. She reached down to pick up the pitcher.

"Let me take that for you." He grabbed the pitcher.

She adjusted Trēs, stroked under his chin. She subtly stepped back a hair.

Draw him in...

He added, "Oh, the name. A lad drowned while trying to retrieve them for his lover. He got swept away by a river but managed to toss them to her so she would forget him not," he said through a poignant look.

She wasn't sure which was more ironic: their name, her aunt's dislike of them, or the romantic gesture associated with them. "A dreadful story."

Health glowed in his brown eyes. The wind ruffled his thick, dark brown hair. She inhaled slightly and smelled sweat, too, as expected from a man on a hot day, but clean sweat. Nobility. Why was he in the market? Most nobles sent their servants. A glance over his shoulder—he was alone.

She could probably get two pence or even a groat from him if she tried.

"Domhnall, whatcha fussing about?" another man said as he sauntered up beside the stranger as if in response to her thoughts. Not alone then.

"You sell trinkets?" the nobleman, Domhnall—it sounded like a Gaelic name—asked, sneaking a peek inside the doorway to her display.

Almost there. Closer.

"Yes, aplenty, and a fortune or two," she said through a bigger smile. He held her look, his eyes calculating. Três squirmed in her arms.

His companion's gaze homed right toward her cleavage. Uncle Oswell would have been pleased. "Domhnall?" he asked, exuding impatience much like her cat.

She offered a dainty eyelash blink to the second man.

"Here's the list for the leatherworker, yonder." Domhnall handed the parchment to his counterpart and pointed across the street. "You get them. I'll look for a gift for Lanie's *cèilidh* here." He turned to Rosalie.

The man with him was no servant. He carried himself differently and gave off an air of intrigue, something she could not put her finger on. His lips twisted into an unsubtle sneer as he parted from them for the leather-worker's shop. "Aye."

She would offer the nobleman the mirror for purchase. Lanie—lover or kin? She chewed her lip.

The man, tall and muscular, had to duck to get through the narrow and short doorway.

She gestured to the counter. "You can place the pitcher there, thank you. Please give me a moment." *Don't leave.* She hurried upstairs and locked Trēs in with snoring Oswell and the other cats. "You rascal." Hmm, he had lured the man to her doorstep. "All right, good kitty."

She hurried down.

The man's gaze darted over the trinkets lined up at the counter, then to her simple table. She didn't use any magical items or elements like other fortune-tellers. Acquired knowledge was her best card. She lacked it on him, so she'd use intuition and observation instead. She had tricks on hand, in case, along with her knowledge of lines and mounts of the palm.

He paced the shop.

"Looking for something in particular?"

He tossed a look over his shoulder. They were alone. "Is the Seer in?"

She blinked. "Weren't you seeking a gift?"

He shuffled around, the floor creaking beneath his weight, perusing, but not touching, the items for sale. He laced his fingers behind his back and inspected with a critical eye. He carried himself well. No concern wrinkled his youthful face—likely a few years older than she—but his body movement said otherwise. He paused at two apple tartlets she'd made this morning for a patron who'd be picking them up soon. He gave a subtle sniff. She hoped the aroma masked the horrid smell of the shop.

"These look delicious. So...the Seer?"

She straightened her posture, broadened her smile, and said, "You're looking at her." She clasped her hands behind her to control the worries within. The poised guise was part of her front, but sometimes she felt her insides might release. Sweat slicked her palms. *No nerves, Rose.* The lies used to be easy. Most of her patrons were crofters, the lower class, who drank in her lies like a good sip of whisky. Ever since Lady Brantingham, her confidence had withered though.

Was it love he sought? The woman Lanie, a tender nickname? Elaine? Elena? Eleanor? None were Scottish names. Did he seek land? She assumed he didn't want for much. No, it was not land or power. Something of the heart vexed him. She contemplated what she could tell him that he would believe.

His eyebrows lifted so high, she thought they'd detach and hit the low ceiling. "You? Aren't you young?" Pink filled his higher cheekbones.

"Not all Seers are decrepit old women."

The flush deepened in his face. He cleared his throat and looked over his shoulder. Nobody came or went, but his friend would return soon.

With a gesture toward the chair on the other side of her reading table, she said, "Do you seek a reading, Sir—"

She slid onto a stool.

"Domhnall's fine."

She regained her composure. "What is it you seek?"

He paused, swallowed. "Don't you require money first?"

"Aye. But it depends on what you seek."

His forehead twisted with suspicion.

She bit her sigh. He didn't know what he wanted. He was a contradiction. It could play to her gain or loss. "Your hand, please." *Assess, Rose.* What would a young, handsome, brooding Scottish nobleman want?

He clenched a fist at his side, shuffling like an antsy child.

"It's part of the process," she coaxed with another gesture to the seat.

"Can you do it without touching me?"

She muffled her exasperation. He dropped six pennies on the table. "Can you?" He took a seat, the rickety table shaking with his movement.

Her heartbeat galloped. That was enough money to pay off Nelda's debts from shoddy work. Lady Brantingham had paid only two pence on her visits, and she'd visited Rosalie three times. Her words caught. "Y-yes."

"Promise, me. No touching." The plea in his firm voice surfaced.

She felt her lips want to turn into a glower. Instead, she said sweetly, "I'm not sick or diseased. My nails are clean." She splayed her hands, her cheeks burning. He had no observable pustules or boils, so obviously his issue was with her. "I have all my teeth." She smiled bigger, bolder. With no information on him, she needed his hands. She was not a real Seer, by God's bones! Seers were not real. The lines, the ridges, the knolls...told many stories. At least something he would believe. She couldn't weave lies from the air!

He exhaled a laugh. "I don't doubt you're well, lass."

What was with Scotsmen calling women lasses? "I *am* well, sir. I'm not an old crone, yes, nor am I a wee lassie."

His eyes lit with mirth. "I daresay you're not. Mistress, then. It's Domhnall."

"You have no last name?" That would at least guide her in a direction. Was he connected to one of the notable clans around Edinburgh?

"What about you? No madam or lass or..." he countered.

He refrained from saying "lady." She remained objective and assured, despite wanting to fan the heat rising up her chest. Woo *them with your confidence, Rose.* "Rosalie." If she had been married, *Mrs.* would garner more respect and sales—lord, she was far from it. Besides, Oswell preferred her to appear "available."

He was full-on smiling. White teeth. Most certainly a nobleman. She inhaled, her ego settled. She scooped the coins and dropped them into her pocket. "No touching, but you must lay both your hands on the table. I'll keep my hands in my lap."

She compiled her assessments. A Scottish laird? No, too young. A laird's son or kin? She was not well-versed on the Scottish hierarchy, but was familiar with a few of the clans around this part of Scotland. He didn't want to give her his last name. He didn't like the title? Maybe.

No limps. No outward ailments or noticeable scars or battle wounds. What troubled this privileged man?

Hesitantly, he placed his hands on her table. When she reached toward them, only to hover, not touch, he retracted them.

"You said hands in your lap."

"Indeed." Something bothered him when people touched him. Her mind ran through scenarios and came up blank.

"Palms up, please. Cup them, like this." She showed him. He did as instructed. "Hmm. I see."

His hands looked—because she could not touch them—smooth, blemish-free, and his nails were trimmed and cleaned. Callouses swelled on the mounts of his fingers but showed no scars or cuts. His plains were smooth. He worked with his hands but had not seen battle. He had well-formed forearms, strong shoulders. Stables, horses? A nobleman who labored? He'd been shopping with a subordinate. A steward? Soldier? This man was mystery, his story full of too many possibilities.

Most of his mounts were equal-sized, but his middle one rose a hair. Insecure, meticulous, sad. Something haunted him. *Doesn't something haunt us all?* "Lay them flat, wide. Good, good. Now, flip over a moment. Yes. Now back."

Loyal, honorable, people-pleasing, rule-follower.

His palm was square, with fingers longer than palm length, and his knuckles protruded, with a lower-set thumb. She wasn't sure she agreed with the attributes the profile held, at least for this man. He seemed hardly the chatty sort. She suspected he was comfortable with the intangible. His thoughts went deep. Why else would he be here? He was open to embracing the unique.

"Air," she murmured, choosing the most applicable of elements for his profile. She'd dare not start with the negative qualities of his mounts. She'd work into them. Her assertions usually hit a mark or two, and then she could move into specifics.

He muffled a gasp.

Good guess. She hit her mark and breathed her own internal sigh. Reading the hand never failed her. "You come from nobility. You seek something." *Vague, Rose...*

"How do you know?"

"A Seer knows."

He snorted. "Not from my attire, weapons, and grooming?"

She straightened. "You came for a reading, but you scoff at me? I can return your coins, and you may seek elsewhere, Domhnall. Mind you, I'm the only teller in Edinburgh." Dear God, a bluff. If Oswell knew, he'd have her head. Six pence was not something to wager. She'd used his name to aggravate him. Add cynic to his list of traits. He both questioned and believed. Or wanted to believe.

Lost in the moment, she didn't notice the other man slither in until he was at Domhnall's shoulder. He was like a shadow. Mother Mary! She chided her racing pulse. She saw past his smooth façade immediately. His simple handsomeness, sandy brown hair, and deep green eyes likely lured women to his bed, and he was a few years older than the nobleman. He was not dressed as finely as Domhnall, so he was of humble birth, despite his haughty presence. Many men would kill to be a noble's liege. She'd bet her coins she was with a nobleman's son, and his vassal, or whatever they were called in Scotland.

The cavalier man thumbed through her trinkets. "Careful, please. Delicate things."

He sneered. "I see naught of value."

Heat burned the tips of her ears. She summoned her best smile. The companion wasn't looking at her, but the dark-haired nobleman was. Show was everything. She would not let his friend rile her.

"I'll wait outside. Domhnall, quit feeding this woman's ruse. We have work. No time to play with a fortune-teller. We do honorable work. The Watch awaits."

The Watch? What was that? A group of soldiers? She would ask Oswell about it. Both men carried swords, but most men of higher rank did. A noble laborer? Rosalie suppressed her retorts. She couldn't risk losing the coins on the account of his pig friend.

"A moment," Domhnall nearly growled. He rose. "The mirror, there. Aye, I'll take it. How much?"

Rosalie stood, too. His friend marched out. "Your reading, sir. There is much to say." His lines, the mounts, all her tricks...now she knew more about him. She needed to earn the six pence. She'd told him hardly a thing.

Domhnall shuffled. "Just the mirror today."

Trēs' unique meow emanated from above, followed by the sound of claws scratching at the door.

"You're being called," he added with a gleam in his eye.

He paid and was off, leaving her gawking like a fool, the six pence and another five shillings—coins she hardly ever saw or felt—heavy in her pocket.

CHAPTER THREE

T he month since Domhnall's visit to Edinburgh had passed slowly. He couldn't shake the teller's reading from his mind.

He wandered the cobblestone paths of Dornie, each step purposeful. Each step soul-cleansing. He inhaled the cooler night air, allowing vitality to rush through his veins.

Air.

She had said air. Wind and air were one and the same. Aye?

As in *the Wind*, the Seer's wind his mother always told him about.

How had the teller known? Most Seers in the towns were frauds. They always told him he'd find glory in battle, coin in his pocket, or a lass in his bed. Nothing original. Nothing a man of his stature didn't usually yearn for. Regardless, he'd spent years scouring the country-side looking for another like him...yielding only vague promises and tales of fortune. All lies. Except...

This one.

She was different. He cupped his fists together and blew a breath onto his palms, always cold despite the evening's warmth. He cast a look around, his night vision rivaling a hawk's, his memory sharper than its talons. Every road and alleyway throughout Dornie sat etched in his mind, no need of flame to light the way. Stone, cobble, rut. His walks were like a faerie dance.

The cold always reminded him of who he was. Everything about his ability was based on stories and superstition. Some would call it witchcraft or demon's work. However, he preferred evidence before drawing any conclusion.

But you have seen your own power. Is that not evidence enough?

He cursed the inner voice.

A brittle peace rested in his mind. Whatever he was doing, he'd continue. So, he shut the visions away. He didn't touch a soul because if he did...

He groaned. Denial wasn't a becoming trait.

A light breeze brushed his skin. It wasn't the Wind. Not the godforsaken Norse words that whispered to him long ago. Nevertheless, he trembled.

Did others like him exist beyond the isles? He'd never met his great-aunt, Venora, to inquire about the whispers of the Wind. Kendrick shared selectively about his mysterious sister Venora. The time had come to press him before his great-uncle met their heavenly Father. Domhnall's ability would only remain dormant for so long. What if when it returned, it would be worse?

Through the years, he'd honed his skills of meticulous observation as a watchman, maintaining order among the peasants and nobles. Kendrick had relied heavily upon his nephew's ability to seek out vagrants, when the Sight had been sharp in the early years of Domhnall's training.

Now, though, Domhnall's keen hyper-vigilance reigned over the Sight. Was it enough?

His doubt caused him to overcompensate. He had to. He had to prove to himself, to all, he was more than his gift. He'd banished it away years ago, after all, and had fared well.

Yet, the Sight lurked in the darkness, threatening to return at at any unguarded moment.

"Och, Domhnall." Hayden materialized on the opposite end of the road, a lantern in his hand. His friend strolled toward him, light-footed. "Anything?"

He cleared his throat. "No, nothing amiss. Perhaps the thieves won't do anything tonight?"

"They've yet to steal during day except once with Mr. MacVinish. I would not doubt anything at this point though. Last week, five of Auld Ysac's sheep were taken in the night. Then Mrs. Clunes reported her silver spoons walked away. They're getting bold. What next?"

The person or group causing unrest in their town always left behind a sprig of fresh or pressed bell heather after each act. Domhnall knew the notable purple flower from meadow walks and his mother's education. Bell heather was also the emblem of Clan MacDougall. Were they the ones committing the acts? Or was someone making them think it was the MacDougalls?

"Should we find our beds soon?" Hayden yawned. "I checked the marketplace already. The peddlers are almost done setting up for the weeklong market."

The late summer market was the biggest of the year in comparison to the weekly markets. More people. More duties. More thefts?

"Let's check again. Then you get some rest."

Hayden grumbled at his side.

"How is your mother?" Domhnall would be remiss not to inquire. His friend was needed at the croft in the mornings to help his mother. Hayden needed his sleep now, not later. Domhnall could at least sleep until midday, though he required less sleep and could never waste half the day on sleeping, not when duty called.

"No change."

Mrs. Iverson worked in their kitchens and received a handsome wage, but lately, her bones creaked and her mind went astray. She had trouble getting out of bed, let alone planning all the castle's meals. He remembered when the same condition happened to Moreen. The downturn had been quick. "Eat greens." His mother had encouraged her good friend and elder confidant Moreen. She had ordered her to rest and take care of herself. The now-deceased kitchen cook—God rest her soul—had held a soft spot for the baked goods. And the weaving of stories about Uist and the Ancients. He loved them as a lad. He'd curl himself in a wool blanket by the hearth, drink warmed milk, and listen, attentive. As an adult, he now understood most of the tales were history of the isles and not fabricated stories for young ears. She had fought Fate's claws for a long time. Regrettably, he'd never pressed Moreen for more truths about the isles. She was a hearty woman and used to sneak him sweet breads.

Aye, and she'd made delicious treats. His grandfather had always enjoyed them. A stubborn ox, Grandda never remarried after Grandmother's death. Grandfather Simon's heart had held room for only one true love. Domhnall remembered his mother's sadness with both the passing of Grandda twenty years ago, and Moreen a few years ago.

He blinked, the memory of seeing Grandda and Grandma reunited in the afterlife glowing vividly in his vision. The dragon-headed ship. Warmth spread in his chest.

His stomach growled, and the tendrils of one of his only pleasant visions disappeared. That moment of serenity enveloping him in shimmery silver clouds left as quickly as it had come.

Hayden dipped a hand into a pouch at his side and handed Domhnall a biscuit.

"Thanks. I'll be by again later to check on your roof. I spoke with the thatcher, and he can do it for less than quoted."

Hayden nodded as he bit into his own biscuit.

They zigzagged through winding shortcuts to the open meadow where, yearly, a grand market of vendors convened. Wooden stalls provided by their town flanked the center ring of tents where merchants from near and far had set up. On his first pass, he counted at least fifty peddlers. Domhnall secretly hoped the English Seer would be among the gathering. Although she had a shop in Edinburgh, many merchants traveled the market route during summer and autumn. Was it a family business? Did she have parents, a husband?

God, was he considering the idea she was a real Seer? And that she'd come here. Daft.

But she had said *air*.

Her mossy eyes had held his with frank honesty.

Either she was true, or a very skilled liar.

Air.

Gooseflesh rippled his skin, and he caught a whiff of words on a draft. *No, stay away,* he reproached, forcing his mind to stay on the task of watchman.

He did another pass around the perimeter. Most folk were camped for the night, slumbering in makeshift tents, and the lucky ones had found lodging with kin or at taverns in town. Part of the Watch's job was to keep an eye on the peddlers' belongings and animals.

"Sleep beckons me, Domhnall. Guthrie and Comroy are here, see. Aiden is watching the western flank." Hayden pointed to the other watchmen monitoring the market ground. "Let's share in delights at the tavern before sleep calls."

Domhnall ignored his friend. Hayden didn't refer to the heady mead or whisky. He wished Hayden would cease suggesting it. After the Isolde incident, Domhnall had sworn off all lasses, and the tavern had felt cursed, as well. The previous owner had not heeded his warning, just like many others...back when he had tried to warn people about what he saw in his visions. And the man had ended up dead. Everything, everywhere, was a reminder of his failures. Perhaps leaving the town would be a better option than staying here and protecting it with only his mind and sword. He was long past an age where it was proper to leave, though. Father expected him to rule as laird.

Besides, this was his home. He belonged here.

Low fires blazed near the peddlers setting up or partaking in a late-hour meal. He kept his distance. By eye of the moon, it had to be nearly midnight. He had his route both memorized and timed.

"You smell that?" Hayden hurried alongside him.

Domhnall sniffed. "Smoke from the fires." His stomach lurched.

"Not from here. There. Look." Hayden turned around, the lantern swinging in his hand.

Gray smoke and red flames stained the sky a short distance from the market area. The flames, both seductive and destructive, enchanted Domhnall.

A woman's scream broke the night's tranquil rhythm and tore Domhnall from the clutches of the branded memory. He jumped to action, already making for the fire.

"I'll stand watch over the marketplace. Go!" Hayden darted his gaze at the fire.

Guthrie and Comroy had seen it, too, and were quick on Domhnall's heels to the fire before he could call for them.

In a matter of moments, they formed a chain of buckets using water from the nearby well. A brigade to the closest stream would have taken too long, so the fresh water had to be used. Abrasive flames heated his skin, and the air squeezed from his lungs. A mule brayed, then whimpered from a nearby pen. Domhnall took the lead to calm the animals, a method he'd learned from Kendrick. He removed his tunic and threw it over the mule's face. He led the animals, one by one, to another paddock while a group of men assisted Guthrie and Comroy with the stable fire. The engulfed thatched roof released sickening pops. A beam fell like a thunder crack.

They worked hard. They worked fast.

Finished, sweat beaded his skin as he took it all in. He shrugged into his sooty tunic. Thank God for Guthrie and Comroy. The roof was gone and could be rebuilt. At least it hadn't spread to neighboring crofts or barns, and nobody was injured. The scent of burnt hay and charred wood attacked his nose. He went around the nearby paddock and vomited as memory unleashed.

The next morning, Domhnall absentmindedly stirred his porridge while Kendrick sat across from him at the table in Eilean Donan's hall, both of them quiet and introspective.

Sometimes intuition and reading body language worked better than his Sight. Domhnall asked, "What troubles you, Uncle?"

"Not enough sleep for my old bones." Kendrick cracked his knuckles. Fatigue dimmed his light blue eyes. Wrinkles carved a deep ridge in his high forehead, but the rest of his skin, tanned by long days with the horses, remained vibrant. In his prime, he'd been a fetching man, according to Mother's stories. It was like Kendrick had sipped from a mystical burn that held life-giving properties. But, the true reason for his great-uncle's longevity had to do with Domhnall's great-grandmother, Caoimhe of Uist. The mystical flowed through their bloodline: Healing, Feeling, and Seeing.

"Do you think the thieves set the stable fire?" Domhnall asked.

Kendrick scooped a bite of porridge, slowly working it in his mouth like he had taken a piece of chewy bread. Though his skin and body had escaped the aging process that would make envious folks want to bottle his enchantment, his teeth had not fared as well.

"I'm not sure. Hayden reported to me that several items were stolen at the marketplace and the thieves left fresh sprigs of bell heather like before. While you lads were putting the fire out?"

He didn't speak with disdain or reprimand, but Domhnall felt it. He tightened a fist. It had been his responsibility. Hayden, Guthrie, Comroy, and Aiden all reported to him. "Bell heather is the MacDougall flower, Uncle."

"Many people appreciate the flower. It grows abundantly in summer. The group might—"

"Have a fondness for leaving it behind? The MacDougalls. They're taunting us."

Kendrick pursed his lips, reflective. "Or someone wants us to believe it is the MacDougalls."

The thieves—for clearly all the stealing had to be a group of men—had used the fire as a diversion. He launched a flurry of questions. "What do you suggest? We watch all night. There are only five of us. Day rounds? Question the peddlers? Recruit more watchmen? I don't think the men in training are ready. Should we use Uncle Crystoll's soldiers for the watchmen's work?" His chest tightened. *Breathe through it. You always do.*

Kendrick turned the question upon him. "What do you think is the best course of action?"

Another test. He dropped his spoon and fiddled with a new handheld wooden puzzle. This one was cylindrical. Athol had made a set last week and wanted Domhnall's thoughts on them prior to the market fair. The woodwright's skills were impressive. The others in the set all had removable parts, composed of different pieces, stained several colors, and cut into various edged shapes. Take them apart...put together. Athol's best yet.

Kendrick added, "If you can solve those wee things, you can solve this."

"Not as simple."

"Everything can be broken down to a simple solution. You've sometimes come up with the best ideas when solving Athol's puzzles, which are complicated, aye, but you find the answer...and then it is simple."

"It's a distraction." From many horrible memories.

From the anger expanding in my chest daily.

Kendrick pressed on. "Motives are simple, too, hidden behind the distractions. Why are these men stealing? That is the first question. Then, how do we fix it?"

"I've yet to figure out who, let alone the why. Don't we want to know who, first?"

"Not necessarily. The why may reveal the who. And ultimately, the how."

Domhnall paused with the next wooden dial, contemplating both its move and the thieves' intentions. "Theft is usually motivated by necessity or revenge. Burning the barn? A distraction. They've never done that before, only stole items or animals."

Kendrick nodded.

"We can't employ the soldiers. Rumblings of discontent with the MacDougall clan keep them on guard. The bell heather? Cannot be a coincidence."

"Usually the simplest answer *is* the answer. Usually. Not always."

Domhnall grimaced with Kendrick's cryptic words. "Father's been preoccupied with repairing relationships with the clan and attending court. Our kinship with the MacDougalls is not beyond repair—yet. Why would somebody else leave the bell heather though? To stir unrest between our clans even more?"

"Perhaps. Or it is another—"

"—distraction."

He nodded again. "We need more minds and bodies on this. If we don't use the soldiers, what do you suggest?"

Click. He solved a second part of the cylindrical puzzle. Four to go. "These past twenty years, Scotland has seen enough strife."

"Och, lad, the wars go farther back than that. Long before my time."

Domhnall's visions from his youth had foreseen death for their country. Why voice their obvious grim future now? He twisted another dial. War. The clans. How can he rally support? The clans were not the problem, but the answer. "We should increase our number of watchmen by recruiting from the neighboring clans who hold alliance with us. We've a strong kinship with the Donalds. We can monitor the day hours, too, with extra men. Instill stricter consequences for people caught plundering."

Kendrick chewed the idea. His thick gray eyebrows furrowed like a caterpillar. "The coin to pay these men?"

Domhnall fidgeted with the puzzle, the answer teasing him. "Tax a penny per merchant for it? They're here for a full week. They're likely to earn well during the market fair." He had never reconciled the numbers with Father because Crystoll assisted with fiscal management and commanding the soldiers.

"Don't they already pay enough taxes to our lairds, sheriffs, and the baron?" He shook his head. "They'd riot if we tax them further. The English and barons bleed us dry.

The merchants are likely to take up pitchfork or hammer and form their own group of watchmen. They could stir an uprising, disorder. Nay. We must help our people, not tax them."

"Aye. I try."

"You do. You'll be an able laird or constable when the time comes."

Domhnall dropped the puzzle to give his mind a moment. How could he be laird if he could not find the solution to this problem? He lifted a bannock, freshly toasted from the oven and slathered with butter and honey. He took a halfhearted bite. Delicious but not the same as Moreen's. "I'm without an answer, Uncle."

"Me, too, and I have over forty years on you."

Domhnall attempted to withdraw from the conversation by eating silently, but it was to no avail. He hated an unsolved puzzle. The solutions, even if simple, still rested in the details. He picked up the puzzle box. Almost there. Twisted another dial. "The market will bring in extra coin. All the merchants pay fees for their stalls. We counted a record number of peddlers this year. It's been a good season. Might a portion of our acquired earnings be given to the other watchmen? Instead of taxing, take some from our revenue?"

Kendrick sipped from his goblet. "I'll ask your father what he can skim off. It might already be accounted for elsewhere. Thankfully, our summer crops are thriving, and the batch of whisky and ales we opened are excellent. The stonemasons repairing the seawall are not bargaining on expenses though. Much coin has been sunk into the project. If your father agrees, you'll meet with the

Donalds, rally men to our cause." He tipped the goblet toward his great-nephew and finished the contents.

"Aye." Domhnall sighed. Failure was not an option. He needed to find the thieves before the problem escalated.

"I never thought to find myself in Dornie, Domhnall," Kendrick said in his crisp voice.

Relief at the shift in subjects loosened the strain building in Domhnall's upper back. "What do you mean?"

"I liked tending the horses." He shrugged with a subdued gaiety. Bright clouds of memory passed over his eyes, which sparkled in fondness. He stroked a gray beard. "Your grandmother Gwyn was a stubborn woman. She thought it was her responsibility to take care of me, protect me..."

Domhnall tried to imagine Kendrick younger, leaner, as a reticent stable boy. Why would he need protecting? For many years, he had been the most able fighter at Eilean Donan Castle. "You've a magical touch, Uncle."

Kendrick hailed from the isles with Domhnall's maternal grandmother, the mystical Gwyn of Uist. His great-uncle had not been a blood relative to Domhnall's grandfather, but Simon MacCoinneach had taken him in, adopted him as his own kin. Called him his brother. Nobody questioned their laird. Kendrick had been born a Norse-Ancient. He had once possessed unmatched powers as a Feeler...like Domhnall's mother, Deirdre.

Until one day, Kendrick had the ability no more.

He should have found solace and camaraderie with both his Feeler mother and great-uncle. Isolation consumed his thoughts instead. They could touch the ones they loved, though Kendrick's wife had long since died and he never remarried nor had children. He happily spent his days caring for the horses, the watchmen, and people.

"Do you miss the isles?" Domhnall chanced.

Kendrick held his gaze. Domhnall had once seen a vision of an epic Norse battle, commanded by a boat with an emblem of a snarling red wolf. Interesting stones had hummed in the vision with an amber-hued healing power. Tall, massive slabs. They sang to him. It was one of his more mesmerizing visions.

This vision had been Kendrick's world once. "Sometimes. I miss my sisters and brother."

He'd had a brother? Gwyn, Venora, and who? A man not once mentioned in the past twenty-five years from what Domhnall could recall. "I'm sorry. It still pains you?"

"No apology, and no more pain." He tapped his temple. "The memories come and go. I once held a delicate power to see into people like your mother. It also pained me terribly. I almost died. I was relieved of my burden by a virtuous Healer, my own mother."

Domhnall had meant the pain of heartbreak, not the physical hurt. Even so, to feel the deaths of others must have been unbearable.

"Deirdre's ability is nearly as strong as mine once was, but she has far greater control of it. She's learned to release the pain of others. And through it all, she found love, no less. You're blessed, your ma and da are so in love...and care for you. One day you'll find it, too." His words held a note of sadness and premonition.

Domhnall had heard about Kendrick's father's cruelty, and he was truly grateful for the gift he had in his own parents. He grunted as Kendrick's story morphed from the physical pain to one of the heart. He almost said *How can I find love if I can't touch her*, but he didn't. He would sound like a whiny lad. There were far greater pains than being unable to touch a woman. "You never remarried."

"I had one love. Venora told me my fate. I didn't bother to test it. I'm not sure we can change our destiny. The truest love for me was of kin, with your grandma and grandda. They were my love, my family."

"More of our kind may still exist." Like a child, he continued to voice the same hope. *I cannot be alone in this, can I?* Venora had been a Seer as well, but she died years ago. He always wondered: if he had met her, would she have been able to help him with his power?

Kendrick swallowed the last of his meal. "I don't know. Many fled south long ago when the Nordmen conquered the western isles. I pray some of my people have flourished elsewhere, on the southern isles. I hope." He rose, his knees audibly creaking and said, "Work demands our attention now."

"Aye." Domhnall hadn't eaten a thing beyond two bites of the bannock. He'd bring it to the stable with him. He downed a half-full goblet of apple cider, last harvest's batch, the drink biting and tart.

Kendrick paused. "You've made us all proud."

Domhnall spun the last twist on the puzzle. "Got it."

Kendrick's smile spread his features wide. "Athol has yet to stump you."

"I wish I could unravel the thieving puzzle."

"You will. You always do. You have gifts beyond the Sight, Domhnall. Trust in them."

With that, Kendrick ably strolled from the hall toward the kitchen entrance, his back as straight as a board, his wide shoulders set and gait robust.

Domhnall retreated to his chamber to begin writing dispatches, restive and pondering the bigger puzzle.

Exhaustion protested in Rosalie's muscles as she maneuvered around their wooden stall in the marketplace to set up their display. Resourceful Oswell had them on a rigorous summer schedule. With open markets across the Highlands, he'd been more than eager to find new buyers. They'd spent the last month, during the heyday of summer, selling and swindling.

Rosalie didn't mind their traveling. She hoped the shop in Edinburgh would be it though, especially if she would have to do most of the work herself. A place to make her home. She had a good feeling about the new place and unpacked all her things there, a first. She wouldn't know what to do with herself if she settled somewhere for good, though. What would life be like not on the road?

The idea made her breath catch. When on the move, she was in control with a simple life of negligible trouble. If one stayed somewhere for too long and got the wrong person upset, it could mean the hangman's noose.

The drawback to being on the move was that she hardly had time for friends, let alone a prospective husband. She felt revered and rejected at once. Settling remained only in her daydreams, she supposed. She would at least enjoy the time she had where she was for now.

Très meowed beside her in his crate.

"I'm sorry, sweet boy, but you can't be nosing about. Uncle Os has plans for you." Duo also trilled. She crouched and rubbed his scruffy fur. "At least I have you two." Sadly, Una had been felled with an awful illness in her third year with them. Quattuor was at the shop with her aunt. Edith, their herbalist and neighbor in Edinburgh, had promised to keep an eye on Nelda. She'd help with the animals and assist Nelda in the shop. Nelda had been ordered by Oswell to limit her excursions into town unless accompanied by Edith. It meant less income in addition to the pence to pay Edith to essentially do their work while they were away. "Maybe I'll find you milk later. Soon, juicy rats for you both."

Meh, how could rats be juicy? Especially those filled with disease? When able, Oswell provided alternative foods for the cats, and they seemed to have an instinct with the rats they caught, knowing which smelled foul and which would be a safe meal. They preferred it when Oswell caught fresh fish.

She assessed her stall with hands on her hips. A simple blue linen, adorned with hand-sewn yellow flowers, lay beneath her display. She had dyed the linen herself, but it had become faded with the sun. How she would love satin or silk! She grimaced at the meager selection. One of her brooches was missing, taken by slippery hands in Edinburgh. It riled her that a thief had snuck off with it.

"Nice castle, this Eilean Donan," Oswell said as he stood in front of their stall, peering at the eye-catching castle on the isle across the way. "I'll inquire if they need a ratcatcher. I've heard this clan is prosperous. I'll see what information I can collect for you, Rosie. Until then, stick with the crofters, no nobles."

Heat flushed her cheeks. "Yes, Uncle Os."

"And no—"

"Eggs. Yes."

"We need the coin to pay Edith upon our return," he reminded.

As if she could forget.

She crossed her arms and looked around. The market grounds were already abuzz with activity and chatter about the fire at a nearby stable last night and rumored thefts among the peddlers. Rosalie had to venture into town regardless. Most men never noticed her, so eavesdropping served well. "Os, I must make the rounds, too."

He waved a heavily calloused hand with a grating cough. "Yes, yes. Be back in a few hours so I can visit the keep. You've a good mind and sharp wit. It will take you far. Be safe."

She stepped out to see what information she could glean.

Lady Edrea Brantingham covered her nose and mouth with a delicate lace kerchief. God Almighty. The smells were worse than the towns and villages in England. Pungent "peat-reek" her driver had told her. Disgusting. She'd hoped the countryside would've improved after she made it safely away from the rabbling reivers in the tumultuous border region, who had nothing better to do than kill, thieve, and fight. An incorrect assumption. The

Highlands were worse. At least they remained civilized, or as much as they could.

The carriage sloshed through muddy, dung-filled puddles. Horrid. How she missed attending court with her dear friend Lady Isabella.

The esquire—what was his name? Who cared? He was another one of Baron Percy's underlings—rode alongside the carriage. He ducked to her level, slowing the horse's gait to keep pace, and spoke through the latticed window. "Lady Brantingham, we've arrived. I'll locate proper lodgings. I suspect the choices may not be"—he sought the right word—"to your liking. I'm unfamiliar with the area."

She suppressed her annoyance while he rode ahead and she remained in the bumping carriage. Wenda, her comely maid, quietly sat beside her, sewing with a steady hand despite the carriage's jostling.

Time bid for imperative action. To rid herself of this nuisance of a girl and get home before her husband Guilbert returned from his summer overindulgence at Alnwick Castle with Baron Henry Percy. Soon Bertie would be dead anyway. He and Percy were always whoring, drinking, and formulating "the next step," as Bertie liked to say. *Predictable.*

He hated their tower on the border as much as she. It was naught but a wretched, simple stone fortification, more tower than castle, on a vast parcel of land. Living there was like being in a prison, as Guilbert oversaw his duties as Lord Warden and Conservator of the Eastern March. They had finer things, but it wasn't the most pleasant home for visitors or hosting festivities. Warkworth Castle, on the coast, would soon be theirs once

Bertie's term as warden ended this year. The king had recently strengthened the garrison. Perfect. Except she needed it now, not in six months.

The Seer knew too much. Edrea's plans, the baby, all of it.

Bertie's sons, bastards, were already dead. Her husband and the girl had to go next.

One blissful time, shortly after her first husband's death, she had relished the benefits of widowhood, she had tasted freedom. Now, new laws gave her even greater power as a widow than as a wife. She'd had but a glimmer of the life she deserved before being married again, her other husband still fresh in the grave—sold off like she was property—to Bertie over twenty years ago.

Soon no more. Warkworth Castle would be hers.

And hers alone.

The king's distant cousin, Lady Isabella, had assured Edrea of her standing in court. All would fall into place. She didn't care about being conservator. She could appoint one of Bertie's men to the job or let Henry Percy handle the details. She wanted the castle. She wanted to control her own fate.

She peered out the latticed window at the bustling town as the carriage stopped.

A groom opened the door and offered a hand. "Lady Brantingham."

She exited the stifling carriage to be greeted with a gray, saturated day in Dornie. First, to get settled. It shouldn't be too hard to find a man willing to kill for a coin or two once she poked around and found the best taverns or brothels. Wenda was skilled at snooping. Soon Rosalie Threston would be a bother no longer.

CHAPTER FOUR

H ayden dodged Domhnall's attack and held up a shaking hand. "A breath."

Winded, they took a break from their sparring practice to recover and gulp water.

"Where is your mind today, Domhnall?" Hayden sheathed his sword. "You fight like you have death in your eyes. And you keep slipping. You've tried all these moves on me." He tapped his nose.

Domhnall leaned against the fence near the stable, lifted his chin high, and closed his eyes to allow the beating sun to warm his closed eyelids. "It's the thefts. I'm angry with myself for not being able to solve the problem. The thefts, the fire last night...I fear it will get worse."

Hayden stood reflective beside him while catching his breath. "Shall we continue?" he asked after a long moment. Always one to listen, but never offer advice, his friendship had its advantages and drawbacks. How could Domhnall also tell his friend, who knew about the Sight and its disappearance all those years ago, that it riled him he could not touch a person? Hayden knew it bothered him. Why verbalize it? At least he had his friend's steadfast companionship.

Domhnall lowered his chin and opened his eyes. Kendrick and Crystoll strode past, deep in conversation. They gave the men a nod.

"Aye, one more spar." Domhnall appreciated their fighting practice. Both had grown skilled after years of instruction under Kendrick as constable of the Watch and Crystoll as commander of the soldiers. Watchmen were trained alongside the armed force, taught the same fighting skills with sword, dagger, and shield. They didn't learn the mace or bow, but the sword and dagger were all they required while on sentry duty. Most miscreants did no harm, only broke the law.

One never knew when they'd resort to the blade though. The fire pointed to a group of thieves willing to hurt others in their endeavors.

Domhnall took position. With Hayden being left-handed, he fought differently. Domhnall could spar left-handed to accommodate his friend, but when they practiced together, they usually used the two-handed method on the lighter longswords or heavier broadswords and varied stances to allow both of them the upper hand.

Hayden started with an empty fade, leaping back, then forward.

Domhnall blocked, lunged. Then retreated.

Hayden smirked.

"You never fall for that one," Domhnall said.

They halted and while catching breaths, circled with their swords in front guard. "What about the bell heather?" Domhnall asked while he passed back and Hayden passed forward, both assessing the other.

They exchanged blows and counters, the metal ringing in the paddock. A cluster of onlookers, mostly Hayden's female admirers, stood along the fence gasping and *oohing* and *ahhing*.

"What about it?" Hayden asked.

"It's the MacDougall flower emblem."

Hayden lifted a brow. "You think a group of the Mac-Dougalls are behind all the thefts?"

"Possibly. It makes sense, right? Why else leave it at each scene? First, it was pressed heather, now fresh sprigs."

"Domhnall," Aileana called from the fence with a wave and snatched Hayden's attention.

Hayden widened his devilish grin at her, then turned to Domhnall just in time to block—Domhnall pulled himself back, preventing a full blow.

"Och! I wasn't ready."

Domhnall tsked. "One should never drop their guard. Don't you feed me the same words?" He hollered, "A moment, Lanie."

Hayden shrugged, his mouth twisting in amusement. "Am I a lost man? The finer half bewitches me." They drew closer, got their swords locked.

"Is it not the other way around? They fall at your boots, Hayden."

Laughter glimmered in Hayden's eyes. "Aye…"

Domhnall grunted with exertion.

"It would help you to release energy, too, my friend."

"This serves well enough." They disengaged, retreating a step, gauging for moves and subtleties.

Domhnall stomped, pretending an attack to bait Hayden to defend.

Hayden overcommitted and couldn't clear Domhnall's sword, swiping air instead, and exposing his shoulder.

Domhnall stepped aside, counterattacked, coming short of Hayden's shoulder. "Do you yield?" He heaved with exhaustion, sweat dripping down his neck.

Despite losing, Hayden seemed pleased with himself. "For today. It's blazing hot...and the sun got in my eyes. Let's see what Lanie wants." He tilted his head in Aileana's direction. "Have I become predictable?" Hayden asked as they strolled to the fence. He swiped sweat from his forehead.

"We both have. Too many spars with each other."

"We'll be fighting the MacDougalls soon enough," Hayden said with a smirk.

"That seems too simple. There is more to the puzzle."

Hayden huffed. "You with puzzles. Sometimes simple is the answer."

"You sound like my uncle."

They removed the protective layers of chain and padded jackets. The midday sun beat down, and Domhnall probably smelled worse than the pigpen. "Swim in the loch?"

The light in Hayden's eyes faded. "Not today. My mother's been raving. I should check on her."

"Domhnall," Aileana said on approach. "Ma is putting a bundle together to send to Gracie at the abbey. She'd adore one of Athol's wee puzzles. Have any to spare?"

"Certainly. Has Gracie sent any letters?" Their youngest sister resided at Dryburgh Abbey for the summer for her education with the monks and abbot. All the Montgomerie children took their turns of education and enlightenment in their formative years. It was Gracie's opportunity, since she had just turned twelve. Domhnall had cherished those years. No worries about accidentally touching someone. Quiet. Serenity. Solitude.

Aileana held out a folded parchment. "One for you."

He took it and smiled at the drawing of a dragon. *Gracie and her imagination.* She was the calm one of the siblings, always reading, drawing, and pondering. She hung on every story Mother shared about the Norse culture.

"Looking forward to the *cèilidh*, Lanie?" Hayden interjected.

"Aye."

"Might you save a dance for me?"

She blinked thick auburn eyelashes, fluffed her bouncy red-brown hair, and smiled broadly. "Always for you." She turned for the keep, Hayden's gaze locked on her swinging hips.

Domhnall almost wanted to tip a finger to close Hayden's open mouth.

But he couldn't. No woman to caress, parents to hug, or friend to knock around. His pulse flittered with agitation. Swords, aye...metal hitting metal. He felt the impact and human contact through the blade. 'Twas the closest thing to touching. The gentle nuzzle of a horse, also fine. People, no. "She's always had eyes for you."

Hayden shrugged noncommittally.

The two were practically betrothed, if Aileana would just make up her mind and Hayden would stop his tavern visits.

"I wouldn't be opposed to taming her spirit."

Domhnall crinkled his face in distaste. "Eww, that's my sister you're speaking about. Think your heart could settle for one woman?"

Hayden released a smooth laugh. "Aye, if it's Lanie. Yes. Well, I'll meet you in an hour. We can walk the market loop again."

After a quick wash by the loch, Domhnall monitored the marketplace while he waited for Hayden to join him. With the day shift covered, he marched off the unrest brewing within.

Rosalie passed the hours alone in their meager stall at the market with the cats yowling to be free from their tiny crate. Oswell had gone to the castle with an ambitious strut in his step. If the dismal business continued on their last stop on the market trail, and he didn't fare well with the laird, she'd either find sewing or kitchen work to cover their expenses, or they'd move on.

Throughout the summer, they'd sold trinkets along the market route and purchased more as needed, Oswell always in seek of a good bargain. But she had acquired no patrons seeking fortune-telling once they realized she was English. Not a soul on this route north. Scotland was not so ripe for the tell as England had been. At least Oswell had been somewhat successful in his rat catching at castles at least. She might be good at lying, but faking a thick brogue accent was not easy. She preferred the blend of people in Edinburgh over the Highlands, too.

"Last stop, then home," she murmured to herself more than the cats. Home. Was Edinburgh her new forever home, or just one more stop on this ceaseless journey?

Regardless, she had perused the grounds of the marketplace and nearby roads, her ears attuned, listening for anything. She'd gathered enough information about the status of the fields and crops, rain, the kinships of clans, and the current town hearsay. She filed it in her memory. She'd also overheard the superstitions and folklore of the region. Glen Shiel was steeped with the history of the Norse and mystical Ancients of the isles—a people with healing and clairvoyant abilities. Interesting. Did she believe it? Maybe, maybe not. Perhaps some tellers were true Seers.

She mindlessly sorted buttons, beads, and pebbles into piles, sliding items around and reconciling her supply, all the while fantasizing about a delightful counting tool she'd seen at the engraver's stand. An abacus, he'd called it. It used the Roman numbers Oswell had taught her, but the contraption was made of pebbles on rods, all within a wooden frame. With time, she'd be able to collect the parts to make her own. The design seemed easy enough.

Her stomach growled, but she ignored it. She repositioned a wooden bowl with copper-edged scalloping and a matching plate to the center. Beside it sat a set of six silver spoons, a pewter dish, and a pitcher. She shuffled her handmade, painted necklaces to the side. Then, she reorganized the bags of herbals Edith had sent along for her to sell, having already memorized the prices. Edith assured her they were finer herbs not readily found in the Highlands. Rosalie knew them all by sight and smell.

Peddlers and patrons, nobles and servants, ladies and gents all strolled past, raising their noses at her fortune-teller sign she had paid good coin for in Edinburgh. A scribe had written it for her. She had painted yellow flowers around the border to match the words. She loved yellow, and it was one of the easiest paints for her to make.

Hardly a soul gave her stall a second look.

A man passed by, scowling and mumbling under his breath.

Two younger women stopped. "Ye tell fortunes?" one asked with a loud bluster and narrowed eyes.

Her companion sniggered under her breath.

"Yes." *Entice them with kindness and confidence, Rose.*

One stepped closer. "How?"

She thinned her eyes and put hands on her hips. "Why does it matter?"

"Ye have witch ways? Make yer patrons drink foul liquid and then ye seduce their minds?" one chided.

"Speak with the de'il, maybe?" the other said.

Rosalie's ears burned. "I read palms."

They both giggled. One fiddled with the jewelry display. Down to one brooch and only her handmade necklaces, pins, and bracelets, it looked...humble.

The prettier woman covered her mouth, appalled.

"Men give their ladies jewels, not slimy stones lads toss across the loch."

The other leaned in with a twisted expression. "We've our own Seer, no need for yer business. Go back to where ye came from."

They clung together with laughter. Neither woman would she consider striking in their beauty, though one had lovely brown hair and fair skin with sky-blue eyes. The other lady was freckled, rounder, and had a large mole on her cheek. Both wore decent clothes of higher commoner stature. She was still unsure of the social hierarchy in Scotland.

"I see no fortune-tellers." Rosalie lifted her chin and brandished her hand toward the market stalls. She could recognize a few letters. F for fortune-teller and S for Seer, plus most displays held a certain look. She'd also made her subtle inquiries to other peddlers. She was the only teller, among the fifty or so peddlers.

An eruption of laughter came from the one woman. The large mole on her cheek and ample bosom danced with her chuckle. "Nor do we. Right, Isolde?"

"Indeed," the prettier one, Isolde, said. She blinked enviable long lashes.

Oh bother, she had tripped right into their ruse. "Where is your Seer, then?"

"He resides there," Mole-face said with a flick of her two fingers toward the isle Donan...and castle.

Her heart raced. The laird possessed his own soothsayer? She internally cringed. Why bother staying now? If Oswell didn't succeed with setting up his rat catching, they could leave. She itched to return. At least in Edinburgh she could meld into the background better and she got fewer scornful looks. She'd already acquired a few regular patrons in her short time there.

"Best luck to ye, selling yer fine things." Isolde traced one of the leather bracelets. They sauntered away, giggling and leaning into each other.

She held in her retort, then busied herself with the cats, while calming her soaring pulse. Why did she let

women like them bother her? Before she'd muddied Lady Brantingham's reading, the former Rosalie
wouldn't have flinched, would have fed them lies, lured
them in, and happily departed with coins.

Curses! She had read into the lady's future too much,
if such a thing existed! Lady Brantingham had been an
easy one to read despite her composed disposition.
The woman had desperately wanted to determine the
fate of her husband and sons. She had seemed dis-
traught even. Rosalie chewed her lip until it almost
bled, biting any chance of tears. Why had she told the
lady about the pregnancy, too?

Why?

She shook her head with disdain. Greed. Lady Brantingham had paid her handsomely.

She'd clearly seen the pregnancy in Edrea's face, for
she'd put on weight since the last visit, even if she had
been far from showing and in the very early weeks of
carrying a child. A servant at the castle had confirmed
Rosalie's suspicion. The lady's hands, too, told many
truths. There was something about a woman's palms
that changed when with child, like with Marin. Telling
pregnancies was one of Rosalie's strengths. She had
thought she'd given the lady hope! Something positive
to look forward to as she lived in a loveless household,
a common reality among many noblewomen. Rosalie
had seen her husband out at the taverns. Not until
after the reading had Rosalie learned about the lady's
own indiscretions. Lord Warden Brantingham was not
the father of the child.

Knowing all the hearsay kept Rosalie alive. Knowing...and telling both truths and lies to people who would consume it willingly...kept her and her family fed.

What good was arithmetic when she couldn't read or write words? She could not do a man's work. What good were her crafts when nobility preferred silver, gold, and gems? Her future rested in the lies she told. The money depended upon her lies. So her focus remained on her fortune-telling.

The lady's sons and husband had been a logical prediction. Aunt Nelda had worked in both the lady's tower house and in Baron Percy's castle on many occasions over the past two decades, as servant, cook, seamstress, and gardener. She had collected information about the Brantinghams and Baron Percy. Rosalie had known of their political affiliations.

But then, she had become too bold. Now, she knew too much.

A short while later, as Rosalie mused, adrift and morose, Oswell stumbled down the path toward her stall, gripping his middle, his tunic torn. He tripped and fell, scattering loose pebbles. She rushed to him and gathered him into her arms. He lurched, knees giving way. "Uncle Os! What happened?"

She almost asked, "What did you say this time?" Her hope fizzled. Was he drunk? Ill? Hurt? Who had he insulted? His tongue had grown sharper with age. His misfortunes were not always his fault though.

Oswell wheezed and coughed. She sniffed. No drink on his breath. He swiped oily gray hair from his forehead. An egg-sized bump formed near his scalp. "Somebody attacked me."

"Os, let me help you." Anger curled in her chest. Who would attack an elderly man? She brushed his cheek. "And I'll repair your tunic." A thought dawned on her. Mother Mary, no. She expected it. "Did he take anything?"

Her uncle had gone to the keep alone, with just credentials and recommendations from other lords in England, without a thing except—

"He robbed me."

Her stomach hardened. *All* their money. They had used some of it to pay for his cough tonics, the remainder of Nelda's sewing mistakes, food, and other necessities to repair their cart. Oswell had carried the last few pennies. She refused to cry. According to Aunt Nelda, she hadn't cried at her birth. Instead of crying, a frustrating fury enveloped her.

A handsome man, dressed in noble attire, sword at his waist, swooped to their side, his form a blur of colors as her mind swirled.

"Let us help. We're watchmen. Did you recognize the person?" He knelt to Oswell's level but didn't assist him to standing. "Hayden." The man beckoned over his shoulder.

"You're who, what?" She turned. "Oh, bother," she mumbled. It was the nobleman who wouldn't let her touch his hands back in her Edinburgh shop. Domhnall. She never forgot a name, face, or hand, and especially a handsome man like him. Soon enough his companion was at his side, too, helping without a word. The man, Hayden, assisted Oswell to standing while Domhnall's gaze assessed their surroundings. The vagrant was long gone, certainly. What good was there in looking around now? She placed her hands on her hips.

Her uncle trembled.

"Come, let's get you a drink," she said, helping Hayden with Oswell. She could prepare a simple tonic with Edith's herbs, and repay the herbalist upon their return to Edinburgh.

They had nothing to drink, aside from some water in her pouch. No food. They had planned to acquire the rest of it in the marketplace today. Thank goodness she'd had the foresight to hide a few pennies in her apron, but it was hardly anything. Not one sale today.

Hayden maneuvered Oswell to sit on the one wobbly stool in their market stall.

"Get a drink for him, Hayden." Domhnall plopped coins into his hand. "Milk for the cats. A loaf of bread, too. Cheese. A bit of dried meat."

Had the man heard Rosalie's stomach growling from yonder?

Hayden's light brown eyebrows slanted over striking green eyes. He didn't question his friend, clearly his superior, as he departed. Rosalie returned to Oswell, her usually steady hands shaking. How had this man known she had the cats with her? The tears begged to come. No, she...couldn't. "What's a watchman?" she said, meeker than she intended.

He did not reply, his gaze rapt on the crowd. He danced fingertips upon his sword's hilt.

Had he been watching her? Those women. Had he seen her humiliating display? Her last shred of hope dissipated.

She tended to Oswell's wounds the best she could with what she had on hand. "It won't require stitching. Just needs time to heal. Let me see your eyes."

He blinked as she held his gaze. His pupils seemed all right. Thankfully, it was just a goose egg. She'd learned long ago that a bump on the outside was a good sign, better than injury in the body with no outward indication. She couldn't afford the healer. "How many fingers?" She held up two.

"Two."

She swiped a hand through Oswell's disheveled hair. Sometimes she worried he spent so much time with rats that he'd begun to look like one. He'd grown as grumpy as one in recent years, too. She suspected his cough was related to his work. Soon...he, too, like Nelda, would cease working.

Her stomach clenched.

She turned. "Thank you kindly for your assistance—"

Domhnall was gone. *Well.* She heaved a breath. She was used to dealing with problems on her own anyway. Steeling herself, she withdrew the coins from her apron and squeezed them in her hand. "Uncle, can you stay? Watch our things, and I'll buy bread and more drink, then make a tonic."

He shook his head, then grasped it, his phlegmy cough worrying her. "No, Rosie. Not your last coins. That gentleman will be back. Perhaps we'll have customers today. Any luck?"

She knotted her fingers together and shook her head. She was about to depart, when Domhnall returned, carrying a flask of something and a stout jar of milk. She had no idea where his friend had wandered off to.

"Here."

He handed the flask to Oswell, and her uncle gladly sipped. "By my balls, good whisky."

Rosalie's cheeks warmed. "Uncle Os, your manners."

Domhnall handed her the jar of milk. "For your cats."

She nodded. "Thank you." Apparently, watchmen watched. He *had* been watching her. Or he'd remembered her cats from the shop in Edinburgh. She pretended it was that, and not him observing her embarrassing display with the women earlier. As she poured the milk into a dish for Duo and Trēs, she asked, again, "What's a watchman, Sir—?"

"You don't have them in England?"

Was it a sincere question or a prick? Scottish mannerisms baffled her.

Oswell responded, "The law, Rosie. They are sentries who guard the streets, maintain peace, make sure no vagrants are stealing things, causing harm, or disturbing the order of the town or village. I've seen a few of them in London, and they've been branching out to other towns. Am I right, Sir—?"

Domhnall said, "Aye. We deter criminal activity, enforce our laws, and work with the constable and sheriff." He cleared his throat. "Can you tell me what happened, um, Oswell, is it?"

He noticeably kept his distance from them. God, did they smell? Refusing first to touch her hands, and now to be near her? Her pride stung.

Oswell shifted on the stool and took another pull from the flask. He hiccupped. "I was minding my own business. I'd come from the keep, you see. I catch rats. They carry pestilence. Dreadful diseases befalling folks south of here. 'Tis only time before it comes north. I offered the lord a fair price, and he said he'd consider it and I should return on the morrow. A dolt came right at me, from behind as I was walking down the path. Nudged a blade tip into my back! He demanded my coin and before I could turn to deny him, whacked me on my head. Maybe he'd seen me come from the keep. I was grinning like a fool. What a nice lord the master was."

"Would you recognize the voice? Did you see him? Did he—give you anything?"

"Give me anything, sir?"

Domhnall grimaced. "Left anything behind on you or near you?"

"All he left me with was a bloody headache and this welt. He took my pouch of coins." Oswell shrugged and scrubbed his leathery face, the ridges in his forehead deeper, the wrinkles around his pursed mouth more pronounced. "Happened fast. He had a mask or kerchief over his face. One moment I was alone, next, wallop. Seeing the heavens."

"Did you get a good look at his clothes? Did he dress in finer things or, uh..." Domhnall drifted off, not holding Rosalie's gaze of contempt.

"Like me?" Oswell shook his head with a blink while he plucked at his soiled tunic. "No, no. Not like me, sir. He wore nice hose and tunic. Leather belt at his waist. Sorry. I've got old ears and eyes, sir. He could be in green or brown, and I'd not be able to tell the difference."

Domhnall exhaled and cracked his knuckles. "I'll relay the information to the constable. I'm sorry this happened. Could I help you to your lodging? Is there anyone else who could assist you?"

"No, we don't require assistance." Rosalie shuffled nearer. Domhnall countered with a step back. The compulsion to check the stables with their oxen tingled her scalp. Their wagon was behind the stall but they'd paid the usual market fee, and with it came supervision of their cart animals in a stable. Unless Oswell garnered the rat-catching job, they'd leave poorer than they'd come. "What about our oxen? Should we be concerned?"

Domhnall shook his head, lengthy brown hair flapping in the summer breeze. "No, no concern. The constable has arranged for men to watch the stables. No, your oxen are safe. I assure you. I can check on them if you'd like?"

"What about the fire last night?"

A frown crinkled his forehead. "The animals will be safe."

She wanted to respond, *But my uncle and I are not?* She held her tongue.

"I reckon you could use a rest after traveling from Edinburgh. May I escort you to your place of lodging?"

Her usual confidence fractured. "No, thank you." She drew closer. He was subtle in his posture but shifted farther away. Maybe it wasn't her. Hmm...he had space issues? Had he his own disease, the evidence not apparent but instead hidden beneath noble clothes? Maybe it wasn't their social stature. She'd bathed yesterday in a loch, as they called the lakes here. It'd been a dreadfully hot day, and the water was cool and refreshing. She did *not* smell. "We're fine. All the peddlers sleep in their stalls or carts or have kin about."

"In your stall or cart?" Wide-set eyes gleamed with surprise. "I can send for the healer to help," he offered.

Again, she declined. "We'll be well. You should be off with your watching." She bit her lip, her ears ringing. Why wouldn't he leave and let them be? His behavior both frustrated her and held her interest. He was kinder than most noblemen.

Hayden returned, a shadow out of nowhere. It sent Rosalie's heart racing.

"I got the food as you requested, Domhnall." He handed a linen bag to Rosalie.

She was speechless.

Domhnall turned to Oswell. "You catch rats, you say?"

Oswell beamed with pride. "Yes. Might you know of other keeps in the area in need of a ratcatcher? My Rosie, she's good with many a thing, too, mending, cooking, cleaning—"

"Uncle Os," she clipped.

"I may. Let me have a word with the laird. Their kitchen is in need of more servants, too, and if I recall, you baked those tarts. Your shop had smelled heavenly," he said with a charming smile to Rosalie. "I'll see if I can persuade him to employ you if you're staying in Dornie for a while?" He swiped a hand through his feathery hair.

"Aye, sir." Oswell nodded. "Work shall keep us here."

"I'd like to come check on you tomorrow. I can call for the healer. You have herbals, too, I see. If you have willow bark or hazelnuts, it would help with the swelling and pain."

"Nay, no nuts around Rosalie. She swells up if she eats any. Once she had trouble breathing!"

Rosalie opened her mouth to speak, but there was no quieting her uncle. The whisky Domhnall had given him loosened Oswell's tongue. Domhnall was knowledgeable about both flowers and herbs? That was unusual expertise for a man of his stature. Her interest stirred further.

Nothing about him appeared usual. Instead, she said, "Thank you for your generosity. We shall be well."

He raised a hand. "I insist. I'll come by tomorrow." She relented and tipped her head. "As you see fit."

He bowed. "On the morrow then."

The afternoon crept along to match Domhnall's rising discontent. The thieves had become bold. Unless somebody else had robbed Rosalie's uncle? They'd not left their telltale bell heather sprig, however. Was it just a misfortune due to the increased presence of people in town? The markets were known to bring in the bad sorts.

He tallied it all. Kendrick suggested determining motive first. Why would a person or group of people do this? It had to be the MacDougalls. What was their motive?

Animals, finer wares, coin. Or revenge.

He needed to speak with Father. The MacDougalls lived in a fractured amnesty with their clan ever since the Norse War. Laird Ewen MacDougall had sided with the Scots in the Battle of Largs, despite having a Norse overlord. So that was all well. Then, the Scottish claimants' war had come twenty-five years ago. The MacDougalls had sided with John Comyn and Domhnall's clan sided with Robert Bruce. A quandary arose after Bruce murdered Comyn. Years had passed, but the MacDougalls were known for their grudges. Father's efforts to arrange a marriage between Brodie, Laird MacDougall's son, and Aileana...were not going as planned.

His sister held a lovestruck interest for Hayden—sometimes. Och, women! His sister couldn't make up her mind.

He was no better, though, allowing distractions to get the best of him. If he hadn't been gawking at Rosalie, he could've bested the scoundrel who'd robbed Oswell. He'd allowed himself to be preoccupied, an unfavorable trait for a watchman.

He kicked the dirt path and clenched a fist at his side as he plodded down a manicured row in his mother's garden, seeking remedies to help the lass's uncle. Some of the summer crop had been harvested, but the herbs he required were in his mother's personal pantry beside the kitchen. However, 'twas summer, and his mother was outside more than she was in. His boots found him on the path toward the gardens, while he mindlessly considered his mistakes of late.

There she was, elbow-deep in digging, lost in concentration, humming beneath her breath. He cleared his throat on his approach.

Delight filled his mother's face when she looked up, dirt tracing her brow. "Sweet love. It's you. Thought it was your father for a moment. Not Lanie...she's off somewhere." She chuckled to herself. "Och, something troubles you." Her smile dipped into a small frown.

Damn, he hated how she could read him. Alas, it was her gift. Sincere eyes beheld his.

A breeze twirled past him, unsettling a few empty baskets.

"Aye."

"I will listen."

As a Feeler, she never forced herself into his mind. She promised long ago to probe no deeper than feeling his lifeblood—the color he emitted—and his surface emotions only. To intuit a person's life energy and emotions was a divine power, one he envied, for she could touch people without harm. Regardless, she respected his privacy, having grown powerful enough to block his sensations. Even when she completely blocked it all, he couldn't stop a mother's intuition.

He harbored so few secrets from her, for power rested in the truth. Except when the truth unleashed hell upon his soul. He scrubbed a hand across his chin. "There is a lass..."

Her spine straightened. "Oh?"

"No, not like that." *Och, yes, like that.* There was something intriguing about Rosalie. He blew out a breath. He could only withhold so much information from his mother. Kendrick apprised his father of all the town's business, and Father told Mother. They'd all know soon enough about the unrest in Dornie. "There've been more thefts recently and today an assault on an Englishman. He is here for the market. His niece is a peddler there." *Not a Seer. Not a Seer. Not like me.*

"Is he all right? Shall I send the healer?"

He shook his head, crouched beside her, and poked at the dirt pile with a trowel. He picked up an onion and brushed off the dirt. "Nay. He insists he is fine. He's the man who visited Father earlier, to offer his services for catching rats. The cooks have complained about rats and mice getting into the pantries. I thought we might hire him...and the lass for the kitchen. To help Mrs. Iverson?"

She paused and blew wisps of white-streaked and black hair from her face. She wiped her forehead, smudging dirt on her brow. "We don't have extra coin for such things."

He scuffed his face. "Aye. I presumed. I—"

"Want to help them?"

He nodded.

"Well, we could use a replacement in the kitchen. I've asked Robena to take leave, perhaps indefinitely. Her ailments have become too serious for my herbals. Does the lass cook?"

The idea of Mrs. Iverson, Hayden's mother, no longer gainfully employed plagued his conscience. Alas, she was incapable of running the kitchen anymore and had become a hindrance. He swallowed and said, "Yes."

"Sew?"

He wiped off another onion. "Her uncle boasted about her skills. Cooking and cleaning and she is crafty. Sells trinkets she makes herself, I think," he said, his words quickening. He released a light laugh, covering his eagerness. "She is hard-headed and likes her cats." *Blazes, Domhnall.*

Mother laughed, too. "Well, then. If she has cats, then she is a good soul. Are they staying in the marketplace or in town?"

He wished to ask permission for them to stay at the castle. He fought the other reason he was drawn to the fair-haired palm reader from the marketplace.

Air.

His skin quivered in recollection.

"She lies."

"What?" He shivered, the grating whispered words scratching his soul.

His mother rested her trowel and turned to him. "I asked if they're staying in the marketplace or town?"

Were his ears playing tricks on him?

In response, the wind gusted, unsettling the dry dirt pile. An onion rolled into a hole. He swallowed the sourness rising in his throat. "Aye, yes, the market-place," he finally responded.

Leave me alone, he admonished the voice in his mind. *You left me years ago. Why return now?*

Kyla, one of the servants, strode down the row, a basket on her hip. She nodded and dipped into a half curtsy. "Good day, sir." She batted her eyelashes, deepening a smile.

He covered a frown with a polite nod.

"Milady, need me to take the basket of onions in?"

His mother heaved a tired sigh. "Yes, Kyla, please. Just a moment."

Kyla knelt and assisted her with plopping the rest of the plucked early harvest onions into the basket.

His mother turned to him, squinting as sun glinted in her blue irises. Lines from years of joy and laughter crinkled at the corners of her eyes. "I can bring herbals and check on this man? What are his ailments?"

"He was a bit torn up. He has a decent welt on his head, was walking funny, but seemed agreeable."

"How were his eyes?"

"They seemed fine."

She nodded with consideration. "Did he have any willow bark and hazelnut-steeped water?"

"I suggested the same. Nay, nuts affect the lass. She can't be near them. So it is better to avoid those in your remedies."

"Interesting. I'll search the tonics in my herbal pantry and see what else he might require." She lifted the basket to Kyla. "Here. I'll be in soon after I check on Robena."

"Aye, milady." Kyla nodded and left for the keep.

His mother turned to him. "I'll inquire with your father about the rats and kitchen needs. I thought to offer the position to Kyla, but I don't think she's ready for it. She can be a bit short-tempered with others. The lass and her uncle can stay in the servants' quarters, if that is all right? I'll ask Cawley what he thinks about replacing Robena. Either way, extra hands in the kitchen are always helpful."

"Thank you, Mother." He turned to leave before she could read the thoughts on his face. Before the Wind spoke to him again.

But it followed him.

Lies.

Golden Lies. Don't believe the lies.

The crabby, limping old man, the one who had haunted his visions for years, manifested before his eyes. Like always, the man carried a basket of yellow roses. This time, a wee bairn's cry emerged from the basket, too.

Domhnall's pulse quickened. Why now? He'd not touched a soul today. Why was the Wind chasing him?

He swiped at the air and covered his ears. "No..." he pleaded under his breath. *Leave me alone.*

The old woman's voice persisted. *"Air. Let it speak. Njord our Wind goddess, our winds are your winds. Blow around us, fill us with your Sight. Steer our paths on the Way."*

Now more than ever, he believed this voice, the woman's at least, to be his deceased great-aunt Venora communicating with him across the Silver Veil.

It had always been a one-way conversation. Not like she, or it, or whatever the hell this was, listened to his pleas.

The Wind taunted him all day, his aunt's encouraging words transforming to garbled foreign words in a venomous breath...of a future laced with lies and gold.

Had hell returned after a ten-year dormancy?

CHAPTER FIVE

T he next day came and went with hardly a customer. Rosalie's spirits plummeted. Not a penny made today. Not even traded goods. She could use a good cooked egg or flask of cider right now.

Oswell dozed in the cart. With a yawn, she put away the sign, tempted to break it over a knee. Her stomach gurgled. All the meat already consumed, she allowed herself one chunk of cheese, imagining it was salted pork or boiled carrots or a lovely berry or apple tartlet. What recipes she could make if given an adequate kitchen! Their new shop was rudimentary with a very small area for cooking. She'd learned many recipes with Nelda while working in castles across England, and felt her skills were wasted. If given the opportunity, she could prepare a grand feast.

As she allowed another bite of cheese, sharp and tangy, she caught sight of—*oh my God!*

She dropped to the ground, ducking behind her display.

How had Lady Brantingham found her?

Her heart raced while she chewed, the only sound in her ears the movement of her jaw as she hurried the dry, choking piece of cheese down. Heat flooded her face. She chanced a glimpse around the display. Yes, it was Edrea, across the way, meandering through the marketplace with a servant beside her.

Go, go, go away! She propelled her thoughts across the dirt path to the evil woman. Why was she here? Lady Brantingham sought finer things, not commoner trinkets found in the Scottish marketplace. Mother Mary, they were nearly to Inverness. Far north in the Highlands, far away from the border marches. Not far enough.

The lady had come for *her*.

Edrea would never travel far north—or to heathen Scotland—unless she had a reason. She usually sent her men out in her stead to do her bidding. The lady had no connections this far north, so why come? She kept to herself, hiding away in her tower house. Her only friend in court, Lady Isabella, lived south of here, on the coast.

Rosalie waited and foolishly closed her eyes, willing Edrea away.

Moments passed. What was she to do if the lady discovered her? Thank God she had removed her sign and Oswell was asleep among the hay in the cart.

She didn't even own a sharp dagger. She had one blade, and it was dull from foraging for herbs and flowers. On her knees, she scoured her crates for it.

"You sleeping there?" a voice came. It was a man.

She craned a look over her shoulder. Hayden. Her heartbeat settled.

"Dropped something," she lied. She rose, slowly, casting a fraction of a look between Hayden and Edrea. The lady continued on her way, farther down the path toward the other sellers. Rosalie deliberately allowed breath to return to her lungs.

Hayden eyed her with suspicion and followed her gaze. Oh, bother.

"Och. I see. Need assistance?" He beheld Lady Brantingham. Edrea's fine brown hair was swept up and covered with a lace headpiece draping her thin back. She walked regally, with an air of confidence and exquisiteness. Older than Rosalie by maybe twenty years, the lady was fair and beautiful, a seducer of men, a queen to bees. One peddler approached Edrea, a fabric spread across his open arms in solicitation. She waved him away. Another man stepped forward, smiled, laughed, said something. She turned the other way as if bored.

Hayden was too perceptive. "Och, you're bonnier than her. Envy is not attractive."

Heat filled her cheeks. "I'm not covetous." Wasn't that the word they'd used in Mass?

"What vexes you then?" He held her look.

She shook her head, her spirit feeling tattered. "Nothing, kind sir."

"Call me Hayden. I am no sir." He lifted a brow over persuading eyes. "What then?"

"She doesn't like rats," she blurted. Well, it was a truth. Just not the one Hayden requested.

"Then she should require your uncle's employment. Does he not catch rats?"

She eyed him. Hayden was hard to read by outward assessments alone. He seemed agreeable, virile, capable, confident, and well aware of his handsomeness. Regardless, something about him unsettled her. Maybe because she felt like he could see through her lie. He wasn't one to be manipulated. Likely he did enough of that himself. "Yes and no. Uncle Os can be gruff with words."

"Offended her, did he? Is she an Englishwoman, too?"

She chewed her lip and nodded. Her guise crumbled around Hayden—why? She longed for his dark-haired companion, Domhnall. She could just *feel* his resoluteness and integrity, even if he tried to come off as mysterious. She didn't require his palm to read Domhnall as a man of valor and honesty. A part of her wanted to visit with him again, determine if the elements from his basic palm reading were correct. She wanted to see if her suspicion about touching was correct. He had soft-looking hands, alluring eyes, and a disarming smile.

Heavens. Where was this all coming from? *Too much daydreaming, Rose.*

Hayden adjusted his belt and swiped clean tunic sleeves. "Consider her no bother. I'll make sure she leaves you alone. Good day, Mistress Rosalie." He bowed and carried on his way.

Straight toward Lady Brantingham.

Feebly, she said, "No. Wait!" with a futile wave of her hand. A wind gust swallowed her words.

Keeping an eye on Hayden, she returned to her cleaning, her mind fragmented. If Edrea turned this way, what then? She readied her feet to run. What about Oswell? The cats? Her things? The oxen were in the stable. Hitching the oxen took time. Could Edrea call for the Dornie watchmen or guards to detain her? Did Edrea have any authority here? But who was Rosalie to these clansmen? She was no one. Always had been.

She shot her heavenly Father a weak prayer. Edrea, thankfully, did not turn around and continued strolling on her way, Hayden at her side, carrying on conversation with grand hand gestures. Edrea snubbed him like all the others.

Farther...farther they went. He looked over his shoulder and cast her the largest smile.

She mouthed, "Thank you." He could have outed her on the spot for her unbelievable lie...for he surely didn't lay credit in it. No, she could tell when her lies didn't work. Some people saw through her. Usually others just as crafty.

They had to leave. Tomorrow, at dawn. Or tonight if she could rouse Oswell from his stupor. Where would they go? The isles north? South into France? When would they cease the running?

No sooner had she returned to her organizing, preparing to put her things away for the day with trembling cold fingertips, than a buyer appeared at her stall. Another finely dressed older woman with striking black hair dappled with wisps of pure white stood before her. A smile crossed her creamy complexion, though it held the color of a person who spent days in the sun. She was no toiler or crofter though. She was exquisite!

Rosalie bowed her head and dipped in a polite curtsy. "My lady, how may I help you?"

After one more glance at the area where she'd last seen Hayden and Edrea, she released a sigh. They were long gone, consumed by the crowds near the taverns and shops. She was safe for now.

The lady in front of her eyed the bags Edith had provided Rosalie to sell. "Are you acquainted with herbs?"

"A little for healing remedies. These are from an herbalist in Edinburgh. She asked me to sell them." She

played with her simple beaded necklace. "I'm more familiar with herbs for flavoring food or making paints."

Intrigue lit the lady's blue-green eyes. "May I sniff
them?"

"Of course, my lady."

The woman ran a finger over the pouches, picked one,
opened, and inhaled. "I certainly enjoy lavender. How
much? Ah, and thyme. Saffron has given me trouble this
season. You travel from England but are in Edinburgh
now?"

"Three pence."

She handed her three pennies for the entire bag of
lavender.

Rosalie tucked the coins in her pocket, then toyed with
the threaded beads around her neck again. "Yes, my lady,
I am from England."

"What a lovely necklace. Did you paint the stones? My
daughter Gracie adores painting."

"This?" She dropped her hand and shoved it in her
pocket. "Oh yes, I painted it. As I did these others. I like
to craft what I find or purchase. I don't sell many of them.
Ladies prefer finer jewelry with gemstones and silver."

"How do you make them?"

"I collect beads, buttons, shells, and pebbles, link them
together with leather or thin twine. Occasionally, I find
a blacksmith to hammer holes into the pebbles or beads,
so I can thread them. I make my own paints with rock
powders, a grinding stone, and mix in egg yolks."

She never had access to precious components. She
had a stash of a dozen shimmering blue glass beads,
hard to come by, in her hidden pouch in her pocket. A
handful more and she could string a splendid necklace.

They had been payment from a Venetian man in London. She smiled, remembering him. He had been pleased with his palm reading. He had doted upon her and asked her to return to Venice with him and be his mistress. She wondered what her life would have been like if she had said yes.

"Ah, resourceful. I know plenty who would appreciate such craftsmanship. What a fine palette of color, and a fetching way to use what we find in nature. My other daughter would love one. How much for this one?" She chose the larger necklace, one of Rosalie's favorites. Tiny golden flowers painted on blue-hued stones.

"Three pence."

"What? Don't ask for less than a shilling. Remarkable work." She plopped the shilling in her hand before Rosalie could protest. A shilling. That was worth twelve pence! More than a month's work in a kitchen. Shillings were rare to come by as most patrons only dealt in pennies.

It was just a string of painted stones. A gold necklace could bring ten to twenty shillings.

"My son said your uncle catches vermin."

Son? Unless Oswell had spoken with the man, surely she meant Domhnall? Was this Domhnall's mother? Though their eyes differed in color and shape, she could see some similar features in this woman's face to his.

Hope returned with sweet abandon as the money in her pocket jingled and she calculated what she could purchase with it. "Yes, my lady, he does. Does someone require his services?"

"I believe we could use his expertise. What about you, lass? We don't require a crafter, but how's your cooking? I'm afraid my cook has become ill and she's struggling with her duties. I'm looking for help. Someone who is flexible and can stay for a few weeks until I find a permanent replacement. I take it your home is still in England?"

"It is in Edinburgh now."

Several weeks' pay! She didn't even ask how much. Why was this woman being so kind? "I—" Hesitation froze her words. Hmm, hiding in a noblewoman's home was better than in the marketplace or on the open road south—the same road Lady Brantingham would be taking home. "Yes, I cook and have worked for many castle stewards in their kitchens. I use a lot of herbs, and I enjoy baking tartlets and sweets, and I can sew, too."

The woman released a throaty sound of inclination. "Lovely, then you must come. Given the detail you put into your craftsmanship, I suspect we won't be disappointed. We have adequate housing, and I insist you stay with us. It looks to be a dreary night ahead. Is your uncle available?"

A snort emanated from the cart. Rosalie cringed and tried to hide behind the length of her locks and not capture the lady's gaze. "I can't possibly—"

The lady's smile deepened, accentuating wrinkles around her rosy lips. "I insist. I've herbal brews. I heard about his injury. Our watchmen are working hard to find the offender. When he wakes, please bring him to the keep and we can make sure he is well."

The keep? "If you insist." She curtsied and bowed her head. "Lady...?"

"Montgomerie, dear. Please, wake your uncle when you can. The laird should like to speak with him about specifics. And our kitchen staff will meet with you. My son spoke fondly of you," she added.

Her throat tightened. Domhnall was the laird's son. She swallowed her foolishness. Before her stood Deirdre MacCoinneach, now Montgomerie through marriage to Laird Alasdair Montgomerie. She was Laird Simon Mac-Coinneach's daughter. She'd heard all about the noble family on her gleaning trips in town. "As you wish. Thank you, Lady Montgomerie. It is my pleasure."

Well, she wanted to hide didn't she? The kitchen of the laird's castle was the ideal place. By God, they needed the coin, too. Autumn fast approached, and the threat of a cold, hungry winter clawed her spirit. Oswell was in poor shape. What about Aunt Nelda back in Edinburgh? Would Edith tend to her and the shop a little longer? They could send a messenger, but that took money and time.

Either way, fortune had finally shone upon them to-day.

For a few more weeks, Eilean Donan would be their home.

Domhnall arrived before supper to escort Rosalie and her uncle to the keep. Thinking he'd find a lass brimming with contentment that Oswell would be cared for, he staggered back at her acerbic tongue.

"You lied to me." She shot him a glare when he approached. Her pursed lips revealed a tiny dimple in one cheek. Her grimace deepened.

He flinched. "Pardon?"

"You are the laird's son," she seethed, emphasizing the Scottish brogue of *lord*.

"I didn't lie. I never gave you my family name." He fumbled on his words.

"A lie by omission is still a lie." Her pink lips tightened, and the dimple disappeared.

Thank God he wasn't a Feeler like his mother, for Rosalie's ire would tear him in two. She loaded the last of her belongings into the cart, already prepared with two yoked oxen. Her oxen looked old, haggard, and malnourished. He scrubbed a hand across his face, the stubble prickling the nerve endings in his fingertips.

"I can have our stable master look at your oxen."

"Why?"

"To care for them, 'tis all. They will moved to one of our private stables. How can I help?"

"You may help by staying out of the way, sir."

She was certainly in need but not incapable. A need he could reconcile. Their stable master Ewan had a thing for horses, but he loved any beast of burden and cared for them like they were his children. Domhnall approached one of the oxen and stroked its neck. He, too, found solace with animals. At least he could touch them. He would see to it that the animals were fostered and fed for her return journey home.

A cat meowed. He bent to pet one of the two in the crate. "Easy there, friends. We'll take good care of you. I've heard we have rats in our pantries. You'll love it. Are you the wee beastie that snuck out of Miss Rosalie's shop?" He brushed a finger under the cat's chin.

Rosalie huffed but shuffled around him. "Excuse me, Sir Montgomerie."

"It's just Domhnall." Shame skittered to the forefront of his mind. He lived a privileged life, hardly understanding the commoner, try as he might by pacing the streets afoot. In his mind, all people were equal, though society and nobles held other opinions of the lesser born. Not him. Not if he became laird. When. He sighed. *When* he became laird. Despite his parents' noble upbringing, they celebrated every man, woman, and child's God-given gifts. All should have opportunity. Here, men and women were treated fairly, as fair as they could get with the demanding barons and the king.

But... He was trying hard to help a woman who maybe didn't want his help. When would he learn he could only help others so much?

Burned. Dead.

He blinked away that pain. Why now? Why remember that awful memory now? What was wrong with him lately?

He'd only been a lad himself at the time. He hadn't understood the power that rested in his visions back then. *And she had died.* He swallowed.

"Here." He grabbed a crate from Rosalie, his hand accidentally brushing hers. Blazes, no!

A cool rush traveled up his fingers to his elbow. Darkness lured him as he saw stars. No, he chided. *Blazes, no!* He commanded the vision to relent. The black curtain crossing his eyes quickly dissipated as blood flowed to his fingers. His extremities instantly warmed. And then it was gone. Gone. Gone?

What was that?

Had he successfully halted a vision midstream? It had been years—years!—since his last true vision, if he didn't count the strange man's reappearance in his mind this week along with Venora's chilling words. Och, plus the misstep with that drunkard in Edinburgh a month ago that quite nearly plummeted him into the darkness. Snippets of visions and whispers of the Wind, but nothing full or true.

He picked up another crate, handed it to her, deliberately touching her fingers, testing the profound idea. His heart was in his throat. Bold. So bold. Nothing. Nothing but an attraction to the golden-haired lass welled within him. No vision. Only interest. Only...

He wanted to try again. And again. Too bold. *Rein it in, Domhnall.*

"Wh-what's your name? Uh, family name, I mean?" He coughed to mask his discomfort. Who was this woman? Why could he stop the vision mid-stream now, of all times? Why did nothing happen with the second touch?

She blew a winded breath. "Why does it matter? I'm not associated with any clans. My name is just a name. I'm not the one hiding behind a family name, Sir Domhnall Montgomerie."

"But it is your name," he said simply. Did she hail from the isles? Was she an Ancient...and a Seer like him? He had wondered it ever since their first meeting.

She narrowed her eyes but softened the glower on her face with his gentle words. "Threston. Rosalie Threston, and you've met Oswell. Aunt Nelda is in Edinburgh keeping the shop with the aid of our neighbor, the herbalist."

"You've no other kin?" He kicked at the ground, cursing his tongue. He loaded the crate with the cats into the cart. "Er, parents, siblings?" *Husband?*

She rushed to the cat crate. "Let me." She cooed and hushed the yowling beasties. "Duo, Trēs, there, there."

"Two and three?"

Her cheeks flushed pink. Blazes, he was embarrassing her when all he wanted was to find a common ground. Something to talk about. She liked cats. He liked cats. He was a Seer. She was—

"Yes. Is that an issue?"

"Is there a 'one'?" He recalled his Latin teachings at Dryburgh Abbey with the priests. Where had Rosalie heard or studied Latin? In Mass perhaps?

"I am afraid not. Una died three years ago. Quattuor is in Edinburgh with my aunt."

He smiled, pleasure expanding in his chest. "You like Latin?"

She shrugged. "I like numbers. I can't read words, but numbers I understand well. I saw a tool at the engraver's in the marketplace. An abacus. Have you heard of it?" Interest replaced her glower.

"I've seen an abacus, yes. You're the first lass I've met who finds joy in calculation." Unless it was inheriting money, like Isolde, who likely saw gold and silver in her sleep. Her flirtations with Domhnall had been pure lies. She had only been after the prestige of being lady of Eilean Donan. He'd given his young heart and body to her. Thank the Almighty for intervening during that one intimate—and soul-shattering—moment when he had lain with her under the rowan tree. He shuddered, remembering the incident like it was yesterday.

They had lain, twisted in each other's unclothed arms, beneath the old tree. Then the inexplicable happened. Visions fell upon visions, raw and intense. Isolde's screech became muted by the screams in his Sight.

Crushed yellow flowers. The bairn in a basket. Hundreds of men marching under an unfamiliar banner. Clanging swords. Weeping women. Blood. An eerie keep surrounded by fields of dead men.

He'd awoken to a pillow beneath his head and Hayden and his father arguing. Hayden had retrieved him, brought him back to the keep, and lied about what really happened.

A cold sweat seized him at the memory alone. Isolde's incident had been the tipping point. It had seared itself upon his heart. After years of seeing death, hundreds of visions, he had forced them away after that fateful day nearly ten years ago.

Now, before him stood a pragmatic, intriguing woman. The pain lifted with the sensory memory of the touch from only a moment before. Was it possible to find another like him? Was that the answer to the pain and visions? He didn't care if it was reckless or daft. He'd chance another touch when the time came, to be certain it wasn't an unusual occurrence, that it held meaning. It was time to try.

He wanted to offer to teach her to read if she was staying longer than a few days, but he bit his tongue. It would give him an excuse to be near her at least.

Full-fledged crimson filled her cheeks now as he stared at her. She dipped her head in a nod, loose flaxen locks bouncing over her shoulders. "I make a living selling and bartering. Numbers are my life."

He had to stop prodding and thinking he was or could be like others. He was as different as they came.

Grace had yet to demonstrate an Ancient ability, and Aileana—blazes, if she had one—was a stubborn lass who hid it well. He asked his mother once, and she'd felt no ability within either of his sisters, though the gifts could appear later in life. For now, it was just him. The anomaly.

He didn't feel so alone when around Rosalie, which was a daft feeling, since he hardly knew the woman.

He wanted to know her more.

He cleared his throat. "My mother loves cats." He scratched one of the cats behind its ear, releasing purrs as the animal pressed its chin harder into his palm.

"Seems you do, too." Her look softened.

He quickly added, "Our cats don't like to hunt for rats and vermin. They spend all day lapping milk or playing in the garden chasing butterflies while my mother works. The wee beasties enjoy sunning themselves a bit too much. Blessed timing you arrived then, aye? We need some workin' cats," he teased.

She thinned her lips, hands on her hips. "Indeed. Lady Montgomerie works in the garden? Does she not have servants for such duties?"

He folded a linen and placed it in a box. "She does, but she prefers to help. We work alongside our servants whenever possible. They are family to us." The stall's contents were nearly loaded in the cart. "Where is your uncle?"

"He's gathering provisions in town." A deep ridge furrowed her brow. "Sir, uh, Domhnall?"

"Aye?" He loved how she said his name with her English accent.

"How long will you be requiring our services?"

He shrugged. "That I do not know. Did my mother say?"

"She said perhaps a fortnight or two?"

He was irritated that his mother had come in his stead. He had gone to his father this morning about his suggestion to recruit men from the Donalds to help in Watch duties. Father had been in a hurry to settle a dispute with the builder who was fortifying the seawall, so Domhnall retreated to his chamber to finish writing the dispatches from yesterday. Apparently, the progress on their new embankment was causing a rift between foreman and castle help. After, he was going to run his theory about the MacDougalls by his father. Then he was going to ask about hiring Rosalie and her uncle. He had wanted to be the one to tell Rosalie the good news. God, he was not good at this. How would he fare as laird?

"Uncle Os's work usually takes a week. I never ask how he does it. It's filthy business, and he uses the cats plus traps, but he's thorough. Lady Montgomerie offered me work in the kitchen. Your head cook is unwell?"

"Aye, Mistress Iverson's ability is limited. She's Hayden's mother. You met him. She's been ill. None of the herbalist's tinctures seem to help. Are you leaving for another market next or returning home to Edinburgh?" *Please say no.* "'Tis a pleasant season to be in the Highlands. Less rain, more sun. I could show you our charms. Introduce you to Ewan's cats."

"We can stay for a while, perhaps a fortnight, at least until Oswell's work is completed and I've fulfilled my obligation to your mother."

"Good. I'd like that."

A different flush ran across her fair cheeks. Countless light brown freckles traced the bridge of her nose and cheeks, and her hazel eyes danced. "You would?"

"I would."

Farther from danger, closer to... Rosalie couldn't put a word to her thoughts. What was she walking into? A refuge? Secure earnings, at least for a short while?

Or something more?

She was accustomed to packing up and changing plans. Nonetheless, her stomach tightened with unexpected anticipation. She'd not worked in a castle's kitchen in a few years, as most of the stewards preferred an older cook, like Aunt Nelda.

She found her mind tumbling to the same thought... If she could woo Domhnall to believe her to be a true Seer, what could result?

The idea was tempting and honestly, she couldn't believe it had come to her mind. A long-term guise? No. Coin, temporary sanctuary, that's all this was. The last time she let greed overcome her senses, she had poked a beast. She nibbled her lip and chanced a look over her shoulder. No more sightings of Lady Brantingham today at least.

She kept pace with Domhnall, the space between them both a chasm and a bubble. He spoke about his mother's gardens, the castle's fortifications, and roles of the watchmen. Maybe her reading of his palm hadn't been incorrect. He was a talkative man—on his terms. She enjoyed it. Too many days lying to people who were not her friends and caring for her uncle and aunt made a young woman aching for freedom, for pleasurable interactions with no end goal or motive. To just...be.

Perhaps, when nervous—though why would he be?—Domhnall put on the opposite façade of chinwagger. People either poured out their hearts when agitated, or the closed up like a box. Her years of reading people had filled her knowledge bank on mannerisms, nerves, and other behaviors, and she found herself even now, assessing Domhnall. Nelda teased her that she truly had the Sight in her, but Rosalie scoffed at such an idea. There was no such thing. She read people. Astutely.

She wondered who the laird's soothsayer was and if she'd need to avoid him as well. Nothing a little snooping wouldn't turn up. Castle kitchens swelled with information.

Oswell met them on the path, climbed into the cart, and took over guiding the oxen to the stable closest to the isle bridge.

"Aren't you to be laird? How can you also be a watchman? Is this normal in Scotland?" Rosalie blurted after Domhnall took a breath from his sharing.

"Och, that's complicated, aye." He shrugged away her question but couldn't hide the stiffening of his shoulders. "Here is good." He took the reins from Oswell while her uncle dropped down from the cart.

Oswell's legs visibly quaked and his knees creaked. He didn't look rested despite his nap. Rosalie steadied him with a hand looped through the crook of his elbow. "Rosie. I'm fine." He didn't shake her assistance away though.

After leaving the oxen and cart with the stable master, she reached for the crate of cats.

"No worries, missus," the stable master said. "Cam, come." He beckoned a lad.

"Oh no, I can manage it, sir." Rosalie rested a hand on the crate edge.

Domhnall gestured to the freckled, brown-haired stable master. "They'll be well tended, like I said. Ewan's been working with the animals since he was a wee lad."

The man beamed. "Aye, sir." He bowed, leaned in, and rubbed Duo. He turned to Rosalie. "He? She?"

She gently swiped a hand upon Duo's brown-black fur. "This is Duo. A boy. His brother, Trēs, especially loves scratches behind his ears. Trēs will wander, but if you have food, he'll return. He gets into trouble when he's alone. I let them out to roam under supervision. Otherwise, they should be in a crate."

"Don't fret, Rosie. They'll be fine." Oswell was already eyeing the keep across the isle with an adoring glint in his eye.

"I'll get Master Murchison to assist with the oxen," Ewan suggested.

Domhnall nodded. "Thank you." He leaned closer to Rosalie without touching her. "All right?"

She liked his emboldened nearness. She hadn't been blind to his subtle brush of her hands when they'd shifted crates. Perhaps proximity to others was not his trouble? She'd answer those nagging questions soon enough.

"They'll be well in the stable with Ewan," he repeated.

She eased herself away from the cats, reluctant, but assured. "Promise?"

"Promise."

She linked her arm with Oswell's and lifted her small sack of belongings over her shoulder.

Domhnall reached for the sack. "I can—"

"I'm able," she countered.

Conversation fell silent as Domhnall guided them across a bridge to the robust castle. Shimmers of late afternoon sun danced in the loch as the water lapped against the shore. Green water plants floated shoreside as gray clouds ushered light across the sky. She wondered if it would rain tonight like Lady Montgomerie had predicted. The loch enticed her. Maybe later she'd gather stones.

Her last question to Domhnall, left unanswered, pecked at her curiosity. Why would he not wish to be laird? Didn't all nobles want such an honor? She'd wait to prod further when he asked for another reading. Given his interest in the first one, she'd bet two hens he'd ask again. And this time, she would be prepared.

His reaction to her observation about air being his predominant element, during his palm reading, was perplexing. She'd only said air because of his hand's finger and palm-length ratio.

Everyone was one of the four elements: earth, air, fire, or water. He didn't match the typical characteristics of air, but she'd hit the mark regardless. Pure luck. Intrigue fed her determination now. Working in the kitchen, she'd glean the right information about Domhnall, his family, and the mysterious soothsayer. Or she hoped, unsure if the Scottish servants would be receptive to her arrival.

On their approach, servants toiled in the interior garden beds. Domhnall greeted them with cordial words or nods. The returned smiles appeared genuine, and a warmth filled her chest at his kindness. She'd seen many cruel lords in England. Not all, but some.

They reached the kitchen entrance. "We've rooms set aside for you. I'm sorry they're modest. My family sleeps in the chambers above, and my extended kin will be visiting this week for my sister's birthday." He scuffed a hand through his wavy hair. "We probably could have fared fine without Robena—Mistress Iverson—but with Aileana's *cèilidh* tomorrow, we're desperate for kitchen help. I hope it's not too daunting for you. I remember the apple tartlets you had in your Edinburgh shop. They looked and smelled divine."

Her cheeks heated. "*Cèilidh?*"

"Gaelic word. A celebration. Lots of music, dancing, and food. It's her eighteenth birthday."

The mirror gift. Lanie. Ah! It made sense now. "I see. This is plenty fine," she said when they reached the small bedchamber occupied by several cots. "Not a worry, sir."

"It's Domhnall." He cleared his throat. "I'll retrieve details of your work from Cawley, our steward. Our midday meal is usually smaller than our evening sup. So they are busy now preparing for that."

"Oh?" Was everything different in this area of the Highlands? Usually the midday dinner was the grand feast, and evening sup lighter fare. She rubbed her temple. She had much to learn here at Eilean Donan and she'd not even begun.

"Aye. We go against tradition and serve a larger sup after the day is done, instead of midday. My grandfather started the tradition years ago. Servants eat before us. Aileana's *cèilidh* will be early evening, tomorrow, to give guests enough time to arrive. Please rest, settle your belongings, and someone will be with you shortly."

That was quite contrary to what she was accustomed in England. She wondered what other cultural surprises lay ahead.

He departed the quarters behind the kitchen, the wind at his heels.

Edrea's accommodations were horrid. This was the best her esquire could find? The scent of god-awful fish and boiled vegetables wafted to her stuffy, rank room. Her lover lay between her and the bannocks on the plate beside her bed. She reached over him to grab one, bit, chewed, and swallowed. Her gaze drifted around the dimly lit room. Wenda had gone downstairs to eat. Meanwhile, Edrea worked on her plan. She shifted beneath the bedclothes, her muscles strained from exertion, her breath catching.

Perusing the marketplace had proven fruitless.

Almost.

Her lover's hand traced along her naked shoulder as she lay with her back to him. Shivers rippled upon her skin. At least he had bedded her well, and it alleviated her morning sickness. Through a deep Scottish brogue, he whispered odd Gaelic words into her ear. He trailed kisses down her neck. She inhaled. He smelled of whisky, sweat, and the afterglow of lovemaking. He would serve duly, she thought, rolling to face him, as much as she wanted to order him to leave. Handsome eyes beheld hers with lust, with intrigue. She quieted his mumbling with her mouth. He tasted good, too. She supposed not all Scots were heathens.

He squeezed her breasts, then slipped below the bed-clothes. She enjoyed a lover intent on pleasuring her...and one far less focused on words. Her money and body would work well on him. He promised her connections. Like all the others, he would do her bidding. He would kill Rosalie if she asked him. Yes, the plan was slowly coming together.

Bertie had left many capable men along the border to fight off the rabble and maintain order at their tower keep. Men she'd slowly been grooming for when she would rule. How easily young men could fall prey to temptations of the flesh. While Bertie had been off fighting his war with the barons against the Despensers and the king—a futile cause that was supposed to have played in her favor with three caskets home, instead of two—she had slithered her way into many of his men's minds and beds. She loathed resorting to this, but her power was minimal. They would listen to her when the time came. Widows held power. She had arranged Bertie's illegitimate sons' deaths. Now to dispose of her useless husband.

She released a throaty moan as her lover reached far lower, his tongue slick and searching on her thigh. She always enjoyed her lovers—heavens, Bertie had been an awful lover. He grunted and thrusted and was done in a matter of moments. Thank God he had stopped coming to her bedchamber years ago.

Early pregnancy intensified her sensations. She bit her lip to suppress an unladylike word. The man was delicious and did all the right things.

Her mind fragmented as pleasure surpassed all thought.

Later, after discharging him with specific orders, she drifted into preparation mode. Once she formulated her story, the laird would assist her with finding that wench Rosalie. She was close. Dornie was the last market north. South, in the town of Garry, she had missed her by one day.

Tomorrow morning, she would call upon the laird and put this matter behind her. As much as she loathed direct interaction and confrontation, she had to resolve this matter. Now.

CHAPTER SIX

"**S**omething troubles you, Domhnall?"

Damn his mother's Feeling abilities.

The evening's hearth crackled beside the long oak table. Servants came and went, clearing the supper's remnants. The flames laughed at him, and he eased himself into a seat farthest from the talons of heat. A storm brewed outside...and within.

Approaching autumn meant more fires. He disliked winter even more. His own body heat wasn't enough to keep him warm, and he couldn't avoid fires then.

She can dull the pain within you, a voice coaxed.

What in hell? He eradicated the voice, but not the idea.

Sitting here, while Rosalie worked in the kitchen, he missed her spark, her nearness. He belatedly responded to his mother with a shrug.

"Hmm," she murmured.

In the chair across from him, she busied herself with sewing a new quilt she'd been working on for Mistress Iverson. He knew his acquiescence didn't work on his mother. She had told him once that his aura, brimming with life, a soft blue, was cooler than most. Coolness didn't necessarily equate to death though, and, in fact, his lifeblood likely embodied what he saw in his visions which was, well, death. Father's lifeblood was red-hot fire, she'd said.

He tore his thoughts from feeling so woeful, and instead pondered this evening's plans. Everyone had their place to be tonight. Earlier, his father had plodded off to his private chamber to draw up documents with Crystoll and Kendrick, and he invited Domhnall to join, but he declined, claiming he had Watch duties to contend with. Letters, deeds, town rulings, dealings with neighboring clans, fiscal management, the crofters' complaints... Domhnall had no ear or patience for it. All he wanted was to find the seditious thieves and arsonists. He added assaulter to the growing list of offenses. What next?

Aileana hurried into the hall, gave Domhnall a "hello," then turned to their mother. "Will you be joining us in the solar?"

"In a short while, dear. Please go ahead with Auntie Caite."

His sister was off to the kitchen in a blink, likely to gather their drinks and biscuits. Her steps were as fast as her arrows most days.

Silence reigned for a long moment. Domhnall found his gaze falling on the kitchen entrance to catch a glance of Rosalie.

"Have you been reading?" his mother asked.

He coughed on a swallow of the ale he'd been sipping for the better part of an hour. "No, not lately."

"Why not?"

How could he tell his mother he'd moved the cursed books from doorstop to table to finally under his bed mattress? There, the Wind didn't chatter his teeth, nor the flames taunt his dreams. No book of Air existed any-way. The metallic emblems on each Ancient book: a tree for Earth, a fish for Water, and a flame for Fire were imprinted in his memory. The unfamiliar Norse words and intricate drawings remained a constant reminder of his difference. He'd expelled the books out of spite and anger. He felt like the Silver Veil was punishing him for a mistake he'd made as a wee lad.

Just a lad!

How could he have known the dark sludge slithering across his field of vision had been the black curtain into the future? Nay. He'd been caught unaware. Death had first entered his life and planted malevolent apparitions in his naïve eyes one cursed day over twenty years ago.

"It's gone, Mother." The lies came naturally, sliding off his tongue like grease but burning his throat like whisky. Perhaps she saw through the dishonesties. If she read into him, she had hidden it all these years. She wasn't one to break a promise. Years ago, after the day with Isolde, he'd cursed the ability away, his body and mind unable to bear the power, the knowing, any longer. Why had it returned? Now? Of all times? Why?

He could only hide from hell for so long.

She pressed pink lips together, fine wrinkles pucker-ing. "The books hold many truths if you allow them to."

He shuffled his feet and stretched his legs. Night called him, but he was on the second shift so he'd grab some sleep beforehand. The streets screamed for his watchful eyes...

A chilling draft blew past him and he shivered.

His mother had the patience of a saint. "Did I ever tell you how your father found my missing book?"

His mouth fell open. "No. You never told me. I thought your grandmother and mother transcribed them all and brought them from the isles?"

"Indeed, my grandmother transcribed them. Aunt Venora gave me the book of Mother Earth, Jörd, and the book of Fire, but my mother's book of Eir—the goddess of healing and mercy, the book of Water—was lost on a journey to the isles many years ago." A sliver of a memory curved her lips into a smile. She exhaled a sigh of fondness. "I thought it was forever gone. Your father, blessed be his determination, found it for me."

He leaned in, intrigued but also suspicious of where her story veered. She didn't ramble without a point.

"There are truths in the books," she repeated. "Sometimes special things disappear for a time until they need to reappear and serve their purpose again."

And there it was.

There are lies on the Wind, he wanted to counter. He huffed and folded his arms. How quickly his visions of the future had twisted into lies. Unbearable lies.

She rested the needle and thread in her lap, then clasped her thin fingers together and held his gaze. "Your book, if it was written, is lost. I'm sorry you never met Venora. She could've helped you with—"

"I don't need help. It is gone, Mother." He ground the words through gritted teeth, his pulse spiking. Lowering his voice, he said, "Gone."

Lies. All lies.

Though Kendrick's gift of feeling was truly gone, removed by his mother's selfless act as the story went, Domhnall's enticed him like the devil's words. If he let down his guard and allowed himself to touch another person...it might return with vengeance. The black terror already clawed to be released, evidenced by the voices and obscured visions he barely controlled lately.

"Why not write the book yourself? I'll help you. Jörd's book can serve as foundation."

"No."

Hurt, something he seldom saw in his mother, shone in her deep loch-green eyes. The evening's firelight danced on her face, and instead of highlighting her beauty, it aged her. White fringed her temple and streaked her long, black hair. A few wrinkles were crescents around her eyes. His sisters were youthful mirror images of Mother and Father combined. Gracie's dark hair and blue eyes like both of them. Aileana had inherited Grandfather's auburn locks and the blue eyes of their parents, too.

Domhnall had brown hair, brown eyes.

He looked nothing like his surrogate father...not much like Mother either. As a lad, he used to pretend he'd been born among the faeries, stolen by his parents, and brought to the mainland. The blood bond with his mother pulsed through his veins though. He was her son. There was no doubt. And Alasdair loved him as if he were his own.

He simmered. "I'm sorry."

Her face softened. "Never apologize for feeling. Never apologize for your ability, or its absence."

Or its dormancy. He shifted in the chair, an icy chill running down his spine. He sensed the cusp of the Sight's return. Like a beast within, scratching to be set free. Why else would the wicked words return now upon the Wind?

And the dreams return as well? It was like a dam, and water was already leaking through cracks in logs.

Though she was not one for diatribes, she pressed on anyway. "I'll remind you, as an Ancient-born, we possess *all* the gifts of the Silver Veil. Healing from Water, Feeling with Fire, and Seeing by the Wind. Jörd runs through our bodies, serving as foundation and guide on our path. Nobody I've known has been able to harness all powers to their full potential, but all are present. Usually one surpasses the others. It dominates. It is our constant and our root to Jörd. Perhaps...it can shift."

Nonsense. He fought the urge to argue. He tried to hide it behind a mask of confidence, but he stooped his shoulders and wrung his hands.

She lifted her chin, her gaze stony, determined, and knowing.

He shivered with her intuition.

She loosened her balled hands. "Wind feeds Fire. Water douses Fire. Water nourishes Earth. Wind churns Water. Fire scorches Earth. All are connected." The flames in the nearby hearth licked in emphasis. A log crackled. It was ironic that she loved fire; he loathed it.

He swallowed sourness.

"You're afraid, but open your heart to the idea. If your visions have left, another ability may arise. Twice, I've healed. Once, long ago, I had visions, too, as I've told you."

His stomach fluttered with her admission. Father and Aileana. She'd healed both. Before he had lost control of the visions, he'd foreseen Aileana's death and told Mother in time. Thankfully, she'd believed him. At one time, his visions had been a gift. A true gift to save lives. His mother had mentioned her visions before. Fire, Wind, and Water all flowed through her. How could she be so blessed and he so cursed?

She tipped her head back, closing her eyes in memory. "The visions are inconsequential now, but they set me on my course."

Servants came and went while they sat in silence. He licked his lips and tapped a foot.

"Go, Domhnall."

"Where?"

She angled her head, a sideways, maternal, and all-knowing look softening her features. "Visit with Rosalie. We have no strict rules. It's not forbidden."

He flashed a half smile to mask his unease at her perception. His mind was exposed and vulnerable around his mother. She only spoke with full regard and love though.

An unnatural stillness fell upon him. Rosalie had read him, too. In a fractional moment, she'd seen into him. *Air.* Curse him for wanting to know more.

"You're allowed to court someone, anyone you wish," she added in an easygoing whisper. "It's—" She didn't finish the sentence.

"I'm not—" He heaved a sigh as he pushed his chair, the old legs scraping the stone floor. "If you'll not be needing me, I'll go."

Her grin soothed his soul. The tips of his ears warmed.

"Go, love."

Instead of going to the kitchen, he procrastinated and pondered what to say to Rosalie next, while taking a round through the castle's hallways first. He checked the locks, storage areas, and the hundred other small protective measures that kept Eilean Donan a safe home for noble and servant alike.

Then he would stop by and see Rosalie, maybe catch her before she turned in and ask how her first night had fared in the kitchen.

Rosalie's wrists ached, and her feet yearned for a dip in a warm soaking tub but a servant's life held no room for luxuries. Sweat dribbled down her back.

"Let me help you finish," came a youthful voice from the entranceway to the kitchen.

She turned to find the laird's stunning daughter approaching. "Lady Aileana, please, I can't—"

Aileana took a heavy clay jar filled with figs from Rosalie.

"I'm fine, my lady." Rosalie shifted weight to balance the sack of flour in her other arm.

Aileana rolled her eyes. "It's Lanie, please. One day I'll be a nobleman's wife, and if Domhnall has it his way, the laird's wife, so he can trudge all over doing his Watch business. Until then, it is just Lanie."

She followed Rosalie into the pantry, and they put the items in their designated places—or so she presumed. The kitchen staff had already finished their work and left her behind to complete a few more duties.

They returned to the kitchen. "What can I get for you, Lanie?"

"I'll gather it myself. Biscuits, honey, and raspberries and mint for an herbal water infusion." She chewed a lip, seemingly accustomed with the kitchen. "Ah, there." She collected clean mugs, the small honey crock, and a plate of biscuits set aside, and placed them on a tray.

"The kettle's cold. I'll put it on the fire." Low flames licked in the kitchen hearth, and Rosalie settled the kettle to heat.

Aileana slid onto a bench at the center table. "My brother is a grouse, but once you get to know him, he's a kind man." She picked at her nails—was that dirt? "How did you meet him?"

"In my shop."

Aileana wore a gown, but earlier, Rosalie had sworn she'd seen her in a tunic and hose and bustling around the stable yard with a few of the workers and soldiers. She gnawed the inside of her mouth, unsure what to say while the kettle heated. She sorted the spices used for the evening's meal to pass the time.

"You mean the marketplace?"

Rosalie fumbled on her words. "No, my shop in Edinburgh."

"Ah. What kind of shop?" Aileana's eyes lit with intrigue, a wide smile tipping her pink lips.

Rosalie retreated to the kettle, urging it to quicken. "We sell trinkets and such." *And lies.* "My uncle catches rats."

Thankfully, Aileana shifted subjects. "Och, I met your two cats."

"My uncle uses them for his work."

"We have a six or eight of them lazing about. My mother loves cats. You've surely met Ewan. He loves the furry rascals, too. Domhnall does, as well. He doesn't like to let people know that he does. He's got a heart for animals. They don't bother him like peop—" She frowned and redirected. "What brings you here? So far from England I mean?"

"Home is in Edinburgh."

"But you're English. You live in Edinburgh? You certainly didn't move north for the weather. And you travel with the market group?"

Rosalie gave a vague nod and played with her necklace in nervous habit.

"Adorable." Aileana leaned in, tracing a finger on the beads. "Gracie would love one. Where did you get it?"

"I made it. In fact, your mother purchased one for your sister."

"Talented. You made it?"

Aileana's exuberant—and scattered—energy and candor, though a refreshing breath, made Rosalie's head spin. There was no need for a palm reading with her. The woman exhibited all her fates and traits clear as day. Rosalie's feet and body screamed for her bed, however pleasant the company. "I could show you, if you'd like?"

"I would love that, thank you. You can teach me, and I can show Gracie upon her return from the abbey. She loves drawing and painting. Unless you're still here in a few months and can show her yourself?" Her blue eyes shone with cunning speculation.

"I am not certain I will be."

"I am certain another person would like it if you did stay for a while," she said with a wink. She twirled a lock of cinnamon-red hair as she checked on the kettle.

Thank God, because heat warmed Rosalie's cheeks. She could not have meant her brother. She hardly knew Domhnall...yet.

Imagine the coin, her inner voice lured. *He hangs on your every word and move.*

Mother Mary, be quiet.

"The kettle is ready. They'll be waiting for me in the solar. Let's spend some time together tomorrow or soon after? My *cèilidh* is tomorrow night, and I'll be distracted by all the handsome gentlemen. I must choose soon."

"Choose?"

"A suitor. I am to be wed soon enough."

"Oh."

"I always thought I'd choose Hayden, but he's a...he's a bit like a tangled knot. I enjoy his company on our walks and such, and he showed me how to improve my accuracy with the bow. He's fine-looking, hardworking, and enjoyable sometimes. But...I do not know how I feel about him. He's always with Dour Domhnall though. You cannot separate the two," she said with a tsk as she prepared leaves and herbs in the kettle. "Besides, how can I marry my brother's best friend?"

Rosalie's ears burned. She'd never met such a talkative lady. Spirited, either. She suspected she shouldn't be listening to Aileana's private ramblings, but she couldn't ask the lady to please hold her tongue either. Eilean Donan was different from other castles. Usually she'd do her work unseen. In one day, she'd already engaged with the laird's wife, daughter, and son. They served meals differently, too. And here now, the laird's daughter was divulging more information in conversation than she would get in a full year working under another family. Nevertheless, Rosalie remained guarded. One never knew.

Use the information gained, later. For readings, her inner voice said.

Really? Her conscience countered. Of all times, it wanted to exploit this young lady? "No," she said aloud.

"What? Oh, Domhnall." Aileana's heart-shaped face broke with a bigger grin. She batted wispy brown lashes. "I saw him watching you in the marketplace. I've never seen him enamored with a lass since—" She brushed off loose chamomile and mint leaves from the counter. "Sorry, I shouldn't have called him dour. He doesn't like the nickname."

Rosalie lowered her eyes. "Is there anything else you require, milady?"

"Lanie."

"Lanie," she relented. "Shall I carry the tray for you?"

"No, thank you. We'll speak soon. To learn painting, aye?"

Rosalie nodded again.

Aileana gathered the tray and hurried through the doorway. Over her shoulder, she called, "And welcome to Eilean Donan, Rose."

With a muffled yawn, Rosalie reached her room and fell onto the thick linens and plump pillow of her cot. Oswell's distinctive snore echoed through the high circulation window between the men's quarters and the women's. The other women had also retreated to the modest, shared room outfitted with six cots. Not one of the lasses spoke to her as they changed out of their kirtles, aprons, bonnets, and working gowns. Earlier they'd all given her terse orders and sideways glares as they bustled about during the evening's meal preparation and subsequent clean-up. Not one introduced themselves, although one younger woman had spoken with her while Rosalie kneaded loaves of bread to be baked.

The laird's daughter had given her a warmer reception than the servants. By the light of a shared lantern, the four other women moved through the nightly ritual of undressing, brushing or plaiting hair, and washing with a basin and pitcher of water, all while talking about their day. Rosalie sat quietly, observing—discreetly. She'd yet to pinpoint the identity of the laird's soothsayer and would need to do more listening to gather information.

She loosened her plait, allowing her hair to fall through her fingers. She withdrew her brush from her sack and worked it through stubborn knots. If she plaited it while wet, it created lovely waves. Today it was a knotty mess.

One red-haired young woman blathered on about the fire in the marketplace. "Did you see how he responded to it? I heard he wouldn't help with the blaze. Grant saw him cower and hide with the animals. What man does such a thing?"

The other older woman responded with a tsk. "A shame. The accident was years ago, and it still bothers him."

"Indeed. I once spoke with Isolde about it. She told me how he blamed himself. He was a wee lad. Surely he should've reconciled his guilt by now." She twisted her youthful face with pity and sucked in her lips.

"Strange indeed," the older concurred.

"For a watchman, ye'd think he'd be...uh..." A Gaelic word came forth under her breath. She brushed her wavy red hair, shadows hiding the golden highlights Rosalie had seen earlier. The woman gave Rosalie a disapproving glare. The women switched to hushed whispers and Gaelic once they realized she had been listening.

Rosalie brushed through her hair with deliberation, letting the strokes placate her mind. Tomorrow's impression was crucial. It was the family she needed to impress, not these hens. She'd acquired enough information to get by today. A handful of servants worked within the kitchen. Two women prepared the food, and two served in the hall. Others minded various chambers, rooms, and gardens. The steward, Cawley, came and left, barking orders throughout the day, and a young lad ran around tending to biddings of any and all. Not nearly as many servants resided here as she'd experienced in the larger English castles.

There, she'd weaved through cooks and scullions who ran the pantry, buttery, spicery, cellar, and scalding-house, to name a few. Eilean Donan possessed a buttery and pantry, and herbal stillroom for the lady, but most other roles such as larder or butcher were outsourced to the village. Several bountiful gardens grew on the isle and within the castle's outer wall. Everyone had a job, and the system worked. She'd only seen them in passing, but the laird also possessed men who tended the stables, soldiers who worked in the barracks, and masons who repaired a crumbling stone seawall. She could lose herself in the activity—in a good way. Lady Brantingham would never find her in the kitchen.

Perhaps tomorrow, one or two of the kitchen servants would thaw their icy welcome. A smile and kindness weren't always enough to woo people though. None of them were outright mean with their discrimination, but she'd felt it in their Gaelic murmurs to each other and slanting glares. She was English, after all.

Someone knocked on the door, three quick raps, and Rosalie dropped her brush. It clattered to the rushes-covered floor. She scooped the brush up.

The red-haired servant, without hesitation, opened the door.

"Tomorrow's list, Kyla," the steward's deep voice intruded.

"Aye." She took the parchment and shut the oak door. She reviewed the page and then lifted a thick auburn eyebrow at Rosalie. "Looks as if ye will be takin' o'er for Mistress Iverson." Disdain darkened her brown eyes.

Mother Mary, Kyla had been the kind one who'd chatted with her while they kneaded bread. Kyla handed Rosalie the parchment.

She tried her best to mask her discomfort. "Thank you."

The words—like scribbles—on the page could've been in another language. The numbers stood out and she memorized them. She identified a few of the easier letters. Oswell would translate it in the morning. She'd draw pictures as reminders. Her memory was sharp—it had to be.

Another knock and the flock of women in the room stopped with their clucking whispers and grooming. Kyla returned to the door, opened it a crack, and peeked out. Her demeanor immediately changed. Straighter bearing, demure smile, a bat of eyelashes. "Och, Sir Montgomerie. Is somethin' amiss?" she asked with a honey-sweet voice. She loosened her shawl to show off her delicate collarbone. Her enviable wavy hair poked from beneath her nightcap. If she went lower with the shawl...it was unnerving to watch.

Rosalie tightened her own shawl, though she was still fully dressed. With no fire lit in the room's hearth and being deep within the ground floor, the cold went straight to her bones. A whistling wind drafted through the connecting high window to the men's chamber. She might just sleep in her work kirtle tonight.

The man at the door whispered to Kyla, his voice a deep timbre, and Rosalie strained to hear without taking a step closer. It sounded like Domhnall, but it could have been another male member of the clan for all she knew.

Kyla's expression curdled. "Och, sir, she's here." Unbridled dislike flickered Rosalie's way with the servant's frown and darted look. "Rosalie, Sir Montgomerie wishes to speak with ye."

She nodded to Kyla and stood, tucking the parchment into her apron's pocket, feeling eyes of daggers upon her from the other three women. This was not how one made friends at all. Sadly, she was accustomed to feeling like the outsider, and being ridiculed for her "profession." She could count on one hand the friendships created through the years with her constant moving. Here, she just wanted to be one of them. Here, she wished to belong. *Futile.*

Her mission here was straightforward: work as a servant, earn her pence, and hide until Edrea Brantingham left Dornie. No friends. No dalliances with the laird's son.

Uncertain steps brought her to the door. In the hallway, she was swift to ask with her chin held high, "Did I do something wrong?"

At the same time Domhnall said, "I'm sorry to trouble you so late. Do you have a moment?"

She released a nervous chuckle. "Of course." She dipped a curtsy and then closed the door behind her. Leave those hens to their nattering.

"This way." He pointed down the dark hall which was illumined by only one sconce. She followed him to the kitchen, her heart racing.

"Why would you think you did something wrong?" He motioned a hand toward the table for her to sit. A set of wax candles in heavy pewter sticks burned on the thick and worn wooden table. Was she supposed to have put them out? Heavens, she knew hardly a thing about her responsibilities. All evening she'd performed mundane tasks while Kyla assumed responsibility as head cook. She'd kept her nose down, had done her job. She slumped onto a bench across from Domhnall.

She straightened her sagging shoulders. "Well..." She cast a leery glance toward the rooms.

His dark brown eyes lit with realization. "Och! Pay them no heed. They *gossib* worse than the ladies in court. You're a newcomer for their chitchat."

His frankness eased her frayed thoughts. "I'm afraid I've been pushed aside today, unsure about my responsibilities. Kyla kindly assumed the lead role in the kitchen." The parchment crinkled in her apron, a reminder. Pragmatism surpassing embarrassment, she withdrew the page. "Might you enlighten me? Or speak with the steward? Or maybe another servant could work in my stead as head cook. There must be some mistake. I am perfectly able in an assisting role, Sir—"

"It's Domhnall."

"I shouldn't. You're the laird's son and should be addressed as such."

He took the parchment from her, squinting to read it by candlelight. "Please. I prefer my name."

Only with her? He hadn't corrected Kyla's formal greeting. "Then I prefer mine. It's Rose."

He rubbed his chin. "Not Rosalie?"

She swatted a hand. "That's my given name, of course, and Uncle Os calls me Rosie. I like simple."

"I like simple, too." Handsome, full lips smiled. Not a speck of beard or mustache traced his clean face. "Life is too complicated. You like flowers, I saw. What a fitting name."

"You as well?"

"Pardon me?"

"You like flowers? The story of the forget-me-nots?" she said. "You seem to know herbals. From your mother?"

He looked up from the parchment, scuffing a hand along his chin. "Och, aye. As you've likely seen already, my mother loves flowers and herbals. She used to talk incessantly about them when I was a lad, with me by her side. I've learned a thing or two. It was the tragic ending with the story, the origin of their name that really struck me."

"Indeed." She nodded. Hmm, a man who adored his mother. Instead of saving it to use, the fact warmed her heart. Domhnall may walk around with a stalwart frown, but a tenderness hid beneath it.

He laid the parchment down and held her gaze. "There is a Christian meaning, too, of course, for the flowers."

"Oh?" She leaned in, closer. The fragrance of cooking oils, seasonings, and yeast laced the stifling summer's air of the kitchen. She wondered if she smelled like food and grease, too, having not yet used the wash basin and linens in the servants' quarters. The thought of food caused her stomach to grumble. Many days on the road in the heat had caught up with her. She'd only eaten what she needed to maintain energy for each day. During supper she ate daintily, not wanting to look like a hungry peasant. She usually gave her extra rations to Oswell and had, without second thought, tucked two biscuits in her apron for him for later.

Domhnall rose, located a pitcher of wine, two goblets, and a block of cheese covered for the morning. He was the laird's son, so she didn't chide him for stealing Kyla's cheese, set aside to be used in a baked egg dish. He sliced a piece and handed it to her. Then he sliced a piece of nearby bread.

She smiled. "Thanks."

He poured the deep burgundy wine. She wondered if Cawley would be cross. He'd apportioned them all in their respective flasks and pitchers with specific instructions to not touch them.

He sipped. "Once, when God was in the Garden of Eden, he saw a blue flower and asked its name. The flower was shy and whispered that it had forgotten its name. God renamed the flower *forget-me-not*, so He, and the flower, would never forget it. My grandfather told me the story when I was a lad."

"Enchanting. Not one you'd hear during Mass." She released a delicate moan after swallowing the salty cheese. Her stomach thanked her. She bit into the crusty bread, wishing for butter or jam, but dared not ask for them. "More pleasant than the departed lovers." She added, "I wish I knew more flower names. I know most by sight and usefulness for paints only."

"There is truth in names."

What an odd thing to say. She shivered, pulling her threadbare shawl closer. With her earnings, she hoped to locate a decent cloth merchant or weaver in town so she could make a new gown and a thicker cloak for winter. The servants in the keep were decently dressed, and here she was, an Englishwoman in her meager attire. "Names are names. Are they not? You find meaning in names? Doesn't it go against the Church? Aren't our names God-given?"

He shrugged. "Not everything is steeped in God's ordinance." He elaborated, "My grandfather Simon put heed into signs, names, and their meanings. I try to find the balance between God's realm and another."

Superstition runs rampant among commoner and noble alike, Oswell's earlier counsel echoed. "Your name? Domhnall," she released it slowly off her tongue, pronouncing it like Donald without the second *d.*

"It doesn't matter."

"If mine matters, yours does," she countered. "I'm a flower. What about you?" she said with a teasing bat of eyelashes.

"The Ancient texts say it means 'stranger,' but the Scots say it means 'world-ruler.' " He struggled on his words. "I'm not fond of either meaning."

"I like both." The Ancients. She had heard of them before. They were the mystical people of the isles. Oswell had promised her they'd fare well here, feeding off the beliefs of the commoner. Perhaps the nobles were just as superstitious? Domhnall, a man of noble and Christian upbringing, had come into her shop. For a reading. She assumed he'd been formally educated by the Church and the abbey aforementioned.

Speaking of names... She knew what hers truly meant. Rosalie Threston. Once, an older woman who'd set up next to them in a market in Northumberland, enlightened her with her name's meaning. The woman, who was also a palm reader, was educated in Latin and Ancient Greek, and dissected names, meanings, and signs. She'd taught Rosalie and Nelda a thing or two about interpreting the night sky and forecasting the elements.

Rosalie. A rose who lies. The worst part...Threston, their surname, meant *twisted.* She'd been bestowed her Uncle Oswell's name when she joined their family. She didn't know Nelda's surname. Nelda had been her mother's sister, though Rosalie must have inherited her father's looks, for she looked nothing like Nelda. She often wondered if they were her true kin. But why would they lie to her?

Even if they lied for a living.

A rose telling twisted lies. God had given her a portentous name, indeed. Her stomach roiled in response. *Shift the discussion, Rose.* She braved, "You were not the most forthcoming of your name when I met you. You thought I'd swindle you of more coin if I had known you were a laird's son?"

A gray shadow covered his finely chiseled features with her insinuation.

She lowered her look and fidgeted with her fingers. "Forgive my boldness. I've inherited the bad habit from Oswell." She took a hearty gulp of the flavorful wine.

He paused for a painfully long moment.

She slid a hand across the table and retrieved the parchment. Oswell would read it to her tomorrow. "I should return to my chamber, sir." She almost stood, but his words halted her.

"You're right," he finally breathed heavily.

"Pardon me?"

"About my name."

"You're noble-born. A laird's son. A clan with a prestigious reputation." Or from what she had learned from purveyors in town. "You've a reputable name, Sir—uh, Domhnall. Please accept my apologies. Long day, strong wine."

He encouraged her to stay with a gesture of his hand.

When he wasn't Dour Domhnall, she liked his company, strangely. Her fingers itched to hold his hand and not for a reading alone. A gentle spirit emanated from him, unlike many uncouth men she'd encountered.

"Our clan is well-known and able. My mother is a Mac-Coinneach, and her father was the second laird at Eilean Donan. My father is a Montgomerie from the south. But..." He faltered on his words. "Alasdair Montgomerie isn't my birth father. My real father died before my birth. This is common knowledge here, though I have always felt like..." He stopped and shook his head.

She gasped and covered her surprise with a light cough. The long drags of wine made her head grow heavy, but his admission woke her up. Domhnall mystified her...captivated her.

He stared at her, his strong chin softening. "I'm not sure why I'm telling you. You're the Seer. Shouldn't you be telling me?

That stung. Had it been an insult or inquiry?

He took the parchment. "Let me read it for you."

"Domhnall?"

Even in the candlelight, pink blossomed on his cheeks. "Aye?"

Mother Mary, his look melted her resolve. She wanted to caress his scowl away from his forehead, stroke the mounds of his fingers...

Heavens, where was her head? She cleared her throat. "I don't know my parents, either. They died when I was a baby. My aunt and uncle raised me." *If they even are my aunt and uncle*, she wanted to add, but didn't. Why did she persist in the questions? A voice in her mind continued to taunt her though.

He exhaled. Then offered a smile. "I like your candor, Rose. Not many women speak as you do. I appreciate your honesty. You'd like my sister, Lanie."

"I've already met her. She is vibrant."

He nearly snorted. "That's a good way to describe her. She'd talk your ear off." His face grew solemn. "I'm sorry about your parents."

"Me, too. I'm sorry about your father. Laird Montgomerie seems an admirable man." From what she'd heard at least, having yet to meet him.

His nearness stirred her. She almost wanted to offer another palm reading...to touch his hand. Getting close to him was dangerous. She knew better.

He licked his lips, then sipped more wine. A fractured silence broke through the humidity of the room. "This parchment." He cast his gaze down, shuffling from the candlelight and closer to her. She could hardly decipher the scribbles in the lower light. Why would he move away from the candles?

He said, "Our steward has detailed tomorrow's responsibilities, meal requests, and number in attendance. My uncles and aunts will be attending, along with cousins, visiting lairds, and their kin. It's my sister's birthday."

"Sounds like quite the festivity."

"Aileana does love the attention. My other sister, Gracie, is south at the abbey for her studies." He tunneled a hand through his hair. "Their names definitely reflect their personalities."

"Oh?" He had shifted subjects on her again.

"My sisters. Their names. Aileana means of the green meadow, and I swear all my sister does is run off places. Not to the gardens like my mother, but she wanders about. She'd rather be with the lads, riding horses, getting into trouble. Loosing arrows at the practice mounds or across the field. Grace..." He cleared his throat and smirked. "Hers is easy. She is the devout one, the most excited of us all to attend the abbey for her learnings."

She enjoyed his digressions, though her fatigued mind struggled to keep up with his fast-moving one. She relished this side of Domhnall more than the sulky one. Something had changed in him since their first meeting. She hardly thought it was her presence or the wine's richness. A smile rounded her mouth, and she quickly masked it. "So...food? The list."

"Aye." He rose, sidled around the table, and sat beside her on the long bench now, just keeping enough space between them to avoid brushing up against her but so close she could smell him. "You like numbers, you said?"

She nodded.

He reviewed the list of foods, where to locate them, and who in the kitchen handled what responsibilities.

He inquired about her abilities and efforts with certain recipes. She assured him she was capable, having learned in other castle kitchens.

Finally, when her mind was set at ease for tomorrow's work, her gumption dared her. "Why did you ask me here? It's late. We could have reviewed this in the morning. If I'm not in trouble, is there something else you require from me?" She quickly added, "I appreciate you reading to me."

A strange breeze shuddered past them as they spoke. Gooseflesh prickled her skin. The air seemed to tingle. She leaned in closer, enjoying his presence, not wanting to sleep, though her body begged otherwise.

He shifted, no closer, no farther, though she sensed he was conflicted. "I've a proposition."

"Oh?"

His voice deepened with a husky yearning. "I'd like to teach you how to read and write."

"I couldn't possibly—"

"It would be my pleasure."

She swallowed, eyeballing his lips as they moved. Speaking of pleasure...

Rose! Where is your head? Her wine goblet was empty.

"Perhaps...you can show me your ways in return."

"Pardon me?" she asked.

"You're a Seer, aren't you?"

His eyes. They pleaded with her. *Now. Tell him.* Her nerves tensed with his projected energy and sincerity. "Yes. I am. It's not something one teaches." And she'd just dug the hole to her own grave. Why did she not just tell him the truth? She bit her lip. Money. It always came down to money. Without it, her family would starve.

"I want to see...if you're like me."

"Like you?"

He quirked an eyebrow but didn't respond.

Dear God—was he the laird's soothsayer? Connections in her mind burst. "What do you wish to learn? I can finish your session if you'd like, but I'd need your hands." Sure, Rose, *that's why you want to touch his hands.* Too bad her reading didn't require a kiss. Oh, her head! How much of that wine had she consumed? "It's how I read. Do you not do the same?"

His body rigid, he raised his eyebrows more. Her pulse quickened.

He said, "Tell me what you know. If you're true, then you will get your answers."

"You'll teach me to read and write?"

"Promise."

Quick, Rose. The wine fogged her memory. *I can do this.* "May I hold your hands this time?"

He placed his hand before her. She reached, and he recoiled.

She locked her eyes with his. Brown, wide, scared. "It will be all right," she said softly, keeping her eyes on his for a long moment while she subtly reached with her hand. She drew his hand into her palm. Her pulse drummed in her ears. *Breathe, Rose. Breathe.* His fingers trembled in her hand but neither of them released the look. She tried to convey trust and understanding with her own gentle smile. When he seemed settled, she turned her gaze to his hand. After a pause, she said, "It is as I said. Air is your element."

"What else do you see?" He leaned in, closer.

She inhaled him like he was a savory confection. Sweat, sage, hmmm...male? Was *male* a scent?

Feeling his eyes upon her, she continued to scrutinize, drawing light touches over the mounds in his palm. "You're somewhat content, though you spend hours alone to get away?"

He held a straight face. "Easy enough facts to guess. I'm a watchman. Fortune-tellers are good in their ploy."

She refrained from arguing. He was on the defense. Understandable. Most people were. He was correct after all. She stroked his fingers and pretended to examine. His hands were ice-cold.

All right, memory. Time to shine. The marketplace fire, something from his youth. Domhnall liked animals. He seemed to not like fire or touch. She chanced the next statement. "Something in your past upsets you."

Again, he was stone-faced. At least his hand had stopped trembling.

She would throw out statements until one stuck. That is what she usually did. Had she been incorrect in her eavesdropping? Surely the servants had been talking about Domhnall.

He chewed his lip and held her gaze.

She paused and pushed the candle closer. "To see better."

He flinched.

Yes. Fire. It bothered him, along with touch.

She persisted. "Something troubles you. A secret. A puzzle to solve."

All things anyone knew. There had been thefts in the marketplace. Her uncle had been attacked—it could have been Lady Brantingham's men, but intuition told her otherwise. The thefts and attack had to be connected. Domhnall was a watchman, seeking miscreants. Of course, he had a puzzle to solve.

He huffed.

"When you were young, there was an accident." Her stomach twisted. *Here goes nothing.* "With fire."

Silence, not a breath.

He abruptly stood, handed her the parchment. "It's late, and I keep you. I need to sleep before my rounds. Let me escort you to your room."

Target hit. Instead of reaping accomplishment, her heart hung heavy.

She pocketed the parchment with shaky hands and followed him from the kitchen without another word.

At the chamber door, he turned to her. "Good night, Rose," he said, drawing closer. Almost within touching distance.

"Good night, Domhnall."

Her mind buzzed with numbers and responsibilities as she nestled on her cot, grateful the other women had already fallen asleep.

Her thoughts fell upon Domhnall. Hardly dour. Dear. Kind. Inviting. Aching?

Her dreams transported her to court again. This time, her wooer held the chiseled, brooding face of Domhnall Montgomerie, as he led her across the dance floor...the smallest glimmer in his deep, brown eyes.

CHAPTER SEVEN

Life teemed in the normally peaceful keep the following afternoon as Domhnall's family prepared for Aileana's *cèilidh*. He didn't understand why she got all this attention. He released a sigh. It was Lanie. She loved it.

"Pardon me, sir." One of the servants shuffled past him, her arms brimming with linens and decorative tablecloths. Domhnall made a fast count of settings in the usually plain, now embellished, room. Fifty guests.

Cawley burst into the hall like a flaming arrow, hovered near the servants at a long table, and blasted orders. They readied platters and trays that would be soon overflowing with food, while others gathered candles and sticks, prepared sconces, and hung cleaned tapestries. Just as swiftly Cawley returned to the kitchen. There was no sign of Rosalie among the servants.

She seemed to be a competent lass but he could imagine she might be overwhelmed by the tasks today. Moreover, Kyla and her trio of prattlers needed to leave her alone, or else he'd put an end to it. They were likely too busy today to continue their poking at least. Either way, he should have warned her about Kyla yesterday.

Hayden strode past, Comroy in tow. Guthrie and Aiden were off shift today but would be on watch tonight. "Morn, Domhnall," Hayden said, cheerful. He had likely gotten more sleep than Domhnall, who could work on about five hours of sleep before or after a shift. Every fortnight, Kendrick ordered him two days off to rest and sleep longer.

Comroy nodded and continued through the hall doors at a brisk pace.

The reminder of why Rosalie held the new esteemed position scratched Domhnall's conscience. "Hayden," he said, lowering his voice and drawing nearer in their usual close-enough-to-whisper-but-not-touch stance. "How is your mother today?"

His friend's posture slouched, and he flinched as if pricked. He shrugged, straight-faced. His alert, green gaze flickered subtly to Domhnall's parents conversing by the hearth, and then upon the busy servants, then to Domhnall. Always watching, like him. Their job required sharp observation, heightened focus, and endurance. Hayden was also especially soft-footed, and Domhnall would forget he was there. Ideal traits for a watchman.

They stood side by side, in their usual stance, and surveyed the room, taking it all in, never dropping their guard.

Shame rose to the forefront of his mind whenever he thought of his friend. Hayden was the sole earner for his family. The burden had been his for years, alongside his mother's deteriorating condition. Hayden's neglectful father had abandoned the Iverson family for a life of whoring, gambling, merchanting, and overindulging across the country many years ago, shortly after Hayden's sister Maisie's death.

They never saw or heard from him again. The old skiver could be dead for all they knew. He was no good when he *had* been around. No, Mrs. Iverson grew more ill by the day, and her healing was beyond the scope of Mother's or the herbalist's concoctions...

And Domhnall had just replaced their cook with Rosalie. Hayden did not seem concerned by it, but when did Hayden ever show his true emotions beneath that mask of charm?

Domhnall tapped a restless finger on his belt. He'd ask his parents if they could also continue paying Robena while she was on indefinite leave. He thought it unlikely though. They couldn't pay two head cooks, especially when one was no longer working. He chewed his lip. More than once he considered asking Kendrick about having Hayden promoted to constable. With it came more coin and prestige. Since Father wanted Domhnall to be laird, it made sense for all.

Except Domhnall didn't want to be laird. Whenever he broached the subject of Hayden rising in rank, Kendrick had refuted it, too. His great-uncle said he was best fit to keep doing what he was doing.

Watchmen also had families to provide for. Mrs. Iverson required constant care, and Hayden was her only family. What if he married? Had children? A match with Aileana suited him. Domhnall hoped she'd choose him tonight. She could settle Hayden's wandering ways.

If Maisie were still alive...she'd be married and raising fat bairns with an able-bodied husband.

He cleared his throat, chastising the demon. He had been a wee lad when she died. There was nothing more he could have done. *You can keep telling yourself that.*

"Ye look a muddle, Domhnall. Jealous, are ye?" Hayden's intuitive voice intruded.

Domhnall shook his head. "Of Lanie?" He chuckled to cover his unease. "Nay."

Hayden's mood grew more buoyant. "Is she eager for tonight?"

"Aye, you know how she is."

Hayden beamed. "Och, I do. She's been nattering to me about it."

Neither mentioned that there would be other potential suitors—competition—coming tonight to woo Aileana. Neither mentioned that Father didn't approve of Hayden as her match for whatever reason. Neither admitted Aileana never fully reciprocated Hayden's ardor, either. She teased his heart. It wasn't becoming of her and she knew it.

"All set with the Donalds?" He'd meant to inquire with Hayden about the plan last night but got distracted by his conversation with Rosalie, then had to hurry on to his watch shift after a short rest. Hayden must've already completed his shift by that time. Usually they would check in as they switched sentry duty.

"I'll confirm with Aiden once he wakes. A dozen have already arrived today. More are coming."

"Good," Domhnall responded. Of all times, this was not one to drop his guard. Hayden always had his back.

"You seem bothered."

"Eh." Domhnall scratched the back of his neck. His mind was a jumble.

Rosalie's astute words from last night whispered. *Air. Accident. Fire. Secret.* She had unearthed them all. How could she be a fraud? How could she know?

Shivers erupted along his arms. He couldn't wait for the next reading. Would he dare to let her touch his palms again? Yes. Tempt fate. He'd already touched her soft hands when moving the crates, and last night during her reading, he'd felt nothing but...serenity. He'd kept the beast at bay. He wondered what else he could do with her.

Maybe the visions were gone? Or...maybe Rosalie's touch didn't cause them? Maybe his absolution rested with another Seer like himself. He knew a perfect way to test his idea.

Touch. Again. He could do this. He *would* do this.

He never felt the energy off people as his mother did, but the motion of the room beleaguered him today. Many people, in one place. The minstrels readied themselves in the corner farthest from the hearth, plucking their stringed instruments in discordant tuning. His eighteenth birthday had possessed marginal splendor, but he did not care for such treatment.

He was twenty-five, still unwed, and uncertain of his future. Mounting pressure to find a wife and claim his spot as future laird hovered like a dark cloud over his days. He could try talking to Father again about Hayden rising as constable in his place. It was the perfect compromise, though not his wish, and it meant reconciling himself to being laird. His father would be satisfied, and Hayden and his mother would be cared for. It was the honorable thing to do.

Of course, Father would argue that Hayden and his family were not Domhnall's responsibility. They'd had the dispute more than once. "A laird's responsibility is to all of his clan and their kin," Domhnall protested.

Father refuted, "Compassion is important in lairdship, but one must be rational. A laird can't show preference for those suffering. Hayden and his mother will be protected and secure living in Glen Shiel, but we can't give handouts to everyone. When in abundance, we provide alms to those in need, but in scarcity, all we may be able to offer is protection."

What about the mercy his grandfather always spouted about?

Did his father not understand that safeguarding Maisie's family was Domhnall's penance?

Why argue? Alasdair Montgomerie was a kind, just laird, who knew his son's pain. His mother had kept Robena on through the years despite her lethargy, mistakes, and deteriorating health and mind.

"I'll report back later." Hayden dipped his head in courtesy and was about to depart but stopped. A sly smile parted his lips as Aileana scurried past them with their cousins at her sides, laughing, carrying her new gown from the dressmaker.

She skidded to a halt. "Och, good day, Hayden." She batted her eyelashes at him.

Domhnall wasn't sure Hayden could handle the sting if she ultimately refused him for good. If Aileana and Hayden were left alone, the other suitors would not stand a chance. Once, Domhnall had found them alone in an alcove. The two had been caught kissing and embracing.

"Might you save a dance for me tonight, Lanie?" Hayden lifted a sandy brown eyebrow, unleashing the charm. He took her hand in his and kissed the knuckles.

Domhnall's cousins all giggled, averted their eyes, or blushed.

Something as simple as kissing a woman's knuckles—would he ever be able to do that again? Yes. He was going to try, dammit. He was. Last night's interaction gave him the confidence to press his fortune with Rosalie again.

Aileana recovered her pluck. "I might consider it." She flashed a grin and fiddled with a colorful necklace. Hayden bowed, and she curtsied, turning to Domhnall. "Rose gave me this necklace. She's a pleasant woman. She said she'd show me how she paints them so I can teach Gracie upon her return."

"Oh?" Domhnall's mood lifted.

"Mm-hmm."

The gaggle of lasses continued toward the stairs in a flurry of swaying skirts.

Hayden's gaze followed them. "No putting off rounds. Until later, Domhnall."

"Aye."

His friend departed through the main hall doors.

Domhnall paused for a moment as his cousins exited the hall. Among the MacCoinneach-Montgomerie clans, Domhnall was the only male heir. Uncle Crystoll and Auntie Caite had the three daughters, and Uncle Edmund and Auntie Fiora had Ellen.

Not one of them presented an ability.

None were like him. None. He wasn't sure how the inheritance of the Ancient abilities passed on. Of Simon MacCoinneach's three children, Domhnall's mother Deirdre was the only child with an ability.

Gracie sometimes demonstrated a gift of Sight, but either it had not fully revealed itself, or her connection to the Silver Veil was weak. Perhaps she was strong only in intuition.

His parents sat at a table, perusing the guest list. Several attendees had been added last minute. He trudged over toward them, dodging two servants who were rehanging a mended tapestry.

Though their roles took them to different areas of the castle by day, when together, his parents were inseparable. Mother oversaw the gardens and kitchen and educated the noble lasses of nearby towns in the glen. She relinquished other domestic roles to Cawley. He managed the household servants. Like Domhnall, his mother's spirit found peace in nature and solitude. It was as if she was connected to the earth, always up to her elbows in dirt.

Father governed Dornie and smaller villages in the glen, traveled to court, collected taxes and dues, handled disputes, listened to reports on harvests and supplies, and oversaw the soldiers, while Crystoll managed their training. Blazes, an extensive list of responsibilities would soon fall upon him. A tightness filled his chest.

He straightened his shoulders. As servants passed, they gave him ample space. They knew. They all knew. Nods of courtesy greeted him as they scampered on their way.

His mother traced a hand along his father's spine as they spoke in whispers, their heads close, shoulders touching. Smiles, sweet murmurs.

Envy mingled with admiration at watching their intimacy.

He skimmed closer to his parents to listen, being sure to stand across from them at the table.

His father looked up from the parchment. "Domhnall, is all set for this evening?"

"A dozen Donalds arrived today. More are on their way."

His father's long, nearly black hair swayed with his nod, coming loose from the thong. Gray edged the thick hair at his temple. He had a long nose, sharp-edged chin, genial smile, and deep blue eyes.

Domhnall continued, "Most of Laird Donald's men will be on nightly watch duties." *To help me apprehend the thieves.* He compressed a fist at his side. "A few can be spared for courtyard posts." He leaned in and whispered, "Have you given my idea more thought?" He'd told Father yesterday about his idea about the MacDougalls and the bell heather being left at scenes of thefts.

His father gave a nod of acquiescence. "I have. The gathering should prove interesting."

Laird MacDougall and others from his clan would be in attendance. Domhnall almost spat, "Let them try anything," but he bit his tongue instead. Father was not convinced about his idea. Who else could the miscreants be if not the MacDougalls?

Father nodded. "You'll be present for the *cèilidh* tonight." It was not a question. He returned to his parchment reading.

His mother offered Domhnall a honeyed, all-knowing smile. "Why don't you check on the kitchen for me, dear, on your way out?"

He covered a blush with a swipe of hand in his hair and subtle cough. "Aye."

One woman has touched me without pain. Twice.

Last night's reading teased and bewildered him. His fingers prickled with want. To feel her fingertips caressing his hand. A flooding ache pooled within him. What did he want more? Her Seeing answers or her affections that made his skin sing and heart leap?

He slipped off to the kitchen to see her. The idea of touching her without ramification seized him like a fist that would not release its hold.

The kitchen hummed in similar fashion to the grand hall. Every hand available was chopping, stirring, and arranging. He sought a glimpse of the lovely tell-tale blonde locks rippling down Rosalie's back.

But, she wasn't there.

He made another pass through the pantry and maze of hallways and rooms abutting the kitchen, almost colliding with Kyla when he turned back into the kitchen. His pulse soared. *Not now. Not in here.* He skidded and jumped as if landing on hot coals. The hearth beside them blazed, its flames angrily baking a concoction.

Touching Rosalie was one thing, but if Kyla touched him—who knew? That was too close.

Sweat traced Kyla's hairline. "Och, sir. Didna expect ye. What might I do for ye?" She hovered nearer, a clay bowl in her hands the only shield between them. Blazes, she knew. They all knew. Kyla was kin with Isolde, and *that* story had circulated throughout town. Bed a lass and nearly die because of it? Not a story that hid well among prattlers.

Don't do it. Don't do it.

She did. Shifting the bowl to one arm, she pressed in close and laid a hand on his forearm. Why now? Why the hell now! Every servant in the household knew better than to touch him, for it would rouse his ire, the ire he fought hard to contain. Annoyance was his mask. How could he explain it to everyone? Being an arse was easier to explain away. He didn't want to come off as a strict master, but if it meant keeping the visions suppressed, then he'd continue the ruse. Couldn't they see? He put on the angry façade to protect them.

But, Kyla was a bold lass.

He sequestered angry words. He flinched. Delicate and tender as her touch may have been intended, he waited for the assault on his soul. "I-I..." He swallowed. Hell, his head rioted. The blackness began to slid across his vision...

Last night with Rosalie had been different. The hearth had been barely a whisper, and not a moving body about. And he had been with *Rosalie*. Her touch had brought only feelings, not visions. No black sludge. No pain.

Now, spellbound, he couldn't move. Kyla's hand weighed a load, like sacks had been heaped upon his forearm. It scalded. *Move your hand!*

He couldn't fight it. Words caught in his tightening throat. Not a cry or whimper. He was a stone statue. His heels felt adhered to the stone floor.

Black licked at his eyelids. No! He screamed internally to his soul. Finally, he broke free from her grasp. And then he heard nothing but the pounding of his heart in his head.

Nevertheless, it was too late. Apparitions glided across his vision. An attractive woman with blonde hair, holding a wrapped bairn. He couldn't see the woman's face. The infant didn't stir or cry. Then a stocky man with a pockmarked face yelled something at the woman. An argument. Blood. He grabbed the bairn. The woman screeched but couldn't rise from her cot. No, it was a bed with fine linens. The man disappeared from the vision. And then the woman vaporized, replaced by the image of a square keep, unfamiliar to him. Suddenly, there was a battle. Men in English armor. Screams. More blood. Death.

His breathing grew ragged. The curtain of darkness reappeared, then disappeared. The kitchen faded before his eyes again, and the old man from many previous visions appeared. Hobbling along a road, carrying a basket of yellow flowers. More bloodcurdling screams.

He blinked. Several times. The vision faded.

He heaved as if he had just run across the moor.

"Sir! Sir!"

Kyla's eyes shone wide, fearful.

Bloody hell. It'd been so long, he'd forgotten how to hide it. Had he moaned? Cried? At least he was upright. Finally he found his words. "Ch-Christ, Kyla!"

"Och! I'm so verra sorry, sir. Are ye all right? Ye were mumbling under yer breath and shaking. Might ye sit and have a drink? I'm sorry, I didna mean to touch ye—"

No one else in the kitchen had turned toward him but he saw the strain in their backs. All stiff and knowing...with their own masks of pretend.

"I'm f-fine. Just a moment of dizziness. It's warm in here. How is everything for—for tonight?" He nearly choked on a foulness in his mouth. Whatever he had seen was gone. *Breathe, breathe.*

The fright didn't leave Kyla's face.

Or was her look one of abhorrence? Did he sicken her? She'd been lovestruck, and now he turned her insides out?

"All is fine, sir. Whisky?" She crept toward the closest table and rested the clay bowl upon it.

He fought the devil within and waved her away. "Nay, I'm fine. Where is Rosalie?" *Pulse, must slow the pulse.* The aftermath was always far worse than the vision. He had to center himself before he fainted on the kitchen floor.

Disappointment soured her expression. She blew a wisp of hair in a huff and rested her hands on her hips. "In the gardens. She wanted herbs for the fowl, but I assured her it's tasty as is. The laird always enjoys my fowl."

He darted outside as fast as his feet would allow. With the vision thrashing at the back of his mind, a sense of foreboding dwelled in his chest.

He inhaled the fresh, earthy fragrance of impending rain. The crack of thunder sounded as droplets began to patter the ground in beat with his boots. He swam through the mugginess, each step determined, each step a liberation from the vapors of the vision. He made for the gardens, steadying his thoughts.

Something didn't feel right.

A commotion drew him to the rows farthest from the keep. Ewan waved frantically toward him. Ewan then crouched by a body, prostrate in the carved garden row.

Domhnall dashed to the scene while others congregated. The person on the ground was a lass in a simple gown.

He jerked his head at the sight of her hands bound loosely with twine, and a sack over her head.

"Sir Montgomerie! Thank the Lord. I came when I heard her scream and—" Ewan's cheeks were splotched with red, his eyes wide and confused as he blinked away the rain dripping down the furrows in his forehead.

Domhnall dropped to the ground beside her and ripped the linen sack from her head. His stomach clenched. "Rose! Wake, lass. My God, Rose!"

"Sir, should I lift her?" Ewan knelt, ready for action.

What the hell?

Domhnall's cowardice to touch people—to help people—shuddered through him with humiliation. Did they all think him an ignorant lout? Did they truly think he held himself higher than them because of his rank? Did they think that was the reason for her terseness, his distance?

No more. Let the visions take his soul.

He loosened the twine around her wrists, lifted her up from the muddy ground, and gathered her into his lap. He was tired of being idle and looking like a haughty nobleman. Or worse, he gave the impression of a dastard who could not face the devil. He would feed fears no more.

"Sir, should I fetch a soldier, or another watchman to assist—" Ewan sputtered, almost terrified to see Domhnall holding someone.

"Get the healer. Send him to my bedchamber." He wasn't going to drag the poor lass to the servants' quarters and cause a stir with the celebratory preparations. Cawley would lose his bowels if Domhnall brought this extra quandary anywhere remotely close to the kitchen or hall.

"Aye, sir." Ewan rose.

"No. No, wait. My mother. Get her, please. Send her, with some linens. We won't need the healer."

A puzzled frown crinkled Ewan's brow. "Sir?"

He released an impatient, heavy sigh.

Ewan bowed.

"Aye, sir." He ran toward the keep.

Domhnall swiped tangled wet hair from Rosalie's forehead. A large, red welt formed on the side of her face, along her cheek. Her skin was chilled. Yet...she felt divine. Smooth, vibrant, and ever silky. Energy prickled his fingertips. The wind rustled in an eddy. *To hell with you, Wind. Release your wrath. I don't care.*

He felt for a pulse in her neck. Good.

He'd forgotten what others felt like. Her hands upon his last night had been the first step. A trickle of need coursed within him. It begged for more. He took a fingertip and gently touched her lips, and hovered close to her face to assess breathing. He wanted to help her. Protect her. Be with her.

Sensation puddled within his soul like a spicy brewed cider ale on midwinter's eve. He'd been cold for so long, fearing fire. Fearing touch. Heat now melted his resolve.

Christ, he was touching a person. A woman. No curtain of gloom crossed his vision like the encounter with Kyla only moments before. His pulse soared in response.

Rosalie finally stirred, then moaned. Her fingernails were broken, dirty from the altercation. Her dress weighed them both down, soppy from rain and mud. He'd forgotten how heavy a person could be.

Other servants hovered nearby. He broke from his stupor and looked at them. "Did anyone see anything?"

They shook their heads. All frowned.

Gallantry returned. "Get inside. Dry yourselves. I have her."

She mumbled under her breath. He belatedly glanced around, beyond the scattering servants. Rain blurred his vision and washed away any evidence of her attacker. Caught in the moment he hadn't done what first instinct always taught him to do as a watchman—to observe the surroundings, the people. Had the perpetrator been among the flock of onlookers?

Blazes. He'd just foiled his chance. This was the second time he missed seeing an attacker. First, her uncle's assault—Domhnall had been too busy watching Rosalie in her stall. Now, he had been to consumed by his own sensations and feelings.

He stood up with her fully in his arms and strode toward the keep. He had to shift her weight, as he was used to carrying sacks of grain or calves or heavy saddles. Never a person. Not like this. He stumbled twice. Labored steps and breathing brought him to the entrance by the servants' quarters, where he could sneak upstairs through a second set of steps, sight unseen. He hoped there was enough commotion within the kitchen to keep prying eyes away.

He reached his chamber without trouble, his muscles straining at the extra weight. The servants who saw him did not question. It wasn't their place. He laid Rosalie on his bed and propped her with a pillow. Mud and wetness soiled the linens. She roused. "What happened?" She gripped her head. "Mother Mary, who hit me?"

"Rest, Rose. Rest. Help is coming."

He paced to his bedside writing table, uncorked the strong whisky he drank to dull his nightly insomnia, and poured a nip for her.

"Here." He lifted her to sitting once he determined she'd not faint. Heat swelled in his palm.

She sipped, coughed, but sipped again.

"A boiled infusion with honey would be better. I'll get you that shortly."

"What happened?"

"I was going to ask you the same thing." He wanted to brush her wet hair from her face, but he resisted. He stood beside her, feet itching to move, to find the scoundrel who'd attacked her. Kyla was a jealous sort. Would she have found someone to do it? Or had it been the devils lurking throughout Dornie, the ones who burned barns, robbed poor men, stole anything they pleased, and now assaulted women? With no answer from Rosalie, he pressed, "Who did this?"

She coughed. "I went to the garden to gather herbs. Thought to flavor the duck," she said, her voice groggy, stumbling upon words.

He ceased his feet's anxious dancing and sat on the bed, being sure to leave space between them. He'd left his chamber door open. All was proper.

To hell with proper.

"Then a sack was over my head. I fought. They—he—whoever grabbed my hands, pinned them behind me. I clawed at 'em. But couldn't find his face. I think I scratched his arms? He tied my hands. I screamed. Then, I-I think they hit me." She rubbed the left side of her head.

"They?"

She shrugged, sipped more, crinkled her nose. "Or him? It had to be a man, right? He was strong. I had trouble fighting. He said nothing to me. Didn't breathe a word. He gr-grabbed my hands with one of his, put the other over my mouth. Tied me. Hit me. He smelled...hmm, sweaty?"

"Did you see him? Or them? Was there more than one? Anything?"

He saw no sign of the bell heather on her soggy dress and apron. He wasn't going to pat her to look for it, either.

She pursed her lips. "No." Fire lit her eyes. Her pupils were dark, wide in the hazel irises. "Domhnall, I must return to the kitchen. Tonight's preparations..."

He clenched a hand. "They'll manage without you."

She slipped her legs over the side of the bed, straightening upright. "I must."

"Rose. Please. Stay, for me? I've sent for my mother."

A frown dipped her lips downward. "You shouldn't have." She tried to stand.

He pressed a firm hand on her shoulder.

"Oh...my head. It spins." She fell back on the bed, closing her eyes. "Why would somebody hurt me?"

"I don't know, Rose. There have been disturbances in town. Numerous thefts. A fire. Your uncle's attack."

"Who would do this? Why?" she sputtered. "There've been other incidents?"

A shudder crawled up his spine. He rubbed a hand across his forehead. "Yes, but we've no link between them all. I'm not sure who's causing this disorder. The puzzle you referenced last night in my palm reading. This is it. The stealing has been going on for weeks. Minor infractions. Nuisances."

"And assaults?"

The grimace hurt his face. "You and your uncle are the first to be injured. And that stable fire was the first of its kind."

Questions flew through his head. What the devil was going on in Dornie? Why couldn't he crack it? Damn the MacDougalls. It had to be them.

His mother rapped on the open door. "Domhnall?"

He turned. "Rose was attacked."

"Please, I wouldn't—" Rosalie attempted to say.

"Christ, Rose. Somebody put a sack over your head, tied you up, hit you, and tried to drag you off." His rage echoed off the high ceiling.

She visibly winced, her eyes shutting.

His mother hurried inside, a pile of clean linens held against her chest. "Let me check her. Then I'll call for the healer if my herbals are not enough."

She handed Rosalie a cloth to wipe away the rain and mud from her soiled gown, neck, and face.

Rosalie shivered.

Domhnall tossed a log on the low-glowing hearth, added more kindling, and ignored his unease around the flames. Stoked it. Blew on it. Then, when it seemed warm enough, he grabbed one of his already solved puzzles from his bedside table and spun the segments while pacing.

His mother sat beside Rosalie on the bed and looked into her eyes. "Do you feel ill? In your stomach?"

"A little."

"Dizzy?"

She shook her head. "No...oooh, yes..."

"Does the light hurt your eyes? Look at the hearth a moment."

She did, then moaned. "Yes."

She reached for Rosalie's head. "Warmth?"

Domhnall groaned. "I already checked. I felt no fever. Besides, it'd be too soon, right? Fever would take a day to set in."

His mother turned to him and spoke in a halting voice. "You touched—ehm, checked her?"

Muscles stiffened in his back. "Aye." He ripped his gaze from her shocked one. He focused on the puzzle in his hand, allowing himself to settle, to let focus rule.

She blinked and returned her attention to Rosalie. "Sometimes, when..." She exhaled, choosing careful words. "We receive a blow to the head, we are stunned. It's a jarring stupor. It can unsettle our insides. You must rest for a day or two while your body rights itself."

"I must work, my lady."

"Rosalie, you are both servant and guest. We aim to treat all equally, as I'm sure Domhnall told you. We would never ask you to work when you are unwell." Nimble fingers ran to Rosalie's wrist. She pressed to get her pulse. Domhnall knew his mother's methods well.

"My lady, I must protest. You brought me here to work. I can't possibly rest."

"It is not a request, Rosalie. You shall rest. Two days." She stood, gave Domhnall a stern look, and strode to the hallway. He followed. They talked out of earshot. "She must rest. Headache, dizziness, fatigue, imbalance. She can't be about in the kitchen. Please assure her that she is not in trouble nor a bother. Sleep, drink, and food will help. I'll prepare her a tincture with berries, beets, and hazelnuts."

"No nuts. She says they cause her throat to close."

She nodded. "Och, aye, you mentioned that. Where is her uncle?"

"He's in the depths of the keep somewhere, been working on the rats. Might be in the wine cellar."

"Inform him in a gentle manner, aye? I'll tell your father, too, after the celebration tonight. He has enough to worry about."

"I must tell Kendrick."

"I agree."

He rubbed his face, swiping dirt and sweat, then tapped a finger on his lips. He exhaled through his nose, calming the inner beast fuming as a result of the hell being unleashed upon his home. Perhaps, since the person or persons had not left the bell heather, the assaults were unrelated to the thefts? Answers lay hidden in corners of taverns, among whispers, and within the least likely places. He'd inquire and would get Hayden to help. "She can stay in my chamber. I'll sleep elsewhere."

His mother donned her all-knowing smile. "I assumed so. I'll make herbal tonics for her, and will send up food. I'll get one of the servants to sit with her."

"No. I will stay with her."

"Domhnall, it's not—"

He cut her off. "I'll keep the door open. Father wants me to be laird, does he not? As laird I would choose to care for any and all. Rose included. She is under my protection."

"Remember you can't be everything for everyone."

His lips quivered, but he said nothing.

Maternal compassion crinkled the fine wrinkles around her eyes. Of all people, his mother knew rules were just rules. Rules were meant to be bent. "Be careful. We have many visiting. You will make an appearance."

"But—"

"Understood?" A commanding tone penetrated her smooth voice.

He nodded. "Yes."

She whispered. "Domhnall?" Blue eyes blinked at him, darted a look to Rosalie, and then back to him. She lowered her voice. "You—you touched her? I mean you were able to..."

He swallowed, lifting his chin. "I was fine. I saw nothing." Never mind he had seen an awful vision with Kyla's mistake only moments before touching Rosalie. He felt nothing but intrigue when he touched Rosalie.

"I see." She nodded before hurrying down to the kitchen.

It hadn't been his sheer mental might and avoidance squashing the visions.

No visions had come when he touched Rosalie several times now. She was the key. Another Seer. Damn him for wanting to press the speculation further.

CHAPTER EIGHT

drea delayed her plans until the evening. Her esquire had visited the castle, made inquiries, and gathered information. Tonight was the perfect opportunity: the laird's daughter's birthday celebration. Laird Montgomerie had extended Edrea an invitation, too. That had been easy enough. How cordial of him. The man she'd hired to assist in her plan had proven himself worthy of the coin already. He filled her ears with much about the laird's family and the happenings of the town. In fact, he was a blathering fool, especially when she had him naked and in her bed.

Oh, heavens, no but he was no fool. A slick animal.

Other local clan lairds and noblemen would be in attendance tonight. Also, the market caravan ended in Dornie. Granted, some peddlers departed, traveling north or east, but many were still here. Her man had confirmed that the wench was here. Rosalie was employed by the castle already. What a cunning twit. Rosalie and her aunt had worked at many castles in England. Why wouldn't they sink their claws into the unsuspecting Scots? Liars, the whole lot of Threstons.

Mute and obedient, Wenda helped dress Edrea in a gown. Edrea's pregnancy remained hidden, but her bodices were tighter and breasts heavier. Wenda laced the back of the gown. Edrea glanced in the mirror. "Up or down?" She ran her fingers through her light brown hair, lifting it off her nape.

Wenda smiled and flicked a hand toward the ceiling.

"Yes. They love to admire my neckline, don't they?" She drew her hands to her bosom, traced the décolletage of the bodice, and gently cupped her aching breasts. It had been many years since her first and only full-term pregnancy, but she remembered the painful swelling. This child would live. It had to! She could make a home for herself and her child and garner the power she deserved.

She missed Lady Isabella. Her only true friend. In a world dominated by men, she'd found one person who understood her. Despite becoming accustomed to being alone all these years, she longed for her time with her friend.

Her pulse raced with the idea of going to this celebration. So many people, a full crowd of boisterous and drunk Scots. She hated being around so many people. This wasn't something she could send her guards to handle though. This was her responsibility. "This dress, Wenda? What do you think?"

Her silent maid nodded with a wide smile.

She enjoyed Wenda's company. No words, dutiful service, and put on the earth to do her bidding. Wenda's presence eased some of the loneliness.

Good riddance to Asher and James though. They were never her children, born as bastards, acting as nobles. Despicable, both, like their father.

Guilbert and his sons considered her to be a barren crone who could not give her husband an heir. With both sons dead, he persisted in the fruitless endeavor of sealing a successor in the beds of Henry Percy's whores. Not if she had her way of it. She knew all of Percy's whores and had paid them each handsomely to not fall with child, or to rectify the matter if they did. Should he die after they secured Warkworth Castle—which should be soon—his responsibility as conservator and steward would fall upon her...and her child, his "heir." Nobody would doubt the child's paternity. Lady Isabella, as the king's distant cousin, had assured Edrea of her standing in court. All would fall into place. This baby would be hers. Perhaps it would ease her desolation. To finally have love, not from a man, but from her child—someone more loyal.

She smiled and rubbed her belly.

Asher and James—were gone.

Warkworth Castle—was almost secured.

Guilbert—would be gone soon enough, or sooner if his weak heart failed him during one of his eating, drinking, or bedding frolics. If not, then her men would make his death look like an accident once he came home.

Guilbert wouldn't return for a few more weeks so she had some time. First, she had to tidy things with the peasant Seer. Bile rose in her throat. She had paid Rosalie handsomely. For lies. The girl had assured her Guilbert would fall in the Despenser rebellion with other barons. Instead, his two sons had died. Granted, she'd sent along well-paid men to see it done. Bertie was supposed to have fallen, too! Mistakes. Complications. A lying wench.

Rosalie had painful knowledge that could foil it all for Edrea. The Seer knew about Edrea's plan to have Guilbert killed. Edrea's men had confirmed that Rosalie's aunt had been employed at the keep before the war. Many servants came and went. How was Edrea to keep track of them all? They had snooped, acquired delicate information about her. The one maid who'd tended her chambers also knew of the pregnancy and confessed to divulging it to Rosalie, too, before Edrea had the maid disposed of. A child who was not the warden's true heir would ruin Edrea's claim on the title and land.

All depended upon whether she could rid herself of a fortune-teller who knew too much.

Rosalie shoved a hand into her drying pocket, her fingertips falling on the bracelet and money pouch. Thank God she had them. Her most important things always remained on her person nowadays. She'd hardly unpacked here, too, and fortune shone on that wise decision. Once able to walk and travel, she and Oswell would take their leave. She would offer sincere apologies to the laird and lady.

And to Domhnall.

Her heart grew heavy with the thought. She liked him. Maybe a bit too much.

Where was Oswell? Was he faring well? What about the cats?

She eased upright in the bed and conjured a believable story while she had a moment alone. Whoever attacked her must've been one of Lady Brantingham's henchmen. Granted, she hadn't seen the lady until after her uncle's attack, so Oswell's perpetrator remained unknown. Perhaps Edrea had arrived earlier and Rosalie had just not seen her. For, who else would have cause to attack both of them? The two attacks were no coincidence. They'd been targeted by Lady Brantingham.

"Oh…" She leaned on the pillow, gathered her breath, and stewed over what she'd tell Domhnall. Weary eyes blinked spinning stars. She was in no condition to make such decisions right now.

She rubbed her chafed wrists and gulped the awful truth. She wasn't safe anywhere. She had to leave. The ruse needed to end. The only lies she told were to herself these days. Oswell and Nelda were unwell. They needed to perhaps find a croft, live off the land, and forget any hope of finer things. Oswell had friends throughout the English countryside. Why not hide away?

Anger and fear mingled like a soured drink in her stomach and pain pinched her forehead.

She ached inside and outside, and wanted to cry. But alas, no tears. Her eyes had been dry since birth, she'd been told. Oh, but she needed the release. Something to dull the pain.

She chewed on her lip. Discovery was inevitable. So, she had two choices. She needed to decide and follow through, without a look back.

Choice one: locate Oswell and leave Dornie fast behind her, along with forgoing good pay to feed them through winter, when her business suffered most.

Choice two: lie to Domhnall and convince him to protect her. He was unmarried, and she'd noticed his—

well, his intrigue with her. He clearly sought her fortune-telling abilities. She could play that angle. He wanted the truth and she could give it to him, or at least what he longed to hear.

Curiosity and hope dwelled in those large brown eyes that made her fortitude go soft. He'd willingly allowed her into his world, and a spark grew within her knowing this. He was also handsome and kind and...

Mother Mary. Option two scared the strength from her. A part of her hadn't the heart to continue the ruse with Domhnall. She liked him.

Staying in one place with Lady Brantingham a hair's breadth away was perilous. However, the keep was a mighty fortress. They had soldiers, watchmen, and clan affiliations. She had made a good impression upon Lady Montgomerie and her daughter, too. Did security outweigh the threat?

She tapped a finger against her thigh as her thoughts tumbled back to Domhnall...

A warmth spread across her chest. She wished she had been fully aware to feel what it was like to be in his strong arms as he scooped her from the garden bed. Her memory only gave her snatches of the moment.

She hushed her thoughts. She liked him but that was no matter.

Lies were her life, and her life was at stake here. May God forgive her. Lord, her conscience grew wearier by the day.

Tamping down her feelings for Domhnall, she allowed mental notes to fly through her swimming head.

Domhnall Montgomerie had his own secrets. *Like me,* he'd said. *He* was the laird's soothsayer! It wasn't like she believed in such a thing. Would he offer her safety if he found out her ruse? Her body vibrated again at the sensation of his hands carrying her.

That was a fool's thought. *Stop that, Rose!* Focus on the task. Safety. Lies. Could she do it?

Blurriness swept across her vision, and sweat rippled gooseflesh upon her skin.

It was this or meet her end with Lady Brantingham. The road home would not be safe. The ride north had been satisfactory because they'd been ahead of her pursuers. Now, now Edrea surely had men posted from here to Edinburgh!

Choice two it was. She would lie.

That was that. No turning back. She silenced her nagging conscience.

She reviewed her observations of Domhnall despite her throbbing skull and fuzzy mind.

She'd learned much since his first two readings. Now, to go deeper. He was loyal, honorable, responsible, and rule-following. He was quiet and solemn and most certainly hiding something. Descriptors bounced around in her head. Observant. Withdrawn. His reaction to the word *air*. There was an accident in his past, a fire—the stable?—and a puzzle—well, that must have been the thefts happening.

Domhnall yearned for a simpler life. Why?

He didn't like to be touched. Why?

He hadn't helped Oswell on the ground though she recalled it had bothered him—his antsy feet, trembling fingers—he avoided direct contact with others like it was a disease. Yet it pained him *not* to help.

He'd touched her though. A few times. He'd carried her to his own chamber. Was it due to chivalry, responsibility, or guilt?

She searched the modest room for clues. The hearth was hardly aflame, and the window was open, but the room held a chill. Cold was embedded in the stone around them. *Cold.* His hands had been ice-cold. He liked the cold? Or he did not like fires?

Beside the bed lay a few wooden puzzle-like contraptions. He'd worked with one when pacing while his mother checked on her.

She blinked fatigue and yawned, her thoughts fading...

His voice woke her. "Rose?"

She must have fallen asleep. She cracked an eye. The hearth was dead and her mouth dry. Light from a nearby oil lamp hurt her head. She moaned. "Hmm..."

She shivered but Domhnall made no move to relight the fire. He paced, a wooden puzzle in his hand again.

"I've brought you food and drink, but you've been asleep for a few hours. Could you try to sit up to eat? My mother says to rest, but don't sleep for too long. I'll make sure you wake every few hours. And check your vision."

She eyed the tray of food filled with part of the meal she'd prepared for the *cèilidh*, which was already ongoing, evidenced by the tunes belting up to the bedchamber. Roasted duck, cooked peas, rye bread, a hearty vegetable stew, berry tartlet, and a large goblet of a burgundy wine. The meal was fit for nobility, not her. Beside it sat a small glass vial with a purple liquid.

"It's for your head."

She blinked. "I see two of you." Food both enticed and nauseated her.

"Then you better drink the herbal tincture."

"From the healer?"

He approached, drew a stool closer, and sat. "No, my mother."

"Is she a healer, too?"

"Not exactly. She's a Feeler."

She yawned a parched mouth. What was a Feeler? The Montgomerie family—the lady was originally a MacCoinneach—held uncommon traits. Something to think upon later.

"Why am I not in the servants' quarters? That is my place."

His throat bobbed with a deep swallow. "You're safer here. I can keep an eye on you."

"Am I not safe?" She played the fool's card. He knew nothing about Lady Brantingham.

"You'll be protected under my watch. I'll find the person or people who did this." Something flared in his chestnut eyes. Unrest? Determination?

"Who hit me?" *Tried to take me.*

He ruffled a hand through wavy brown hair. "I don't know."

She reached for the vial.

"Please don't leave," he said.

"I won't. But I must work."

"My mother said to take the herbal with food, especially meat. Please try to eat. How is your stomach?"

She sipped the fruity liquid and puckered her lips at the tartness. "Not so well."

His stare unnerved her. "Is there anyone who would wish you harm?"

Be firm. Lie. It's what you're good at, after all.

"No."

Lady Brantingham was the obvious answer, but what about Kyla? She was number two on her list. Number three, the miscreants Domhnall had referenced. She doubted this attack had been random.

"Shouldn't you be in the hall?"

He folded his arms across his chest. "No."

"Or performing your watch duties?"

"All is managed."

"If you're going to sit with me, at least eat something."

He just shrugged.

She wanted to shake her head in frustration, but her head ached too much. "You don't eat or sleep, do you?"

His eyes narrowed.

She ate in silence, taking in his every move and pondering him more. He valued friendship with Hayden. Liked his sisters. He also had a strong relationship with his mother. What about his father? She had yet to see the laird.

Choice two reminded her she had work to do. "Would you like me to finish your reading?"

She expected a rejection but was not surprised when he said, "Yes."

"Then I'll need your hands—"

"Later? You must rest."

He reached forward, swiped a hand across her head. Icy hands met tepid skin. There, he'd touched her again. What had changed his mind? Or perhaps she had misread his hesitation for touch.

His face gleamed with kindness. "No fever yet. Keep eating. I'll come to check on you in a few hours. Rest, Rose."

After he left, questions and theories beleaguered her mind.

What secret vexed Domhnall Montgomerie?

Domhnall hardly slept. After assessing the grounds, assuring the watchmen had any weak points covered, then partaking in mindless talking at the *cèilidh*, he fell into a fitful sleep on a cot in Kendrick's room. His mother ordered him to rest while she took shifts waking Rosalie and checking her wellbeing. He woke before sunrise while shadows still lurked in the castle hallways, and he walked another round, followed by roving the keep's interior.

Once the time was proper, he grabbed a tray of food Kyla had prepared and plodded up the stone stairs to his chamber to greet Rosalie.

"Come in," a sweet but groggy voice beckoned at his knock.

Sunlight filtered in through the open window. Rosalie sat in a plush seat, gazing outside.

"Would you like to walk today? How are you feeling?"

"I should return to the kitchen."

Daringly, he closed the chamber door behind him.

He laid the tray on a table beside her seat. "Hungry?"

"Famished." She lifted a spoon and ate the porridge and plum jam, pausing to sip the oat milk.

"Has your uncle come to visit you yet?"

She nodded between bites. "Yes, this morning. The cats are enjoying their work here." She smiled.

The way her subtle pink lips turned up, and how the light played on little green flecks in her light brown eyes was sunshine to his gloomy mood. "I am pleased to hear that." *I wouldn't have found you if not for one of those cats,* he wanted to add. Curiosity alone had not brought him to her shop though. Coincidence did not exist in his world. Fate had brought him there.

He flicked a glance heavenward, remembering the vision he had of his grandfather years ago. The Ancients and their Silver Veil reigned in years' past. Mother had spent years enlightening him—or trying to. He spent just as many denying his heritage, his truths. Seeking logic, not some mystical abilities in a dead culture. But maybe she was right...

He cleared his throat, beholding Rosalie. Her hair had dried damp, and waves fell about her shoulders. She still wore her soiled gown and apron from yesterday. A healthy glow filled her cheeks. Cheeks he'd touched.

His fingers tingled in remembrance. He picked up one of his puzzles to occupy his hands.

Her bag of personal things sat beside the bed. He'd asked a servant to bring it up last night. In fact, Bethia, one of the maidservants, had informed him that Rosalie hadn't unpacked anything whilst staying in the servants' chamber.

"Do you feel well?"

"Yes."

Good sense told him to wait, but impatience ruled today.

"What are those?" she asked, pointing to his puzzle.

"Puzzles that Athol, our woodwright, makes for me. I found one in Edinburgh, too. They keep my mind sharp and hands busy."

"Interesting. I tried one last night. Made my head spin."

They shared a chuckle.

He plunged deeper into an abyss of no return. "It's not often I find one...like me. In fact, you're the first."

Her jaw dropped. She clamped it shut. "What do you mean?" She cocked her head to the side.

He drew in closer, trying to read her by observation alone. He held her gaze. Faint flecks of yellow edged the green in her eyes now, as the sun continued its ascent through the open window. "You know of what I speak."

She licked her lips and crinkled her fine-haired eyebrows. "If you're like me..." She never said the word. The internal thought played clearly on her face, her eyes brighter, her mouth twisted. She was measuring him.

Seer. Soothsayer. He knew many were frauds. Some *thought* they had a power. Perhaps she was a liar, too, like all the rest? His heart raced when he was near her, though, offering him an awakening. She had said she was taken in by her aunt and uncle. Her parents could have hailed from the mystical isles, too. It was a reach, but he was willing to dig for it.

He trembled as his insides vibrated. The evidence bewitched him.

A gust shifted through the window, fluttering her hair gently.

The Wind spoke to him. *I am here.* It eddied in the room with their combined powers.

She visibly shivered, drawing a blanket on her lap closer to her chest. A trace of perspiration beaded upon her high forehead.

He channeled it, all the while holding her gaze. A vortex danced around them.

The claws of coldness seeped into his skin.

Breaking free from the Wind, he plopped his puzzle upon the bed. He dragged the stool closer to her seat, and sat in front of her, knees against knees. "Will you read me again? That is—if you feel better?"

His pulse raced in his skull. Foreign words screamed on the Wind begging for him to come back, to channel it into being.

Rosalie sat as calm and confident as one of her cats. Maybe she didn't hear the Wind the way he did?

"If you wish it." She blinked, dubiousness furrowing her brow. "Your hands, please."

Steadying his mind and centering his heart, he splayed his hands on his knees, palms up. She leaned in, lifted one of his hands in hers. Graceful fingers scaled the mounts, ridges, and lines of his hand. Then, she moved to the other hand.

All the while, the storm raged. No blackness veiled his vision. Her touch aroused a new curiosity and yearning within him. He wondered what a kiss would trigger. He licked his lips and nipped the thought—for now. That was the next step. "You'd mentioned fire."

"I said your element was air," she said, not looking up.

He stared at the strawberry freckles on her cheeks and mentally connected them to make known star constellations. One grouping looked like a cat. They were so light, he had to lean in closer to see.

He pursed his lips, biting frustration. "You said fire, the other night. An accident. How—?"

Maisie. Did she know? Nobody would have told her. Hell. Or had they? Kyla's mouth ran off faster than Aileana in a foot race.

The old man with the yellow flower. He flashed behind his eyes. Was it a buried memory of a day past or a vision of something to come? Was it a memory *of* a vision?

"Do not believe the lies," the man's voice warned.

Not now. Bugger off.

"I saw it in your hands," she said.

He cleared his throat, and the man and flower vanished. "You see this all with my hands?"

"Yes. Your left hand shows what God has given you, and your right shows what you have done with it."

"Tell me."

"You have much untapped potential."

She found a ticklish spot in the center of his palm, and he muffled a giggle.

"At times, you've had serious doubts as to whether you've made the right decision or done the right thing. You have regrets, Domhnall."

He dropped his hands from hers and stood, the stool falling. He righted it and flopped onto the bed with a sigh. The truth hurt more than the lies.

She pressed on, her voice firm. "You run from something. From responsibility, from the truth. You hide your true feelings from others."

"Tell me, Rose. Do you see this all in my hands, or is there more? Do you see..." *Don't say it, don't say it.* Christ, he must. The painful whisper escaped his lips. "Visions?"

Her eyes widened, and she inhaled. She breathed, "Yes, sometimes."

"Will you tell me about them?"

"Why don't you tell me about yours? If you're a Seer, like me," she said, brows sharply angled, her stance resolute. "Are you testing me?"

Was he? *I want to believe, Rose, so much.*

She drew her look downwards, a ripple of hair falling beside her face and teasing the neckline of her gown. Her chest heaved with a racing heartbeat. "My head—" She grabbed it. "I am weary."

He exhaled loudly, chastising his manners and his requests. He'd always promised to not abuse his authority. Shame pierced his heart. "I'm sorry. Thank you. Why don't you rest, and then we can take a stroll later? I will keep you safely by my side. My father always says that walking is good for healing. I could also send up a bath, warm water."

Slowly, she lifted her head, her gaze meeting his. "No, thank you."

If others can, I will, too. He took her hand in his, kissed the knuckles. He saw nothing but the beauty before him. "I'll see you in a few hours. I've brought a quill, ink, and parchment. I could start to show you writing later, mayhaps tomorrow, once you feel better?"

"Yes, please."

Rosalie woke up from a nap, plagued with guilt.

My God, the lies had been water plunging over a cliff. One after the other they'd fallen off her tongue like a serpent. Certainly, she had started with her skills, but then she lied. The statements she had told him weren't unique. She'd used them on people before. She had a specific list and adapted them for readings.

Shudders shot through her at the ease of it, too. He was the soothsayer spoken about by the women in the marketplace. Did he exhibit early signs of what ailed Nelda—delusions of the mind? She'd heard of it striking people younger. Seers were not actually real, were they?

She'd hit all her marks: fire, secret, accident. Obviously, they were common threads in life. People died, were hurt, got sick, kept secrets. She'd put it all together: Kyla's story, the hearth, the barn fire, and Domhnall's own demeanor. This was no Sight, just observation and deduction. An accident with fire, in his past, haunted him. He felt responsible. He refused to touch people, for he feared it would cause his visions. And, try as he might, he could not escape the burden of being laird.

She was pleased with herself. Her readings had been successful.

Then why did a knot grow in her chest?

And Domhnall...was a Seer with visions?

A knock on the door stirred her from her reflections. A servant—not one of the kitchen help, thank God—poked her head in. "Rosalie?" Timid and young, she entered, nodded, and brought a tray. "Sir Montgomerie said, if you're better, to please join him in the inner garden before the evening meal. I could set your bath after supper?"

"Thank you, but there is no need."

The woman grabbed the finished meal from the morning and was gone.

After a swallow of herbal-infused honey water, she grabbed her sack to bring it to her appropriate lodgings. She was staying but she belonged in the servants' quarters. Thankfully, she remembered the way through twisting hallways, enough that she avoided the actual kitchen itself. At a turn, dizziness hit her. She supported herself with a hand against a wall. She blinked cloudy eyes. Her knees buckled, and she skinned her palm while righting herself.

Work would distract her.

First she stopped at Oswell's room. She knocked and blew on her stinging palm. Nobody answered. He was probably working. She paused in the women's chamber, and dropped her bag on the cot. She ran a brush through her air-dried knotty hair and attempted her best to refresh herself. Her gown felt tacky having been wet and muddied, then dried on a chair in Domhnall's chamber. She'd have to wash it later. She swapped it and her apron for the other set. She only had the two homespun dresses which were naught more than work kirtles.

She smelled the aroma from the kitchen. Meal preparations were underway. There was no time for a walk with Domhnall. She'd love a leisurely stroll—with him—but how could she indulge in that luxury when she'd been hired to work?

Bracing herself for any evil glowers or terse words, she entered the kitchen. A formidable wall of heat from the hearths knocked into her. She stumbled. Servants bustled about in the kitchen. Bethia kneaded bread. Kyla didn't look up from chopping vegetables. Rosalie stepped around Kyla, her head feeling like a weighted sack. Was it this the ailment Lady Montgomerie had mentioned when one hit their head? "What may I help with?" she croaked.

"Seems ye've done enough, Rosalie. We dinna need yer help."

A tingling ran up the back of her neck and across her face. "Has the steward provided today's daily report?"

Kyla gritted her teeth, and tossed vegetables in a pot. "Aren't ye supposed to be resting?"

"I'm ready to resume my responsibilities."

Kyla crinkled her nose, a bead of sweat trailing the side of it. "The stew needs stirring. The tartlet in the hearth needs checked. Cawley will be in shortly with today's wine and ale to decant. I usually set the tables with the trenchers," she said with a chin flick to another table, "but since Mistress Iverson is sick, and since you are unwell, I've done it all myself. We've more mouths to feed this week with the visiting clans."

"Thank you, Kyla, for your diligence." She ushered sluggish legs to the hearth, choosing not to ask about how last night fared. She'd had nearly everything prepared before the incident in the garden. Sudden unrest agitated within her. Had Kyla been the one behind the assault? The woman clearly had an interest in Domhnall and saw Rosalie as a threat. Was she capable of asking someone to—?

No.

She busied herself with decanting wine once Cawley arrived and then with setting the tables in the hall. A servant had already prepared the grand hearth for the evening, more for light and ambiance than heat. Shivers erupted within her, followed by a horrible flush. Her mouth tickled. She licked her lips, and fanned her face. Her sleeves felt tight and her skin...itchy.

Oh, no...

She'd felt this way only twice, both times after eating nuts. The second response happened sooner. This time, it felt delayed. She'd eaten hours ago. Had there been nuts in her food?

The drink she'd had a few sips of before leaving the bedchamber had tasted strange, earthy.

She usually recovered after mild discomfort, but the second occurrence had been worse than the first time. This one felt even more so. Her throat tightened. A wheeze captured her breathing.

"Rosalie, are you well, dear? Why are you not resting?" A sweet, older woman's voice floated near, muffled by the ringing in her ears.

"No. Nuts..." She gripped her middle, stomach clenching like she might vomit. Was a basin nearby?

The drink. Had Kyla prepared her infused herbal?

Preventing her fall, arms were upon her. Two blurry faces, the lady and somebody else with dark hair, but not Domhnall. "I-I can't breathe. The herbal drink. Somebody gave me nuts...I can't have..."

"Alasdair! To my herbal pantry. Get the dragon's petal tincture. She must drink it straight away."

The man disappeared.

"Please, dear, focus on breathing in, breathing out." Hands like bird wings danced over her wrists, face, and neck and loosened her painfully constricting front laces.

"Bethia, a wet cloth, please."

Time moved slowly, excruciatingly, but she fought to remain awake. She was prone on the hall floor now, her head resting in a woman's lap. The vaulted wooden ceiling blurred above her. "Everyone, out, please," the woman ordered sternly.

The woman's voice—familiar—said to someone nearby, "Why did you bring me that?"

A gruff male voice. "I thought you might want the healing stone, too."

She exhaled loudly, and lifted Rosalie's neck. "Rose, drink this first."

First?

It tasted putrid, but she forced every drop down her narrowing throat. A snake wrapped around it, luring her toward blackness. If she couldn't swallow the foul remedy, she was dead.

The man pleaded, "You've done it, twice, Deirdre. Remember Lanie as a bairn? Remember me, love? You can do it again. Take the stone."

Deirdre? Rosalie's mind was fuzzy, but she remembered all names, all faces, all voices. This was the Lady of Eilean Donan, Domhnall's mother. And his father? Heavens, the laird.

She tried to sit up.

Lady Montgomerie pushed her down, firmly. She placed a hand on her forehead, a sort of stone cupped in her palm. Shadows seduced Rosalie. Fierce heat flooded her lungs on the next inhalation, expanding them to fullness.

Then she closed her eyes.

CHAPTER NINE

Mother Mary, she was in Domhnall's bedchamber, again. Familiar scents and sounds and textures brought her back to the present.

Exhausted, mind numbed, and frustrated beyond words, she rolled to her side, then sat up and commanded her legs to the edge of the bed. They felt like logs. The chamber was dark, the hearth glowing low in evening's shadows. She fumbled to the door.

She opened it with a shaking hand.

"Rosalie, why do you stir?" Hayden came toward her, his arms outstretched. "You're to rest. The laird and lady's orders."

She gritted her teeth. "I must work."

Or leave this place of misfortune. So much for choice two if somebody or somebodies are intent on harming or killing me.

"You must rest," he repeated, looping her arm in his. He ushered her into the bedchamber. She lacked the strength to protest. "If you're to go anywhere, you're to be escorted by me, Domhnall, or a watchman."

Escorted? She was a servant. Was she in trouble?

"My uncle?"

"He came by. Should I send for him again?"

She nodded, mute.

This place was not safe. Hiding had done nothing to help her. Choice two was turning out poorly. It was time to reevaluate her first choice: leave and pray they made it through winter with her work.

A man cleared his throat in the doorway.

"Lass thought to return to work. I told her to rest," Hayden said sternly.

Domhnall approached and gave his friend a grateful smile. "Thanks, Hayden. I'll take the night's shift with Rose if you coordinate with Guthrie about the watchmen for tonight? We have Donalds remaining in town who can assist."

Hayden nodded. "Aye." He was out the door, quick on his feet and silent. Domhnall's boots swished through the rushes, while Hayden had paws like a cat. Heavier burden, heavier step?

Rosalie returned to the bed but sat upright. "What happened?"

"You tell me."

Her pulse soared. Was he irritated? "I tell you? Twice somebody has tried to harm me." *Kill me.*

His lips tipped into a frown, and his forehead furrowed. "Are you saying someone put something in your drink or food? My mother said you were raving about nuts."

She wanted to cry. But couldn't. All she wanted were a few tears. It sounded daft, but mounting pressure begged to be released. Nothing. Not a drop.

A tender swallow confirmed her response. "Yes, nuts." She scratched a patch of irritated skin on her forearm. Her lungs rattled with a wheeze.

"I asked Kyla, and she denies it. I questioned the rest of the servants, too. What is this madness, Rose?"

He paced, and must have been riled, for he didn't pick up one of his puzzles to mess with.

"You think I'm lying? So I could stay in your lavish chamber?" She made to stand. "I have a cot of my own, and my things are there. It's where I belong. Not here. Oswell will finish his work, and I'll take my leave. I've changed my mind. I am not safe here. In fact, I would rather be anywhere but here!" Admitting those true words deflated her spirit. She always knew her place. Domhnall didn't understand. She was nothing like him.

A *Seer*. A voice in her head whispered. He only liked her because he thought she was one, too. The tears pricked the backs of her eyes but refused to come.

He reached for her, but his hand met air as she wiggled away. He massaged his neck and exhaled—loudly. "You can be convincing."

"Are you bloody kidding me? You think I did this to myself? I cannot have nuts. I will die! I told you. Somebody overheard it or knows." Realization smacked her harder than his accusations. She lowered her voice in a painful, confused whisper. "How am I alive, Domhnall? I've managed before, but this time was far worse, albeit delayed. I couldn't breathe. I felt death's claws upon me."

"My mother."

Her mood simmered. "How did she help me? The foul drink? A special herb? No remedy exists. I have searched around."

He opened his mouth, then closed it. "Well..." He released the arms crossed against his chest. He dragged over the same stool he'd used for his reading and slumped onto it. Dark brown eyes held hers and she felt a heat well in her belly at their scrutiny.

He had accused her of lying, making up the entire charade. Well, he wasn't completely incorrect. But she was not lying about the nuts or the assault.

"She has a gift. She is special like me. She's been taught in healing remedies."

"Didn't you say she was a Feeler?"

"She doesn't heal in the traditional sense."

He knelt and dragged three hefty leather-bound books out from beneath the bed. "These hold the answers." He released a whoosh of a sigh that could fill the room. "I can show you a few similar letters to our Latin, Gaelic, and English, but the books are written in Norse and another language of the Ancients. As I promised, we can still work on your reading and writing. We can work on that while I watch over you?"

It was a question, not a suggestion. "Watch over me? I'm under guard now? Because you do not trust me, or is it for my safety? You just accused me of doing this to myself! I said I was leaving, but not because I am guilty. I am not safe here."

"Please don't leave, Rose. Give us time to find who did this. You might not be safe alone or traveling."

She grimaced.

"I'm your guard tonight," he said with a half-boyish, half-something else smile. The heat from her belly radiated to her limbs. He plopped the books on his table with a thud. "I'm sorry I accused you. Please forgive me, Rose."

She lacked the energy to argue more.

Like me, he had said. Before her stood a mystical-born Seer. Did she believe it? His mother was some kind of magical Healer *and* Feeler? Rosalie believed in her Holy Father, listened to weekly sermons, but never found her steps drawn to confession. She swindled people of hard-earned coin with her lies. She was no saint. If the Church had authority in all their teachings and ways, it was purgatory or worse for her.

Domhnall's mystical religion intrigued her. Seer, Healer, and Feeler. True to their bones.

Her own abrupt words drew her from her musings. "Do you think it's all connected?"

"What...all?"

"The thefts, fire, me, and Oswell. All of it." She paused.

"I've ideas about the thefts and the fire. Your and Oswell's assaults don't make sense. Does somebody wish your family harm?"

"No." *Yes, but...* Somebody was trying to kill her.

Kyla? Had she poisoned her drink? Lady Brantingham? Or someone else? Had the lady infiltrated the castle staff with her influence? She could not ask Domhnall about Edrea without drawing more suspicion.

His brown eyebrows curled with a frown again. "The thefts all point toward a group of people working together."

"There are always going to be thefts when times are difficult. The border wars...Robert Bruce..."

"Aye. But these all only began happening a few weeks ago."

"How do Oswell and I play into this?" She twisted a finger around her necklace, shielding her eyes from him. "I've done nothing wrong and have no coin to be stolen."

"I'm sorry to have accused you," he repeated. He rose and paced again. "We'll keep you under watch."

"My work?"

He strode to the window and peered out. "Your employment is no longer required."

Her heart sunk. "What do you mean?"

"We gave your responsibilities to Kyla, and we've inquired in town for help."

Was this exactly what Kyla had wanted? Fatigue and dizziness erupted in her head, but blood rushed to her temple. Her pulse faltered. "I need to work. Not everyone is as...has the resources you have."

"We'll pay your uncle handsomely for his work. Trēs and Duo are doing a thorough job." He released a half-hearted chuckle. "Cute wee beasties. Sorry. I don't mean to make light of it." He sat beside her, leaving space, but then took her hand in his. Squeezed it.

She didn't retreat. His nearness steadied her racing mind and she enjoyed his touches, even wished for more.

"We have more rats than we thought. They've been raiding the stores. Robena, er, Mistress Iverson, the former cook, usually kept watch on the stores, but, with her deteriorating health and with Cawley being overrun with all the planning for Lanie's *cèilidh*...och, it will get worse when winter comes. We might require your uncle's services indefinitely."

Hmm, back to choice two again. Lady Brantingham had to return home at some point.

Dear God, she'd never felt so indecisive in her life. Staying on the move meant easier choices. Settling befouled everything. These incidences proved it. "My aunt can't keep the shop alone for too long. Our neighbor, the herbalist, is helping her, but we are paying her. I'll leave once my uncle finishes." There went all the coin for her work here. "I am capable of working, Domhnall. How can I help?"

"I'd prefer you to stay by my side until we find these people. If not with me, when I must leave to walk my rounds, then with Hayden or another trusted soldier or watchman. We're trained to protect."

Seemingly done with the conversation, he reached for one of the books and handed it to her. She traced a metal fish on the cover. He said, "Why don't you peruse these, and with the parchment and quill write letters or words you're familiar with. You'll be able to pinpoint any letters you might know in the side-translations."

"I know a few."

"Good. It will give me a starting point. I have other books in our library, in Latin and the common English. Mostly religious texts, but I'll look for something that is pleasing to read. Which do you prefer?"

"Latin or common English? What do you think? The best for doing business."

"We write in Latin, English, and Gaelic. Speak in English and Gaelic. You don't want to learn Gaelic. Tough words, tougher pronunciations." He smiled fully.

His smiles and determination pushed the storm clouds in her mind away. "Indeed. Let us try the common words in English first? Whatever would be most useful for me."

"That is wise."

He hesitated at the door. "I'll send your things up. My chamber is yours. No more of this shuffling around, aye?"

She sighed.

"Please?" He gently bit his lip as his fingers dancing at his side. "We'll always have guards posted. I'll supervise the preparation of your food and drink. Our home is your home, Rose."

"I can't possibly—"

He talked over her refusal. "Feel free to walk the grounds, but a guard must be with you. My mother will check on you shortly, and then I'll be back." He waited for her response.

She'd bet all her coins he'd win in a match of patience. "As you wish. But truly, Domhnall. Just a few more days or a week at most, then I must leave."

He smiled and departed.

This compromise worked. She'd consult Oswell later about it. Sleep summoned her. Then, she'd look at the books. For now, she was safe under Domhnall's guard. The closer she stayed to him, the better.

CHAPTER TEN

T he next morning came with clarity. Never one to waver, Rosalie weighed her long-term options, went for rational yet cautious, and followed through without a look back.

First, Lady Montgomerie tended to her and confirmed her suspicions: the concoction she'd swallowed helped her with the reaction to nuts, but the lady had also healed her with her own hands. Despite her intrigue, Rosalie refrained from asking more about her methods. To heal with touch was astounding. And powerful.

It wasn't proper to question the lady of a household, so Rosalie had nodded along during the her explanation. Mystical power? So be it.

Second, Oswell visited, brimming with satisfaction. His work always buoyed his step and mind.

He clapped his hands. "This is fortunate."

"Fortunate I was attacked? Poisoned?" She lowered her voice. "That Lady Brantingham is here?"

He stepped lightly around the room, lifting and touching items. "Of course not those things. The laird's son has taken a liking to you."

"He has not."

"You're in his chamber, Rosie."

She muffled a guttural groan. "What about Nelda?"

He tsked, lifted a clay goblet, sniffed its contents, and then smiled. He ran a finger along the finely constructed dressing table and embroidered seat. "She has Edith."

"She needs us, Uncle Os. Edith will only take care of her for so long."

"We can request Laird Montgomerie to send a message to her with one of his sentries along with some of my coin. They've already paid me for half of my work."

"I'm no longer employed in the kitchen. What about that coin?" Was Edinburgh her home? Did she have a real home? Meekly, she suggested, "What about France? We can go there. That was an idea before. They might be more accepting of us."

He scratched at his growing gray beard. "We must stop moving so much, Rosie. Nelda is not well, and me, my bones creak. No. I've decided. We'll stay here. Let the man court you and protect you. We can move our belongings north. Here, to Dornie."

"Uncle Os, you've hardly thought this through."

"We've moved for lesser reasons. We're not safe if we travel to Edinburgh. That witch will send her henchmen after us on the journey. They are still in town."

"Is Nelda safe?"

Surprise dashed across his face. "Of course. It's not Nelda Lady Brantingham seeks."

Humiliation stole her voice for a long moment. She coughed. "What if I refuse?"

"I've never forced you to do anything against your wishes, Rosie. Think upon it. Think. You are good at thinking. You have done so much for us, my darling flower."

She chewed her lip. She had already thought plenty upon it. Her uncle was right. Her arguing and musing had grown irritatingly unsuccessful.

Oswell approached the bed and sat beside her. "I'm sorry I couldn't provide for you more, Rosie."

"You've provided well."

He snorted. "A ratcatcher for your caregiver? Your aunt's mind." He shook his head. "Her wits are sideways these days. This—what we've made you do? Teaching a trade of lies? It was not kind of us to make you do that. You are good at so many other things."

"I wanted to, Os." Nevertheless, her gaze darted to the closed door. Nobody could hear their conversation.

In all the confusion, she hadn't realized Oswell's cough had dissipated. Granted, she'd hardly seen him in the past few days. "How is your cough?"

He gleamed. "Better. The lady gave me a tonic." He tapped his chest with a fist.

She smiled. "Blessed be." She reached in and pulled out her mother's bracelet from her deep pocket, cupped it in a palm, and traced every striation with her fingertip. "My parents...you don't remember them?" She'd asked it a hundred times. They always told her the same thing. There was a cottage fire. She was a baby.

He gave a hard, deliberate swallow and looked away. "We found you."

"In the fire."

His cloudy gray eyes teared. "I'm sorry, Rosie. You're always askin' me. I grow weary in my age. I can't die with this lie on my soul. I said your parents died young in a fire and that your mother was Nelda's sister. It's not true." He exhaled, loudly, almost painfully through his nose. "You were abandoned, found like Moses himself, in a basket, with a blanket and the bracelet."

"What? Found? What about my parents? Nelda is not my aunt?" He told her this *now* after years of asking? Why? "Are my parents alive?"

She was no Moses.

"I don't know. Nelda found you. We never had children of our own, so..."

Her parents hadn't wanted her. They had just left her? A coil tightened in her stomach. Somehow, she had always known.

He added, solemnly, "You're meant for more, sweet Rosie. Fortune-telling can be put behind you now."

She sniffled but sequestered the absent tears. "What am I to do?"

He shrugged. "Like I said, the laird's son seems taken with you, and do not worry about your auntie. You've got splendid—*seeing*—eyes. You have skills, and people like you. You'll make an able lady."

"Uncle Os, what did Lady Montgomerie put in your drink?" Uncle. Auntie. They were not her blood.

"He likes you. I'm growing deaf and losing my sight, but some things I can see, Rosie. If it doesn't fare well, then we will find work. Here." He smacked his knee with decisiveness. "You're a talented cook and skilled with the beaded things and with numbers. We'll find you a virtuous job. What laird's son would not want you though? My betting days are behind me, but if I had the coin, I'd put it on you two."

"I hardly know him. He only wants me for my seeing ability." A blush warmed her cheeks. Why would a man want her if her own parents hadn't? It was a shadowy decision. For the first time in her life, she hated the game. Hated the constant uncertainty of where the next coin would come from.

"As you wish it, Os. We can stay longer for now."

Domhnall. He was a real Seer. She was anything but.

Rosalie sat in the garden with Aileana, showing her how to make her paints. A pleasant sunny day shone upon them. One of the watchmen, Aiden, stood nearby. It was nice to be outside after days within the castle.

Aileana passed restless fingers over the mortar and pestle, various ground colors obtained in town at peddlers' stands, and the bowl of eggs. "You use....eggs?" She crinkled her nose.

"Yes. It is simple. Crush the mineral color first. Many I gather from rock powders or flowers, and then I use my grinding stone or something like the mortar and pestle your mother provided. Then, mix in egg yolk, just right." She cracked two eggs, divided the yolk from the white, and whisked them. "I love trying new colors. If I can afford it, I purchase darker, harder-to-come-by color powders."

"What do you paint, beside the pebbles?"

"Anything I can get my hands on. Canvas and parchment if I have it."

Today, several palm-sized, flat stones sat on their tray.

"Gracie draws dragons and faeries and all sorts of fabled creatures. She'd love to learn how to paint them."

"It would be nice to meet her."

"You will," Aileana said, sorting the simple horsehair brushes provided by the lady.

"Here." Rosalie handed her a brush. "Try the blue. A suitable color to use on these paler rocks."

Aileana hummed to herself as she attempted to paint, but then grew flustered, wiped a rock with a cloth, and then tried again.

Rosalie balanced a piece of slate in her palm. First, she painted five long petals of yellow, her favorite color. Then she chose a slender brush and put blue dots in the middle.

"Gorgeous. Mine looks like—" Aileana scrunched her face, sticking a tongue out. "Mmphmm. A blue splat." She giggled to herself. "Give me a bow and a target instead."

Rosalie chose another stone and began a different flow with a pink-purple paint. "You know how to use the bow?"

"Verra well. Hayden taught me. I'd attend hunts if my father allowed me." She huffed. "He's afraid I'll get hurt."

"I'm sure he's only concerned about your well-being."

Aileana flopped on the blanket, shielding the sun from her eyes with her arm. She twisted a finger around curly, auburn tendrils of hair. "I said no to Hayden."

"No to what?" *Rose, don't pry.* Her brush slipped. She took the cloth and fixed the edge, then reapplied with focus.

"Marriage."

"Oh."

Aileana nibbled on her thumbnail. "He's patient with me, sweet with words, a sweeter kisser, and agreeable, but he has a wee temper. He doesn't like Ma's cats either." She fell quiet. "He can be frustrating sometimes. Likely too much time with Dour Domhnall."

Rosalie wondered if there was another suitor after Aileana's heart, one she did not speak of.

"Tell me about your business, Rose."

Rosalie's hand skittered. "Pardon me?"

"You're not just a kitchen hand. Mind you, your food was all the talk at my *cèilidh*."

"I take whatever work the Lord provides. Cook, clean, sew. I sell trinkets I've bartered for or acquired. I don't sell many of my own crafts. Ladies want finer jewels."

"You're a fortune-teller...who travels. Scotland is not your home."

Mother Mary.

Aileana sat up. "Your secret will not leave my lips. The servants talk. Do you see? Like, *see*? Have the gift?"

Rosalie hyper-focused on her painting, feeling Aileana's stare upon her. "I read palms."

"Ohhh, it's by touch, like Domhnall. Intriguing. Will you read mine?"

Well, her conclusion about him was correct. Not that she needed the confirmation at this point. She laid down the brush and turned toward Aileana. "Maybe later?"

"The palms tell you things?"

"More or less."

Aileana smiled without any guile. "You are among like folk here, Rose. No one will question your ability."

Rosalie returned to the painting while Aileana moved on to the next subject, and the next. Rosalie adored Aileana's company, but how much longer could she continue the farce?

Domhnall guided Rosalie on a stroll through the village. He kept her close by his side but didn't loop his arm within hers. When separated, he missed her presence already. He wanted more.

Wariness reigned regardless. Would the visions return if he pushed their physical interaction? The idea of kissing her rosy pink lips sent a roaring wind through his veins and lungs. Was this foolish young enchantment? Did he feel a true connection to her? He was hardly the young dolt he'd been years ago with Isolde, but this was the first time he had felt anything with anyone again. Was it only the lure to be able to touch someone without the affliction cursing him to misery?

He purposely avoided the gardens—the location of her attack—as they crossed the stone bridge connecting the isle to the mainland. "Ready for a test?"

She faltered. "A test?"

"Words, letters. I'll take you past shops with signs. See what you know."

She nibbled her bottom lip. "Do you think I am ready? We've only just begun."

"You're a quick study. Especially your control with writing the letters."

"My painting skills help my hand. I'll admit, the drawings in the Norse books intrigue me more than the transcriptions."

"Curious, aren't they?"

So far he'd shown her the three books of the Ancients. There were English translations on the side...and a part of him wondered if any of it might seem familiar to her...that it would trigger some memory of being from the isles.

His mother had told him the stories about the books, their origin, and her own ability. His parents had a unique bond, she'd said. She'd told him about visions of the "man from the wood" she had seen in her dreams...long before Alasdair Montgomerie stumbled upon their village years ago. Visions. Mother not only had visions and was an astute Feeler, but she also accessed the power across the Silver Veil to heal. She'd exhibited the healing power three times in her life already: with his father long ago, Aileana as a bairn, and now Rosalie. His mother's ability to harness all the powers demonstrated the magnitude of the Silver Veil. How could he not believe that fate and the Silver Veil brought him to Rosalie Threston then?

"Domhnall?" Rosalie's kind voice intruded on his thoughts.

"Aye?"

"Which way?"

He shook his head. "Och. This way."

He guided her past shops, his arm linked with hers now, enjoying the relief and bliss of her presence...and her touch. No black nightmare crossed his eyes.

He pointed to the first sign.

She squinted. "*Ahh-paw-th*..." She faltered over the middle TH when trying to pronounce the word.

"Apothecary," he finished.

She fanned her hand at her chest, pink rising up her neck to match a glow in her cheeks. "Mother Mary. Simpler next time?"

They strode past the carpenter and the bronze smith, engraver, butcher, fletcher, tavern, and a handful of other shops, with each one, he sounded out words or pointed to the occasional sign for her to read.

"My head is spinning. Many letters, many words. I prefer forming the letters with the quill over reading them aloud."

"You do have a good hand for it. You're doing well. I want to show you something else first before we head back."

"I'll be seeing letters in my sleep." She covered a yawn.

"No words, I promise."

She pressed her lips together into a receptive smile, revealing a sweet dimple he'd love to kiss. Maybe he would.

They weaved among crowds, and he stealthily avoided touching anyone else but her.

She leaned into him, her own arm tense within his suddenly. "Could somebody be lying, Domhnall? About the drink?" Her gaze shifted, warily taking in their surroundings like a skittish mouse thrown into a den of feral cats. He needn't be a Feeler to know she was still unsettled after both attempts upon her life; being out of the safety of the castle walls certainly could be unnerving. At least she had finally stopped asking to be put to work. He relished his daytime with her—reading, writing, and walking.

"Why would anyone lie to me?" He squeezed her arm and leaned in close to her ear. "You are safe here, at my side, Rose. Always."

"You believe them? Nobody would lie to you?"

"I want to believe it, yes."

She scoffed. "Even Kyla?"

He nearly snorted. "She wouldn't hurt anyone. A jealous hen, she is, aye, but no, I don't think she'd wish you harm."

They continued farther through the village, on an open path along the loch.

A sound came from behind a nearby bush. An unmistakable cry like a young child, but not from a child.

"What's that?" Rose asked.

"Let me see." He grasped his sword's hilt, ready to draw.

He heard teeth grinding, thumping, and a moan and knew before he saw. "Rabbit, caught in a trap."

Rosalie came nearer.

He waved her back. "Wait there a moment. It is already upset," he said, stroking the rabbit's head. One of its hind legs was ensnared, and it looked to be in terrible pain. "The rabbit will die a slow death if left here. I need to release it." He worked with the snare.

"Isn't that somebody's trap?"

"Aye, but it shouldn't be close to the keep and loch. We have strict rules for catching. Also, it's a leg-only trap, which we forbid. The animal suffers."

Released, the rabbit dashed off into the trees, only a slight limp to its hop. "It will be well."

"Won't someone be upset you took their meal?"

"They know the rules."

The pebbles crunched beneath their feet, and the sounds of village life diminished as they continued on.

His wariness relaxed with his step. Keeping Rosalie close was both necessity and reward. He breathed in her feminine scent of rosewater.

A twig snapped nearby and she startled.

He paused, listened, looked. "I'll protect you, even from furry wee creatures," he said.

"I don't wish you to feel obligated," she said stiffly.

This entire stroll Rosalie seemed unsettled. He wondered what more he could do to reassure her. "Rose, I want to. It's not only my responsibility spurring my words." He ran a hand through his hair and rubbed his chin. He was no good at courting. Is that what this was? He wanted to protect her. "Look. We're here." He loosened his hold on her and hurried ahead to the water's edge.

He squatted, running fingers through a tidal pool. She came closer. "What is it?"

"I thought you might like these stones. For some reason, this spot always has an abundance of unique stones, pearly, shiny, and interesting colors." He swept a hand to the horizon as he stood.

"Hmm."

He pointed west. "Skye is that way, and then the deep wide sea beyond it. Then the isles from where my ancestors hailed."

"I see." She squinted in the distance. He turned to face her. Contemplation furrowed her forehead.

He wiped a wet hand on his tunic and took her hands in his. *Cheeky.* He wanted to tempt fate further, and repeatedly, like a child rebelling against a commanding parent. Living life on the periphery, protecting himself from the pain, had become a suffocating blanket. It was time to live. Time to jump.

He drew a finger down the hollow of her neck, softly. "I thought you could use some of these stones for your necklaces. I saw the ones you sold in the market, and my mother told me about them. Lanie said you showed her how to make paints. Your work is beautiful."

"They're just stones."

"Even stones can hold power," he whispered. "And it is like the stones here vibrate…"

She swayed on her feet.

He must have sounded like a fool…all this talk of Seers, and Feelers, and magical stones, and sharing those books with her.

"Do you speak of the Ancients?" she whispered.

He nodded. "Aye."

"What exactly is a Feeler?"

"A person who can see inside you…see your inner most lifeblood and your emotions. Each person emits a color. My mother can read people, the true person they are. No masks, no shields."

"Lifeblood?" Gooseflesh rippled across her feminine neckline.

"We all emit a color. It is our life force. I do not quite comprehend it myself."

"Ahh…"

"She can discern intention from malice, truth from lie."

Brazenly, he traced a finger over the embellished stone necklace she wore around her slender neck, its length dropping above her décolletage. The crinkle extended from her brows to the middle of her forehead, forming a wee crease in a sea of pale softness. Instead of being intrigued by what he shared, she looked bothered.

He laid one hand softly on the small of her back, and drew himself closer. He kissed the deepening crease. He preferred her smile to her frown, and longed for its return. He brushed feather lips upon her skin. A spark jolted him, but he absorbed it. He inhaled her scent, retreated slowly, and then drew his finger from the necklace to her cheek.

"Domhnall, I don't think..." She didn't finish the sentence and, instead, held his gaze, then closed her eyes while he stroked her cheek.

He stopped, as difficult as it was. "Let's find you stones, shall we?"

She opened her eyes and nodded. "Yes, please."

He removed his boots and rolled his hose. Lacking modesty, she removed her work shoes and allowed clean toes to venture into the loch's cool water. She inhaled sharply, as did he. This water was always so cold.

They spent the better part of an hour picking through rocks and pebbles and pond plants on the shore, locating unique pebbles. Domhnall shared stories of his youth, of trips with his father, and his explorations north and south. Rosalie chatted about her own travels, and her passion for rocks, crafts, and numbers. He loved listening to her animated voice.

"Do you like visiting new places?"

She shrugged. "It's all I know."

"You don't wish to stop, and choose one place to call home?"

"One day." Rosalie squealed with delight. "Look at this one!"

She hovered intently over a pool, turning over rocks, not a care in the world as the hem of her simple gown grew soppy and her fingers muddy. She held a pebble up, her face brimming with pride.

He drew nearer. "Bonnie. I see blue and opal."

"Why are the unique ones here? They're all round and smooth. So different from other places."

He continued digging, thoroughly enjoying himself. "I do not know. There's plenty of lore about our region of Scotland. Magic in stones, some say," he said, echoing his earlier statement. "I believe the answer is rooted in nature. The lochs and rivers flow to this spot, and perhaps it has something to do with water's movement and the rock composition. Others proclaim this area as both a man-made and magical gateway to the isles. My grandfather always told me stories of Norse warriors and bloody battles. It's a mystical place, some say, like a doorway that opens to an even greater mystical place, to the isles. Even the mountains have a story to their creation."

"Maybe the water is magical, too?" She toyed with a sweet smile. Her dimple appeared again. He liked that she at least indulged him.

He wanted to kiss the dimple. He felt less foolish sharing with Rosalie about his family's stories and heritage. They both worked quietly, lost in thought for a little while longer. The late morning's sun dappled gold in the choppy blue-green loch. He gloried in the day's coolness, a break from the unusual heat, and the momentary respite with Rosalie. He loved her inquisitiveness. She was unlike any lass he had met before.

"I can have our village stonemason bore holes in the pebbles for you, for easier threading."

She was right beside him. She jerked her head up. "That would be kind—"

Their heads collided. "Oh." She clutched her forehead and stumbled.

He dropped the stones from his hand and grabbed her before she could fall into the water. They toppled onto the pebbly shore. He laughed, she smirked.

"I've heard of hard-headed, but graces." She rubbed her forehead, the crease returning in a pink spot where they had cracked heads.

His head rang, and not just from the bump.

Her chest heaved from exhilaration and she frowned. He kissed the corner of her mouth. "Sorry," he breathed, holding her, close.

"It's just a bump. I'll be fine." She rubbed her head with emphasis, not taking her eyes off his.

"No, not that. For, er..." Blazes, why could he not string his words together when around her? "For kissing you. I should have asked permission. Please accept my apology." His words said one thing, but his body said another. He didn't release her.

"No apology needed. And not everything needs to be proper or planned."

Neither moved. His heart raced. "I..."

She stopped him with a kiss of her own, full on his lips. Not only was she resolute, Rosalie did not play demure games. He cupped the nape of her neck, drawing her closer, allowing himself to disappear in the kiss. The only blackness across his vision was his own. No damning words, hissing Wind, or blood and death. Only a rousing from within. She tasted like the earth, pure and humble. A hint of honey on her tongue from the sweet pies they'd eaten at the village baker's. He dared to part her lips and enjoyed her deeper.

They were alone, lacking escort or guard. This most certainly was not proper, but his parents weren't concerned with courting rules anyway. They always told him to chase love. Domhnall made his own choices, and he was not one to corrupt a young, naïve lass. Rosalie was hardly unsophisticated though. She was a person of the world, like him.

A sigh escaped her throat, and he moaned in return. He should stop. It had been too bloody long. By his Holy Father, he wanted to do so much more though…

They both drew back simultaneously. A smile tipped her lips.

"I—" he breathed.

She blinked over a frown.

Her look crushed him. Had he overstepped? These frowns tortured his heart. He helped her upright from their seated positions on the shore. She fluffed her layers of skirts, and huffed like a frazzled hen. "Domhnall, I must tell you something."

She didn't reciprocate the feelings. Shame flushed his cheeks. He'd been too forward, too eager. "Aye?"

She swallowed, licked her lips, and busied herself with gathering the pebble pile, dropping stones into a linen sack. She spoke in a flurry. "In England, there was a lady of a castle. She err, she eh—" She whimpered, the crease digging deeper in her forehead.

Dammit, he wanted to kiss it again, to make whatever vexed her go away.

"I tried to tell her what would happen if her husband went to war. The Despensers' dispute. I tried."

She seemed on the verge of tears, but he'd never seen her shed one not when her uncle was assaulted, nor when she was hurt in the gardens, not after the nuts in her drink, not even when he saw Isolde and her friend bother her in the market. Not one tear. She was a braw lass. She formed fists at her sides and halted in her fretting.

He stepped closer. "I'll listen. Tell me."

"I think I know who attacked me."

Well, he didn't expect that. He approached, took her hands, unable to control himself anymore.

She sniffled, eyes filled with unrest. "I told you about my ways with reading palms. Well, they're not always perfect. Fates can be hazy."

He nodded. "Mine, too."

"Lady Brantingham was awfully chafed by her reading back in England." She didn't elaborate. "She wishes me harm." She lowered her gaze. "Or she wishes to abduct me and exploit my—my ability."

"An English lady?"

Her lower lip trembled.

"She's followed you all the way here?" He cast a look over his shoulder, though they were alone, far away from the nearest person.

"I saw her in the marketplace earlier this week. I didn't think she saw me. But now I am not sure. She would never stay in Scotland for this long without a reason."

Her visions. His visions. Did he believe her? Yes. "You think she's behind your attack? The drink was indeed tainted? That she infiltrated the castle help?"

She shrugged. "Who else would it be? I doubt your thieves have any interest in harming me."

He mulled over the idea for a long moment. The thieves—clearly the MacDougalls—would have no reason to harm Rosalie or Oswell. Perhaps he had two sets of evildoers on his hands.

"I should've told you sooner."

"Aye." His fingers itched. He needed to solve this. 'Twas time to uproot all the miscreants, let them see justice. Keep Rosalie safe. "Do you think she was behind Oswell's assault, too?"

She tugged her bottom lip with her teeth. "I don't know. He was robbed. Lady Brantingham wouldn't have done that. She prefers to send messages in other ways."

"You think she is capable of...murder?"

"Very. I know too much about her. I believe she had her husband's sons killed."

Illumination filled his mind. His thoughts had been elsewhere during Aileana's *cèilidh*, but he recalled an Englishwoman among the guests. She had been in the castle.

"Tell me about her."

Rosalie bit her lip. His legs fought him, told him to pace, untangle the mess by movement, but he made them stand still.

"Aunt Nelda used to work in her castle—a tower house on the border—in the kitchen. Edrea came to our shop a few times, for readings. She'd heard of my abilities. Are you familiar with the Despensers?"

"No."

"Many barons with powerful allies led a revolt against King Edward and Hugh Despenser after the king took their land. There was, and still is, much strife in England. One of the men in the opposition was Warden Brantingham of the marches, Edrea's husband. She, hmm, she does not have marital relations with her husband either. There's no love in their union. My vision showed him dying in the conflict. Instead, his sons died in battle, and he returned home. She was furious. Came to our shop, hurt Os." She lowered her voice to a whisper. "We left and moved to Edinburgh."

"His sons are dead by her bidding?"

She nodded. "And she still plots to see her husband dead. She is with child. It's not his. She knows I know this."

"This is quite a knot, Rose."

"I know. I believe now that she wanted all of them to die. She is sly, Domhnall. She doesn't usually confront people. She is quiet, keeps to herself. I believe she only came to me for readings out of desperation. She exploits others to her causes. She has naught but one friend in court, and from what I hear, her standing is shaky with nobility after the revolt. She does not draw attention to herself, as it would soil her reputation."

"So she wouldn't just confront you?"

Rosalie shrugged. "Not likely. She wouldn't engage with me in public unless she must. She'd find another person to do her bidding. I should return to Edinburgh. I've brought trouble to your home."

"Disturbance was here before your arrival. Lady Brantingham just added to the unrest." His attempt at good humor did not work.

She clutched the bag of pebbles against her stomach. "Os is almost done. We should take our leave."

"No. We can offer you full protection. How can you return south now, with her men about? She will only follow you there."

She grimaced.

"I have an idea." He wrapped a hand around hers, guiding her from the loch toward the castle. This idea had, admittedly, entered his mind a few times, but he thought it rash. Now...now not so much.

Laird Alasdair Montgomerie had a dominating presence in the hall as he stood, arms crossed, in front of the low-glowing hearth. "Full protection. You understand what it entails, Domhnall?" His voice echoed off the rafters.

"Aye," his son replied, equally resolute.

What was with him and Domhnall and "protection?" Rosalie dipped her chin, unable to hold the laird's powerful dark blue gaze. She felt like a child caught doing wrong. Or worse, a person on trial for all their sins. First the kiss, and her lips still hummed with Domhnall's touch. Oh, his tongue. Dear God, his tongue. His hands all over her. She hadn't expected it. She hadn't rejected his advances. Her stomach rumbled with turmoil, not hunger. *Concentrate, Rose.*

Then her confession: guilt had brought her words forth in a flood. She'd spent her life lying and running. She couldn't carry on the charade much longer, at least not with Edrea Brantingham in town. Now she sat in front of the laird and lady of the keep, seeking full protection—whatever that meant—like a coward.

His mother explained. "To be fully protected, under Scottish law, you must be one of the clan, Rosalie, dear. Domhnall has brought your issue to us. Returning home is an option, if you wish. My son is..." She paused, finding choice words. "Insistent."

Home.

She had none.

Was Edinburgh her home?

Rosalie brought her chin up, met both elders in the eyes.

Lady Montgomerie expounded, "English laws are different, but here, the clans reign, even with our king. Clan and marriage bonds create strong unity."

She didn't like how this was going.

Domhnall said, "Marriage."

Why yes, he had just said that.

Her jaw dropped open. She clamped it shut. "My lady and my laird, I cannot ask such a thing. Protection is fine, but this?" She turned to Domhnall. "This was your idea? Marriage?"

"Not marriage, but handfasting, yes. You'd fall under my protection—our entire clan's. The lady cannot touch you without ramifications."

"Hand-what?"

"We won't make you marry against your wishes," Lady Montgomerie said. "You can plight your troth, publicly, in a handfasting ceremony."

Rosalie's face must have affirmed her lack of understanding.

Lady Montgomerie turned to Rosalie, her gentle tone and tender smile calming. Was this part of her gift? Did she induce serene placidity over those around her? Did she use this ability to coax people to do as she wished? "It's a ceremony of hands, like a betrothal, an exchanging of future consents. It would be documented, recorded on parchment, and made official. Then you live under our protection."

"How is it different from marriage? And isn't the Watch's protection enough? They've been staying by my side. I agreed to supervision for the remainder of our stay."

"That was before you told me about Lady Brantingham. This is serious, Rose," Domhnall said, his voice resolute and tinged with desperation. "My men's guard are not enough. You need more protection. You were attacked and poisoned. You think you'll be safer on the road and alone?"

Lady Deirdre exhaled. "It's only a step toward stronger protection, having the law on our side. Marriages don't always result from a handfasting. This adds a layer of safety."

Domhnall interjected. "We have two choices. First, a few days after the handfasting, we proclaim by formal decree that we decided to continue with the consent and we have said the vows in a private marriage ceremony in our chapel, or second, if a year passes and you wish it, we can make the union real."

A year? What happened to a few weeks? "You mean...?" Rosalie's breathing quickened.

"You lie," Lady Deirdre said, turning a sharp look to Rosalie but softening it with a hand wave. "A wee lie. In this case, we tell everyone you two exchanged vows in a private ceremony. We stretch the truth. The handfasting must be public. It is binding."

Rosalie's thoughts eddied. A sham? A pretend marriage? It wasn't as if she hadn't already spent her entire life pretending.

She beheld Domhnall's gaze. It was sincere, adamant, almost pleading. She then turned to the laird and lady. "I can't ask you to—"

Domhnall broke in, "You're not. It was my idea. My parents agreed to it."

Lady Deirdre's look stabbed her. She was a Feeler. What did she feel inside Rosalie's soul in this very moment? Did she know this was all one lie? How much of Rosalie's "ability" had Domhnall disclosed to his parents? Was the plan to trap her deeper? Send her to the gallows? Use their son as bait? Oh, how her mind tumbled to some dark places. No. Domhnall would not do that.

Silence fell upon the room. All servants had been ordered away.

"There is one stipulation." The laird directed his gaze to Domhnall only. "If the handfasted union is consummated prior to speaking the wedding vows, the marriage is real, effectuated before our Lord. No words need to be said in the chapel. You understand, aye?"

An unfathomable chill engulfed them all, as did Rosalie's half-suppressed gasp.

Lady Deirdre passed her husband a sharp look. Rosalie would bet her meager coins that there was a subtle meaning behind his declaration.

The laird almost appeared bashful at his wife's glower, his cheeks brimming with pink behind his stalwart appearance. He cleared his throat and eyed Rosalie then Domhnall with a firm look. "We will stand behind whatever you two decide. I've inquired about Lady Brantingham.

She is powerful. Like you said, manipulative, not one to confront us directly. She could have men about, watching you, watching us."

A blank expression sat on Oswell's aged face. Rosalie had forgotten he'd been beside her the entire time.

Oswell poked Rosalie in the side. He would never speak for her like a father would. This was her decision. Nevertheless, his thought on the matter influenced her mind like a cloud beside her. Money, security, home. He coughed.

Yes, she knew his thoughts. He'd made them clear already, before this handfasting idea had been laid upon them. He was fully ready to stay here long-term.

Rosalie broke the fragile silence hovering in the room. "Yes. I'll do the handfasting, but only if it's what Domhnall truly wishes." May God forgive them all. Her confessions to the Almighty stacked higher and higher by the day.

Her suitor pushed the chair from beneath him, stood, and said in a raspy whisper, "Aye, then. I do."

"We could still leave before I go through with this. Get my things, Uncle?"

"Hogwash. This is a wise decision. We stay. A home, Rosie. I can travel to Edinburgh with the laird's soldiers, retrieve your auntie. Make a new home in town. I like it here. Nice master, Laird Montgomerie. You could—will—be his son's wife. Just like I suggested a few days ago. Just as I predicted." He tapped the side of his temple.

"I can't possibly do this." Her hands shook, and she dropped her hairbrush as she found herself again stuffing all her belongings into her sack, an action opposed to the verbal agreement she had given the laird and lady of the castle. It was like Domhnall had wanted her to stay in his bed. In his bed. As much as she felt like she belonged on the cot in the servants' quarters, working in the kitchen...she liked his bed. "Mother Mary. The laird and lady. My head hurts."

"This is so unlike you, Rosie. This man has affected you?"

The cats meowed in their crate. She bent and rubbed Trēs and then Duo behind their ears. She'd asked for their company the night before. It was difficult and lonely in a big chamber by herself. "You keen beasts. Proud of you little boys." She withdrew a small square of salted venison from her apron and broke it, giving parts to both.

Uncle Oswell paced. "They like the stable. I was going to bring them there."

She sighed.

"A laird's wife, Rosie. Isn't this what you always wished for?" Oswell helped her fold her things, reluctantly. Her other gown lay on the bed, clean from fresh laundering. Somebody had washed and dried it for her.

She didn't say what she thought. *I'm a child with no parents. With a rat-catching uncle. A sickly aunt.* Her whole life was lies, and she was being asked to tell another one? To handfast, promise to be wed, and pretend to be wed to a laird's son. Was she ashamed of herself and her upbringing? Yes. God forgive her, yes. Her childish dreams to dance in a hall with a lord or knight were the dreams of a little girl. Tears threatened. The first time in years—years—no! She would not shed a drop. Not now, not ever. Whenever she begged them to come, they hadn't. Now they chose to try to break through?

She wished Oswell and Nelda had never found her as an infant.

"Don't overthink it. I see the cogs in there moving. No more fortune-telling. It's your chance. Our chance at a better life."

Our.

She would do this for them. "You'll retrieve Nelda?"

He nodded. "Yes. I'll leave in the morn. The cats are almost done with their work. We can leave them with the stable master, Ewan."

"I must tell Domhnall the truth."

"Let him simmer. Let it fade, Rosie. In time he will forget all about it."

She had the sneaky suspicion Domhnall Montgomerie did not let things fade away. She nodded, biting her lip. Truth hid among the lies. "Very well. I shall do it."

CHAPTER ELEVEN

The next day Domhnall led Rosalie to a nicer bedchamber beside his. She insisted on moving out of his room and repeatedly offered counterarguments when he suggested she should stay. Oh, his stubbornness rivaled hers! He would not have any of it, so this relocation was their compromise.

A part of her missed her stay in his bed, short-lived as it had been. No longer in the bed perfumed with his unique scent—hay from the stables? Heather?—but beside his chamber now...so close, and so far. She licked her lips and distracted herself with the memory, again fleeting, of his kiss.

Hmm...

A kiss could go deeper if they allowed it.

She'd touched many hands but his said more than all the others. His kiss told her even more.

He was real. This was real.

Oh, what had she gotten herself into?

She paused in the doorway. "I can't possibly displace anyone again—"

"You're not displacing anyone. We keep this chamber for my uncle and aunt when they visit. They've already returned home."

He rounded the bed, plopping her bag—and all her worldly possessions within—upon it. He smirked. "I'd ask if you require help, but you'd just say no and argue with me again."

She released a huff. Well, he was right. She nearly tripped on the rushes carpeting the floor, grabbing his elbow to prevent her fall. He didn't pull away. "This is the only way?" she asked, yet again. "Me, here, the handfasting?"

His look held hers. Thankfully, he was keeping her upright or else her knees might give. "Can you think of something better? I want to protect you. I want you to stay. With me."

Her heart caught in her throat. "I want to be here with you, too." Domhnall fractured her confident façade. She found herself blundering over words.

All was set into motion.

Oswell had just departed for Edinburgh with a few of Laird Montgomerie's men to gather Nelda and their possessions. He'd close the shop, sell inventory no longer needed, and move north to Dornie in the autumn. It was done. The future lady of Eilean Donan was a peddler, a farce, a liar. A woman with nothing to her name.

She rubbed the bracelet in her pocket, the gold warm and almost humming to her. Somebody of importance had left it in her basket when Oswell and Nelda found her. Like Moses. She cringed internally. There'd be no parting seas or burning bushes.

Stories. All these years, her uncle and aunt had told her fabricated stories. Lies most certainly ran in their blood.

Irrational thoughts assaulted her now and she asked again, "Take me through this, Domhnall."

"Through what? The room? Over—"

"No. The handfasting. In England, couples can pledge an intent to marry, in a small blessing ceremony, which is then followed by a religious ceremony in the Church. Is handfasting similar?" She busied herself with opening the shutter to allow in fresh air. She had said yes. She could have said no, under no pressure from Domhnall, his parents, or Oswell. But, she said yes. She had to follow through.

"We're in luck it's market week."

She clenched her hand at her side and turned to him, confused.

He elaborated. "The handfasting ceremonies are usually performed at the annual summer market to ensure ample witnesses. Other couples will be there to plight their troth and declare their intentions. Several neighboring clans are visiting, too."

She muttered, "How fortunate for us."

He snorted. "Indeed. My parents will host a *cèilidh* in the hall afterward."

Another big meal. She should be cooking, not unpacking.

"What about Lady Brantingham? She'll surely hear of it." Her stomach twisted.

"That is the point, aye? If she is as cunning as you say, she'll make certain she is there to witness it. I'll be there, along with the rest of our clansmen, the watchmen, and my father's men. We will all be there for you, Rose. By declaring our pledge, you will be one of us. You will be a Montgomerie and MacCoinneach, on my mother's side."

This was all too much. She fidgeted with the edge of her apron. "I didn't ask for this. Domhnall, I'm sorry I brought this upon your family. This was not my intention when I told you about Lady Brantingham." Unshed tears welled. *Too late, you little beasts! Do not fall*, she chastised them. They obeyed. She was accustomed to life's cruelties.

He approached, the stiff posture of his shoulders relaxing. He took her hands, his beseeching eyes upon hers.

Trying to stay detached had not worked well. His caresses melted her insides like butter.

He issued slow, purposeful words and motions as he rubbed his thumb over her fingers. His eyes glowed a deep brown. "They tie our hands together, knotted like so, with twine." All edge left his voice as he mimicked the tying movements around their interlocked hands. "It's symbolic. We say our intentions—the priest providing the words—and the contract is sealed with a handshake." He eased out a smile, his teeth hidden behind pressed lips. "All agreements require a shake."

She swallowed, trying to remember the taste of his lips. "Naturally," was all she could murmur.

"The couple used to pass their hands through a hollowed stone and link them, then shake. The ceremony has its roots in the isles, with the Nordmen." He was closer, his thighs brushing against her skirt. Near. So desirably near. For a man who a week ago had cowered at her proximity, he could not keep his hands off her now. Her pulse quickened. She didn't dislike it. Why push him away when she, too, had never felt such attraction...or been touched in such a tender way? Oswell and Nelda were not open with displays of affection. The occasional tap on the shoulder. A rare hug. They loved her in their own way. She had never a kissed a man before, well, not in the way she had kissed Domhnall.

He continued, "In a year, we proclaim our intentions and hold the marriage ceremony in the Church..."

"Why a year?" She swallowed the unladylike thoughts prancing through her mind.

He shrugged but kept his hands knotted with hers. "Mostly so the couple can learn to live with each other, I suppose. Learn to love each other?"

"Do all couples handfast as a form of betrothal? And then they live together?" The idea dumbfounded her. Why lead her to a separate bedchamber then? Shall they not share a chamber once handfasted? They lived together but did not share the same bed?

He shook his head. "Many do. Some forgo the handfasting and marry, their hearts already steadfast and true. Or, they make their proclamations in the handfasting ceremony, and shortly thereafter, the marriage takes place in our chapel."

"I hope to not hinder you for long. I'm sure there's another woman who holds your heart."

"There is no other, Rose."

His words and actions were as erratic as a summer thunderstorm. Dark one moment, sunshine the next. The sun increasingly came out in her presence now though. She liked it. He didn't have to say it, but she understood. He wasn't forcing her into any long-term commitment. He was giving her a chance to leave later if she so wanted it. That gesture alone made him all the more desirable.

She floated on his words as his smoldering eyes riveted her to the spot. "Are most unions arranged?" she asked.

He broke the moment, released their interlocked hands, and then strode to the window. He looked out at nothing in particular. "Some for alliances. Many are for love. My parents married for love, but, it was a complicated courtship. They broke a few rules." He smiled to himself.

And that sly smile sent shivers down her spine. Was Domhnall a romantic?

Love. *What of your heart?* she wanted to ask. *Nonsense, nonsense, nonsense.* What man would want her?

"If we err, hmm..." A rush of warmth shot up her throat to her tongue. She fussed with her hair and fanned herself, instantly hot as her look fell upon the bed. She knew what consummation was. A young married woman who worked in an herbalist's shop at the mouth of the Tyne had told her plenty about it. She educated her on the specifics. How and what. Even drew pictures!

She knew that a woman could find pleasure with her husband, with time. Rosalie was not naïve at her age of twenty. On the rare occasion, she would overhear her uncle and aunt. Cramped lodgings concealed nothing. She cringed with the thought. Ailments and senility aside, all people had physical needs.

He finished for her. "Aye. If we share a bed, the handfasting is dissolved and we're married in the eyes of God, the Church, and clan. No requirement for a ceremony, but my parents would have my head if we didn't get married in the Church. Even if we..." He gave a hand flourish, his rigid back turned toward her. "...aye, we'd celebrate the sacrament nonetheless."

Her breath hitched.

He tripped over hurried words and turned blazing eyes upon her. "Your bedchamber is yours alone. I-I won't...you don't need to worry about..."

She turned toward her bed and began to rifle through her things, hiding her embarrassment as heat scaled her neck to her cheeks.

He approached and shocked her by embracing her from behind, resting his chin on her shoulder. He gently slid his hands down her sides and settled them where her waist met her hips. His chest pressed lightly against her, and his heart thrummed into her back. Sweet breath escaped with his words. "If you wish to dissolve the union before a year, once Brantingham is no longer a threat, I'd understand."

She nodded, wordless. He kissed her cheek, then, boldly, her neck. His lips delighted her skin with a riot of gooseflesh on a ticklish spot behind her ear. Energy coursed to her toes and she released an unladylike moan-sigh.

"Ahem."

She jumped in Domhnall's embrace and whirled out of his arms to find the steward standing in the doorway, his regard lowered and his larger ears tinged pink on the tips. "Sir. All is set." He coughed, cupped a hand to his mouth, and cleared his throat. "My lady," he added.

My. Lady.

A commoner no more? A lowly nobody, an English peasant no more. She hadn't wanted nor planned for this.

Oh, but you did, an evil voice within chided her.

She must have looked at Domhnall blankly.

"We'll be there in a moment, Cawley. Inform my father."

The man bowed and left.

"Now?" Her legs would not move. The tender moment, the pleasure of his comforting hands upon her waist, his heated breath upon her skin, disappeared. "Uncle Os has already left for Edinburgh."

"He'll return in a month. Besides, we're only declaring intention, like I told you. At any point you may dissolve it. If it comes to the point of the marriage ceremony," he said, thoroughly studying her for—what? fear? assurance? attraction?— "he'll be here. The market ends in a few days. They moved the handfasting ceremony up to today, for us. We need to do this now, so Brantingham sees that you are protected"

Was she the only one who saw the enormity in all this? Domhnall hardly seemed unsettled by it. Was this routine for him? Had he done it before? Mother Mary, this was practically marriage! Did nobody see that? The Church forbade divorce. At least in England.

Intentions. Contract by handshake. Marriage if they shared a bed. Was there a chance of turning back? *Word is everything in the Highlands*, Oswell had always told her.

Apparently, handshakes, too.

"Rose, rest assured. All will be fine. Once the Englishwoman sees the entire breadth of Clan Montgomerie and Clan MacCoinneach behind you, she'll leave. We can nullify the agreement any time. I promise you."

Nullify. Why did that option unnerve her just as much?

Because I want more.

"You've not met her. She won't relent."

Rosalie imagined Lady Brantingham and her pack of dogs—the dreadful soldiers who worked at her beck and call—circling the keep, waiting for the moment to catch her alone, unguarded. Certainly, there'd be ramifications if she were found dead. There was no undoing death. Even if Edrea were caught, it would be too late for Rosalie.

"She will. Life will call her away. All opponents eventually bore of the chase when something prosperous summons. She won't stay in Scotland long."

"What if she doesn't desist?"

"Then you have me, and us. The watchmen and clansmen will fight for you."

A rock fell to her stomach at his declaration. She whispered a prayer under her breath and played with her necklace. Now she was being taken in by another family, not by blood, but by union. The line was so thin, it would break if she blew upon it.

She thought about changing into a nicer gown. She owned none so her regular gown would suffice. She shrugged off her apron and draped it onto the bed...her bed. She quickly swiped fingers through her hair. There was nothing she could do about it. "Should I change into something finer?"

"You look bonnie to me. My mother can provide you with a few more gowns and such, too. I believe she is already speaking with her seamstress about it."

Heat stole her voice. She had a borrowed pair of Lady Deirdre's slippers already. Domhnall's eyes watched her with intrigue as she swapped her work shoes for the dainty slippers. He'd already seen her barefoot in the loch while they collected pebbles but his look upon her actions caused her fingers to tremble.

He wore his everyday outfit of simple tunic and hose, leather boots, and belt. His brushed, dark brown hair matched his eyes. He had a cleanly shaven face, staunch countenance, and looked devilishly handsome.

He approached again, grazed his fingers upon her chin. It sent ripples of warmth to join the rock expanding her stomach. "It will be all right. We'll do this together."

She nodded through a loud exhalation. She sank her hand into his, and they departed for the marketplace.

A roaring sensation blew through Domhnall's body. He tried to mask it around Rosalie, but disquietude revolted within him. A betrothal. He wasn't one to have second thoughts, so a betrothal was it. Marriage came next. He would say his vows in a year, or whenever they all decided. Rosalie would be his wife, if she decided the same. If. This was the definition of madness. Some arrangements were made on far less though, he had to remind himself.

Too bad a betrothal concluded with a handshake. To feel her again, to cradle her in his arms, to brush his lips against hers, to push limits with intimate touches...

Nothing—so far—had resulted in a vision. His skin prickled with memories and flashes of warmth for her. Was she the one? His fated mate? Like his mother's visions of Alasdair? He'd not deny his feelings anymore. The Silver Veil had decided he could touch but one person, and he was grateful that person was Rosalie. She was the one.

She had a gift, too. He cared for her. Loved her?

The summer's breeze upset his hair, like fingers teasing his scalp, reminding him of the omniscient Wind. He fidgeted with the sword at his side, never parting from it. Especially not after the attacks on Rosalie. Consumed by the wheel of events in the past few days, he'd nearly forgotten about the criminals tormenting their village, stealing and setting things aflame. All he wanted—in this moment—was to kiss Rosalie, keep her close. Bring her to his bed.

Blazes, a year. Maybe.

Unless she returned the feeling. What was stopping them once they became promised to each other? They could seal their fates tonight if they wanted. He'd never force her to do a thing she didn't also yearn for though.

They made their way to the market center. Midday's sun shone brightly as cheery commoners, nobility, and clansmen gathered around the central stone, leaving space for the couples. He recognized three other couples ready to profess their love.

Unlike the hollowed stones in the story he'd told Rosalie about, this stone held its foundation in the history of the clan. It was the first marker for Glen Shiel, laid by his grandfather Simon, when the king had bestowed the glen officially upon their family after the Battle of Largs in 1263. It served as reminder of their heritage. White speckles and striations adorned the lichen-covered gray stone, smoothed from the oils of hands touching it for good luck.

The symbolism meant more to him than its superstition or history. One side held the carved Montgomerie motto: *Guard well.* MacCoinneach on the other: *I shine, not burn.* The irony of both mottos stirred him. He clenched his free hand at his side, upon his hilt. He would guard Rosalie to his death. He would honor his town, guard them as watchman and laird. He would shine, not burn... Alas, he hated any reference to fire. Could he be a shining light for his people?

With the union of both MacCoinneach and Montgomerie, his parents had considered renaming the clan into one unified surname: MacKenneth. It wasn't uncommon for names to change with time as clans merged. Great-great-grandfather Kenneth Lonn MacCoinneach, great-grandfather Alroy Kenneth MacCoinneach, and grandfather Simon Kenneth MacCoinneach all wanted the Kenneth lineage to live on. This was technically MacCoinneach land. The Montgomeries hailed from the south. With the name change, Father honored the first true lairds—Kenneth—of the glen. Such a change wasn't an easy task and would require permission from surrounding clans' elders, the glen's baron, and court.

Domhnall, descendant of the Kenneths, and the first Laird MacKenneth.

It sounded...too real. Pressure mounted in his chest with the responsibility and honor.

The crowd faded to a blur. Familiar faces greeted and nodded. Where was Hayden? Domhnall had ordered him to scour the perimeter of Dornie with the Donald clansmen. Father's negotiations with Laird MacDougall were at a standstill, so few of their clan were present this week. The accusation of wrongdoings had worsened the animosity between their clans. Laird MacDougall insisted his clan wasn't behind the thefts.

Pig manure. Domhnall would see about that.

He scanned the crowd for Lady Brantingham. There were too many faces and noises as the other couples found their places. His throat tightened, begging not another soul to touch him. Rosalie was his anchor. The Wind had stopped and was replaced by a frightening but seductive calm.

As long as his arm was within hers, all was tranquil. No voices, no visions. When he touched her, all was...right.

Had he the courage to test it? Could he touch another person while not linked with her? But then he remembered Kyla and her touch. No. Not yet.

The true test rested in taking his union with Rosalie deeper when the time came. Meeting her had emboldened him to test fate. Kisses and handholding were one thing...but what would happen when their flesh joined?

His ego wanted to protect her. Did he love her? Was this love?

Was he using her for selfish gain?

Here he was, stating intentions he would never rescind.

The couples smiled at him, all dressed in their finest, their youthful faces brimming with adoration. John and Marrie, a crofter and common lass. Comroy, another watchman, and his sweetheart, Elsbeth. Lastly, two Clan Donald folk. He, a laird's son, among the many. Would he be a just laird to them?

His path lay before him and around him. As he beheld Rosalie, his heart unleashed a rapid set of palpitations.

He was ready. For any and all.

His parents stood on either side of the stone. One unreadable and the other glowing with happiness. Their young priest, always a picture of serenity and hope, stood off to the side. Rosalie froze in her steps beside him, only paces from the central clan stone. Stock still. "Rose?" he whispered. Had she changed her mind? "If you—" He followed her wide-eyed gaze.

A noblewoman pushed through the crowd, elbowing others out of her way. Two strapping soldiers, fully decked in armor and weapons, flanked either side of the likes of Lady Edrea Brantingham, he'd guess. They eyed Rosalie like she was a bug to be squashed. He clenched his hand into a painful fist around the sword's hilt and tightened his looped arm within Rosalie's. He gave the menacing and unshaven soldiers a daring look. *Make your move, you beasts.*

They smirked. Her goons were outnumbered twenty-fold by all the men in attendance armed with weapons. Clansmen—MacCoinneach, Donald, Mathieson, even a few of Clan MacDougall—soldiers, watchmen, crofters.

A few wrinkles edged the lady's shockingly blue eyes, almost crystalline in their color. She was womanly figured and stunning, clad in a low-cut, deep burgundy gown, embellished with lace and buttons, and her golden-brown hair was swept into an elaborate plait. Pearls dangled from her ears, neck, and lace hairnet.

A shudder rippled through him as he caught her evil glare. Later, he'd ask his mother about the woman's lifeblood since his parents had met with Lady Brantingham during Aileana's *cèilidh.* He could almost sense it himself. Cold slapped him in his face. He blinked and blue-white flashed beneath his eyelids. He glanced at his mother. In unspoken agreement, he gave her permission to read his emotions with a nod. Confirmation flickered in her all-knowing eyes.

There'd be no waiting if this malicious woman was about.

Let her attend! Let her see Rosalie fall under their protection. Brantingham would be gone soon enough.

Hayden materialized from behind a mob of people and strode to Domhnall with a harried breath. He whispered, "Sorry I'm late. You know I'm always punctual. I left Guthrie and Aiden to watch the borders because Comroy would be with his lass and you with Rosalie. The Donalds are watching the western and northern flanks, Domhnall. All is well."

The coils in Domhnall's back relaxed with his friend nearby. He broke his stare at Brantingham, who was paces away, and said to Hayden, "Keep an eye on that woman for me." Hayden followed his look. "I'll tell you more later. Follow her. Tell me where she goes after the handfasting."

Hayden nodded. "Aye." His own fingers danced on his sword's sheath.

Rosalie whispered, finally emerging from her frozen stance, "Domhnall. If I leave, trouble leaves with me." Her lower lip trembled. For the entire route to the stone she had been silent, perhaps fear surmounting all other emotions. Her voice was pensive, unlike her.

It was not proper to kiss her, not here, and not until they were handfasted. But he wanted to melt her fears with a touch. Instead, he whispered, "You're safe with me. Always, Rose. All will be well. Say the word, and we end it all. But if we bow out, I can't promise full protection of the clan. My power is limited without them."

He tried to sound convincing. Instead he came off as a dastard. Or worse, condescending. He inhaled, the sharpness of grassy herbs appeasing him. She smelled floral and green from her time in the gardens. His mother may have given her an herbal-infused oil for her hair, too. The desire to smell her skin in all her fine womanly places rose from within. He cleared his throat. "Should we call it off? Say the word. I can protect you another way. You will have my sword. I don't want to see you fall to harm. It's your decision, Rose." He squeezed her elbow. All he had were words and promises.

Round, swelling eyes captured his. He could not read her. He would not seek the help of his mother, as easy as it would be. He would not invade Rosalie's thoughts. He'd contributed to the mess. She nibbled a pink lip, color filling her cheeks.

"Rose...please. I need you to say something. Yes or no?"

"Let's proceed." A timid smile broke through the squall on her face and the heaviness in his chest fluttered away.

They moved through the motions, his arm linked in hers, the other couples also standing around the clan stone, all repeating the words on their turn. The priest officiated, with joyful approval, speaking in both English and Gaelic. First, he explained the tradition of handfasting, but sounds whirred in Domhnall's ears and he tuned it out. Sweat beaded on his forehead as the sun bore down through a cloudless summer sky.

Rosalie stood erect, not moving a muscle, carefully listening to the words.

Intentions, declarations, God, honor...the words glided off the priest's tongue.

"On this day, I, Domhnall Alasdair Kenneth Montgomerie, give my consent, plight thee my troth, and intend on one year hence to be married before our God in the Church, under His holy ordinance."

Rosalie spoke in crisp, clear words: "On this day, I, Rosalie Threston, give my consent, plight thee my troth, and intend on one year hence to be married before our God in the Church, under His holy ordinance."

The other couples repeated their vows.

The priest nodded toward the grouped parents, who had surrounded the clan stone. They all came forth, twine in hands, and tied it around their respective children's interlocked right hands. Domhnall's palm grew slick in Rosalie's as his father approached and tied the twine. Rosalie squeezed his hand, the squeeze of reassurance. They shared a look. Her eyes reflected trust, her smile sincerity, and her posture unwavering independence.

He blushed under his mother's wise eyes and maternal beam. He was touching another person. Here he was. Not a flash of dark, no curtain of death. Just his future bride glowing in an amber sun. Bronze and honey highlights swung in Rosalie's long hair as a breeze swirled. Strays caught in her mouth, and she shoved them aside with her free hand. Pink blossomed in her cheeks. She was radiant and he felt fate's blessing in that moment.

First up, they stepped toward the clan stone and flanked it, hands joined, arms spread across the formidable, robust symbol of their clan. The priest hovered his hand over theirs and stated the unifying phrase. Together, Domhnall and Rosalie repeated, "Our hands we bind, a symbol of our love entwined. Blessed be our union."

The other couples repeated the words and movement.

Finally, the priest grinned as if Holy God stood among them. He raised his hands in emphasis. A bird squawked, and the wind blew harder. "One may be overpowered; two can defend themselves. A cord of three strands is not quickly broken."

Domhnall was familiar with the verse from the Bible, for he'd heard it recited during each handfasting ceremony.

Then it was done.

His father added, in a deep and commanding voice, "Two are strong. A clan is stronger. We are all bonded by blood and marriage. May God bless these unions. May our clans provide for, nurture, and *protect* these couples." He passed a glance over everyone, repeating the clans' mottos, "Guard well. Shine, not burn."

Domhnall watched his father's subtle look that paused a moment longer upon Lady Brantingham. His father had never added the last part before.

Protect.

Yes. With his body and sword, Domhnall would protect Rosalie.

The lady blinked, pursed her lips, and lifted her chin.

Good. Let the witch squirm.

And then it was done.

The couples unfastened their twined hands and paraded through the merry crowd, exuding contentment and eagerness of what would come in the next year. A flutter of hopeful expectation danced in his chest. For once, he didn't cringe—too awfully—at his proximity to the people. Many would head off to family homes for celebrations.

His parents scooped Rosalie into an embrace, and Hayden gave Domhnall a sideways look with a flick of his head, and then stepped aside with him, cognizant of Domhnall's need for protective space. How long had it been since he and Hayden shared an embrace? A wrestle in the field? Or hand-to-hand combat in training? Years. Domhnall missed the touch of friendship as much as he yearned for the intimacy of a woman's touch.

"Domhnall, what am I to do about—" Hayden began.

"Sir Montgomerie," Lady Brantingham interrupted. Her soldiers were close behind.

She laid a hand on Hayden's forearm and squeezed past him.

Domhnall bowed. "Lady Brantingham. I hope you enjoyed the festivities with us this week. Dornie is far from Northumberland. You've come during one of our busiest weeks of the summer."

She wrinkled her nose, an uncomplimentary look for her lovely features. It gave her the air of a spoiled five-year-old lass told she could not have a golden trinket. He almost chuckled.

"Let's not pretend about why I'm here. Your heathen ceremonial protection doesn't mean anything..." She flourished a hand for him to insinuate her meaning. With a puff of her chest, her bosom heaved. The longest gold chain circling her lengthy neck, with a teal tear-drop pendant, dropped right in between her breasts. "Laws are different in England, and she is an English peasant."

Heat flared off Hayden, and his friend's fingers danced on his sheath while he shuffled his feet. A deep scowl ridged in his forehead.

Domhnall whispered, "*Socair ort, a bhràthair.*" *Easy there, stand down, brother.*

She unleashed a wicked snigger and twisted a slender finger on her necklace. "You won't be able to protect her all the time." She flashed a prickly smile at both. "I've heard miscreants are troubling your home, Sir Montgomerie. It is a shame the watchmen can't protect their own town."

She portrayed the image of refined beauty, but the snide voice and her threats made her downright foul. He pitied her husband.

A less honorable man would spit at her insult. His heart raced, but his spirit was only momentarily bruised. He'd not give her ploy any power.

She continued. "What watchman is afraid of fire, too? The life and breath of the men who patrol the streets? Next you'll tell me it's because of an incident with a dragon." The soldiers at her sides smirked.

Curse the whispers among the townsfolk.

He would not let her get to him.

She whispered, venomous, "Or an accident years ago."

His palpitating heart skipped a beat, then tightened like a fist. It might have burst from his chest if he hadn't seen Rosalie, his anchor, his mystical answer— beginning to make her way through the crowd toward him, unaware of whom he was speaking with. Others greeted Rosalie, shook her hand, and welcomed her with joy. She glowed at each stop, disappearing into embraces.

He bowed, his tongue fighting for words. "Good day, Lady Brantingham. May your journey home be safe."

He turned around to greet his betrothed, a forced smile on his face, while passing Hayden "the look." His friend knew. *Follow the lady. Get information. Do not let her out of your sight.* Hayden would always have his back.

Then, he took Rosalie's awaiting arm in his before she saw Lady Brantingham again, and they strode to the keep.

CHAPTER TWELVE

T he celebration in the hall, though not as grand as Aileana's *cèilidh*, was lively and crowded. Guests chatted and danced, minstrels belted harmonious tunes, and servants weaved through crowds with platters of fragrant food. Energy vibrated among attendees. Another *cèilidh*. Domhnall wanted Rosalie for himself, to abscond to an alcove with her and test his physical limits, but his sister, cousins, mother, and the other ladies had pounced upon her, surrounding her with preening, titters, and hand gestures.

He covered an indulgent grin on his face, his chest tight with something unfamiliar, something he couldn't name. He resigned himself to engaging in the usual political and local conversations with the men. Kendrick hovered near, observant and sipping his wine. When the topic turned to the thefts and fire, Domhnall's pulse flared. There was no mention of Oswell or Rosalie.

No need to rouse the others about that situation.

Blame wasn't placed upon him, but unrest boiled in the group. Something had to be done, they all said. Laird Donald offered more men to add to the Watch. Others asked: How had their home become a place where people were beginning to fear for their safety?

An hour later, and not needing to feign fatigue, Domhnall broke free from another argument about current crop demands in the glen and eyed his escape to the kitchen. Kyla nearly brushed into him, awkwardly managing a pitcher and goblets in her hands. He grabbed a goblet before its crash. Pink-cheeked from the heat of the crowded room, she blew a wisp of cinnamon-red hair from her face. "Och. Sir, thank ye kindly."

"Never a bother." He tried to smile despite her unnerving presence. With his declaration to Rosalie, Kyla would give up on the chase. A bonnie lass, she'd make a lovely wife to a crofter or soldier. She damn well better not touch him again. He stepped back, noticeably.

She dropped her look. "Sir, I-I..."

He tried to not cringe. *Blazes, lass. Leave me be.*

She resettled the goblets in her arms and wrestled with the half-full pitcher. She chewed on her lip and rocked in place, then flung a brief glance around them, it landing on Hayden and the men in the corner. "Sir, if ye have a moment..."

An ache from consuming too much spiced wine made his head heavy, his mind confused. "Kyla, I'm promised to Rose now. You'll make a fetching wife to—"

She shook her head, and her cheeks nearly matched the color of her hair. "Och, no, sir. 'Tis not that." She fussed with the pitcher, nestling it upon her hip.

Her demeanor aroused his suspicion. Kyla was never short on words, nor looks.

He began to take the pitcher from her to help carry it to the kitchen.

"Nay, I mean...och..." She heaved, her bosom lifting with emphasis. She shuffled a step—away from him. "I need—need to tell ye something. In private. About—"

She was cut off. Hayden appeared, out of nowhere, nearly causing Domhnall's bladder to empty. Through all these years, he had never grown used to his friend's stealth. Hadn't Hayden just been in the corner? "By the—Hayden, you must stop sneaking up on me."

He shrugged, smugly. "Domhnall, we should talk." Hayden tossed Kyla a brief, almost annoyed, look.

She curtsied and departed, mouthing to Domhnall, "Later."

He needed to excuse himself soon. Too much wine with not enough food made him feel woozy. "Come." He directed Hayden toward a quieter corner.

Hours passed. The world spun. Talking, questions, movements, sounds, smells. Rosalie prospered among the energy of busy places, but tonight she wanted one thing.

Domhnall leaned against a wall in the corner, talking with other men. Earlier she'd seen him with Kyla, and she found herself surprised when jealousy clenched her jaw.

He caught her gaze. His dark eyes flashed a nearly sensual look. Or was it one of exhaustion? Courting was an unfamiliar place for her. She read peoples' hands and body stance, not eyes. At least, not gazes like *that*. A smile curled the corners of her lips. He reciprocated with a grin that broke all her resolve. That definitely was not exhaustion.

A group of ladies surrounded her. Rosalie was skilled in her façade, but she wanted nothing more than to escape, find a quiet spot, rest, and be with Domhnall. She fanned herself and nodded and answered yet another question from the flock.

She wanted to touch Domhnall again. To slip her hand into his, hot meeting cold. She wondered why his hands were always cold. Except for during the handfasting, when his palm had been slicked with sweat.

They were now promised to each other. Her heart had not ceased racing since saying her words of declaration. Instead of reluctance or dread, despite having seen Lady Brantingham in the crowded marketplace to watch the ceremony, joy had sung through her veins. Domhnall wanted her. Perhaps she, too, wanted to be his. Now. Forever?

The past few weeks had been a whirlwind of highs, lows, and uncertainties. She had never spoken to this many people in one day, and the welcome reception fulfilled a longing she'd wanted her entire life—to be one of them. To belong. The cynic within triggered alarm bells. She couldn't allow herself to get too close to any of them. As quickly as they'd come into her life—parents, sisters, cousins—they could be snatched away. Life held no guarantees.

Besides, she didn't truly belong here. Anywhere. Her time here was temporary.

Remember that, Rose.

She excused herself from a droning conversation with another cousin who rambled on about a scandal in court—and sought refuge where she knew she belonged. She weaved through the dancing crowd to the kitchen, her slippered toes tapping all the way. She wished Domhnall had asked her to dance. She passed him a suggestive arch of the eyebrow. He gave a shrug of acquiescence, captured by the people around him in deep manly discussion. She wanted a moment alone anyway before they considered broaching the next step in their union.

Dear God, she was betrothed to the heir of Eilean Donan, future Laird of Glen Shiel. She wondered why Edrea had not warned the laird about Rosalie's sham or tried to soil her reputation or tell them the truth. Maybe she had, but the laird and lady didn't believe her? A passing look to Lady Montgomerie showed a woman as calm and exquisite as ever.

Rosalie dove through the kitchen doorway, her steps frantic, her breathing rapid. She hushed the pessimist in her mind. *Take each day.* One foot in front of the other. Approach each challenge life flung at her. She would do the same here. Prudence was her middle name, or so Oswell liked to claim, after he once attended Mass where they discussed the cardinal and heavenly virtues.

A part of her wanted to sneak to the stable and check on her cats. Oswell had left them with Ewan. It was a foolish idea to check on them with Lady Brantingham's soldiers about. Perhaps she could do so in the morning with Domhnall. For now, the castle was her fortress. Even if someone from within had tainted her drink. Domhnall had supervised all her meals' preparation since then.

A draft of air washed over her in the busy kitchen as she allowed her mind and body to settle. She ducked into the empty pantry behind the kitchen. The scent of yeast and herbs loosened tight muscles in her neck. The room, sedate and homey, grounded her. It brought her to where she felt best. Alone with menial tasks. She almost wanted to pick up a utensil and do...something. Knead bread, work the energy in her fingertips begging to be released. She blinked, hit by a surge of dizziness.

She still wasn't quite herself after the attack and drink incident. She gripped a table. Mayhap it was from all the energy in the hall tonight. She'd lost count on fifty people in attendance. Perhaps a hundred? She fanned herself to catch her breath, clearing spots of blue and yellow from her vision.

A whimper emerged from the hallway leading to the servants' sleeping quarters. Was someone hurt? She crept from the pantry, her feet achy and swollen from the tight slippers. How could women work in such fancy things all day?

Alas, ladies didn't work. They sat, socialized, sewed, and talked. However, Lady Montgomerie and Aileana proved otherwise. She loved that about them.

She heard a few moans, then a shuffle from down the hallway. A giggle? Or was it a cry? She grabbed an empty candlestick from the table. Why were they here? They belonged in the kitchen with the other decorative settings. They were probably pushed aside in the hurried frenzy before the *cèilidh*. Her fingers fell upon the rough amber stones embedded in the enameled base. It was an eye-catching candlestick and would get a lovely sum in market. Mother Mary, her mind was always working, wasn't it?

Scruples more than curiosity drew her light-footed down the hall, heavy candlestick in hands. Ready to meet an opponent. She'd heard stories of scoundrels in the dark, snaking halls of castles, attacking women in a corner. During her employment in castles in England, she always stuck by her aunt or uncle or the other servants when venturing from the kitchen or a bedchamber or the gardens. She doubted Eilean Donan was a place filled with drunken, misbehaving men though. Hmm. The town was flooded with visitors. Who knew if anyone lurked in the hallway. Besides, somebody had attacked her. Poisoned her. The keep and its grounds were not safe. Trepidation lingered.

She paused and listened, ready to bolt. She should get help from the kitchen. This was not her place.

But then a throaty moan emerged with Gaelic-sounding murmurings of a man. Quickly followed by a giggle from a woman. Yes, a giggle. One peek and she'd be gone to be certain this was just some consensual merriment…

The steward had already lit the sconces in the hallway for the evening. A man and woman hid, partly down the hall, among shadows.

The man had her shoved up against the wall near the alcove. She watched for only a moment, heat flooding her cheeks at her audacity. She wanted to be certain the woman was not being harmed.

Kyla's face came into view, her trademark red hair tousled about her shoulders and across her forehead. She nipped on the man's ears. Kissed his neck. He dipped his head, burying it in her half-unlaced bodice, her breasts spilling over. He squeezed both eagerly. He lifted her skirt with frantic hands and grunted in hungry lust as he pinned her against the wall. His hands skimmed all of her: arms, breasts, hips, and then finally slipping between her legs.

"Och, Hayden..." Kyla cooed as they rubbed against each other. He cupped her bottom and lifted her, drawing her deeper into the alcove and out of Rosalie's field of vision.

Rosalie dropped back behind the corner. She chided her racing heart. With all the events of today, she thought her heart might stop and leave her dead on the floor. Two enamored people in a passionate—and very intimate—embrace, that's all she saw. Aileana had said her interest in Hayden had waned. Perhaps he sought solace with Kyla? Rosalie prayed he didn't leave Kyla with child.

She scurried to the kitchen, overwhelmed with what she'd witnessed. They were adults, and if they chose to rut like animals in the hallway, she wasn't one to stop them.

The kitchen was empty—momentarily, as servants were still coming and going. She nearly collided with Domhnall at the arched entrance on her way back out.

"Rose," he said, grabbing her arms to steady her. His touches had become expected, and she'd forgotten how much he'd avoided her initially.

"Domhnall," she breathed, clutching the candlestick to her chest.

"What's wrong?" He eyed the candlestick, then her. His set jaw and pressed lips hinted of suspicion.

She adjusted her posture with his help and avoided his gaze, placing the candlestick upon the table. "I needed to escape the crowds." She summoned a smile.

He beheld her a moment, then said with a gentle chuckle, "Me, too. Let's make our escape?"

She nodded, too shocked to speak. Too ready to flee the scene behind her.

He was about to take her the back way, past Kyla and Hayden. She froze in her steps.

"Shouldn't we be supervised?"

"Nay." He continued, leading her toward the hallway.

Think, Rose, think. "It's dark in the passageway, even with the sconces, and I saw a man and woman, er..."

"Och, I see. We can dash through the hall. Maybe skirt the walls, avoid well-meaning family." He full-on smirked, and she gloried in the eagerness in his face. An easygoing glint appeared in his eyes. "Don't make eye contact, and they may not stop us." He laughed to himself.

She wondered how much wine he'd consumed. Regardless of the rules of their betrothal, she wanted to kiss him. Kisses were allowed, right? Reminded of what she had seen in the hallway between Kyla and Hayden, her insides throbbed and she felt a rush of heat with thoughts of her and Domhnall doing such a thing. Her bedchamber was directly beside Domhnall's.

They could steal a kiss or two, couldn't they?

She almost crossed herself with such thoughts. What would people think of her? What would Domhnall think? With their hands linked, his ever-present cold a strange comfort, they bypassed the throng in the middle of the hall, only stopped once by an inebriated distant relative visiting from Inverness asking Domhnall a question in a stuttering blather. They dodged, weaved, and ran across the hall, her heart beating to the quickening pace of her steps.

They made it upstairs and flopped upon her bed, full of laughs. She laid a hand across her chest, as hiccups escaped.

"I've never had to d-d-do—" A hiccup. She covered her mouth and laughed. "—something like that."

"I've mastered the skill."

"What? Evading?" Bubbles rose in her throat. She held her breath to suppress them and rubbed a stitch in her side.

Laughter danced in his eyes, but they sobered. "It's why I work the Watch."

She sat up. "What do you mean?"

"I enjoy the silence and darkness of night. I like being alone. Avoiding."

She hiccupped as her heartbeat settled. "I'm alone a lot. Not by choice."

He sat beside her but didn't make a move to stand or leave space between them. Her chamber door remained open after all, and boisterous music drifted up the stairwells to her room—the two guests of honor no longer in attendance.

"Why do you like to be alone?" She wiggled closer to him, their hands no longer linked, but hips intimately close.

"Why do you move so much?" His eyes clung to hers, imploring. "Is it for the markets or did you come to Scotland because of Lady Brantingham?"

She knotted her hands together in her lap but found solace in his proximity. "It's what we've always done. Os's work requires us to move. And yes, because of her."

"Not anymore." He threaded a hand through hers. He cradled one finger and ran a thumb over the mounts, sending shivers through her entire body. Then he moved on to the next finger. His gaze studied her palm as he caressed each finger methodically. His fingertips were like silk, a fine fabric she'd only felt in her hands when mending a gown for a lady of a keep. Her own hands held a heightened sense of touch memory, and Domhnall's touch upon hers planted its permanent spot in her mind. She'd be able to feel it with her eyes closed.

She pleaded for temperance, the cardinal virtue controlling thoughts of flesh, of sensuous appetite, to rein her fantasies in. Perhaps it was the music, the intrusion in the kitchen hallway, or the quick escape stirring her. Warmth swelled in her chest. Below the tight confines of her bodice, her nipples tingled. *Was this desire?* She'd once had a minor infatuation with the blacksmith's son, in Brumleye long ago. A stolen and chaste kiss under the oak tree. Then her family had moved on. That kiss had been nothing like the one she shared with Domhnall. And she wanted more. Many more.

She was here. In one place. She seized the moment and leaned into Domhnall, tentatively kissing his lips. He sidled closer, wrapping his arms around her. His lips touched hers in a whisper. An unexpected yielding groan escaped her throat. He took her bottom lip into his. Inexperienced, but letting nature—and not the cardinal virtues—guide her, she parted her lips, and savored his taste. Burgundy wine, spices from the sup's fowl, and...a new hunger. She craved his strokes. He gently deepened the kiss with his tongue.

He danced fingertips down her spine, erupting tingles along her skin. He lifted one of her hands that rested in her lap, unsure what to do with themselves after his sensual stroking of each mount and tip. He planted her hand upon his cheek. He retreated briefly, his breathing uneven. "I love your hands on me."

And I, yours. She rubbed his cheek with her thumb, then traced her fingers along the edge of his chin. She stroked a spot behind his ear, where his thick hair curled. Twirling his hair in her finger, she then caressed the nape of his neck.

"Nobody's touched me in so long," he whispered, coarsely.

She emerged from a heady haze. "Why?" She kissed his chin and shifted but did not retreat. "Why are you afraid of touch?" She knew the answer already but needed his confirmation.

"I don't hide it well, do I?"

"No."

He exhaled. "It's a long story."

"I'll listen."

He leaned in, kissed her cheeks once more...as light as the wind. "You'll think it daft."

A hundred ideas floated through her head, but all came back to her original deduction. Touch triggered his visions, even though her rational side still fought believing in such a magical ability. Being healed by the lady of the keep had not just been from that tincture though, her irrational side refuted. Lady Montgomerie had accessed a greater power and healed her with touch, so why couldn't

Domhnall be a true Seer? "I believe a lot of things. My mind is open." And for once, she quieted the rational voice within, and believed.

He drew back, to her chagrin. "I couldn't touch anyone until you came along."

Instead of asking "why" again, though burdened with a cloud of confusion, she waited patiently.

He played with her fingers, compulsively. She didn't mind. She had her own compulsions, too. Sorting, numbers and calculations, orderliness, refusing to unpack. Lies. That wasn't a compulsion, was it? More like survival. Her job had become her undoing.

"I've told you about my gift. The gifts run in my family's blood. You've experienced my mother's healing, and she has the gift of feeling into a person's being, their lifeblood, like I said." He paused. His gaze lay focused on her hands.

"What an amazing ability."

"I am a Seer, but unlike you, my visions stopped years ago. I believe touch sparked them. I stopped touching, and they ceased."

Nausea crept up her throat but she had to ask. "What did you see? In your visions?"

He shot a look at her, frowned, then returned to her hands. "Death. So much of it. The future. It grew distorted. I hear—heard—things, too. Voices. Warnings."

He heard things, too? Her heart hammered. "You stopped touching people to make the visions and voices disappear?"

He stilled. "Does touch cause them for you, too? Is that why you read palms?"

Mother Mary, his eyes beseeched her. His gaze was a poker through her heart. She chewed a lip. "No." She quickly added, "I don't always need to touch. I read the palms. They speak to me." Was that even a partial truth? By God, did she fool herself these days? To tell lies for so long she believed them. Wasn't that a sign of illness of the mind? People were thrown into prison for such ramblings.

His forehead creased with skepticism. "You hear things?"

"Not exactly."

His voice thickened, clearly frustrated with her vague answers. "My mother thinks I was predestined to find you." He slid a hand on her thigh. His hand was no longer cold, and heat warmed her leg through the layers of gown and shift.

Damn all the cardinal virtues tonight.

"Predestined?"

He shrugged. "I've blocked the visions for years. I've never seen you. But I've seen...oh, you'll think it—"

"I won't."

"I saw golden flowers, yellow roses."

She inhaled sharply. *Holy Mother of God.* "Me?"

He shrugged. "You." He sat in a long silence, then gave an audible swallow. "The visions became corrupt, drenched in blood and pain...and they misled me. I couldn't tell fact from fabrication, and when I tried to act on the premonitions, bad things happened. I was wrong. I tried to save people and couldn't stop fate. Only once, when Lanie was a bairn, did I save someone. I'd told my mother, and she was able to act, to save her life. After then, the Wind, or as you call it, air, lied to and teased me. Touch triggered chaos in my mind." Tiny tears welled in the corners of his eyes.

The Wind? The air. What she'd seen in his palms. He believed the wind spoke to him and showed visions of the future. Had she betrothed herself to somebody more delusional than her aunt? He believed what he was saying. But, did she? "Do you want to share with me about them?"

He shook his head. "Not now."

She recalled the Ancients' books. Fire for Feelers. Water for Healers. She'd learned that much from them. Wind for Seers. Interesting. Perplexing. Spellbinding...

"I stopped touching people years ago."

Her heart ached, shifting from doubting to believing in a moment. He was not daft. This was real to him. He'd suffered for so long. Not a hug from his parents? The kiss of a young love? A tap on the shoulder from his best friend?

He said, "Until you."

"I don't cause the visions?" Her pulse quickened.

He answered by capturing her lips. He said, hot, and heavy, "No. I'm free from the shackles when I'm with you. And though our ways may differ, I believe it is the Sight that connects us."

Oh my God, but she had no true Sight! She voiced the obvious, at least to her. "Maybe the visions all just left? It's been so long. They're gone. It can't be me. Like you said, you blocked them. You stopped touching and stopped seeing. Could this ability leave a person? For good?"

He scrubbed a hand through his thick hair. "No. I-I ran into Kyla the same day you were found in the garden. She touched my arm by accident. Another vision came to me. It's like they were dormant. Waiting. Waiting for me to touch another person." The flames of anguish and anger laced his usually tepid tone.

She fought the trembles, sensing there was far more to this confession. She took his hands into hers. She, too, couldn't help herself. Their connection was unlike anything she'd experienced. Maybe she was naïve, foolish. She'd met many people in her years. She read people. Too well. People lied all the time. Domhnall was telling the truth.

"It must be our shared ability," he said, firmly now.

Her hope dropped like a heavy stone to the bottom of a bucket with a thud. "Perhaps," she said in a feeble croak. It was all she had. One moment, laughing and reveling in the moment, the next...the conversation soured.

He ran his hand through the lengths of her locks. Her scalp prickled. *Do you want to...stay with me, tonight?* Instead of saying that, she said, "You should leave. Someone could come."

He released her, and she was instantly cold. "Aye. I should."

"What lies ahead for us? I mean, for tomorrow?"

"More writing and reading? I've found a book in the library you'd like."

"Lovely."

He gave her one more peck on the mouth, brief but meaningful. Her lips hummed. She wanted to taste him. She loved learning but she loved touching Domhnall Montgomerie more.

"We can do whatever we want."

How she wished it were true.

CHAPTER THIRTEEN

After showing Rosalie a book written by Grandfather on number calculations and a ledger on information about the land, town, farming, and fee collections, Domhnall moved on to the books of the Ancients again, more for him than her. Could they figure out this puzzle together?

"Is it awful that I'm more fascinated by the drawings than the words?" Rosalie repeated with a full smile, tracing the emblem on the book of Eir, the goddess of healing and mercy. A metal fish adorned the leather-bound book.

"Would it be awful if I feel the same?" he said with a smirk. He kissed her cheek. She leaned in closer to him. "They've sadly served as doorstop more than education. I was..."

"Avoiding," she finished.

"Aye."

"The covers alone are beautiful and speak to a person." She traced the metal emblems. The flame, the fish, the tree...

"They're impressive stories," he agreed.

"Most stories are based in fact," she said. "The Ancients are profound people."

She'd asked him ceaseless questions about the Ancients, Uist, and the Norse legends again today after the awakening conversation on their betrothal night, three days ago. He gladly told her all he knew. Years of listening to his mother and great uncle had filled him with knowledge. During the past few days, the weight in his chest lifted with Rosalie's presence. Lady Brantingham had been reported gone, per Hayden. No more thefts or assaults had occurred, but Rosalie remained under constant supervision regardless.

He spent much time with her, alone. Breathing, talking, touching.

"Tell me the truth...how am I doing?" She spread a parchment page in front of him with practiced letters, numbers, and words.

"Your letter formation is astute."

"My wrist is used to the precision, with painting, I suppose."

He took said wrist and kissed it. Delicate, fine. Irresistible.

They were alone in the library, sitting intimately close at the desk. He placed his finger over hers as she outlined the vowels. "Your touch is..." A release? Freeing?

"Hmm," she cooed. She leaned into him and kissed his cheek. "You're well when I do this? No visions?"

"Aye."

"And this?" She weaved their fingers together.

"The dark only joins me when I close my eyes to sleep." Excitement vibrated in his bones. Her lips were sweetened from the honeyed oat milk sitting beside them. He feather-touched her hair and the nape of her neck.

Fine sensations stimulated his fingertips at her body's gooseflesh response.

Daring, Domhnall.

Not once in a hundred small touches and dozens of wee kisses with her had a vision passed across his sight. He could go further. He *needed* to.

"Why don't you take me on your route?" Rosalie asked as they lazily ended the embrace a moment later.

"My route?"

"Where you go every night. Your watchman's route. I'm certain you have a memorized route, don't you? Or do you change it daily?"

"You know me already?"

She looped an arm through his. "I'm keen on judging character."

A short time later, they crossed the bridge to Dornie. They stepped over a sloshy puddle, breathing in the fresh air today after the night's rain, a welcome respite from the itchy heat and annoying midges. His walks used to be for work, but now they were for pleasure. Rosalie's company was a cleansing breath, a rejuvenation of his soul.

"Tell me about your sister Gracie."

"Aye, she's south in Dryburgh Abbey doing her summer's studies. Each child in our family visits the abbey for learnings. Latin, arithmetic, the arts, and enlightenment, I suppose. I especially enjoyed the silence and being left alone. Lots of ground to walk. Priests are quiet, aside from chants in worship."

"Naturally." She furrowed her forehead. "Enlightenment of?"

"A religious education. The priests spend most of their days copying holy texts, farming, trading, and praying. Our parents send us south to the abbey to learn about the divine path, to understand the Christian ways. We appreciate both upbringings...the ways of the Ancients and the ways of Christian Scots. Interestingly, it's my mother who insists we travel to the abbey in the summers. This is Gracie's first year there. You'd like her. She adores painting and drawing."

"I saw an abbey."

"Oh?"

"When we crossed the southern border. Jedburgh, Oswell called it. We didn't get to visit, but I saw it from the road. Looked magnificent poking from the trees. I'd like to see it one day."

"That's not too far south from Dryburgh. I could take you there sometime if you like, once..." He heaved a loud sigh.

She squeezed his arm with affection. "You will find the answers. Maybe it was the other clan, as you suggested to me. Most have traveled home, right? The incidents with me..." she said with a shrug. "Lady Brantingham's gone, too." Rosalie's steps seemed lighter.

He'd give her credit for her confidence. It was catching. Unrest had left his every thought since the day of the handfasting. He pointed for them to turn. "I usually take the same route each night—you were right—but lately I've been trying different paths, attempting to get into the mind of the troublemakers. To solve this bloody puzzle."

"You'll solve it," she repeated with gumption. "No Dour Domhnall." She poked him in the rib.

He chuckled heartily. "You've spent too much time with Lanie."

"She's a lovely woman."

"Ha! I've other words to describe her. Am I truly dour?"

She squeezed his arm. "No. Anything but. Dutiful. Diligent. Dedicated."

"My uncle suggested I keep it simple. Consider motive first. Find out the why before the who." He sighed. Always one to not let something go. He shook his head. Damn.

Rosalie humored him. "Motive to steal? I'd say for survival or need."

"Or revenge...for a wrongdoing," he added.

"Ah. Scots are notorious for revenge."

"How do you know all this?" he teased. He admired her half smile lifting one side of her face into her adorable dimple.

"Cow-stealing and such? Stealing lassies? I overheard many stories at our *cèilidh*. Scots are chatty folk."

Our. After the handfasting. A marriage of hearts. What about a union of bodies...? He thought of the parts of her he would like to kiss, the parts beneath her gown, the delicate skin behind her knee, her smooth stomach, those lovely breasts... Would she want to join him in his bedchamber one night? Perhaps, they could declare their marriage before God, and not wait the year... He cleared his throat. "Indeed. Cows. Grandda told stories of my great-uncle Desmond's love of his cows and how once he nearly lost half a herd to the MacDougalls."

"Your family's stories are rich. I love hearing them. I've always appreciated learning by listening and observing. Soon, I'll be able to read the stories." She glowed with the statement.

They continued around a bend, both drifting in reflective silence.

Guthrie ran toward them, red-faced, and winded. "Domhnall, sir. You're needed."

"What is it?"

He nodded to Rosalie. "Milady." Then to Domhnall. "Auld Mac an Bhaillidh, got in his cups again at the tavern. He's been tossing chairs and breaking things."

Domhnall released an audible sigh. At least it was manageable unrest. "Escort Rosalie to the keep, will you?"

Guthrie nodded, a thick patch of brown bangs dancing loose over his brow. "Aye, sir."

Domhnall planted an apologetic peck on her cheek. "I'll see you at supper."

The days passed with a new sense of normal, and a welcome feeling nestled within Domhnall.

Contentment.

Having finished his daily afternoon rounds, he headed straight for the gardens edging the keep's outer walls. His mother had insisted on placing the vegetable beds here years ago. The best sun, she'd stated. He hated how they were outside the keep's primary fortification.

He hoped to take Rosalie on another stroll along the pebbly shore of the loch to help her gather unique stones...and for him to gift her more kisses. Maybe quiz her on another grouping of words. Maybe convince her to have her next lesson in his bedchamber...

Whenever they were apart, his fingers yearned for her touch. Eagerness wrapped itself around his chest, squeezing the air from his lungs with anticipation. The more he touched her, the more he needed it, a force driving him out of his wits.

Every night after his rounds, he'd come upstairs and if the candlelight shone through beneath the door, he would knock, enter, and they'd talk. Kiss. Touch a lot. Always in her room, never his. He wished to bring her to his bed. Make her his wife for real. Forget waiting.

Kendrick approached from the kitchen entrance. "We must speak."

Domhnall pinched the bridge of his nose. He hesitated. Rosalie hovered beside his mother by the raspberry bushes, both of them dropping the summer crop into a wooden bucket at their feet. She was safe with Mother. He breathed easier, and Rosalie's demeanor had relaxed since Brantingham's departure.

"They've struck again."

Kendrick's blunt comment jolted Domhnall to the present. He turned to his uncle. "What do you mean? Thefts?" *Please don't be another attack.* His glance went to Rosalie.

"Aye."

"None of my men reported anything to me."

"Cawley reported it, just now. At first, he thought it was a mistake, with two celebrations going on over the past fortnight. Items get misplaced." He scratched his head, reluctance weighing his words. "A few wares went missing from the cupboards holding our pewter, silver,

and candlesticks, so he came to me. He drew up a list."
Kendrick tapped his pouch with emphasis.

"He looked everywhere?"

"Aye. None to be found."

"Someone stole from within the castle?" An attack in
the garden, tainted drink, and now thefts? All within the
formidable walls of Eilean Donan? He clenched a fist.

Kendrick nodded as they passed the corner tower and
strode through the portcullis into the inner courtyard.
Mud squished beneath their boots. He eyed the sky with
a heavy sigh.

Domhnall knew his look. Kendrick was already planning around the weather...whatever was on his master
planning list as constable. The market was in the middle
of teardown, and many peddlers and clansmen were on
their way home. The Watch's responsibilities included
assistance with disassembly, protection from elements,
and returning labor animals to carts. They were both
guards and helping hands. His uncle's mind must have
been moving at a gallop.

Kendrick scratched gray-brown stubble on his chin.
"I've not told your father. I thought we might handle this
first, quietly. He's got enough going on with the Mac-
Dougalls."

"What do you mean? He ruled them out as offenders. I
don't agree."

"Och, you didn't hear? Brodie MacDougall asked for
Aileana's hand."

"What? When?" He scrubbed a hand along his jaw. "She
turned down Hayden, but not Brodie? That red-headed,
freckled...er..." He held in his consternation. It would take
a man of equal temperament to woo his sister.

"The two have had a hidden courtship. After witnessing your handfasting, Brodie came to your father, asked for Aileana's hand in marriage. Might finally put an end to the rift between our clans." He smirked. "But with the secrecy of the courtship, Laird MacDougall was irate. He blames your father and Aileana for hiding it and left angry. In the wake of our accusations of thievery." He shook his head with disdain. "Your father departed this afternoon to make amends with the laird. The yearly tournament fast approaches, and it would be good to put this trouble all behind us." He lifted his gaze heavenward, crossed himself, then returned to the task at hand. He shuffled along, his steps keeping with Domhnall's as they made their way to the kitchen. "If it fares well, they will handfast during next year's summer market fair. Then a wedding shortly thereafter." Kendrick's sky-blue eyes gleamed with plotting. "We might have two weddings next year."

Domhnall sighed. He'd not been the best brother lately, ignoring his temperamental sister. He shifted back to the issue. "The list, Uncle." The thieves had stolen from within their keep!

Kendrick spoke from memory, and his voice drifted to a whisper as they ducked through the kitchen entrance. Nobody was about. Bread baked in the hearth, and something fragrant bubbled in a cauldron. "The amber-embellished candlesticks—the gift from King Alexander to your great-grandfather—your mother's emerald brooch and her gold heart necklace, your father's *sgian-dubh* with the garnet hilt, a set of pewter goblets and serving bowl, and other items from the kitchen we use for special occasions."

"That's a long list. And fine items that are worth the coin. You think it was a servant? Not the same group who's been causing hell in Dornie, who attacked Rosalie and her uncle?" He shook his head. "Bloody hell. Are we dealing with one person, a group, Lady Brantingham's men...or...or? This is a damn mess. I can't help but think it's my fault."

"How is it your fault? It falls upon me."

"It falls on all the Watch."

A shadow crossed Kendrick's face, instantly aging him. "I've faced evils far worse."

"I'm sorry."

Kendrick repeated from his recent conversations with Domhnall, "Never apologize. The past is the past. Lairds do not apologize. They make difficult choices and uphold justice." He added, "As do the Watch."

The past. His uncle certainly referred to the heathen Nordmen. The horrors unleashed upon the people of the isles had been unimaginable. The Ancients were gone. South or dead. He always wondered. "Are they all connected? I've considered motives like you suggested. I still believe the MacDougalls are behind the thefts. But Oswell and Rose...Brantingham had to be behind their assaults."

"I agree with your father. I don't think it's the Mac-Dougalls. I'm as perplexed as you. I agree about Brantingham, at least for Rosalie's attacks and maybe her uncle's, too."

Amber, emerald, garnet. Jewels could be sold or used into other jewelry. Silver and pewter and the like. All valuables. What was the motive? Coin?

"If not the MacDougalls, who?"

Kendrick shrugged. "It could be a thief among us, wishing for profit. We've had many travelers through the town lately. It doesn't explain the incidents prior to the market's arrival, however."

"What a stew. I feel like we're missing something. Something or someone connects them all."

"Aye."

Hayden rushed into the kitchen from the servants' hallway. "Domhnall!"

He spun around, and Hayden nearly collided with him. His friend skidded to a halt on the kitchen's stone floor. He held his hands up, shielding himself from Domhnall as if he were a flame and would burn his friend.

After all the caresses with Rosalie, Hayden's response irked him. "What now?" Domhnall snapped, his voice resonant.

Hayden didn't cower at the agitation in Domhnall's response. Green eyes, sharp and hooded, eerily placid, beheld his, nearly staring straight through him. No furrow in his brow, no alarm in his tone.

Dead. Calm.

Ice slivered down Domhnall's spine, and his fingers tingled, the blood draining.

"Kyla. She is dead."

Rosalie stretched and reclined in the pile of dry straw. Duo pawed at errant, crunchy pieces of straw as a late afternoon wind blew in through the stable's open doors. She released an "ahh" as she allowed the shadows of the stable to cool her. Sweat trickled down her back from laboring in the gardens with Lady Montgomerie today.

Trēs purred and curled in Rosalie's lap. She covered a yawn and whispered sweet nothings to him. It felt good helping in the gardens. It felt lovely to just relax here and feel the fruits of her labors. Her role as head kitchen cook had been passed on to Kyla, to her chagrin and Kyla's glee. The glare the red-headed woman had given her the morning after the handfasting ceremony was a look of daggers. Didn't she have Hayden's attention now?

"You're like my mother, Rose," Aileana said as she settled a saddle on her mare.

"Oh?" her voice croaked. What a comparison. Rays of the setting sun broke through the stable doorway.

Aileana flipped her hair, gathered it into a low knot, and plaited it with deft fingers. She pulled her cloak hood over her head. "Cats. My mother and her cats. She's always talking to them while she gardens. She likes you. Gracie will love your painting and crafting. Domhnall...adores all of you. He's far less dour this week. You're part of our family now, Rose."

One of them. Her heart rejoiced.

Aileana drew her horse outside and mounted it.

Rosalie stood and swiped loose straw from her skirt.

"None of Ma's lazy cats are keen on rat catching like your wee fellas," Aileana said with a fresh-faced smile. Duo meowed as if in response, then hopped into the straw pile, instantly burrowing in.

Duo was an energetic one. He caught the most rats of all the cats in her uncle's litters. Trēs was mischievous while Duo was productive.

Rosalie eyed Aileana. She wore men's work trews. "Where are you going? It's nearly sunset."

"Brodie returns home soon, so we thought we'd take a ride through the pass before nightfall." She winked at Rosalie. "Don't tell Domhnall. Though I doubt he'll notice." The horse pawed at the ground with its front hooves.

Rosalie's cheeks warmed. She waved a piece of straw at Trēs, who was snuggled neatly in her arms.

"Ye're the first lass to come along in a long, long time, Rose. He's fond of ye." Aileana clicked under her tongue. "Ta." She whipped the reins and was off in a heartbeat, grinning brazenly at Rosalie.

A brief moment passed as Rosalie waited for the stable master's return. After a quick transfer of the cats to their crate and assigned accommodations in the corner of the stable, she meandered to the keep wondering what interesting words Domhnall might teach her tonight. She almost blushed. There would be kisses, too.

Domhnall approached from across the bridge. The bleak frown on his face dampened her delight. She wrung her hands. "Something's wrong?"

He looped his arm through hers, their new normal, and guided her to the keep. "Aye," he said, winded. "I couldn't find you."

Hayden, Domhnall's great-uncle Kendrick, and Domhnall's other uncle, Crystoll, held equally taut faces of alarm when she passed through the portcullis. Several armed men encircled Kendrick, listening to orders.

"What happened?" she whispered. Domhnall drew her away from the gathering of nearly twenty men.

"There's been an accident—" He cursed under his breath. "There's been a death. A murder."

Her heart nearly stopped. "Wh-what? Who?" She pressed a hand to her lips, squelching the gasp. "L-lady Brantingham is gone." She tossed another look over her shoulder. The men, all armed, scrambled in orderly fashion to various spots along the wall, the bridge, outside the bailey, to the battlements, and into town. A few, who wore armor, clinked in their deep strides. All departed briskly, ready for action.

"You must stay inside. Stay with my mother. One of our guards will be with you two at all times."

She tripped. Curse the fancy slippers she wore today instead of her work shoes! He almost didn't catch her this time. She righted herself.

"Are we in danger? Who, oh my God, who, Domhnall?" She hated the squeak in her voice. Somebody was dead.

"Kyla."

She released a breath. "Do you think Lady—?"

They hurried through a tall, vaulted doorway into the hall, and he kept on walking. "No. She left days ago. Somebody else did this."

"Why would anyone want to kill Kyla?" She added, "Maybe Lady Brantingham is not really gone."

The stone walls passed in a blur, sconces flickered, her head reeled. He nearly dropped her in the solar without another word. A guard was posted at the door. Lady Montgomerie sat within, looking inward and blinking rapidly.

"Wait, Domhnall," she tried, her hand on his arm.

He beheld her gaze but pulled away and dragged his steps from her.

"She, uh, where? Why?" she asked, her voice shaky.

His usually calm countenance twisted into a dark scowl. Quakes rippled in her stomach. This wasn't Dour Domhnall. This was Devil Domhnall.

"I don't know." The words seemed to both cripple him and spur him. He'd progressed from a man perplexed by puzzles to a man dead-set on absolution. He'd solve it. She knew he would and could.

"I'll be with Kendrick." A flicker of fragile control passed in his brown irises. "Stay here. The last thing—I can't lose you, Rose. I need you safe. You understand?" He squeezed her hand. His face almost broke with the words. She nodded, mutely.

He wheeled around and was gone, a whoosh of wind behind him.

She released a pent-up breath.

"They've gone to gather potential offenders," the lady said in a steady, relaxed tone. Though Rosalie enjoyed her presence, almost as peaceful as a grassy knoll on a summer's day, her words held no comfort.

A room usually bathed with light, as evening fell, dimness shadowed the corners. Candles flickered as the wind drafted across the room, its momentary coolness a respite on her cheeks.

Lady Montgomerie patted a spot on the bench beside her.

"Gather offenders?"

The lady settled a knitting hoop into her lap and laid the needle down, the thin string getting lost in the deep green of her skirt. "People they suspect of Kyla's murder.

They have a few in mind. This might lead to answers about the thefts and other incidents, too."

Rosalie chanced, "The MacDougalls?"

"We don't know."

"I wonder if everything is connected?"

"The entire situation is complicated." Her hand shook. "Our town has been fortunate to have been spared strife since my father's reign." Lady Montgomerie glanced out the window. She chewed on her upper lip, thin lines and wrinkles compressing her mouth. "I wish Lanie would join us. I don't know where she is."

Panic tingled in Rosalie's chest. "Lady Aileana went riding a short while ago."

Lady Montgomerie bolted upright, her hoop and fabric falling to the floor with a clack. "Where?" She was already hurrying to the door. "Christian!"

The soldier poked his head in. "Milady?" She shot Rosalie a hopeful look.

"She said she was going for an evening ride with Brodie in the pass. I'm not sure where that is." Was it the same pass she'd traveled through on her way here? Her map was in her room. Domhnall had been helping her write the names of locations on it.

"Tell Kendrick," the lady ordered, and Christian was gone with a quick nod.

"Blazes, that child will be the death of me. All my grays and wrinkles, mind you, are from her." A forced chuckle escaped her tight lips. She returned to the chair, her gaze rapt on the window.

Domhnall swayed, running through every swear word he knew. Foul, ungentlemanly words. Many in his mind. A few tumbled out.

Of course, Aileana had run off. When a group of thieves, fire-setters, and murderers was unconfined in their town.

Of. Course.

He and Hayden broke from the watchmen and soldiers to search the path through the pass.

Inky blue fell upon the glen as they galloped to the pass and night hastened. Hayden was quiet with his own musings. How could Domhnall apologize for his sister having chosen Brodie, a MacDougall, over Hayden? He gripped the reins harder, working the horse past its limit, an ache etching a spot in his skull.

"This way." Hayden's words and sudden shift in direction startled the hell out of him.

"What do you see?"

They brought their horses to a halt and rested them for a moment to convene. If Domhnall's night vision was near perfect, Hayden's *was* perfect. His friend pointed to hoofprints in the mud. More than one set.

"Good. Let's go." He dismounted, eager to throttle his sister.

"No, look."

All Domhnall saw was red. He blinked and examined the gloppy mess.

"There's at least one other set of prints. Somebody followed them into the woods." Hayden flicked his chin to the grove of trees, their green summer leaves transformed into shades of blue and black in the night's darkness.

"Where are the horses?"

"Something happened. They must have ridden through the copse where it thins."

"Someone came upon them? Startled them and they fled into the copse on horseback?"

They tethered the horses to a tree, withdrew swords and went afoot, weaving through trees as silently as the leaves would allow. "Here," Domhnall whispered despite the noise their blades made.

Hayden fell silent, his step aligned with and behind Domhnall's. Pressed bushes and broken branches proved somebody, or somebodies, had come through recently. He stifled the desire to holler for his sister. Instead, he turned an eye upon his friend. They nodded unspoken agreement and separated, each scouting a different way around the rocks ahead.

As he tackled an unwieldy gorse bush, a crack sounded a few paces off to his right. He flinched, then discerned a shape in the distance. The summer moon was full, bathing the copse in light where trees thinned out.

The person stood near a collection of large granite rocks. One person.

The outline of long hair, a woman in a gown.

Aileana?

He assessed the area. Brodie had left? Who did the third tracks belong to? Had their pursuers left already? Why was his sister alone?

He gripped the hilt of his sword with indecision. Before hollering Aileana's name, somebody surprised him from his left. Quick as a whip. Domhnall turned. Too late. The blow caught him square on the back of his head.

An explosion of color and pain...then all went dark.

Rosalie suffered through a bleak supper with Lady Montgomerie and a few others. She made sure to finish her plate of food, even if her stomach disagreed with her. She wasn't used to always having a meal. Aileana reappeared—thank the saints—at the end of the meal. She rushed into the hall, flustered, but outwardly unscathed. Mother and daughter shared a hug as the lady ran a hand through Aileana's hair, and stroked a cheek.

"Domhnall and Hayden are returning the horses. Someone struck Domhnall, but he's well," she assured them at Rosalie's gasp, "and whoever it was got away. They must have followed me to the pass."

Lady Montgomerie, likely too relieved for her daughter's return, did not chide her about running off with Brodie.

They finished the meal in silence with no sign of Domhnall.

Now, Rosalie paced the rushes bare as she chewed her fingernails, a habit she'd ditched years ago when she'd been promoted to fortune-teller.

All the men were rounding up miscreants and standing guard, keeping Dornie safe. Long past midnight, commotion sounded in the courtyard, but she lacked a clear view from her window. There was a better one from Domhnall's chamber. Brazenly, she went into his room, lit candles, and peered through the window, having to lean far on the deep ledge. Horses, orderly energy, grunts, and angered curses. The men had returned. Words she could never decipher, likely Gaelic curses or phrases, rumbled through the men.

She waited, twiddled her thumbs, and drank from the herbal infusion she'd prepared herself. The fire waned, almost out. Her eyes grew droopy as the candle burned into the wee hours, wax melting in a puddle on the bases of the candlesticks. She sat on Domhnall's bed.

She awoke in the morning in her own bed. Hurrying to Domhnall's chamber, she found him pulling on his boots.

"Domhnall, what happened?" Fatigue circled his eyes. "Did you sleep? Are you well? Lanie said you were hurt."

"Just a bump to my head."

She reached for him. "Let me see."

"It's cleaned. The healer looked at it. He gave me a few stitches."

Her jaw dropped. She looked anyway, her feelings bruised. He must have washed his hair, too, for it smelled freshly fragrant with the herbal soaps Lady Deirdre made.

She firmed her stance and gently felt the crown of his head. A bump, the ripples of sutures. He winced.

"What about—?" she began.

He threaded his fingers through her other hand and squeezed it. "It will be all right, Rose. I didn't want you to worry."

"It's your time to rest like you made me," she attempted.

Her lightheartedness didn't bode well. "We've gathered offenders. Questioning comes next."

"Rest."

"I can't." He made to stand.

She held him down with two hands on his knees. "Stay, with me. Please? We can—"

He kissed her. Hard, fervently. She reciprocated. Finally, short of breath, he extracted himself from their interlocked arms. "I want nothing more. Except duty calls. I hate it, Rose."

"I know."

"I—" He held her gaze, eyes saying what words could not—yet.

She blinked and thinned her lips, also wordless. She was depleted of advice and encouragement.

He kissed her cheek and stood. "I'll be up when I can. Stay near my mother. We have extra guards posted. If anything happens to you..."

She brushed his cheek while in a confident voice, her usual guise, said, "It won't." Inside she trembled.

CHAPTER FOURTEEN

Two somber days passed after Kyla's simple funeral and the misadventure in the pass. Though Rosalie was not a prisoner, a morose haze shadowed her morale. After a dreary sup, Domhnall escorted her to her bedchamber, pausing. "May I come in? Just to talk."

"Please, yes," she said too animatedly. Her eagerness to be alone with him surpassed the usual interest to learn words. She'd rather test a few words, physically. Perhaps in turn it could release some of the strain upon his mind. Physical labors of work—or pleasure—could have that effect, could they not?

Under constant watch, they all toiled through daily tasks, Rosalie helping in the kitchen again, to Domhnall's protest.

"Leave her be. We need her, and she likes to help. We'll find another head cook," Lady Montgomerie had scolded him during supper that evening.

He strode into the bedchamber behind her, closed—and bolted—the door. Interest aroused, Rosalie settled onto the bed, her feet aching from the day. She preferred the garden labors to the cooking, especially with the summer's stifling heat near the kitchen's hearth.

Outside she'd catch the loch's breeze and a whiff of fresh air. Regardless, she loved keeping busy.

Her wardrobe had grown in the past week, too. The lady insisted on providing her with two new gowns, work and formal, slippers and work shoes, apron, and necessary undergarments. Her room bloomed with a bouquet of fresh flowers, a handheld mirror, silk ribbons and lace for styling her hair, thick fragrant wax candles, ewer, water pitcher, wine, and heavenly comfortable bedclothes. It was a lady's chamber.

She leaned over to pull off her worn-out work boots but paused. Her gaze fell upon the bedside table. "What is this?"

"I hope you like it."

She couldn't mask her shriek of delight. She rubbed fingers along each smooth and recognizable loch pebble, all bored with holes, and aligned in a wooden abacus. "These are the ones we picked—?"

"Aye. I had Athol, the woodwright, make it with the pebbles we collected by the loch. It's my handfasting gift to you. I thought you could paint them, too. The way you'd like. Different colors for ones, fives, tens, and hundreds like the one you saw in town."

"It's lovely!" She turned, hugged him, and squealed, giddy. In their lessons, she stumbled through the reading, but Domhnall couldn't stump her on the sums questions. Breathless, she said, "I didn't get you anything."

"I have all I want."

His blazing look went right through her. She fell onto the bed to control her wobbly knees.

Like a fool, she shifted subjects. "Do you want to talk about—?"

"No. There is no update. We rounded up men, and each will stand a fair trial of questioning. We take every matter seriously. My father should be home soon to question them all."

"I see." She reached again to take off her work boots.

He sat beside her and said, "Let me." He removed one boot, then the next. Clunk, clunk to the floor.

"But my feet smell and are dirty," she said, squeamish.

"So are mine but not nearly as dainty." He stroked the arch of her foot. Tickles shot up her leg.

He reached for the nearby stoneware ewer and poured the steaming water, prepared by a servant for Rosalie's nightly grooming—God, she was being treated like a lady. He dipped a cloth, then proceeded in cleaning her feet. She wiggled but relented to pleasurable waves.

"Who do you think attacked you? You never said," she asked.

Cease your prying, Rose. Her damn curiosity.

He dropped the soiled cloth beside the ewer and returned to his stroking of her cleaned feet and toes. "I saw a woman, in front of me in the woods. I thought it to be Lanie, but I wondered if it was Lady Brantingham. It was getting dark, late. It was hard to tell."

She gasped and not from the ticklish spot he traced with his finger.

"I can't imagine a woman like her in the woods, alone. Why? It was probably Aileana. Whoever hit me had full strength behind them. A man, likely."

"Brodie?"

"He'd have no reason to hit me."

"One of Lady Brantingham's men? Maybe they stayed behind? You think Edrea was after Aileana, now, too?"

He gave her a curt nod. "Or the MacDougalls are riled about Brodie and Aileana's courtship. So many disturbances have happened in the past few weeks, but who is doing this? Who? It's like hell has come to Dornie, Rose. I think it's more than one person. I don't know. It doesn't all add up. I suspected the MacDougalls, but now, I question everyone."

"Everyone?"

He gave a half smile with a tip of his head. "Not everyone."

"Domhnall, I..."

His lips found hers. He stole her courage.

He fingered the front of her bodice, played with the laces, but didn't advance.

She swallowed the taste of his mouth, of his tongue. She wanted to inhale all of his male scent. His closeness stirred all her senses and she wanted to pull him back upon her, right here on the bed, feel his warmth pressed against her.

Recovering her breath and not retying the loosened laces, she eased back. Her body begged to be free of the confining garments, to lie in a shift, enjoy the evening breeze fighting through the window to cool her room. Her body also pleaded for his touches.

Handfasted. Married. Nearly the same in her mind.

He heaved a deep breath, shifted upright, and returned to caressing her feet. She reclined on the bed, a plush pillow behind her head, and released a sigh. Firm, adoring hands stroked each toe, the inside of her ankle, and slowly worked their way up her calf. He pushed her hem higher and higher.

She closed her eyes, savoring his hands upon her skin. A stifled moan escaped her lips as his own lips dripped kisses on her calf, then behind her knee, the gown creeping ever farther up. Desire forbade her to resist. She wanted him to kiss her everywhere.

They could venture deeper if they wanted; they could seal this marriage by joining of flesh.

Oh, yes, she wanted that.

She cracked an eye open. His gaze asked her permission to go further. In response, she licked her lips and drew a hand through his disheveled hair, mindful of his injury.

God, she probably smelled like the garden. Dirt certainly smudged her calves. As if he read her mind, he dipped the cloth, wiped her calves, her knees, behind the knees...up her thighs, softly, sensually. Then he returned his mouth to its wanderings. He slid off the bed, taking her lower legs with him so they hung over the edge. He knelt in front of her, his head disappearing. She enjoyed his traveling kisses, not abashed at her allowance of it. Her delicate thread of fortitude, of chastity, was so thinned it might break with his caresses.

Her dress fully ruffled to her knees, she finally spoke. "Domhnall, we are only..."

His hands slid up her thighs. Farther. With assurance and hesitation. "We can do plenty that is not considered consummation," he offered in a throaty voice.

She cooed, "Are you an expert in this?"

His tone patient and lowered, he said, "Nay. But only once, long ago. This is new to me, my golden rose. Do you wish me to stop?"

"Yes." She gulped. "No."

He chuckled. "I can stop. Say the word." His fingers and lips halted.

"Oh...we cannot..."

"We won't do *that*," he assured. His fingers teased the inside of her thigh and grazed higher.

Her body throbbed with want, with indecision. Her heart drummed in her ears. "I-I must return home eventually. This—you and I—can't be...can't...be..." She swallowed her own words, her breathing catching.

"It can be. If you want. You can stay in Dornie and be my wife."

He stood lazily and then lay beside her. His hand rested on her abdomen. He kissed her mouth, and she wholeheartedly returned his affection, her tongue dancing with his. She ran hands through his hair, massaging his scalp. A longing hardness pressed against her hip. He wanted her, too.

"Let me show you." He drew a kiss to her throat, to her collarbone. Her nipples hardened beneath the remainder of the tied laces, aching to be free. He beheld her, his brown eyes like pools of dark water. She grew hot under his stare. He shifted, his hand returning to her knee...then higher.

She nibbled a lip to stifle the unladylike words while he watched her face and reaction to his touch.

He rubbed the core of her being, and an ache grew in the spot. Nerves in her body prickled to attention. His eyes never left hers as his fingers explored further...deeper...

Her heart joined the growing ache in belly and thighs as she writhed and gasped.

She shifted. She wanted more, so much more. Her hands grazed his side, then back, his muscles taut and responsive through the tunic. She wished to see him naked. Kiss his chest. She stroked along his tunic and hose, found his hard longing, and rubbed him, surprised at her own audacity. He gasped, then took her exploring hand. Brought it to his mouth, kissed her wrist. "No. This is for you tonight."

She panted as he stopped and brought his hands up to her bodice.

His look lingered as he unlaced her bodice the rest of the way. He kissed the round swells of her breasts, then gently each nipple. She bit a moan as he took each into his mouth, licking and teasing in turn. She could not take more. Sensing her yearning, he shifted lower.

And lower. Lower where his hands had been stroking.

She abandoned herself to the sensations as his mouth found flesh, burning and waiting for him. She held in a sigh as he...*God, did he.* She had no words for it.

He freed the restraints of body and heart as the flooding ache released.

Rosalie awoke alone.

Had she dreamt last night? No, the residual pleasure remained. She lay in her bed, down to her shift, buried beneath bedclothes smelling of him.

Was that consummating? Were they married now in the eyes of their Lord? *Foolish girl, no.* She understood the workings of lovemaking enough. He had not...No, he hadn't done that.

Yet.

The feel of him still tickled her skin and warmed her soul.

He'd liberated a burst of sensations from her. It had been nothing like her friend in England had described about lovemaking. Where was the reciprocating? Usually, she had said, women lie there while the man went about his business. Her friend had said most women did not find joy in it at first. Last night was far from unpleasant.

Her body tingled with recollection. She wouldn't have minded venturing further with him. Was she willing to be his wife in full?

No.

Yes.

Maybe?

A riot of shivers skipped down her spine as she contemplated staying longer, staying forever.

Domhnall passed through his day with a tender hunger growing within. He needed to be with Rosalie and not hold back. The taste of her skin, of her flesh, of her everything made it difficult to walk.

"Last stop," Hayden's voice intruded. "Your uncle said Muirfinn was causing a disturbance at Barrie's Tavern."

Barrie's was now run by his son. The original owner, despite Domhnall having come to warn him all those years ago, had died before his eyes. Just as his vision had prophesied. The man had been yet another person he couldn't save.

They veered down a heavily trodden path. Since Kyla's death and the gathering of potential offenders, most trouble had ceased. No more fires or attacks or thefts. Brantingham was confirmed gone, for certain now. They'd inquired again and searched the glen.

All was dead quiet. Was it the calm before the storm as the captains say of the Northern Sea?

Or did the perpetrator sit in the cells of Eilean Donan? The cells held a few miscreants and dastards, mostly MacDougalls who'd stayed behind, causing mischief in the local taverns, bragging about glories, and boasting about the superiority of their clan.

Muirfinn was local and he liked his drink. He got rough when in his cups.

Domhnall itched to question the prisoners, but the responsibility fell upon his father and Crystoll. His job, along with the other watchmen, was to detain the wrongdoers and keep the walkways and roadways safe throughout the glen. Justice fell upon the laird, who would be home today, likely.

"Do you think it's over?" Hayden asked.

"The marketers are gone. The MacDougalls, Donalds, and other visiting clans left, too. Lady Brantingham's exact whereabouts are unknown, but at least she's not in the glen anymore. She fled south. The potential lawbreakers are locked in the cells. Puzzle solved, right?" Hayden said with confidence.

"Aye. I am not so sure about Brantingham. *Did* we successfully quell her plan? Discourage her from pursuing Rosalie?"

"I think so. She is gone. Women are like that. We took away her toy and she got bored." Hayden shrugged.

"She could be hiding, waiting."

Dornie, their remarkable town in the western corner of the Highlands, had fallen back into routine. Soldiers monitored the perimeters and key vantage points in the keep and on the battlements as watchmen maintained their roles in the town and dale. Had order returned? Were the misfits who'd caused him hellish grief imprisoned in the belly of the keep? Was it really that simple?

"I still have my concerns about the thefts within the castle." The solution was so close, he could taste it, feel it. He no longer fell upon his hand puzzles to keep his mind sharp. He had a wife to protect and that alone was enough to keep him focused.

A wife.

Not yet—exactly. Soon.

"Simple motives like Constable always says," Hayden agreed.

"Aye. The thefts are either out of necessity—times have been harsh for some—or they are retribution."

"Aye. Your father can update us after his return from meeting with Laird MacDougall. The bell heather? Clearly the MacDougalls were taunting us. It had to be," Hayden agreed.

Domhnall nodded as they turned a corner through town. "Oswell's robbery—maybe the MacDougalls, likely Brantingham. Rosalie—definitely Brantingham."

"The witch is powerful and vicious."

Domhnall scrubbed a hand on his chin. "She must have had someone inside the castle help her. Kyla?"

"Maybe. And then dispose of her after using her? I would not be surprised."

"I'm sorry about her, you know. I know you two had a...were..." Hayden had missed his chance with Aileana and Kyla, now, too. Blazes, the poor man. He hoped some sweet spirit would come along to ease Hayden's balms and calm his wayward ways.

"Och, well. Aye." He gestured nonchalantly. "She was a bonnie lass. But conniving, too."

"I think Brantingham bribed her to poison Rose. Kyla was bothered, skittish during the handfasting *cèilidh*. Seemed like she wanted to tell me something. Did she say anything to you?"

"Nay. She preferred *not* talking..." Hayden said with a sheepish grin.

Domhnall postulated aloud, "It would explain Rose's herbal infusion being tainted with nuts and Brantingham knowing Rosalie would be in the garden. Kyla was there, the time I spoke with my mother about Rose's concern with nuts and Kyla knows her way around the pantries and my mother's herbs. She also knew Rose went to the gardens."

"Kyla had access."

"Indeed. What about the missing items from the cupboards?"

Hayden paused. "Why would Kyla steal?"

He'd seen the amber-jeweled candlestick in Rosalie's hand the night of their celebration. Had Rosalie pilfered it? Was stealing not beneath her? The street and market life of a commoner was not an easy one, and before the handfasting, Rosalie seemed content to leave when her uncle's work finished. What about her uncle? He'd left town recently…and the items were still left unaccounted for.

Domhnall hadn't been completely truthful last night when he told her not everyone was on his list. His mind swiveled with too many possibilities. Rosalie was innocent. She was not a thief or liar. She'd been caught up in the madness, that was it. How could he doubt her innocence?

The missing items in the kitchen were easy enough for Kyla to take. Why, after all these years?

His fingers fidgeted with belt loops. Maybe he still needed the wooden puzzle boxes. Or he could busy his hands with Rosalie later… A blazing heat returned to his stomach.

They turned another corner, past shops on a narrow road, the patrons rowdy in the evening haze in front of Barrie's Tavern. The scent of boiling fish wafted through open windows. The air curled around his head like fog. Women laughed, men joked loudly, all in the usual jolliness. They were all blissfully unaware of the problems plaguing the laird and Watch.

Could Rosalie have poisoned herself to garner sympathy, to coerce Domhnall into protecting her by handfasting? To worm her way into his home? A woman like her… He was an easy target. She saw right into him, as a Seer.

Did she exploit his weakness? Use him? He'd been used before by Isolde.

Christ, where do these thoughts come from?

As if reading his mind, Hayden asked, "How is Rose? We must rule out all possibilities. You don't think—?"

Domhnall clenched a fist at his side. "No."

Rosalie was a kind, genuine woman. Curse himself for even considering her as the offender. No. Not her. Nor her uncle. The unrest had begun before Rosalie's arrival.

They turned into Barrie's Tavern, and Domhnall exhaled. Muirfinn was passed out in the corner, smelling of his own vomit. "Gather him up, Hayden. We'll bring him for questioning." Domhnall flicked a hand to another acquaintance he recognized, James, who assisted. He wasn't ready to test his chances of touch beyond Rosalie.

As they left, he reconciled his thoughts.

The MacDougalls and likely perpetrators—caught. To be questioned.

Kyla—sadly, dead. She acted out of jealousy, likely bribed by Brantingham.

Lady Brantingham—gone.

Rosalie?

She had not stolen a thing. Except maybe his heart.

With the laird having returned, the men retreated to Laird Montgomerie's working chamber for discussion after the meal. Rosalie assumed it might take most of the evening, and she didn't plan for Domhnall to visit her despite her desire for it.

Lady Montgomerie and Aileana excused themselves to the solar, and so Rosalie joined them.

A low fire crackled in the hearth. Knowing Lady Montgomerie was a Feeler, Rosalie fought all thoughts of Domhnall and last night's passionate moment. Did the lady know? How could she read into people?

She quieted her incessant thoughts. *Think upon the mundane.* Sweet things. Gathering pebbles, strolls around town with Domhnall's arm linked in hers, her family in Edinburgh, her cats lazing their days in Ewan's stable. Writing and reading. Domhnall. His touches. Oh, bugger.

Birds squawked in the setting sky, and voices drifted up from the courtyard as men prepared for evening shifts. Growing bored with quilting, Aileana excused herself for bed.

Rosalie, too, stood to leave, when Lady Montgomerie said, "We've time alone, dearie. Let us speak in private."

Thwarted.

"You know," Rosalie said, her throat tightening. She sat on the bench in front of the hearth. She fanned her face, unreasonably hot. Time to suffer the consequences of whatever last night had been. Would the lady call for the priest now to marry them?

"I've known since the day we met."

What?

Rosalie played along. "How?" She reached for the pitcher of a cooled herbal infusion with mint leaves, mashed raspberries, and honey. She'd made it herself.

With shaky hands, she poured two goblets and handed one to Lady Montgomerie. She tried not to gulp her drink.

"I know an Ancient when I meet one. I also know pretenders."

Rosalie gagged on the hearty sip. *Mother Mary.* "Lady Mont—"

Domhnall's mother sipped the drink. "Please call me Lady Deirdre, or just Deirdre. I grow tired of titles. Never liked them."

That seemed to be where Domhnall and Aileana got it.

Her hands shook. "My lady, I never claimed to be an Ancient." She had not denied Domhnall's inference either. How much could Deirdre see within her? Truths? Lies? Feelings? Thoughts claimed her as her insides shook.

"When will you tell my son?"

"It's too late for that."

"It is never too late when the heart is involved."

"He won't forgive me." She rested the goblet on the nearby table and drew her gaze down. "I didn't mean for this to happen." What was the point of explaining? To the lady of the keep, she was a fraud, a liar, and had exploited Domhnall to work her way into higher standing. How could anyone forgive that? Even if she'd not done it on purpose.

In all truth, she had lied, yes, but she had never asked for any of it.

"He has a heart for forgiveness. Except for when it comes to himself."

"What do you mean?"

"It's better if he tells you about it."

"The accident? When he was a child?"

"He told you?"

Rosalie couldn't lie, not now. "Servants talk. I pieced it together, short of the details."

"Ah, is that how you do your readings? *Gossip?*"

Heat stole Rosalie's voice for a long moment at Deirdre's either inquisitive or condescending—she wasn't sure which—tone. "Some of it. I have an ear for information. I rely on weather and evidence..." She almost said superstition, political talk. This didn't make her sound any better. "I do it to help people, to give hope and reassurance, not to swindle." That wasn't the full truth. All she did was lie and swindle. She dropped her look to her sweating hands. "I'm sorry. I never meant for any of this."

They sipped in silence, only the crackle of the fire breaking it.

"I should retire for the night." She stared at the elegant shoes on her feet. "I can leave on the morrow." Her pulse spiked with the declaration.

Leave. You don't belong. You don't belong anywhere.

Deirdre flourished a hand. "You'll do no such thing. I've been known to tell my own fib or two, and it all worked out fine. Like I said, love will see past the wrongs. At some point, Rose, you must divulge the truth. If love rests in your hearts, it will shine through. He's already told you about me?"

She nodded.

"I see inside you, dearie. You have a genuine heart, a vibrant color, with conflicted but true emotions. I understand why you deceive. You have elders to take care of. But you understand why you must tell him?" she said firmly but kindly.

Rosalie curtsied. "Yes. I do. Good night, Lady Deirdre."

Her legs couldn't bring her faster to her room. Tonight, she extinguished the candle and bolted her door. When Domhnall knocked a few hours later, she burrowed herself deeper within the bedclothes. He knocked again. She did not answer.

He felt her presence before she entered the room. A golden yellow to match her flaxen hair and ruddy complexion. Felt? He could no longer deny the truth anymore as the secondary gifts slowly revealed themselves.

She was his golden rose from his visions.

"Rose?" he croaked, shuffling out of his bed, always on alert, hardly able to reach a deep sleep. When was his last solid slumber? He dragged a hand across his chin. Months ago.

The vapors of a dream disappeared, like licks on the skin taking a moment to evaporate in the warmth of summer. Licks? Had he been dreaming about Rosalie? He moaned, moved slowly as if underwater. He moistened dry lips. "Rose?"

A silhouetted woman stood by the window as he blinked himself awake.

What had the dream been about? He searched his mind for clarity. When was the last time he had also dreamed? Most nights, chaos filled his restless slumber. Rosalie came into better view as a shaft of moonlight crept across the room. Her back faced him.

She turned and glided to his bed, then touched his forearm. "Domhnall."

Remembrance burst behind his eyes at her gentle trace of his skin. Bright colors ruptured in his eyesight. He couldn't stop it and closed his eyes. "Aye…"

The Wind groaned through the open window.

With it, the vision. A young woman, fair and simple in an indistinguishable room or cottage. Stone or wood? Sitting in a bed. Crying. A bairn in her arms. A nearly lifeless bairn. Not a cry or whimper came from the bundle in her arms. Dead? Sleeping? Was he in a castle? Obscure and foreign, he couldn't tell. A man entered, took the bairn. The woman reached…collapsed. A pool of blood. The bairn was deathly quiet.

Shock froze him. He'd had this dream-vision before. When Kyla touched him in the kitchen. The woman presented differently now, and the setting was muted, garbled…confusing. It was not a vision from touch. He had dreamed the vision. Rosalie's touch returned him to it. Why?

He emerged from the black curtain as the image of a square tower came, then faded. Grassy moors. The bairn in a basket.

Then nothing. He blinked, and all was clear. Rosalie was beside him, speaking.

"Domhnall?" she repeated, alarm in her voice. She removed her hand. "Are you well? I didn't mean to startle you. I'm sorry about earlier. I was tired."

He came to full awareness. Sweat moistened his temple and palms, and his heart raced.

More bloody visions in his goddamn dreams now! He hung his head in his hands.

"Domhnall! What's wrong? Is it me? I can leave."

He wiped the edges of his eyes. "The visions have returned, Rose. I told you how I experienced one, when Kyla brushed against me. There have been more recently. Small ones and voices following me. Now...in my dream I saw it again. I'm sure of it. Same vision, but altered. I won't ever be free of them, Rose. I thought you were key. You were my salvation."

"I'm no savior."

He managed a smile. "You're a godsend. I'm still safe in your touch. I love you, Rose."

The room lay blanketed in darkness. He was no damn Feeler, but Christ, he felt it, too. He felt the tenderness within her.

She made an audible swallow. Her hand softly fell on his thigh, his bedclothes long since tossed aside, and he wore a long sleep shirt. "I love you, too, Domhnall. Do you want to tell me about your dream?"

Tension released from him, like a weight lifted. "Later."

He moved with ease, with want. He could wait no longer. Dornie had been cracking around him but slowly returning to normal, he hoped. His mind grew fractured and the Wind whispered death in his ears, but when he was with Rosalie—he was free. He scooped her into his arms. She erased all the pain and worry with her simple, rational view of life. "I want to be more than handfasted. I want you to be my wife, in spirit and body. I want us to be married. We can say our vows any time now. If we wish."

He waited, his embrace around her fierce.

She shifted and her face illumined in the moonlight. Green eyes stared, milky and lost in time, in place, in...doubt? What stories and worries hid behind her heart? He knew she longed for family and connection. She was an adaptable woman, able to move on, run her business, or take on a new role, but he knew she longed for a steady place to call home. "Can I be your home, Rose?"

Not an ember burned in the hearth, nor a candle flickered on the bedside table. Only the near-full moon dipped its fingers into his room, casting a beam across Rosalie's face, shift-clad body, womanly curves, and his crumpled bedclothes.

She nodded, hair swaying in the glow. "Yes?" It came out as a question.

Her breathing grew ragged and moist on his face. He held her tighter, brushed his lips against hers.

Louder, firmer, she said, "Yes."

"Yes?"

She kissed him with fervor.

He was slow, careful. He didn't move nearly as fast as he'd wanted to since the first day they'd met in her shop a few months ago. Was her arrival in Dornie fate or coincidence? She was his. His wife. They would declare their vows in the Church as soon as her uncle and aunt returned from Edinburgh. Let the eyes of God bless their union tonight.

He released a throaty grumble as she kissed him, hard, tongue seeking. Warm, wanting fingertips lifted his nightshirt over his head, and he shivered. Her kisses and caresses erased the vision-dream like it had never existed. She smelled like ripe fruit and nighttime slumber as he also lifted off her shift. He caught a whiff of rosemary from her cooking concoctions—which were as delicious as she. He remembered the other taste of her, and he grew harder. Christ, he needed her now.

Round, perfect breasts rubbed against his chest. He moaned as he laid her on the bed and shoved his bedclothes aside. He wanted to see all of her. Parchment-hued moonlight rippled over her round breasts, curved shoulders, the hollow at her throat—a quick kiss there—down her abdomen, across her thighs.

She writhed under his scrutiny, but she didn't close her eyes, which were like dark rocks in the shadows. He paused and contemplated the woman in front of him.

"What is it?" she asked.

"Admiring."

She released a nervous laugh.

He gave her another chance. "If we do this...it means..."

She pressed two fingers to his lips. He nipped them, took them in his mouth, and sucked the tips. She nearly purred. "Yes. I'm aware of what it means."

She drew him closer, her arms on his shoulders, eager, wanting. He stroked the essence of her, and she moaned louder. He found her ready and wanting. His fingers teased to make her want him more. Her reaction warmed his entire body.

Mouth found breast and nipple, then the other. She arched her back as he brought her closer. Then, ever carefully, he made her his wife. With the care he gave everything, Rosalie deserved it. She welcomed him in.

All his subconscious thoughts surfaced as the burning captive within him yielded. Her scent infused his mind. Sweat, the humid evening, and the Wind blowing across his backside sent his skin erupting with gooseflesh.

Visions, jumbled, both familiar and foreign, glinted behind his eyes. Yellow roses. A wagon. Rainy moor, a square drab tower. The fire in the kitchen with Maisie. A young boy smirking near the flaming hearth. Opposing blades. Feet upon cobblestone. An island with windswept shore grasses. A ship with a dragon's head on the bow. Standing stones.

He opened his eyes, quelled the dark hell. Not with her. Not with his Rose.

Golden flowers. Roses.

The visions disappeared as he willed them away, allowing only the sensual smile on her face into his mind. The Wind died, no longer a scratch on his back. Gone. The visions left—momentarily, for he knew they would return—while he moved with urgency, with completion. Their union lifted him as if he left his body and transported him to an unknown place. He drew his lips to join hers. She sighed and rocked with him. They both moaned into each other's throats as she urged him deeper, harder.

Bursts of color exploded before his eyes, and they both fell to stillness.

Rosalie loosened herself from their tangled limbs, located her shift on the edge of the bed, and shook it. Her golden bracelet tumbled to the rushes, falling from the secret pocket she'd sewn into the linen. "Oh." She got on her hands and knees and recovered it.

"What's that?" Domhnall shifted in the nest of his bed-clothes.

She drew the shift over her clammy skin, it cool and sticky from evaporated sweat, and slipped beneath the fur and quilt with him. "Something I was given as a child. Os said he'd found it in my basket as a baby. I think it was from my mother."

"Basket?" He rubbed a hand over the bracelet.

She tucked it back into the pocket. "Like Moses?" She muffled a somber laugh with her hand. "After Oswell's attack, I sewed the pocket into my shift for safety. It has always been the most precious thing to me. Thieves could steal my coin, but not this."

"Why don't you wear it?"

"It-it's too hard to explain."

He stroked her cheek. "I understand. It's lovely. Your mother, wherever she is or whoever she is, must have loved you."

"She left me."

"Circumstances call for difficult decisions. I'm sorry." He kissed her neck. "I can be your family, if you'll let me."

Now, Rose, before it's too late. "What happened to you, Domhnall, when you were a child? I've heard..." She couldn't expound.

He kissed her forehead. "*Gossib* in the castle? People should let history be."

"I didn't mean to offend you."

He squeezed her tighter. "My great-uncle, Kendrick, always says the past is the past. But that is not easy. I can't quiet the ghosts." He heaved a breath, sweet and hot on her cheeks. "It was a fire. I saw a vision of Maisie's death in the hearth in the kitchen. I was too young, unsure what to make of my visions. She died before I could convince my parents it hadn't been a dream. She was the first of many deaths I couldn't prevent. I blame myself. Fire...it pains me so. Sparks the memory, the pain, my guilt."

"Who was Maisie?"

He reached for his bedside table and took a long drag from his goblet. "Hayden's sister."

"Oh." She laid a consoling hand upon his arm. "You were young. You can't blame yourself."

"When his sister died, his father took it out on him and his mother. Blamed them. The loss drove his father to drinking, bedding anyone his coin would allow. He lost all their money to gambling. Sold everything. My father helped his family the best he could, but money is scarce some years. Hayden has worked hard as a watch-man. He has hopes to be constable one day. Granted, it's something I've always wanted, but it won't happen for me. I'll be laird. I will promote Hayden to constable. It's an admired position, and usually someone of his stature cannot achieve such a rank. I wish to see inequity abol-ished when I'm laird. And my guilt eats me so. I want to help him and his mother."

"You were a child. It wasn't your fault."

"Tell my heart that."

"I would love to see such equality. I have no doubt you'll be a compassionate laird who will make it happen." She ran a finger along the curve of his shoulder. "Do you trust Hayden?"

He glanced at her throat and swept a hand down her back. He held her gaze for a short moment. He set his jaw. "With my life. He's got a temper sometimes, but he is loyal."

She wiggled in his arms, slumber seducing her. "We should retire soon." She adjusted, nestled her bottom snugly into his groin. He was hard again.

"Rose..."

"Yes?"

He sniffed her hair. He twirled a few locks in his hand. "Maybe fate guided me to find you. You're my golden rose from the visions."

Even roses have thorns.

She fell asleep trying to work out the best way to tell him the truth.

CHAPTER FIFTEEN

E drea paced her room, wearing her mind thin and ignoring the disgusting rushes on the wood floor. The boards creaked beneath her. She had each annoying sound figured out, expected, and timed. By God, pregnancy made her mind spin. She was not crazy. She wrung her hands together, then shook them frantically while mumbling under her breath.

It was unlike her to obsess, and she prided herself on her educated and persuasive nature, but the pregnancy wreaked havoc upon her body and spirit. The initial surprise, then delight, at the news of finding herself with child after years of barrenness had soured with the swollen ankles, hands unable to wear her rings, stomach in an uproar after every meal, and dreadful fatigue. She exhaled and inhaled, then leaned over and retched in a bucket beside the thin-mattressed, half-clean bed in the godforsaken tavern.

Why had she agreed to meet the imbecile here?

Edinburgh offered limited finer lodgings, but money was never a concern. She always found the best place to stay. But...she couldn't chance being seen with him. She'd allow no possible link. The save in the woods, in the Highland pass, had been close. So close. Brash Domhnall Montgomerie had almost recognized her. Yes, she'd chosen the right person. The man's quick action had protected her from discovery.

If he didn't hurry with his task though, she'd dispose of him herself. Could he not do this simple thing?

Calloused pain had left its sores upon her heart. Desperate times called for her to act, time her biggest rival. Once Rosalie was dead, and Bertie, too, she'd take her place as ruler of the Eastern March. Why had she trusted this fool? Trust always failed her. It's why she had no friends, except for Lady Isabella. The only person she could truly trust was herself.

She eyed the jeweled, silver-hilted dagger sitting on her bedside table. If the fool brought no good news soon, she'd slit his throat. She sat and rolled the dagger around in her hands. She ran her finger along the sharp edge and pricked her thumb with it. Pain awakened her senses. She stared at the droplet of blood as it pooled on her fingertip.

This was maddening!

She'd yet to return home. Tomorrow she would go back to the marches, back to Bertie when he returned from his fornications. She imagined tying him up, poking him with the blade in his fat belly, enough to make him bleed. Then she'd cut off his errant limb, which was likely diseased from all his whoring. She'd show him her belly swollen with child, and then stick the blade right through his compassionless heart.

She rubbed her thumb and middle finger together, smearing the red blood between the two, then grabbed a cloth from her bedside table and cleaned her fingers.

She sucked on the thumb until it stopped bleeding, the metallic taste appeasing.

Panic gripped her womb like a kick of a bastard wanting out, and she retched again. Her stomach had nothing left to throw up.

"Where the hell is he?" she said through a gasp.

Wenda announced her presence with a knock, then poked her head in, a tray of food in her hands.

Edrea waved it away. Wenda nodded, laid it down anyway, and returned to her separate room.

Relenting, Edrea picked at the heel of bread, chewing and swallowing small pieces of it. Then she drank a smaller sip of wine.

She bounced fingers on her lips, willing the nausea to cease.

Hours later, sleep deprived, and after waking with every sound below or on the street, she knew he wasn't coming. She ruminated over her options.

Should she wait longer? She waited for no man, especially a Scot.

Or return to the border? The fool knew the plan. If he hadn't made it to their meeting point, there had to be a reason. She had promised him riches he'd never see in his lifetime. She had opened her legs to him, allowing him to dine in her earthly pleasures. He could still bring the girl to the tower keep. She had given him that alternative, in case.

Killing Rosalie had been the easiest choice. However, Edrea always had an alternate plan, shifting tactics if needed. Sometimes murder was not the clear solution, not when she could exploit the person. She would use the fortune-teller to her advantage instead. Bertie was the most superstitious Englishman she knew. Rosalie would tell him a prearranged lie. Her plan would then align into place for her. Then she'd see the girl, her husband, and her Scottish lover all three dead.

"It's time."

Rosalie hesitated in her steps as she entered the hall. "For what?"

Domhnall leaned in and kissed her cheek at her appearance. The servants had already set the tables for supper, and delightful scents—mostly her doing— wafted from the kitchen. "Your next test of words. At least on what we have learned so far. Your written hand is exquisite. Now to check the spelling and pronunciation."

Her pulse didn't settle with his lighthearted answer. "Should we talk to your parents? About..."

"We will. Your uncle won't be back north for a few weeks." He looped his arm in hers.

It had been two days since they made love. Dear God, they were married in the Lord's eyes. Rosalie pinched her nose, her mind a tangle of what to say, what to do, how to tell him. She could not carry on the Seer farce any longer. She'd spent two days spinning her story. There was no story, only the truth. She had to tell him. "Test?"

"Your first set of lessons are done. I gathered a meal for our supper. I'm taking you to your test. You've been inside, working, being under watchful eye. Let us escape this suffocating keep."

"Please no more shop signs," she said, half smirking, half scowling.

He chuckled. "No. Better."

"Are we safe? To go about?"

"Order has returned."

"Have there been confessions?"

"No."

She grimaced. "What has come from the men below?"

He thinned his lips. "Men can be stubborn. We're working on it. Lanie said she'd speak with Brodie Mac-Dougall and see if he can help us draw the truth from the men we're holding. Seeing he has given her his heart, he is more willing to help our cause. The discord between our clans has not improved."

"What if the guilty persons are not the Mac-Dougalls?"

Frown lines dipped down his forehead.

She didn't ask about the rest of the uncertainties.

Kyla. Lady Brantingham.

The mystery wasn't solved, but she had faith in Domhnall.

"I packed us a basket while you were changing. Come. We can enjoy the sunset, too."

She wrinkled her nose. "I am not ready for a test."

"I think you are. Besides, I would love your company."

His words sent shivers down her spine...in a good way. Her body reacted to all of his words and touches more each day.

They made their way to the pebbly beach where they'd collected her abacus stones. Ashore sat a rowboat and oars. He took her hand as she stepped in, then handed her the basket.

Curiosity awoke within her. "Can you believe I've never been in a boat? In all my years of travels, we've never crossed a river or lake other than by foot or wagon on a bridge." She was experiencing many firsts with Domhnall Montgomerie.

"The water is a peaceful place."

"A place of healing." She teetered, grabbing the sides, as he shoved off.

"See, you've been reading the Ancients' books. Water is a conduit for Healers."

Her cheeks warmed and not from the late afternoon sun as it lazed its way toward the horizon. "I'm good at listening, and you told me about it. Plus, the drawings tell more of a story."

"You see the hidden messages in them. I see scribbles or art of the creative, 'tis all."

"Your mind has been closed off to it for so long."

He smiled. "Perhaps."

He rowed them leisurely across the loch toward a spit on the opposite shore. The wind tickled her cheeks and ruffled her hair. Rosalie enjoyed the peace as oar sliced water, and Domhnall grinned like a young boy and it was devilishly handsome. The boat rocked gently, offering her a new welcoming sensation as she focused to remain steady with the strokes.

After making shore, Domhnall guided them a short distance up the sandy shoreline to a patch of trees and rocks. He withdrew a blanket from the basket, laid out their bountiful spread of food, and lastly, a rolled parchment. He fell onto the blanket with a sigh, and she followed suit.

"Ah..."

"Questions first or food?" He tapped the parchment.

"Food with test?" She reached into a clay jar for a piece of salted meat. Her appetite had grown accustomed to eating regularly since her arrival at Eilean Donan.

He uncorked a flask and offered it to her. Parched, she gladly sipped a pear wine, the added spices dancing on her tongue.

He unrolled the parchment and laid it flat with stones. "First, reading."

She groaned. Her least favorite. She sweetened the labor with a bannock already cut and slathered with honey and butter.

He pointed. "Read each line."

"Sentences? I'm not good at that. I hardly know the letters and just a few sounds."

"Try? Just words. Nothing difficult."

She munched and picked through the food offerings: bread with fresh-churned butter, dried and spiced venison, hard cheese, dried plums, and a raspberry tartlet.

"Stalling?"

"The food is tasty." That was not a lie. The herbs grown in Dornie were plentiful.

"You made some of it. Pleased with yourself, are you?"

She swatted at him.

He pointed to the page.

"If I must, Dour Domhnall."

He covered his heart. "Lanie's brought you over to her side."

"There are sides now?"

He leaned in, hovering near, stirring her to remember two nights ago. A trace of honey touched the corner of his lips. He licked it away. "Words."

She stuck out her tongue. He laughed. She focused on the first sounds. "Green."

"Your eyes." He pecked her cheek.

"Yeeloo. No, yellow."

He ran a hand through her hair, pausing to tickle the nape of her neck. "Your hair."

"Reeb. Reb."

"Red," he corrected.

She groaned. "Oh, the *d* and *b*. They stump me each time."

He circled his arm around her, his hand falling on her hip. "Your lips."

She felt herself blush. "Is this all about me?"

"Nay, read on...First, colors, aye?"

She looked at the next pair of words. "See. And...uh, say?"

"Close. *See* and *sea*. Spelled two ways." He pointed to the loch and then to her face. "One way means to see with your eyes."

Mother Mary, or a Seer. She internalized the stab of guilt.

"...and the other is the sea, like the open ocean."

"Two words spelled differently with different meanings but sound the same. Language is...oh, bother."

He grazed her finger. "Next."

"Live and love. What's this?" She pointed to the word.

"Life."

Her heartbeat quickened.

"You bring life to my days, Rose. You bring love to my heart."

Heat flushed her chest and raced up her throat. She read the next word. "Rose. Now flowers? I'd love to learn flowers and herb names. Oh, can we? We could read your mother's tonics and bottles. What is the next one with the D?"

"Splendid idea. Your name, Rose, not the flower. It is the first thing I taught you. You are my golden Rose. Domhnall is next to your name." He spelled his name aloud.

"Oh, my goodness, the Gaelic way! Thankfully, you're not teaching me that."

They shared a laugh.

"They're all about me. I was right." She swatted at his chest.

He tumbled backwards, carrying her with him. "Och, all right. Some of them are about you."

She giggled, giddy from wine and feeling almost childish with their banter. "These are not the words you were teaching me. What about all the sounds? The easy *a* and *e* and *o* vowel sounds. You're throwing new words at me. Though a few of these were in the books."

He held her close. The laughter vibrated from his chest to hers. "You're doing fine."

He kissed her, deeply. Wind tickled her bare arms with gooseflesh. She lay atop him and didn't let go. His tongue searched. His hands, too.

Breathless, she retreated for a beat. "Are we...alone?"

"Nobody comes here."

"Hmm." She wasn't fully convinced, but desire begged her to kiss him.

"The sun sets, my sweet Rose. We are all alone. 'Tis only us and the breeze." In response the water lapped softly against the shore.

Eager fingers unfastened her laces. She surrendered to his kisses everywhere. Her inner wrist, down her neck, her ear lobe...

"You taste of salt," he said, not stopping.

"I've been in the gardens all day."

"I like a salty wife." He rolled over, switching spots with her.

She lay back, enjoying his eyes upon her, only a tad self-conscious of their intimacy in the fading daylight. Before, they'd lain by moonlight. She glanced around. "Are you certain?"

"Only way here is by boat. Land is mucky on foot. The birds won't mind if we make noise."

She trembled under his touches.

He hadn't hurt her the other night—there had been only mild discomfort, replaced by pleasure—and she hoped this time it'd be even better. He touched her like a gentle, but hungry, wind. He shrugged off his hose, lifted his tunic, and fumbled with her gown layers. His chest was chiseled from labor, almost too thin despite the muscles. She hardly saw him eat. She'd have to remedy that.

He too, tasted of salt and labor.

He teased her nipples with finger, then tongue, and she writhed, eager and receptive. She caressed the strong muscles of his neck and upper back as his fingers explored her body while his mouth traveled down her abdomen. She fidgeted, moaned, shivered.

Delight puddled in her belly.

Her pleasure was pure and explosive as she anticipated it this time.

She went languid for a long moment, heaving. Boldly, she lifted up on her elbows, and gave him a look. "You," she said with a push of her hand against his hard chest. He was naked, and she took a moment to switch spots with him—her on top—to admire him. She was half dressed, her breasts unburdened by tight laces, her nipples taut and hungry for his mouth again, and her skirts a mess, hitched around her hips. She dripped kisses upon his throat, to his chest, abdomen, and lower.

He gasped.

She tickled and teased and did whatever her heart wished.

Throbbing in many places, she returned to his mouth. He kissed her hard, so hard, she almost fell with the intensity. He caught her, holding her neck, pressing chest against chest. She followed his lead as he brought her up and onto his length, slowly, despite the roaring desire pounding in her heart and body that ached for quicker, harder.

As an orange-pink sun set, splashing low light and long shadows over their blanket, Domhnall's chest was aglow with shimmers as they danced to their own rhythm.

He guided her through the motion as a hot current of passion roared through them, the only sounds the lapping of the loch and liberated moans.

"A few silver settings are missing, sir," Cawley said the next morning.

Distracted, seeking Rosalie in the garden, Domhnall almost kept on going. "Wait—what?"

Cawley lowered his look and dipped his head. "I've searched everywhere, sir. Perhaps I missed them a week ago when I inventoried all the missing items."

"Thank you, Cawley." The steward bowed and departed.

Hayden traipsed past from the direction of the seawall, finished with his night's shift. He yawned. "Christ, your face, Domhnall. What is it?"

Domhnall tucked in his upper lip and shook his head. "More items stolen."

"More? How is that possible? The thieves are gone or locked up."

"I don't know. Bloody hell. More stolen." Kyla? Had she taken them? Hidden them? Nobody ever searched her room. Perhaps Cawley hadn't noticed before. "I've an idea."

He reached the women's servants' quarters. He knew the women were all about for the day but he knocked first. With no answer, he pushed open the door, harder than intended. Kyla's bed lay empty, her blanket folded and awaiting a new servant to join the ranks. He held a breath as he looked under it. Nothing. He tossed the mattresses, threw off the bedclothes, and bent to look in corners and under things among what limited furniture the room possessed. He should have done this sooner.

"Did she keep anything elsewhere?"

"How would I know?" Hayden shrugged.

"Because you were—" He squeezed a fist at his side. "Because you were intimate with her?" He snarled, his patience depleted. Perhaps Aileana was smart in not choosing Hayden. He'd become more brazen in the past year. If he wasn't careful, he'd turn into his father or end up with several bairns with all this bedding.

Hayden blinked, nonplussed. "She only kept things here, I believe. It's not like she ever came home with me."

No, they just fornicated in the hallway. He shook his head. "Blazes, Hayden. Check the men's quarters." Hayden slipped out with a curt nod.

Domhnall found Rosalie's empty cot and mattress. He knelt and looked beneath it. Something. In the dark corner, far from the naked eye.

There.

Behind a rolled-up blanket. A heavy sack. Her sack. Why wasn't it upstairs? Did she have another sack, from Oswell?

By all that was holy, was this why she'd insisted on being down here so much? To guard the things she took—

No. No. No...

He found the pewter goblets and serving bowl. He tugged and withdrew his mother's gold heart necklace from between mattress and cot. His father's *sgian-dubh* and his mother's emerald brooch were unaccounted for. Sold already? The amber-embellished candlestick sat in his hand. He clenched it, white knuckled. He had seen her holding it the night of their handfasting. At the time, she'd quickly replaced it on the table. Caught in the act?

No. This could not be!

He slumped against the wall, his head hung low. Hayden returned. "Nothing in there—oh my God. You found it all."

"God, Hayden! She didn't. She couldn't. It can't be." His heart squeezed. Her bracelet, and the story about her parents. Was that all a lie? A ploy? Was it even her bracelet?

"All along it was her?" Hayden curled a lip, then crinkled his nose. "Is it all there?"

"No."

"Maybe the old man took the rest with him to Edinburgh?"

"Why? What if Kyla had done it, hid the items, and was going to accuse Rosalie? Implement her? She was a jealous hen. And maybe the poisoning hadn't been Kyla. It had been Lady Brantingham all along."

"Too complicated. Remember, simple? Nobody saw Rose get attacked nor admitted to the tainted drink. Who knows if it had been poisoned at all. Sorry, Domhnall."

He leaned against the stone wall in the hallway and breathed through the riot of emotions. None of the MacDougalls had admitted to anything—the early thefts, fire, and assaults. Somebody had to have done those. Somebody who was not Rosalie. This was driving him to madness!

Lady Brantingham had to be responsible for the later misdoings. Rosalie? Had she fabricated the story with Brantingham? No, even the noblewoman admitted her ill-regard for Rosalie. But...what if Rosalie had embellished the story, making it seem worse than it was? What if she lied about the attack and drink?

He stared at his palms as if they held the answers.

Only one person would know. He strode to the gardens to find his wife.

"Domhnall's looking for you," Aileana said, with a flick of her chin over her shoulder. "Seems none too pleased."

Rosalie's stomach hardened. "Oh?"

Aileana drew in closer and gestured to Rosalie. "Come." Rosalie dropped her basket. Her palms sweaty, she balled her hands into fists and hugged her middle and waited for impact.

"I'm not a Feeler like Ma, logical and task-minded like Pa, or an intuitive Seer like Domhnall—and heaven knows I cannot heal nor stand the sight of blood—but I listen. People think I don't pay attention, but it's the contrary. I cross paths with many different folks. I do my own watching. My mother is aware of your *ways* isn't she?"

Mute, Rosalie nodded. Why lie?

"Aye, and she doesn't care, does she? She adores you." Rosalie gave a half nod.

"A-dores you," Aileana emphasized. "Domhnall is be-sotted. Fully. You're no Seer like him though." She arched an eyebrow. "You use other ways to intuit."

Rosalie's mind returned to an earlier discussion with Aileana. Had she suspected all along?

"People talk. I've watched you do your own observing. It's your craft. You're not a fraud like many of them, telling them about massive fortunes, glories, or whatever suits their interests. I reckon you collect information and give people hope."

"I try." Her voice fell quiet, like a mouse. Her guise was falling into a bottomless chasm.

"He thinks you're real, from the isles?"

Disgrace brought her eyes down with a nod.

"Rose, tell me. Are you involved with any of this madness? Did you come here purposely to deceive us?"

Rosalie shuffled her feet and darted her gaze around. Nobody else was near or listening. "No! I came with the market, with my uncle, to make coin, work our business. His rats, my fortune-telling, and crafts. I didn't mean for anything awful to happen. What I told the laird and lady about Lady Brantingham is true. She is after me. That's all!"

"I believe you. I'm not the one you should worry about though. He's told you about Maisie?"

She swallowed and nodded like the fool she was.

"Talk to him. Tell him all. Today. He will forgive and let it go because he loves you." Aileana hugged her and scurried off.

Rosalie stumbled to her bedchamber and waited. Her stomach was queasy, so she would skip supper. She could not face them all at the meal. She packed her bag.

Ready to face the truth.

Tired steps brought him to her room before supper.

"Domhnall, I must tell you something," Rosalie said as he came in and closed the door.

His stomach hardened. He expelled his breath as if pained. "You stole from us. The things under your cot."

Us? Wasn't she one of them now?

"Stole? No. What things under my cot? I'm here, in this bedchamber."

"Hayden and I found missing silverware, candlesticks, and other personal valuables in the servants' quarters, under your cot."

Her face blanched like she'd been slapped. "No. I would never steal."

He let his head fall. Thank God.

"How could you think I stole from you?"

Och. "I didn't really...well, maybe. We found them under your cot and I saw you with that candlestick and..."

"I've lied, Domhnall."

He brought his eyes to meet her gaze. "What? You said you didn't steal those things."

She paced the room, fidgeting with one of his puzzles he'd left. She chewed her lip. "No, I've not stolen a thing. That is not a lie. I have never stolen a thing. I pay or work for whatever I have."

"Then what did you lie about?" As the words left his lips, he knew. Blood pounded in his temples.

She lowered her gaze, but then stared directly at him. "I am not a Seer like you. I'm a fortune-teller only. I read palms. I do not have visions or hear things like you."

"You lie? Like those other..." He bit back an uncouth word.

She sniffled but shed no tears, though her eyes glistened with them. "I don't tell blatant lies. I gather information. I read into people. I use all my learnings of the sun and moon, and political banter, and superstitions, *gossib*, and, and, and…" She trailed off with a shake of her hand. "I give people hope. I disclose only things I am mostly certain of. I never create stories. I'm sorry, Domhnall. I never wanted to lie. You held such hope."

I still do. The Wind whispered in his ears, "*You can touch her. She is the one.*"

She approached, then backed away. "I can leave. We don't have to tell anyone about this." She gestured to the bed. "I will leave. Lady Brantingham is gone. You've honored your end of this deal."

"Is that all we were? A deal?"

Pleading, sad eyes stared back. She didn't agree or disagree.

He wanted to hold her, throttle her, kiss her. "Why didn't you tell me? I would have understood." Would he have? That was a lie.

She shook her head slowly, regretfully.

"I need to think. Give me till morning? I-I…" He tripped a step, his knees wobbly. "Don't leave. Please?"

She crossed her arms. "Until morn, and then I go if you wish it." Her shoulders shook. "I'm sorry, Domhnall."

"Me, too."

He left, skipped sup, and went straight outside for a night round. Not only had she lied, she manipulated him. Just like Isolde. The inescapable truth snickered in his mind. He was alone in his nightmare. There were no other Seers out there.

And the woman he loved was a fraud.

Raw, primitive feeling spiraled him to the place he'd vowed never to visit again.

After the castle stilled for the night, Rosalie got out of bed and retrieved the abacus, parchment, and a quill from her table. She dressed fully in what she had arrived in weeks ago, her threadbare cloak and old working shoes a reminder of who she truly was. She gathered her few personal items.

With her rudimentary learning from Domhnall—how ironic—she wrote an apology:

I'm sorry, Domhnall. I stole your heart. I stole the truth.

She hoped she'd spelled the words correctly.

She tiptoed into his room, and placed the letter and abacus on the table, caressing the stones one last time. *Meek liar.* She passed a glance to Domhnall, asleep in bed. She wanted to kiss him goodbye. She sent a prayer heavenward instead. *May he find a better woman, Lord.*

She just as quietly left the room.

A lone tear, salty and warm, rolled down her cheek to her lips as she closed the door behind her. Ache swelled her breast as she choked her sobs.

Finally, the tears came. All these years, and a broken heart was all it took.

She leaned against the cold stone wall in the hallway, trying to silence the panting as she struggled for air. She closed her eyes as the tears flowed.

She was a wretch.

A long moment later, she wheezed and hiccupped. What was she doing? He hadn't turned her out on the dirt road. He had asked for time to think. She owed him that.

With a sniffle, she opened her eyes to return to her room and sleep—to honor his request.

In the darkness, a clamped hand upon her mouth squelched her scream.

Hayden stood before her.

Domhnall pondered his choices as the creamy yellow sunrise broke through his window.

Yellow. He saw it everywhere. *Daft Domhnall.* Forget Dour. Daft was more accurate. The golden rose. Rosalie. *Don't believe the lies*, his visions had warned. Damn. He shook his haggard thoughts away. Had his visions been warning him all along?

Rosalie was not a Seer. She was a fake who exploited others. It was her true profession. Selling trinkets had been her cover. She never denied her job as a palm reader, but she never admitted to being fake either. She led him to believe what he wanted to believe.

Fortune-tellers preyed on weaknesses: pinpoint a person's need, reveal their deficits, and exploit the hell out of them so they could survive. God, she was good. She had wormed her way into his heart, into his bed...

Empathy was a sword cutting through the bitterness. Rosalie was just trying to survive like the rest of them.

Shame foiled him, and he slumped onto his bed. Weren't they all just trying to make their way through the world? To find love or comfort in home, partner, and family?

His pulse wouldn't settle. Answers. He needed answers. Another damn puzzle. Christ, was nothing straightforward? Did she love him, or was it all part of the charade? He had not asked her that last night.

He found her room empty after discovering the abacus and note in his chamber.

He read the parchment over and over. Well, her penmanship was superb. She spelled most of the words correctly.

Vanished.

Like the Wind. One moment torturing his soul, driving him to a point of sweet oblivion...then in a blink, she was gone. This was his fault. Could he do nothing well?

She'd left behind all the clothing his mother had provided her, neatly hung in her dressing cabinet. Her wine pitcher sat full, the goblet unused. The water ewer was dry, her cloths neatly folded. He ran a hand along the bedclothes and brought his fingers to his lips. Inhaled. Nothing. Could he not even be left with her scent?

He hung his head in his hands. She had not simply gone for a stroll or respite on an early sunny morn. How had she gotten past his guard? Had she left in the night or at daybreak? Who had been on duty last night? Hayden, Guthrie, Aiden, or Comroy? He scratched his head and inhaled the last tendril of her he could from his fingertips, hair, and clothes.

Had she been real? Had any of it been real? Was he living in his own nightmare, caught in a vision that would not cease? No. Awareness reigned. Rosalie Threston had been here, been in his bed, been in his heart. He'd seen her as a bairn in a basket in the vision. He knew. That infant was Rosalie. He was sure of it now. Fate had brought her to him, and he would not let circumstance take her away.

He plodded to the table in his room and traced the beads of the abacus. Picking it up, he squeezed it so hard his knuckles hurt.

He could not—would not—let another failure befall him. Not Rosalie. Not his heart. He laid the abacus down calmly. He sat on the bed and conjured the Wind.

Come to me.

Lay your hands on my soul. Show me.

Patience succumbed after a few minutes of silence.

He stormed from the room and headed straight to the stables. He'd reach her before she got to the next town afoot. He found his friend in the stable readying a horse.

"Where do you hurry off to so early?" Domhnall asked.

Unperturbed, Hayden turned. "Och, I was going to ride to MacPherson's to check his broken fence. What's amiss? You look—not well." He wiped his sweaty forehead with a kerchief, though the morning was crisp. He reached for his outer tunic which was draped over a post. Scratches tracked one forearm. He must have caught Domhnall's gaze. "Och, the cats. Nasty mongrels. One thought to steal my cheese when I wasn't looking."

On cue, Rosalie's cats poked their heads from the straw pile in the corner of the stable. One meowed. "Those harmless things?" Domhnall chided. He was in no mood for Hayden's sour dislike of animals. Frankly, he grew more tired of Hayden's disdain. What was wrong with cats?

Confusion froze him. Rosalie wouldn't leave the cats behind. But how could she carry them if traveling on foot? An unsettling enlightenment rippled through him.

Puzzles should be straightforward. Simple motives. He blinked a hint of darkness as it crept across his vision. Fire flickered in his mind's eye. The kitchen hearth. Maisie's screams. A short shadow—a lad?—in the corner.

But he hadn't touched a soul. Now the visions came without touch, like in his dreams! Would he never be free? The Wind had answered his earlier summons apparently, just not in the way he intended.

"What happened?" Hayden pulled his tunic over his leaner than usual upper body, readjusted his belt, and picked up his satchel. "You look green, Domhnall." He handed him a flask. "Drink something."

He gulped the whisky. "I think she was taken."

"Who?"

"Rose. She's gone. She left a note, but she would never leave her cats behind."

"What about the stolen goods? Do you think—?"

"I don't know." Nausea gripped him. He wanted to lay a hand on Hayden. To see. The most obvious offender is usually...

Hell. Bloody hell! He clenched a fist instead.

First, he had suspected Rosalie and her uncle, now his best friend? Desperate. Daft!

He stumbled and grabbed the beam nearest him. "Is there coverage for—?"

"Aye, Constable MacCoinneach has all posts covered. Your father has already identified one of the prisoners as the thief. I was going to tell you when I saw you next."

"Why wasn't I told?"

"Your uncle informed me, in passing, on my way here."

Domhnall clutched the beam harder, white knuckled.

"Drink. You'll feel better." Hayden offered the flask again. Domhnall gulped more, the whisky fumes burning.

He blinked, hit with dizziness. A rustling sound drifted out from the far corner of the stable. A moan? The Wind? A person? He couldn't discern reality anymore.

Hayden said quietly, "You loved the lass despite her lies. But this is for the best, Domhnall."

Reluctant, Domhnall downed half the flask. It washed away the sour realization. He loved her, but she didn't love him. She'd left. It was what she did after all.

His mind churned unsteadily. The drink was not helping.

Hayden's voice, always calm, always ready, brought Domhnall to the present. "Maybe you should go inside. You look..."

CHAPTER SIXTEEN

T he next town came...and went. Rosalie made a mental note. She wished she could assess their route on her hand-drawn maps. The road seemed familiar from her ride north a month ago, but she needed her maps to confirm it. Dizziness still plagued her from Hayden's blow to her head and the foul drink he'd forced her to consume when she had awoken the first time in the stable. She pitched sideways on the horse, hungry, thirsty, tired...

He caught her before she fell.

She broke away from his grip with a huff, more alert now. The scratch marks on his arm gave her a little satisfaction. She had tried at least.

She repeated the same questions to herself. How far were they from Dornie? How had he escaped without anyone seeing a thing? Had he bribed someone to help?

They passed through another lochside town without stopping. He didn't acquire food or offer her lodging. Evening drew upon them. She knew better that to ask if they were stopping. Two days of riding in the saddle with him resulted in her questions unanswered, a mounting ire at being tied up at night, and constant watching even while she relieved herself.

Intuition had failed her with Hayden. Why hadn't she trusted her initial thoughts about him?

The horse clopped along the shoreline, which by her mental map had to be Loch Oich if the town they'd just passed was Garry. Civilization disappeared behind them as they entered another glen. Her mental map—of her written maps—slowly returned to her. They traveled south toward the bridge in the town on the River Spean. The dominating peak of Meall Dubh hovered behind them. It sat between the two glens.

He didn't stop.

He was taking her south. Far south. To Edinburgh?

To…

The marches.

She loosened her grip on the saddle as the terrifying realization washed over her. Hayden trudged beside her now, resting the horse from the burden of two. *Stay calm. Wait for a moment.* The last town was not too far back. Could she run? Would she make it with Hayden hindered by his sword and light armor?

She had first thought he had abducted her out of spite. God, she didn't know. Of course, he was working for Lady Brantingham. It all made sense now.

Her look darted to the woods flanking them. What about the loch? Run that way, get herself lost in the brambles and thorny bushes? Hide? Flee toward the people of the town? She was hardly experienced enough to bolt with the horse. It would likely toss her if she whipped the reins and gave it a good kick. Hayden was a cunning man. He sauntered upright, confident, and he masked his dubious ways with caution. He knew the land. He was punctual or arriving at the most convenient time. He was never around when bad things happened but showed up to help. All the evidence slapped her in the face.

Sly dastard.

She lacked a strong plan. Reaching into her gown pocket, she grabbed a few of the smooth water pebbles she'd gathered with Domhnall by the loch in Dornie. 'Twas a blessing she had painted them in bright colors. They'd catch a watchful eye. Domhnall's eye. She carefully dropped them on the road. He'd see. He'd see. If he followed. She prayed. She'd been dropping them for two days along their route. Hoping.

Hours later, they stopped to water the horse by a stream that forked off the loch. She dismounted, an ache sliding up her backside.

Hayden knelt, rolled up his sleeves, and splashed water on his face.

Maybe she could smash him on the head with a rock?

He dipped a pouch into the stream to refill it with his left hand. Nestled in his belt, his sword's hilt rested on his right hip, and when they'd rode together, he had held a hand around her waist, using his left, dominant hand, to hold the reins.

A flash of memory caused her to stumble.

Hayden was left-handed. Her garden attacker had been left-handed. It had been him all along.

He looked at her, his grin without humor. He was almost too handsome. It made for the perfect charm or ploy to unsuspecting people.

"We're not different, you and I," he said, rising, plugging his pouch, and then attaching it to the satchel on the horse. "At least I know we'll never be like them. Wise up, my thorny Rose."

She swept a hand across her eyes to shelter herself from his penetrating look. Her leg muscles tightened as she readied her feet to run. They were nowhere near a town. She expelled an almost painful breath. All her methods, all her fallbacks...evaporated. Mother Mary, in the previous town she would've had a chance. Not here. Not against him, a wall of lean but strapping muscle and a dangerous mind.

He scoffed, "A fake Seer. You're like me. You lie. It is how we survive. And you're damn good at it." He approached, thumbed her chin, and locked his stone-cold brown eyes with hers. No empathy. No feeling. No remorse. "Granted, Domhnall believes many lies. And you are such a bonnie liar."

She jerked her chin away from his touch. "You killed Kyla. You attacked me. You had Kyla poison me. Did you attack Os, too? All for what? Money?" Her skin crawled.

"You'd fetch a reasonable price on the market, but the noble bitch paid better."

The market? What was she, a pig or sheep? People sold people? She hugged her arms to her chest, suppressing the welling fury. Then, with a furtive glance, she evaluated her best routes to escape. He never took his eyes off her.

"My thorny Rose. You know better." He tsked. "You have nowhere to go."

She recoiled from his nearness. He hovered but didn't touch her. His overbearing presence dominated his words and actions. How could she argue with a lunatic?

"Liars don't belong among them. We have our own place. It's not in the keep of Eilean Donan." He gave her a brutal stare and held his ground.

Domhnall had explained motives for stealing. He said they were usually simple. Usually for security and money or for retribution. Certainly, Hayden hadn't been hurting for money? But... His mother was ill.

Rosalie had taken his mother's job in the kitchen.

Retribution?

Maisie. His sister, dead in a fire years ago.

Hayden knew about Domhnall's ability. Did he blame his best friend for the death of his sister? Was this revenge? Years later? It didn't make sense.

She chastised herself for not listening to her first instinct. She had ignored the signs: a prickle in her scalp, a twist of her insides. She'd always known. Finally, she found her voice. "Where are you taking me?"

His forehead creased. "Like you don't know. People like us deserve better. I'm afraid that might not happen for you. Edrea has a plan for you before she kills you."

Plan?

Her face must have shown her confusion. "Och, Rose. You're not dimwitted."

"She wants me dead."

He chuckled and rubbed his cleanly shaven chin. "Oh, she does. But there are many who believe your lies. I suspect her husband would. From what I hear, he's a gullible dolt. Edrea is a complex woman. Retribution alone doesn't drive her. She is a planner. Like me. At first, I thought you a nuisance, but it turns out you're my deliverance."

Shivers erupted upon her arms at words eerily echoing Domhnall's. Is that all people wanted from her? She'd manipulated people for years. Was God serving her penance now? Domhnall, Hayden, and Edrea all wanted her for something. "I am nobody's deliverance."

He grabbed her by the arm, brought her to the horse, and planted her in the saddle.

"Domhnall—he didn't mean to... You need to forgive him for Maisie," she tried. "He was a lad. He didn't know about his visions yet."

Hayden laughed, the sound sickening. "I don't blame him for her death. My sister was a twit. 'Twas her own fault she got too close to the hearth. Her own fault she didn't follow the rules when we played our games. Domhnall's visions left long ago, but I knew they would not sit dormant forever. Eventually he would have seen the truth."

If any food had been in her stomach, Rosalie would have vomited then and there.

"You—you killed...?" His own sister.

"Yes."

Three days passed. The landscape softened as Hayden and Rosalie drew closer to the borders. They were far beyond Edinburgh and the rugged crags of the Highlands. With each passing town and familiar landmark, her hope dwindled more. She had managed to retrieve the rest of her colored pebbles from her sack, loaded her pockets with them, and whenever they made a turn, she left one. Domhnall finding them or at least one of them was close to impossible. All she had was hope though, so she persisted.

If he was even looking for her. She hadn't been able to retrieve the parchment with her apologetic goodbye. He probably thought she purposely left. He probably wasn't even looking for her.

She rose, after relieving herself behind a bush, under Hayden's watchful eye. At least he'd kept his hands to himself. He seemed to prefer a naïve woman, somebody willing to fall for his charms.

As she strode toward the road, she clenched the last of her pebbles. Leave it? Or one more stop? She lifted a quick prayer and dropped the stone casually. It clacked, hitting a large rock by the roadside.

Hayden's ears were sharp. He passed a glance between her and the ground and saw the blue-painted, out-of-place stone. He pocketed it. "You think you're smart, don't you?" He backhanded her across the cheek.

She released a muffled cry as pain radiated through her head, shaking her teeth. So much for him not raising a hand to her.

"You think he is going to come for you?"

She pressed a hand to her aching cheek. She didn't know what to think.

Domhnall picked up another painted pebble. These had to be from Rosalie. She was alive, heading south, and she was with Hayden. Domhnall was at least a day behind, due to his poisoning by Hayden and his need for rest and recovery. He was thankful for Mother's herbal treatments. His stomach twisted in remembrance of the tainted whisky.

"Bless her wit," Kendrick said over Domhnall's shoulder.

They stopped in Edinburgh only because their horses needed rest, and with his father's insistence. If Domhnall had his way, he'd keep going. However, logic trounced emotion. Domhnall paced the tavern's crowded room, bouncing the handful of pebbles in his palm. He could almost feel her golden hue, her lifeblood, in them.

"Sit, Domhnall," his father ordered.

"Shouldn't we at least speak with her uncle?" Kendrick voiced later over their subdued meal.

Domhnall scooped a bite of bland stew into his mouth, knowing his body needed it.

"We'll leave at first light," his father said. "And yes, we should speak to her family."

Domhnall dropped his bread. "What can they do? All it would accomplish is worry."

"What if I stay back?" Kendrick took a long sip from his goblet. Today, his age showed. The journey pressed him. "As guard to her aunt and uncle, in case Lady Brantingham sends more men north?"

"Good idea," his father said.

Domhnall forced another bite. "What *is* our plan?"

Father sipped. "I'll inquire with my contacts in town, ask about the warden's post in the Eastern March. I might be able to recruit a few able-bodied men. We have kin here."

"You think we should try to negotiate or enter by force? Or sneak in?" Domhnall drummed his fingers on the wooden table. He tore off another piece of bread and dipped it into the stew, his mind a blur of emotion. Rosalie's food was tastier than this slop.

Father, always logical, said, "We're dealing with an uncertain woman, willing to do whatever she pleases, crossing country borders. We could get the king's men involved, but they have other concerns right now, and frankly they won't care. There's also the issue of Hayden."

"Dastard. He was always the best watchman." Kendrick spat. "He fooled me too, lad."

Aye, but you weren't his best friend.

Domhnall almost retched at the naming of his best friend and betrayer.

All. These. Years.

Thank God Aileana had not succumbed to his temptations. Her rejection of him must have spurred him to madness. *He's been mad all along,* a voice told him. Domhnall's heart—his trustfulness—hadn't allowed the truth. He brushed a hand over his chin. "Sneak in?"

"Let's wait on that decision." The stool scraped the floor as his father rose. "I'll make my inquiries. Kendrick, you see to her aunt and uncle. I'll find a friend in town who can watch over them with you. Maybe Iagan?"

Kendrick nodded. "Aye."

"Domhnall..." His father's look implored. "Rest."

In the upstairs room, Domhnall did everything but rest. He paced. He threw a puzzle at the wall, watching it break into its components with a crash to the floor.

A fool no more.

One of the miscreants they'd gathered in the prison confessed to helping Hayden with thefts. They'd gone to Hayden's croft and spoken with his mother. She knew nothing of his misdoings. The remainder of the missing possessions not already discovered under Rosalie's cot sat in plain sight in Hayden's cottage. Candlesticks and other kitchen wares, Domhnall's mother's emerald brooch, and items stolen from other crofters. Mrs. Clune's silverware. Hayden couldn't hide the pigs. They must have been sold. His father's *sgian-dubh* was still missing.

Hayden or Kyla had planted the other items under Rosalie's cot. Kyla had been working with him. She'd panicked and wanted to confess.

Then Hayden killed her.

He must have stolen to help support his mother.

Watchmen made a moderate wage, but the Iverson croft needed a new roof—one Domhnall had promised to help repair—and their puny fields reaped little harvest. Mr. Iverson had sold nearly all the property and wares to pay for his bad habits. Hayden was a masterful watchman but a poor farmer. His mother no longer worked at the keep. Her medicines cost a hefty sum. Domhnall's mother was talented with herbs, but Robena's health was beyond her healing skills. She'd told Hayden this, repeatedly. They'd done all they could.

When had been Domhnall's last visit to the Iverson croft? He shook his head in shame. It had been too long since he'd checked in on his friend. He'd been so consumed with helping Dornie, finding the thief, that he'd forgotten about helping his best friend.

Why else would Hayden have done it? He stole to help his mother. It made sense and deserved empathy. Reason argued with truth. But Hayden had taken it too far.

The attack on Oswell...the attacks on Rosalie. Kyla's murder.

Maisie.

Blazes, had Hayden killed her? Who was the little boy in Domhnall's vision?

Murder warranted no sympathy. It demanded justice.

He attempted to tally the good and bad in Hayden, but the bad tipped the scales...

Hayden needed to care for his mother and home. Maisie, the sweet lass had been just a child! Kyla had done nothing wrong. Hayden's playing and whoring. His dutifulness, always by Domhnall's side. But he hadn't been helping, had he? He had been lying, stealing, massaging his own desires...to be sure his friend didn't recover his ability to have visions. To see the bloody truth.

Their friendship had only developed after Maisie's death. It hadn't been a friendship. Instead, Hayden had been silently observing and exploiting his opponent. Hayden had been waiting all these years. Waiting for Domhnall to recover his visions. Waiting for the right person to come along to help his memories reappear. He had been *watching*.

Who else had died mysteriously in the last twenty years under their watch? Domhnall could list at least a few people.

He pumped his hand, coaxing the blood to flow into his fingers, allowing heat and pain to awaken his senses. Hayden was the epitome of a puzzle.

A fire glowed in the hearth. He approached and stoked it, teasing the flames to light bigger, brighter. To hell with fear. He stared into the hypnotic flames.

He allowed the sweat to build, his tunic sticking to his skin. The insect-humming outside intensified and sounds of people in his memories and visions argued, cried, and begged. He summoned the Wind. *Send a message to her. Show me my golden Rose.*

He released a primitive growl. The Wind quickened, whirled about him, swayed his disheveled hair, and scratched at the ache in his heart and mind. He squeezed his eyes shut and focused on his Sight. No longer angry, no longer sad, no longer pathetic.

He whispered to it. "Please come to me. Guide me. I am ready to accept my fate."

The answer came to him.

He slept hard.

Edrea surveyed their stretch of the Eastern March from the highest point in the tower house.

More like a prison, her cell for twenty years. Punishment for choosing the wrong man. Punishment for being a woman. Punishment for not providing a worthy male heir.

Upon her return, the soldiers she'd left in charge had informed her that the border reivers had ceased with their constant thievery, fire-setting, and disturbances...for now. Peace was usually a good thing, but not in this case. Her choices of ways Bertie could die without suspicion had decreased. The plan had been to blame it on the reivers.

He hardly ventured anywhere without a protective force, too old, too round to pick up a sword himself. He didn't hunt. He had no men, save for the border patrol, to command. He indulged. Using poison was a thought, but she preferred him to be killed in action to leave no room for speculation of cause.

It was fine. She had other ideas of disposing of him and making it look like an accident. It depended upon the girl's cooperation. Hayden stealing the girl instead of killing her played in her favor. Use her first, then kill her.

She tapped two fingers on the window ledge, peering at a whole lot of nothing. The hills certainly were lovely in the spring and summer, rich in shades of wheat and moss. But she longed for the fresh air of the sea. She longed for the companionship of Lady Isabella, too. She prayed Guilbert would bring home the promising news Warkworth Castle was in their possession. She cradled her swelling middle. Nobody would deny the child was his accept for Bertie himself.

She'd grown accustomed to staring out the sliver of a window in their drab tower, waiting and conspiring. Loneliness numbed her. Bertie would be home any day. She had precious hours to get the girl to agree. Threat of death wasn't working.

She had offered clemency in return for white lies fed to Bertie. The girl refused. Did she not understand her life was at stake?

Hayden snuck up from behind, nearly making her jump from her skin. He ran his hand along her shoulder. She swatted him away. "Dear Almighty, make your presence known next time."

"You've not asked me to your bed, and we've been here a week. I want to taste you again." He kissed her neck, and her body mutinied against her mind as she tilted her head to one side, allowing it. Thankfully, her nausea had passed. "Nobody's here," he added. He slid one hand around her waist, pressed downward, grabbing her through the layers of gown, kirtle, and shift. Seeking.

He did have very good hands…

Hidden by undergarments and gown, her abdomen was rounded, evidence of the child within. Bertie wouldn't ask her to his bed, so he wouldn't see it, but in a few months he would notice it even with her gown layers.

She wriggled in Hayden's touches, both loathing and longing for him. He twisted her around, devoured her lips, the taste of salted meat on his roving tongue. He pawed her roughly, drew her toward him, and unlaced the front of her gown. He shoved a hand down the top of her bodice, squeezed, hard and demanding. She didn't mind it rough, but she was in no mood for his play. He was well-endowed and adequate at addressing her demands in bed. He pressed hard against her, then startled.

Inquiring green eyes, almost angry, sick with his own delusions, stared back. "Is it mine?"

It took the fool long enough to realize it… When they had been naked, had he not seen her belly stretch and grow firmer? The bump had just started protruding this week though, as if overnight. She gritted her teeth and took his lips in hers and bit them, hard, hungrily. "No."

"Good." Cold, unfeeling eyes bore into hers. By the king, she liked the madness raging in his soul.

He ruffled her skirts upward. Curse the hunger heating her veins with the pregnancy. With the nausea subsided, her body begged for physical pleasure. Instead, she pushed his hands down. "Later."

Then she heard the horses below. Guilbert's entourage. *Perfect.* Now to deal with him and explain the girl locked in the cell below the kitchen. He'd readily consume her lies—if Edrea could just convince Rosalie to say them. Bertie was a superstitious louse. He had been the one who usually visited soothsayers. Granted, most found a spot in his bed, too, after manipulating him. A blonde seductress had been the one to convince him to join the Despensers' cause after all.

She'd need to make it seem like his idea. Rosalie was another blonde, another beauty.

Let him rest today. Then he'd listen to the lies tomorrow. He'd see the girl.

Hayden scowled, and muttered Gaelic words, unyielding. He knelt, shoved her gown up with no regard for ripped fabric. "Ah, your beloved is home. One more taste before I must return you."

"I said..."

Her words fell upon deaf ears. She'd give him that. He was persistent and a delightful lover. She leaned against the window, spreading her legs, allowing him to pleasure her with his divine mouth and tongue. This, oh this she would miss when she had to get rid of him. He was smart, too. She ventured her next statement, curious as to what he might suggest. "She..." She stifled a moan. "...won't do it."

"I've another idea if she won't relent." His words grew muffled as he lost himself in her layers of gowns. The burning within her rose and she released once, then he stood, stared at her, holding her gaze while his fingers ravaged. Oh, she'd found her equal.

He brought her to a higher release the second time. She broke from his powerful gaze and bit his shoulder to muffle her own cry.

"Oh?" It was a shame she'd have to dispose of him, too, but she'd leave no loose ends. She hadn't hired him for his bedding skills.

He spun her around, shoved her gown up higher, and pressed into her roughly, harder than she'd ever felt him. She drew near a peak again as he grunted behind her. She watched Bertie's men ride to the stable, unaware of the passion happening in the tower. She almost wanted to wave to him. Let him see she could be as cunning as him. She bit her lip until it bled. "Tell me..."

He nibbled on her neck, almost painfully. He ripped open the front of her bodice further, pushing sleeves down her arms. He grabbed both breasts and squeezed. She rocked her hips, pressing harder against him, allowing him deeper. She gripped the window ledge.

He spoke in a ragged breath. "The Montgomeries will come for her. Domhnall is seduced by her charms. We kill your husband in the skirmish. Blame them for his death."

"You know he will come?" she rasped.

He gasped with his thrusts. "He is too pigheaded. They'll be here soon, for the girl. We then kill them all, your beloved included. Nobody will question it."

It was a grand idea. All that bloodshed. He thrust harder, with determination, as if the death of them all pleasured him, too.

She peaked, and bit back a scream. She then cried out as they both finished together, and her mind spiraled into the darkness, a relief from the torture. She leaned over more. Her breasts squished against the cold stone of the window ledge. Perhaps she'd keep Hayden. He had his assets and had proven to be worth the trouble...and not a bad amusement.

She suspected he'd likely kill her in her sleep one night, and there was only room for one ruler at Warkworth Castle.

She let her mind fragment with the idea of finally being free from Guilbert and this dreadful place once and for all as Hayden fixed his clothes and left without another word.

Two days of watching, and Domhnall's distress wouldn't settle.

Warden Brantingham's force of men had doubled with his return yesterday.

"I'd hoped the men from Edinburgh would've arrived by now," his father said.

"What about negotiation?"

"Brantingham is not one to negotiate. She doesn't confront, and she gets others to do her bidding. That's likely why she had employed Hayden's services. Too cowardly to do it herself. We could try the warden. He's resigning from his position soon, moving closer to the sea. He has nothing to lose. He won't raise a sword to us. We could request an audience, explain the situation, and retrieve Rosalie."

His father rubbed graying stubble on his chiseled chin. "You think he'd release her? I don't trust the English. We need something to bargain with."

Predictable words. Domhnall stepped back from his vantage point in the trees. "We do have something."

His father shook his head. "No. It won't work. Trust me."

Domhnall never questioned his father, but now he would. "That was another time and place. You and Mother...it was a different situation." He didn't voice the story he'd heard repeatedly from his parents. His mother had offered herself in trade for her sister, who had been taken by a rival clan and sworn enemy. It hadn't turned out as they'd planned, though lives were spared. "This is a different kind of trade. Rosalie told me about the lady and warden. I will use my Sight. I will touch him. I am ready."

A vision danced across his mind, but he silenced it. His power of control had grown stronger in the past few days, once he'd permitted the Sight in again.

His father's face hardened. "We'll ride to the gate as guests, present our request, and see what the warden of the Eastern March has to say. No exchange of body or blade. We will follow the ways of the law. If needed, we bring the matter to their baron or earl. I've connections in Northumberland."

"And?"

"We must try to earn his favor first, Domhnall."

It was a good enough compromise. Domhnall minutely shook his head. A Seer for a Seer, after all. He was their bargaining piece. He crossed his arms. "Aye." He had no intention of leaving without Rosalie. Father's suggestion was highly unlikely to succeed.

They mounted their horses, making their way to the primary road to the tower's entrance.

"How do you know she is alive, Domhnall? If it was revenge the lady wanted, then she had it. Didn't you say she wanted Rosalie dead?"

A scratch tickled Domhnall's throat. "I saw it. She's alive," he lied. He didn't like lying, never had, but some lies must be told. "If Lady Brantingham thinks Rosalie to be a genuine Seer, like me, she needs her. The Englishwoman is anything but dumb. Manipulative, unscrupulous. She'll use Rosalie to further her cause until she can't."

"And Hayden?"

Domhnall shrugged. "He's a..." He couldn't say it.

His father frowned. "I'm sorry, son."

"Me, too."

A stiff silence passed between them as the horses clopped on the approach to the gatehouse. Domhnall slowed his horse and tried again. "I think we should expose her as a fraud and convince Warden Brantingham to make a trade for me, the real Seer. He'll release her if I promise to do his bidding and answer his questions."

"Son, you think she—" His father didn't finish.

Domhnall's heart broke considering Rosalie's mistakes. She had not used him. She had reciprocated his love, he was certain.

Father said firmly, "He might listen to reason. Let him know you two are handfasted. This is all a tragic misunderstanding. Although English and clan law differ, he might show pity upon us. She is your future wife, after all. We will negotiate first."

Wife in body already.

His father always drove a hard bargain.

The idea of humiliating Rosalie didn't sit well with Domhnall. What other choice did he have? He needed to get her at any cost. Between the Englishwoman and his deranged friend, she was caught in the den. And the wolves were hungry.

Starving, filthy, and achy from shackles upon her wrists and days of sleeping on a hard, cold dirt floor, Rosalie stumbled beside a guard as they trudged up the steps from the dark bowels of the tower. He didn't help her. She wiped soiled hands on her gown. Was she being brought to her death? Noose or beheading? As she emerged into a meager-sized kitchen, daylight shining through a slat window blinded her for a moment. A pain shot through her skull. She suppressed a moan and licked parched lips.

An elderly woman approached, arms filled with linens, slippers, and a gown. She crinkled her nose and high forehead. "I must ready her for presentation."

The soldier nodded and followed the servant and Rosalie to another room off the kitchen, a chamber with a table, hand mirror, and no window or hearth. Two cots sat to one side. Servants' quarters. The soldier unlocked the shackles and allowed them to drop to the dirty floor, gave the woman a warning look, and left the room, closing the door behind him. Two candles burned on the table, providing less light with the door closed.

Rosalie rubbed her chafed wrists. "I'm to be presented?"

The servant nodded and got to work, lighting tapers. She poured water into a basin, soaked a half-soiled rag, then scrubbed Rosalie's wrists, hands, and lower arms. "Undress. I've another gown for you."

She winced at the vigorous rubbing of pink wrists. The shackles were excessive. Sores and blisters covered the bottoms of her feet—and she suspected her behind, too—from riding and walking, and from sleeping on the dirt floor the past two weeks.

"Let me." Rosalie took the rag and dipped it in the tepid water. She finished with her washing, trying to find a clean corner of the rag to dab at her face. "Lady Brantingham likes her prisoners to be cleaned and dressed nicely for their execution?" she said tartly. She slipped off her boots, happy for once to have finer slippers provided. Tremors erupted within her at the thought of dying. How had it come to this? She wanted to cry. Apparently, it had become her new habit.

The servant clucked as she untied Rosalie's gown, removed the filthy apron, and mumbled under her breath in disapproval. "You're to be presented to Warden Brantingham. You best do what milady wishes, Miss Threston. I've never seen her so irate."

"You know me?" She didn't think Edrea would be one to divulge a prisoner's name to her servants.

"Indeed, I know you. I know your auntie. And you've the look of your mum."

Rosalie dropped the linen. She twisted around much to the servant's consternation. "You knew my mother?" She pressed a hand to her chest.

"Darlin', Lady Brantingham waits for no soul. I'm Constance. Call me Connie." She switched to pushing the sleeves down the dress because Rosalie's arms remained limp at her sides, shivers prickling her fingertips.

Heavy footsteps paced outside the room. Armor chinked.

Rosalie stood frozen. Trembles bubbled in her belly as she whispered, "If I'm to be presented to the warden and God knows if she, if she..." She couldn't say it aloud. Edrea had been eerily composed with her demands, not the hotheaded fury Rosalie had imagined. Edrea had come in to see her in the cell but once to issue commands—orders that Rosalie had refused to follow. Edrea never was one to make unnecessary appearances.

Rosalie had not budged with the lady's threats even. Edrea had promised leniency if Rosalie told specific, provided lies to the warden: a false "vision." Did she have the strength to tell one final lie? To save herself? "I can't lie anymore. I can't..."

"You must. If you wish to live. I've not spent twenty years under her iron fist not knowing what's what."

Rosalie nodded as tears dribbled down her cheeks.

Connie softened her tone. "I used to talk with your auntie, Nelda, when she came to work. You see, the lady only hires old crones like me now. No fair-haired beauties allowed anymore. Not with the warden's roaming eyes and hands. Oh, Nelda, a lively spirit! Is she well?"

"Yes." More or less. Rosalie stepped into the dusky pink gown. Connie laced her in, pulling tight on the bodice. Rosalie swiped at her disheveled hair.

"We can comb it, dear."

She clutched Connie's frail hands. The woman must have been years older than Nelda. She held a sharp awareness in her clear blue eyes and thin-lipped smile. "Please tell me. Does she live? My mother?" She reached into the pocket of her gown on the cot. "My bracelet. It was found with me when I was a baby, found by my aunt and uncle. How could my mother have owned such a bracelet? Was she—? Was she a noblewoman?"

God, please say she wasn't a thief. Or liar like me.

Connie gasped but didn't touch the gold bracelet.

There was a cough at the door.

Connie drew Rosalie close and whispered, "I can't say more. I'm sorry. But...I suggest you wear the fine bracelet when presented to the warden."

She brushed Rosalie's hair, used a comb to pin it half up, brushed her face with a sort of face paint, and departed without another word.

Boldly, Rosalie slid her hand into the bracelet and settled it on her chafed wrist as the soldier escort reappeared. If ever there was a time to wear the bracelet, it was now.

She had no plan. All she had were the orders given to her by Edrea. She was to take the warden's hand, read his palm, and lie.

The final lie. Then, no more.

CHAPTER SEVENTEEN

W ith deliberate, mindful breaths, Rosalie stepped into the hall, ushered by the soldier. Hardly a window was dressed, nor wall adorned with tapestry. Cooler late summer brought shivers to her uncovered arms. A simple chair at the end, almost like a king's throne, sat empty, facing dilapidated tables and benches. One hearth glowed low on the far end of the modest room. The keep was a march post and stood taller than the usual castle. It consisted of two tall towers, one larger than the other. A walkway with archers' windows to watch, aim, and loose arrows connected the towers. It was more fortress than home.

As if summoned by her thoughts, Edrea entered from a rear door, her arm tucked within her husband's. Behind them came guards, five of them, followed by Hayden.

Her grit dissipated. She wondered what convincing lie Hayden had used upon the warden to explain his presence. She suspected how he had charmed his way into Edrea's claws. Reflection perplexed her: who was her fiercest opponent? Edrea, Hayden, or the warden? Of the people before her, the warden seemed the one she'd find most favor with, though he was a stranger. She curtsied, feeling like an imprisoned swan in her gown. "Warden," she said. Was he a lord, too?

The stout man, many years Edrea's senior, cleared his throat, released his wife's arm, and hobbled to the simple throne-like chair at the head of the room.

At least she understood a warden's role, the purpose of this tower, and all the political unrest. Her informal education by Oswell still served as an asset.

"My wife says you're a soothsayer," the warden asserted, his deep voice piercing her to the bone.

She nodded, deepening the curtsy and lowering her gaze from his penetrating brown eyes. "I am." The soldier beside her poked her in the shoulder. She took one timid step closer.

"Come forth, girl. Don't waste my time."

She crossed the distance, each step harder than the previous, her pulse pounding. She rubbed her hands together, encouraging warmth. "I must see your hands, Warden, for the revelation to come to me."

He scowled but offered a hand.

She traced the lines, ran a finger along the mounds. His hands showed many years of hard work. Thick, rough. As a soldier, not laborer. Cuts, callouses, and lines worn from use. Instinct told her to rely on proven methods, spout off traits she'd already acquired from Edrea, then draw on the elements, his strengths, and his weaknesses. Instead, she repeated the lies, tweaking them. "I presage an unfortunate future for you, my lord. A death by blades. Men from—" She paused. Edrea had ordered her to say from the north among the heather and peat, but she couldn't do it. No, she would not implicate any Scot. She swallowed, closed her eyes, and wrestled the suffocating sensation trying to close her throat as the lie consumed her. "—men from afar. You must strike first."

"See. I told you. She's a powerful one," Edrea said, stepping forward, triumph in her eyes.

The warden ignored her. He withdrew his beefy hand from Rosalie's, not wavering in his visage. "You a witch?"

She wobbled. "No, my lord."

"How do I believe you?" He cocked an angled look. Pink flushed his heavy cheeks and wrinkles rippled a high, balding forehead. "I've visited many soothsayers, and you are by far the youngest and the first to suggest my demise. What have you been promised?" He glared at Edrea, then Rosalie.

Then, he snapped his fingers. A servant appeared, carrying a tray with a goblet and pitcher.

Rosalie cast not a look at Edrea, Hayden, or the soldiers with their sharp swords and spears. Instead, she held the warden's eyes. They were chestnut brown with flecks of green, wide set beside a nose with large pores. She neither feared nor found solace in his countenance. She knew enough about the warden's indiscretions and his authoritarian rule over the border. "Visions come to me. I portend the future."

Vague. Lame.

A man from behind interrupted their conversation. "Lord Warden? We have visitors."

All turned to the slender servant. He dipped a bow.

"For Christ's sake. First, I acquiesce to Edrea's insistence I meet the girl, and now visitors? Who? Nobody knows I've returned. Percy's men?"

The man clasped his hands into a ball. He kept his gaze drawn down to the uncovered stone floor. "A Laird

Alasdair Montgomerie and his son, milord. They come from Eilean Donan, Glen Shiel of Scotland."

The warden's face soured. Rosalie's heart nearly stopped.

"That's far into the Highlands." He rubbed a chin covered with gray whiskers. He shot Rosalie a hard look. "These men? Did you see them? Are these the men from afar?"

"I...uh..." Rosalie faltered, aghast. They had come. Into the trap. No! She cast a look around for help, for hope. Hayden's mouth hitched as he leered at her. The arse seemed pleased with himself.

A scowl deepened a ridge across the warden's high forehead. "What is their business?"

The servant said, "They request an audience with you."

"With no explanation? How many are with them?"

"It is just the two, warden. No soldiers. They rode to the keep peacefully under no banner."

The warden released a throaty growl. He looked at his wife with a hooded gaze, then to Rosalie with a glower. "Did you see these men, girl?" he repeated.

Edrea's look would kill if it could. She pursed her lips tightly. No nod, no mouthed words. The order had been clear.

Rosalie swayed, dizziness assailing her. "No, my lord. It's not them. The men I saw came from much farther away. Across the sea."

Edrea stepped forward, her gown swaying with the sudden movement, then back. She pinched her lips harder.

The warden regarded Rosalie with either the patience of a priest or the disdain of a man who had no qualms with issuing execution orders.

The fine hair lifted on her nape, sweat joining her quickened heartbeat in her chest.

The warden waved permission to the servant waiting near the entrance.

A moment later, the visitors strode into the hall with regal poise. Domhnall gave her not a glimpse, his face staunchly forward, toward the warden. Exhaustion circled his eyes and paled his normally ruddy complexion. His stance appeared strained, forced, but to the other observers, his tension likely wasn't obvious.

"Laird Montgomerie, what brings you south?" the warden asked without pretense.

"Lord Warden," Alasdair said with a respectful nod. "We believe the lass has been wrongfully imprisoned by your wife, and we ask for her release."

The warden's demeanor held no surprise even if it erupted within him. He sipped from his goblet. "What matter do you have with an English peasant?"

"She was caught north with her ruse, swindled several nobles in the glen of good coin."

"Ruse?" He darted his look to Edrea, then gave Alasdair a condescending one. "You Scots will believe anything, won't you? Superstitious fools."

Wasn't he just as superstitious? *Bite your tongue, Rose.*

Domhnall stepped forward. "She is a fraud. A liar."

The warden released a booming laugh. "A fraud, you say? She's an English peasant and is subject to our laws, not yours. I will decide what she has or has not done, on our soil."

"We ask for her to return with us, to be tried in our court, Lord Warden," Alasdair pressed.

Rosalie rocked in place, her fingers twitching. Trial here, trial there. They argued over who would see her hung?

The warden leaned back in his chair, tenting his fingers under his chin. "What proof do you have of this misdemeanor?"

Domhnall released clenched hands from his sides. "A Seer knows. She lies, but I do not. I can offer myself in her stead."

Rosalie shifted from foot to foot. "My lord, I—"

"Silence!" Edrea hissed from across the room.

Hayden's hand subtly went to his sword. Edrea's face could not have gotten any darker with the squall crossing it.

The warden gripped the arms of his chair and leaned in. "What in the king's name do you mean? In her stead?"

"I'm a real Seer, hailing from the Ancients of the isles. Let me read you, and you shall see," Domhnall said with smooth confidence.

Rosalie practically flung herself in front of Domhnall. "He lies! I am true, Lord Warden."

Domhnall pushed her aside, roughly. "She lies. She is a peasant looking for coin."

"I have two lying Seers in my hall now," the warden countered. His voice thickened, growing coarser by the moment. He waved his hand into the air. "Be gone. I'll deal with the girl."

Domhnall grabbed Rosalie's wrist, the one with the bracelet. "She is a peasant. She lies and steals. You think a woman of her stature could own such a thing?"

Recognition contorted the warden's face. "How did you get that?" He tilted a glare to the gold bracelet. "Step forward, girl. Now."

Rosalie found her voice, albeit, it quaked. "It was given to me by my uncle. He said it was my mother's. I-I did not steal it, Lord Warden. I'm not a thief."

Edrea gasped. Realization must have struck her too, for she entered the mix in front of the warden, no longer able to contain her façade. "She is the Seer. The bracelet was payment from me. She—she saw truths. She saw the deaths of Asher and James...she told me after the war," she quickly added, covering her mistake.

The warden silenced his wife with a cutting look, then frowned at Rosalie. "You knew about their deaths? Anyone could have told you. It was common knowledge in this region."

Domhnall gave a quick squeeze to Rosalie's hand, then dropped it, kneeling before the warden. Two soldiers stepped forward, spears in front position. "Let me read you. I'll show you the truth, Lord Warden." He lifted submissive hands in the air, now at the warden's side. One soldier grabbed Domhnall from behind to restrain him. "Take my sword. Please, lord. You have only to gain. Give me a chance, and if you're not satisfied, we'll leave without the lass."

The soldier took Domhnall's sword.

The warden pursed his lips and relented with a groan. Domhnall reached and laid a hand upon the man's shoulder. The warden halted his soldiers with a wave, allowing it.

A long moment passed. Rosalie could not tear her attention from the scene. She kept her gaze steady on

Domhnall and the warden. All did. A wind blew through the open door, and she trembled, hugging her elbows, chilled to the bone. Domhnall was dead still, almost in a trance. His eyes stared into a far-off place. She wondered about the darkness and pain he was feeling.

Finally, he released his hand, exhaled as if breathless from a run, then whispered in the warden's ear.

Shock, then realization lit Guilbert Brantingham's eyes. He turned a fierce look upon his wife. She blanched. "I thought the bracelet looked familiar. You lying whore!" He waved a finger in a circle, and the soldiers immediately made their way to Edrea.

"No! He lies. The girl is the true Seer. She saw James and Asher. She saw it all. She tried to warn me before the war."

"Warn you? You went to her *before* the war? You knew my sons would die? You expected me to fall, too. So you could get your hands on my land, you—you..."

Nobody came to Edrea's defense, not even Hayden.

Edrea pleaded, "Please, Bertie. Please. Have mercy on me. I didn't..." She turned a wrathful stare upon Rosalie. "She's another one of your whores' children! I sent her to a better home."

The bracelet. Edrea knew? She knew about Rosalie's mother?

The warden's voice boomed off the rafters. "You lie. This man has shown it to me. You ordered her dead. Drowned. One of the servants showed pity upon the child. Sent her with the bracelet I'd given the mother."

Edrea wept. "You killed her. You killed our daughter, Bertie. She was born on the same night. The midwife was off tending to your whore's birth. That girl," she said with a long-fingered point to Rosalie, "lived, and my child died in her stead. I bled too much, and our only child…died."

Guilbert shook his head, his lips flattening, a deep V in his forehead digging down to a cold, flint-like gaze. Whatever Domhnall had said held more power over the warden than Edrea's pleas or Rosalie's farce. "Take her to the prison."

Edrea fought the guards. She spat and said to Rosalie, "Your mother was nothing but a whore. A lowly servant in my kitchen." She growled to Hayden behind her, "Why didn't you tell me about the bracelet, you imbecile?"

"Enough, Edrea! You think I'm stupid? I know what you've been conspiring," her husband said.

Edrea's face crumpled at being betrayed as she beheld Hayden's smirk. "He's a Scot. You believe him?"

"Money goes farther than opening your legs, wife," the warden chided.

She clawed at a soldier trying to restrain her. "Bertie. I'm with child. Your son grows in my womb."

"More lies. You threatened the girl with death. I only agreed to let her read me to see if she'd say what you'd ordered. I knew before I entered the room, Edrea. I needed to see for myself to what level you'd reduce yourself." He tsked. "Percy was always right about you. I had an enlightening conversation with Lady Isabella, too, while away."

The girl. The lass. The fraud. Rosalie's heart withered. *I have a name. It's Rose.* All this talk of her like she was a pawn, a criminal. Was she? "My name is Rose," she whispered under her breath. A whore's child.

Edrea's complexion grew ashen. "Lady Isabella? Bertie, please! We can raise our son…our son," she whimpered.

"That night, Guilbert, my husband, after we received the news about your sons. You came to me. You returned to our bed, drunk as a stone. You don't remember. But I do. Your seed grows within me."

He shook his head. "Take her away. I'll decide what to do with her later."

Edrea spat at him as she was brought past. "You don't deserve me."

Rosalie's pulse would not settle as the men disbanded and spoke. Alasdair strode to the warden, bowed, and offered condolences about his sons, and the travesty before them. Rosalie stepped farther back, almost tripping on the longer gown, away from Domhnall, shielding her heart and shrinking from the hurtful truths he had unleashed.

Peasant. Liar.

Now what?

The kitchen servant, Connie, materialized beside her. "It'll be well, darlin'." She tapped her arm.

"How will it all be well? What about my mother?" she nearly squeaked, too ashamed to return Domhnall's quick glance from beside his father as they spoke in whispers with the warden.

She was a liar. A bastard.

"You are the warden's child. Whoring and drinking aside, he is a decent man. He'll see you cared for. The bracelet. I've seen it. He gave it to her, your mum. Master always had a weakness for the fair-haired beauties. Mr. Iverson might have told the warden about the lady's plans, but I was the one who informed him of the bracelet, just before we came in here. You're fortunate Lady Brantingham didn't see the bracelet until now. She would've had you killed. The warden adored your mother, the best a man of his stature could."

The warden was her father. Edrea had known her mother. Her head spun, and she thought she'd collapse if Connie hadn't been holding onto her. She collected herself and returned her focus to the swarm of men near the throne-chair.

A shuffle, terse, heated words, a scuffle. "Seize him," the warden ordered with a chin flick to Hayden.

With lightning speed, Hayden withdrew a dagger and sliced one soldier in the stomach. Caught another across his face. Before either Alasdair or Domhnall could retrieve their swords, Hayden ran out a side door. Two men made chase.

Rosalie knew they'd find nothing but the wind.

CHAPTER EIGHTEEN

Rosalie waited in a private chamber, a nicer room than she had changed in only hours before. She rubbed her raw wrists.

Connie entered, a thick cloak and new boots in her hands. "Milord says you may keep the gown, and these are for you. The cloak will keep you from catching chill come harvest. New boots."

"I'm leaving?" A strange sadness curdled her thoughts.

"He offered for you to stay for evening's sup, but your men insisted upon leaving. They convinced him of your importance north. The Seer, he is your husband?"

Your men. Your husband. She didn't know how to answer. "I am to go? With them?"

"Yes, mistress."

No sweetheart or darling or fraud or liar or peasant. Mistress.

"It's for the best."

"He—the warden—doesn't want me." Her father. Did nobody want her? Her stomach hurt. All she'd had today was a bit of bread and cheese brought to her when she'd been swept up to this high chamber in the tower dominating the grounds. She grew tired of being whisked off to chambers. "My family is home in Edinburgh. My aunt and uncle. Will I be taken to them?"

Connie shrugged, holding the cloak for her. "That's for you and your husband to determine, I suppose. Take heart, mistress. It's not you. It's the warden. He likely doesn't know how to handle it all. You being his child. Besides, he needs a son, an heir."

Sent away. She had been dumped in a basket as a baby, and even now nobody wanted her. She sniffled.

Damn the tears. The floodgates had opened. "My mother? You knew her well?"

Connie nodded. "I did. Her name was Elizabeth. She preferred the nickname Lillie. She was as fair-haired and beautiful as you, with the same eyes. Kind eyes. She enjoyed flowers, especially blue ones, like forget-me-nots. She chose your name. Rose. Nelda must have changed it to Rosalie when they took you away."

A knock stirred Rosalie from her melancholy. Connie curtsied and left the room. "Sir," she said to Domhnall on her way out.

Hesitant steps brought him to Rosalie's side. "Rose."

She fixed him with a stare. What could she say? She placed her palm over her lips to stop the unbidden tears. "I didn't steal a thing. But I told horrible lies. I-I was going to leave, left the note, but changed my mind, and then Hayden grabbed me."

"I know."

She sucked in her lips. "You needed for it to be true. I lied. It got out of hand. I didn't mean for any of this to happen. Domhnall," she said through a hitching chest, a cramp in her stomach, "I'm not a Seer like you. You are the true one. I'm not your answer. I'm not your fate."

He slid his hand around hers and squeezed.

She turned it over then drew a finger along the mounts and ridges that spoke to her.

"You read people, Rose. Better than I can. I never suspected Hayden, but I imagine you did, didn't you?"

She nodded, blinking through wet eyes. "But he was your friend, so I excused it, I accepted that maybe he was genuine."

"I was a fool. Thought it was just his way. I was always making excuses for him, too. He was a friend. Or at least I thought he was. I believed what I wanted to see as true." He shook his head, loose hair swaying and a shadow crossing his serious features. "I should've seen it, but I didn't. He killed Maisie. He killed Kyla. He lied for years. He kept near me, not as friend, but as adversary. He was waiting for me to regain my visions."

"I'm like him. I lie."

"You did it to survive." His eyes darkened. "And you are nothing like him."

"But you—"

He repeated, firmer, "You did it to survive. I try to pretend that I'm like all others, but I was born into nobility, and born different. I was wrong to think I could understand the commoner's plight. Rose, I'm sorry for what I said, downstairs. I had to convince him to release you. I didn't mean any of it."

She weaved her fingers through his. "I'm sorry, Domhnall."

"I am, too. I-I—" He heaved a sigh. He lowered his gaze. "We were fated to find each other. Maybe your instinct and skill are grounded in something else, beyond what we can explain on earth, but we were fated, I swear it."

"I don't think so. Practice and intuition...are nothing like your ability. Mine is all learned."

He drew her to a cushioned bench. They sat for a long moment, caressing each other's hands.

"Did you see my mother and Lady Brantingham in your vision? What you told the warden?" she asked.

He massaged his temple with one hand, keeping the other hand interlocked with hers. "Aye. I can control it better now. The visions come immediately with touch or when I call for them, but I can temper them. I've spoken to the Wind. We have come to an understanding. Sounds daft." He choked on his words, tears stifling them. "If I embrace them, I can manage them. I won't fear them any-more. With vision comes enlightenment. I had to open my mind and heart to the power of the Silver Veil."

"That's good?"

He nodded. "Aye. The warden is your father, Rose. I saw it. Your mother was a servant here, and the warden, well...anyway, she gave birth on the same evening as the lady, but Brantingham's child took no breath. You didn't either, at first. Not a tear. Your mother wept, thinking you were dead. You were taken in a basket, and your mother placed the bracelet within—it had been a gift from the warden. A while later, you woke, were breathing, but your mother never saw. She thought you were dead. Edrea ordered you to be disposed of, but Nelda snatched you, said she'd take care of it. Instead, she left, took you as her own."

Hope filled her chest. "Is my mother alive?"

"No. She died a few years later. I'm sorry, Rose."

Lillie. At least she had a name now. A memory to cling to.

She took her hand from his and stood. Languid legs brought her to the window. The setting sun cast hues of orange across the rolling countryside. "He does not want me."

"He asked for you to stay. He offered you a home near the coast if you'd want it. Mentioned a man who could marry you."

She spun around.

He was quick to soothe her unsettled pulse. "I told him we are married. He seemed relieved you'd be provided for. It sounded like he cared about your mother. He was not a faithful husband, but I think he cares in his own way."

She understood. "He doesn't wish to see me? To say goodbye?"

"I'm sorry." He came to her and cupped her chin with a finger and thumb. "What about our future? Tell me my fortune, Rose. Tell me all you see."

Was he teasing her? "Why do you belittle me? All you said in there—"

"Was a lie. I love you. Come home with me."

"I told you, I can't see the way you do—"

He traced her fingers, the knolls, the lines. "I'll tell you what I see instead." He leaned in to kiss her. "I see you with me," he breathed as his lips homed in on hers.

"You do? I've wronged you."

"I've not been the most forthcoming or understanding. I've put expectations upon you. I tried to see something that was not there. I owe you an apology. I was first drawn to you as a fellow Seer. I thought we could find solace with each other. I could get answers." He gestured with an aimless hand. "I wanted to find another who suffered like me. Who understood my grief. This…" He pointed to her heart, then his. "This is more. Better than what I had tried to force. You are real. You are here. You are my truth."

"No more lies," she said, taking his lips in return. "Truths only." He squeezed her, heart against heart, both beating hard, steady, and true.

Autumn arrived in splendid color in southern Scotland.

Domhnall paced the hallway abutting the open, grassy courtyard of Dryburgh Abbey. His legs held a different kind of restlessness today. Rosalie had always wanted to see the abbeys, and what better place for their wedding ceremony? The priests had spent a few weeks with her, during the wedding preparations, showing her their trove of ancient texts and teachings. With her quick mind, she devoured the learning, utilizing his teaching as foundation.

His father clapped a hand on his shoulder. "Nervous?"

"Aye."

He didn't know why. They were already married in heart and body. His mother approached, giving off her bright yellow lifeblood, which Domhnall now felt. He felt many lifebloods. She hesitated touching him, so he drew her into a hug. The burst of a vision danced behind his eyes…a good one. Of his parents, together, well-aged and content.

"Och, your lifeblood glows stronger than I've ever felt." She embraced him fully, suppressing tears of happiness as she leaned her head on his shoulder. "It brings me incredible joy to hug you again, love."

Without ado, they strode to the grand cathedral of the abbey, its stone walls rosy and robust. His grandfather had been fond of the abbey, and Domhnall felt he not only fulfilled Rosalie's wish to visit one, but he paid homage to his grandparents by having the ceremony here. His entire family was in attendance: Mother, Father, Great-Uncle Kendrick, aunts Caite and Fiora, uncles Crystoll and Edmund, his sisters Gracie and Aileana, and all his cousins. Hayden had disappeared into thin air.

A hole carved by the betrayal sat within Domhnall. But he silenced that pain.

Afternoon warmth blessed the sanctuary through the speckled glass of the rose window. Incense perfumed the air, and the congregation settled their talking.

Rosalie awaited him near the altar, radiant in a pale-yellow dress, matching her buttermilk blonde locks. His yellow rose. She had never pervaded a vision in her bodily form, but the yellow roses always had, and still did.

Fate? He liked to think so. His mind was open to the world of the mystical, to the Silver Veil. He stood beside his bride, clasped her hands, and smiled. Before him stood the truth. Love and releasing control to the fates had brought him here.

Domhnall twirled Rosalie around the grassy court-yard as the music emanated from a trio of string musicians in the corner. She laughed, panting as he remained by her side the entire evening, hardly un-linking his arm or hand from hers. She was dancing. At her own wedding. Oswell and Nelda, both in good spirit, had been present for the nuptials and feast.

Hours passed in a blur of contentment and mer-riment. Breathing heavily, Domhnall pulled her aside to a corner of the courtyard. "Shall we make another escape?" He cocked an enticing dark eyebrow.

"Oh?" Like at their handfasting *cèilidh*, she squeezed his hand as they navigated around congratulations and gaiety. She burst with giggles as they neared their room in the abbey. Many of the guests would sleep in lodgings in the nearby town, in tents on the lawn, or within the cottages or spare rooms in the abbey. Never had the abbey hosted an event of such grandeur.

A low hearth glowed in their room. Domhnall swiveled with a dreamy flare, then closed and locked the door. "My wife." He swooped in, capturing her lips.

"My husband," she responded, eager hands unclasp-ing his belt, then lifting his tunic, pausing only for a moment to admire the golden embroidery on the cuffs and V-shaped neck. He had looked regal and noble in the full attire, standing beside her in the abbey's chapel. She kissed his broad chest, glistening with a hint of perspiration. She wanted all of him. "I can't believe we're here." She teased a nipple with her tongue. She inhaled his fresh, clean scent.

He moaned. "I can. You're my fate, whether we believe in it or not."

"Fate, am I?"

"My golden rose. My fair Rose."

Serenity chased away all doubts from her mind.

He unlaced the front of her gown with playful precision. He nestled his chin in her cleavage, gifting her with kisses all over her neck and collarbone. Riots of good shivers scaled her arms and legs. He undressed her seductively, driving her closer to the brink of impatience. Too many layers. She'd never felt more decadent. At least for one night. Tomorrow, she'd happily don her usual homespun gown for the journey north to Eilean Donan. A life as lady awaited her. Like Domhnall's mother, she looked forward to her time among the gardens and kitchens and townspeople. Together, she and Domhnall could maintain the simpler life in Dornie, where commoner and noble worked side by side.

She stood in front of him, naked as her final layers fell to the floor. He cast her a hungry look as he unhurriedly untied the lengthy laces on his boots. Firelight glinted off his molded shoulders, chest, and abdominal muscles. Finally, he dropped his matching hose with a deliberate, downright tempting, air. With a hand, she brought him to the fur spread on the floor in front of their glowing hearth. "The fire, are you all right with it?"

He kissed her in response and cupped her bottom, lifting her into his full embrace, his own need pressing against her belly. She muffled a squeak.

"I am if you're with me. You bring out the fire within me, my fair Rose." He laid her upon the rug and stroked the length of her unplaited hair, curling tips around his finger. He brought her hair to his nose. "You even smell of rosewater." He massaged all her curves, his hand warm, the eternal cold absent. His heat matched the fire.

They spent the night on the fur, making love, embraced in each other's warmth, wrapped in completion.

"Where are you going?" Rosalie asked, her voice laced with sleep.

The hearth cast dim light in the room. Domhnall had put logs on to keep her warm. He strapped his belt and sword on. "On watch. I want to check the perimeter."

"The priests don't have much in the way of a guard, but your father has men on posts. I saw." She rose in the bed, the thick bedclothes falling below her perfect breasts.

He kissed her on the forehead. "He does. I—"

"Need a walk," she finished, already knowing him.

"Wait, first, my gift for you." She slipped out of the bedclothes, her hips swaying as she shuffled to the near table. She lifted a linen and turned around with a box in her hand.

He took it, his cheeks hurting from the smile. "It's beautiful. The different woods and stains...where did you find it?" He traced hands over the ornate wooden puzzle box, shifting dials. "It rivals Athol's work."

"The priests helped me find one by a local woodwright. Do you like it? I never gave you a handfasting gift." Firelight flickered in her eyes as she nestled beneath the bedclothes.

He leaned in and kissed her full, hard. "Love it. I'll be back soon. Promise. Love you."

"Love you, too."

One final puzzle to solve.

He took the river path, the water's splashing tune soothing, his body fully relaxed from being with Rosalie. She was his other half. Seer or not, she was the one he had been destined to find. His fingers danced on the sword in expectation. When he caught the rustle behind him, he turned, not surprised. He had seen it after all. More than habit and compulsion had brought him outside this night.

"My friend," Hayden said to him.

"I'm not your friend. You've always liked to sneak up on me. But I've learned a lot since you left."

"Have you?" Hayden stepped closer in challenge, his longsword held out before him in both hands, ready. He angled his right foot forward for his usual stance.

"You want to do this? Here? After everything?" Domhnall kept his hand on his sword's hilt, ready.

"Yes."

"You couldn't just stay away?"

He gave a shrug of acquiescence.

"Why did you kill Maisie?"

His wide smirk reflected the moon's glow. "Did I need a reason?"

Domhnall hoped there had been one. The stealing, he understood. Nothing else made sense. Hayden's abusive father, his lower standing and class rank, his hardship as a child...something must have transformed Hayden into a monster. His father's abandonment aside, Hayden had an adequate upbringing with a mother who loved him, taught him good moral standing.

In front of him stood a stranger. On the outside, even to him, Hayden had been a charmer. Inside, a sick man who killed for money, for prestige, and for no real reason? Could a man be born this way?

Who killed without cause?

"Don't," Domhnall encouraged, his hand up.

"You always blamed yourself...you and your cursed Sight. I watched you punish yourself over and over. Like a fool. You should've let it go. But you wouldn't."

"All the other things? The stealing, Kyla, Rose?"

"Because I wanted to."

Hayden's explanations made no sense. He was a man with a tortured mind. Deranged. A person who felt justified doing wrong. How could a person kill for no reason, with no motivation? Just for pleasure?

Hayden made the first move, passing forward while attempting a strike. Domhnall sidestepped, unsheathed his sword, and blocked Hayden's next attack. Both paused.

"Hayden, don't do this." He couldn't let him go. Hayden had to see trial. See justice.

"I don't leave business unfinished. You're a fool, Domhnall. You had it all. You had a gift, and you denied it. The power you held! You have parents who love you. You could be both laird and constable. What about me?"

"I tried. I was going to promote you when the time came. You know this."

Hayden sneered and rolled his eyes. "Lame attempts. I stood by your side in everything. You couldn't keep my mother employed. Lady Deirdre can heal and chose not to save my mother. Lanie chose that dolt, Brodie, over me." He chuckled to himself. "Watching you try to solve the puzzle was entertaining though. All of it right under your nose! Then Edrea came along and provided me with the perfect opportunity to see this matter done with once and for all."

They flowed through the fight as if in memory, synchronized movements from their practices together. They parried, sloped, cut across, and countered moves.

Domhnall stomped, pretending an attack to lure Hayden to defend.

Hayden did not. He laughed. "Not this time. I've learned. I'm always learning. You are not."

They exchanged blows, both growing winded. Hayden purposely rammed him in the shoulder in a brutal tactic. Flashes of visions blinded Domhnall, but he carried on through it, letting an internal awareness guide him along with Hayden's steps. The Wind roared in his ears.

"I see that you've gotten better with controlling the visions?" Hayden sneered. He took a passing step while in Domhnall's thrusting measure. Hayden responded to the thrust with a panicked parry, trying to recover his step. He stumbled, and Domhnall brought his sword within slicing breadth of Hayden's shoulder.

Domhnall stepped back and lowered his blade.

"You're weak. Never one for follow-through," Hayden said with his familiar sneer. He coughed and winced in pain. "You always chose to avoid, took your walks all day and all night, to hide instead of facing the challenge directly, like a braw man." He spat blood.

Domhnall lifted his sword in a feinted move, luring him in. Hayden never backed from a chance to bring his opponent down. He blocked Hayden's advance, holding his sword in place, then kicked him in the groin.

Hayden tripped, dropping his sword, and hunching.

"You will see trial." Domhnall kicked the sword farther away. He did not sheathe his own. Nor did he raise it to kill his former childhood companion, his brother of the Watch. Grandfather Simon always said mercy was more powerful than blade.

Hayden scowled, getting on all fours, then rising with a painful gurgle. He withdrew a hidden dagger and attempted to strike.

Surprised, Domhnall moved in time to prevent a lethal blow—by his father's own *sgian- dubh*. The dagger caught him on his arm. He winced at the searing pain but recovered and knocked the dagger from Hayden's hand.

"You can come out," he hollered over his shoulder. Hayden would be tried. Domhnall had seen it in the vision while they fought. Hayden would see the end of a noose. Kendrick and two other clansmen appeared at his side.

Hayden's shoulders slumped as he rose. The charm had disappeared. Before Domhnall stood a man beaten by his own doing, a weakened spirit, a man who had controlled every move, calculated every day to serve himself only.

"You've your grandfather's compassion," Kendrick said. He sheathed his sword while the two others restrained Hayden and walked ahead of them.

"I heard Grandfather Simon was a killer, hellbent on revenge before he met my grandmother Gwyn." Grandda had talked often about being a merciful laird and ruler, but Simon MacCoinneach had a tainted past, when sword had ruled his life.

"Nothing love couldn't cure." Kendrick nodded and stood beside him as the soldiers hauled Hayden to the abbey.

"Rumor has it there is a prison cell in the depths of the holy sanctuary." Domhnall cradled his injured arm.

"Aye, there is."

Domhnall sighed. "I'm not meant to be laird or constable."

"Mayhap," Kendrick agreed.

Domhnall snorted. "Thanks for the confidence, Uncle. I try too hard to be like the commoner, to rule with no bias, and I try too hard to watch and command men. I can't do either well."

They walked with weighted steps and minds to the abbey. Kendrick said, "Maybe you need to be with your kin for a while before you discern your true path. You need to learn more about the Silver Veil. Hone your gift. You've time to decide about being laird. You've seen it. Your father has many years left in this world."

"My kin? I am with you and my family. Dornie is my home."

"I meant your mother's side. The Ancients."

His chest constricted. "They're all dead. We're all that's left."

"No. I've spent many years searching for the brothers and fathers who'd fled my home isle of Uist when the Nordmen came."

"Oh?" Domhnall's pulse flickered.

Kendrick's face stretched in an aged, wise, and content smile. "I've found them."

"Where?"

"The Isle of Barra."

EPILOGUE

A crisp spring morning cloaked with sun-light—with hope—met Domhnall and Rosalie as they disembarked in the bustling port town on Barra. A turquoise sea crashed against a glistening alabaster beach in the wide bay. Kelp draped the shoreline of grass-covered dunes. Boulder-speckled and rounded crags surrounded the town, as guardians of a sleepy village, guardians of secrets.

Like his mother had before him, Domhnall needed to meet his kin, see with his own eyes. See the truth from the lies. Certainly, Kendrick had enlightened him on many things over the past six months. There were others—like him—who saw death, saw life, saw the past and future. Others who had been displaced and massacred for their gift from the Silver Veil. Distant cousins and blood family. Did they truly exist or was he one of the last?

The truth bellowed within his bones.

After a quick rest and meal, they rode through the village of small homesteads. His steed carried a satchel loaded with the three books of the Ancients. The time had come to write the book of the Wind.

Rosalie sighed with exertion as they brought their horses to a halt after a quick ride across the isle. "Almost there?"

"Yes."

With no hesitation she asked, "What do you see, Domhnall?"

All he had to do was close his eyes to access the Silver Veil now. No more unbridled death. He had harnessed full control of his gift in the past few months.

In the darkness behind his eyelids, splashes of yellow disappeared, and he saw with astonishing clarity. "I see life. I see kindred spirits." *I see our future. Children, family, warmth, and love.*

The tugging wind crossed the coastal land and sang in his ears. He'd heard of the place where the wind never settled.

She drew her horse beside him, leaned across, and took his hand. "Will they accept me, too?"

He opened his eyes from the vision and beheld his wife. His love. "Yes." There were only truths between them now.

"All of us?" she asked, rubbing her belly. "Our child?"

"Yes."

"You won't tell me, will you?" She smirked.

The bairn, the daughter growing in his wife's womb. He teased, "Never." It had been their ongoing yarn for the past four months. She wanted to know whether she carried a son or daughter. Och, she might get the truth from him yet. He could hardly say no to her for long. He could not tell a lie. For truths were all he knew now.

She huffed, but her smile broadened. Exhaling, a frown replaced her grin. "Domhnall, I'm not like them. Like you."

"It doesn't matter. You're my wife, my soul's mate. You are my fair Rose."

Glory stole across her face as her brown-green eyes lit with life.

People emerged from the crofts dotting the tranquil seaside village. Wide, understanding looks held his gaze. They all knew.

One young man who appeared to be Aileana's age, with chestnut hair and a cluster of freckles across his nose and cheeks, approached. "G'day, Domhnall. We've been expecting you. Welcome home."

His heart raced and a smile warmed his cheeks. They had sent no message ahead. He dismounted. A flurry of people surrounded them. Young, old, wee lads and lassies.

"Home?" Rosalie whispered to him after she untangled herself from an elderly woman's doting embrace.

He swept her into his arms. "Home. For us both." His first home would always be Eilean Donan, his family a week's sail and ride away. All would fare well. He'd seen his parents' vibrant futures, after all. They'd visit. For now, Barra was their home.

Rosalie deserved a new beginning, too. A final place to settle. He drew his head down for a kiss. Her lips were chilled, tasted of salt, and were ardent in return.

"Home," she breathed, her face aglow with serenity, with peace.

JOURNEY THROUGH THE HIGHLANDS...

People, clans, and places...oh my!

Want to learn more about The Hundred Trilogy? Visit my website (www.jeanmgrant.com) for some book extras. Learn about the MacCoinneach & Montgomerie family lineage, the clans, culture & lore, places, and so much more with a glossary, Scotland map, and family/lineage chart. Be warned! There may be spoilers. Read with caution...and sweet abandon.

Purchase the rest of the series at various retailers online:
https://www.jeanmgrant.com/bookshelf

Want to know when the next book is coming out? Sign up for my newsletter on my website at:
https://www.jeanmgrant.com/contact

Read on to continue the journey through medieval Scotland.

The Hundred Trilogy

Norse invasions, Scottish wars for independence, and the plights of the mystical isles' people come together in The Hundred Trilogy. In each standalone book, delve deeper into the mystical powers of the MacCoinneach clan...a powerful family descended from the Ancients of the Isles. Each person is gifted with an ancient power—healing with water, intuition with fire, and prophecy with wind. But with each gift comes a curse. Can they overcome their afflictions to bridge peace...to find love?

A Hundred Breaths

1263

Gwyn of Uist is a merciful Healer but loses breaths of her life with every healing charm. She barters an alliance with a Scot bent on revenge against her Norse kin, in the hopes to save her brother from their abusive father. But can she and Simon MacCoinneach outwit her betrothed and bring an end to the Norse-Scottish bloodshed when it will take all her breaths to save Simon on the battlefield?

A Hundred Kisses

1296

Deirdre MacCoinneach feels the lifebloods of everyone around her...but vows to discover if her gift killed her husbands—twice. Under the façade of a trader, Alasdair Montgomerie travels to Uist with pivotal information for a claimant seeking the Scottish throne. A cruel baron hunts him, leaving little room for alliances with the lass he meets along the way. Amidst ghosts of the past, Alasdair and Deirdre find themselves falling together in a web of secrets and the curse of a hundred kisses...

A Hundred Lies

1322

Rosalie Threston's fortune-telling lies have caught up with her and she's on the run from a ruthless English noblewoman. Rosalie finds refuge in the halls of Eilean Donan castle deep in the Highlands, and in the arms of the laird's mysterious son, Domhnall Montgomerie. Terrible visions plague Domhnall and he avoids all physical contact to temper them. When an accidental touch reveals only delight, he wonders if Rosalie is the key to silencing the Sight. Mystical awakening unravels with each kiss. But can Domhnall embrace his gift in time to save her life, even if it means exposing her lies?

Seeker

A novella, part of the Mortar & Pestle series

1322

Aileana Montgomerie lacks the mystical ability of the Scottish Ancients like her kin. She seeks a purpose but what good is her bow and arrow if she is denied the right to fight for her clan? Brodie MacDougall is ordained to be the next war chieftain of his clan. Chronic pain and nervous vapors force him to spend his days alone, not lift a sword and charge into battle. Can his strategic skills alone keep him one step ahead of his conspiring brother? After magic cast by mystical Mortar & Pestle, the seat on his brother's council is no longer dependent upon his health...but on Aileana's strength. With rumblings of unrest among their clans, will their love foster an alliance or be a step toward war?

ALSO BY JEAN M. GRANT

A Hundred Breaths
A Hundred Kisses
Chasing Roses
Letters to Nobody
Seeker
Silent Creek
Soul of the Storm
Will Rise from Ashes

About the Author

Jean has a penchant for the misunderstood, be it sharks, microbes, or wounded characters. A scientist by training, she now spends her days as an author and champion for her children. She draws from her interest in history, science, the outdoors, and her family for inspiration. She serves on the local library board of trustees and is an advocate for community, inclusion, and diversity.

A nature enthusiast who adores the national parks, Jean also writes for family-oriented travel magazines and websites. When not writing, she enjoys gardening, tackling the biggest mountains in New England, and going on adventures with her husband and children, while taking snapshots of the world around her and daydreaming about the next story. If she were stuck on a deserted island, her three essentials (besides family, food, water, shelter) would be: coffee, lip balm, and endless pink sticky notes.

Find out more about her books by visiting her website: www.jeanmgrant.com

SCOTLAND
1263-1322

www.ingramcontent.com/pod-product-compliance
Lightning Source LLC
Chambersburg PA
CBHW032114310726
48972CB00001B/225